GIDEON FALLS THE BLACK BARN

LAYOUT & PRODUCTION BY RYAN BREWER

IMAGE COMICS, INC. • **Robert Kirkman**: Chief Operating Officer • **Erik Larsen**: Chief Financial Officer • **Todd McFarlane**: President • **Marc Silvestri**: Chief Executive Officer • **Jim Valentino**: Vice President • **Eric Stephenson**: Publisher / Chief Creative Officer • **Corey Hart**: Director of Sales • **Jeff Boison**: Director of Publishing Planning & Book Trade Sales • **Chris Ross**: Director of Digital Sales • **Jeff Stang**: Director of Specialty Sales • **Kat Salazar**: Director of PR & Marketing • **Drew Gill**: Art Director • **Heather Doornink**: Production Director • **Nicole Lapalme**: Controller • **IMAGECOMICS.COM**

GIDEON FALLS, VOL. 1. First printing. October 2018. Published by Image Comics, Inc. Office of publication: 2701 NW Vaughn St., Suite 780, Portland, OR 97210. Copyright © 2018 171 Studios & Andrea Sorrentino. All rights reserved. Contains material originally published in single magazine form as GIDEON FALLS #1-6. "Gideon Falls," its logos, and the likenesses of all characters herein are trademarks of 171 Studios & Andrea Sorrentino, unless otherwise noted. "Image" and the Image Comics logos are registered trademarks of Image Comics, Inc. No part of this publication may be reproduced or transmitted, in any form or by any means (except for short excerpts for journalistic or review purposes), without the express written permission of 171 Studios & Andrea Sorrentino, or Image Comics, Inc. All names, characters, events, and locales in this publication are entirely fictional. Any resemblance to actual persons (living or dead), events, or places, without satirical intent, is coincidental. Printed in the USA. For information regarding the CPSIA on this printed material call: 203-595-3636 and provide reference #RICH–815925. For international rights, contact: foreignlicensing@imagecomics.com. ISBN: 978-1-5343-0852-7. Big Bang / Forbidden Planet Exclusive ISBN: 978-1-5343-1171-8. Newbury Comics Exclusive ISBN: 978-1-5343-1172-5. Kinokuniya Exclusive ISBN: 978-1-5343-1175-6. LCSD Hardcover Exclusive ISBN: 978-1-5343-1184-8.

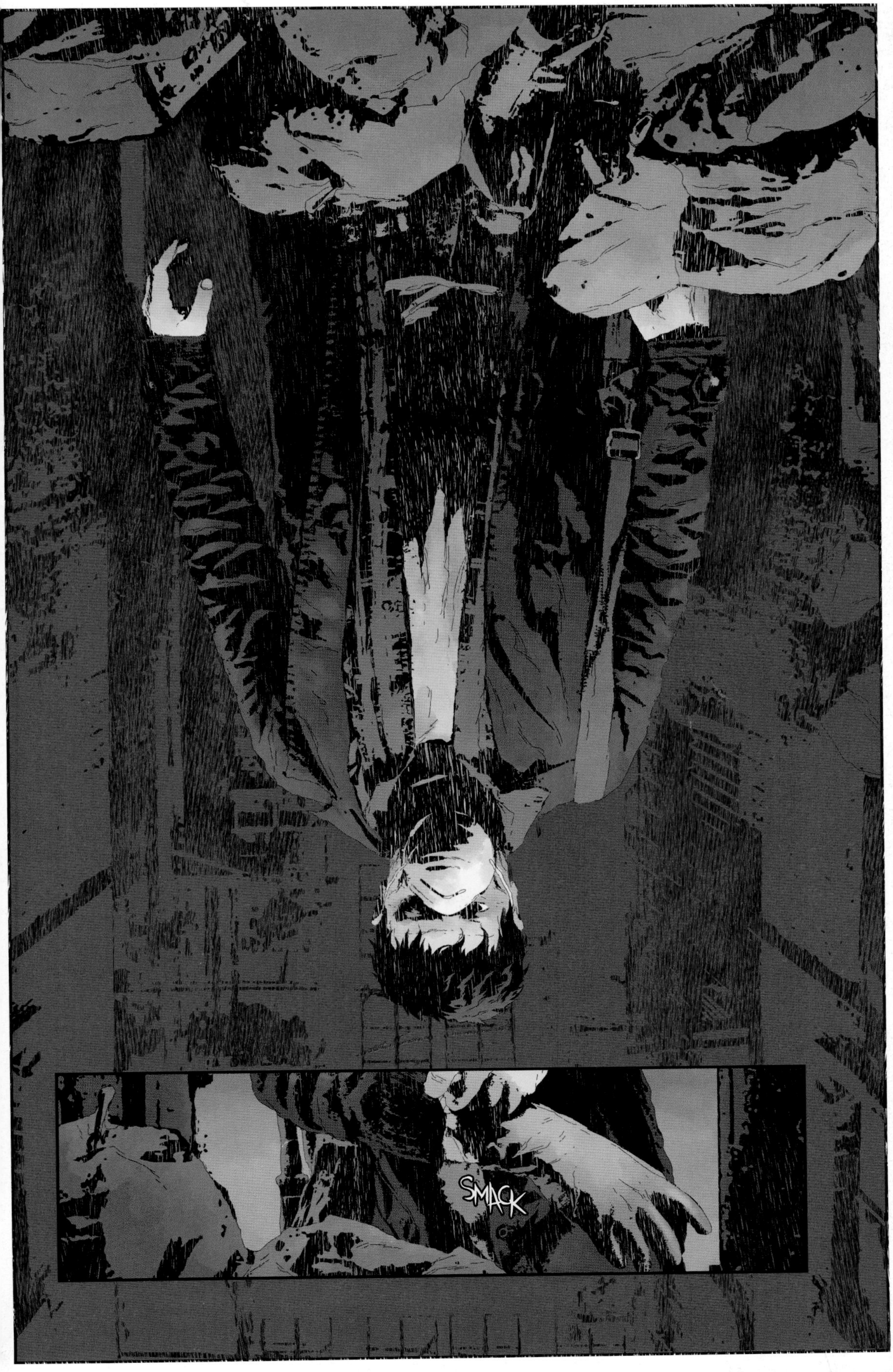
SMACK

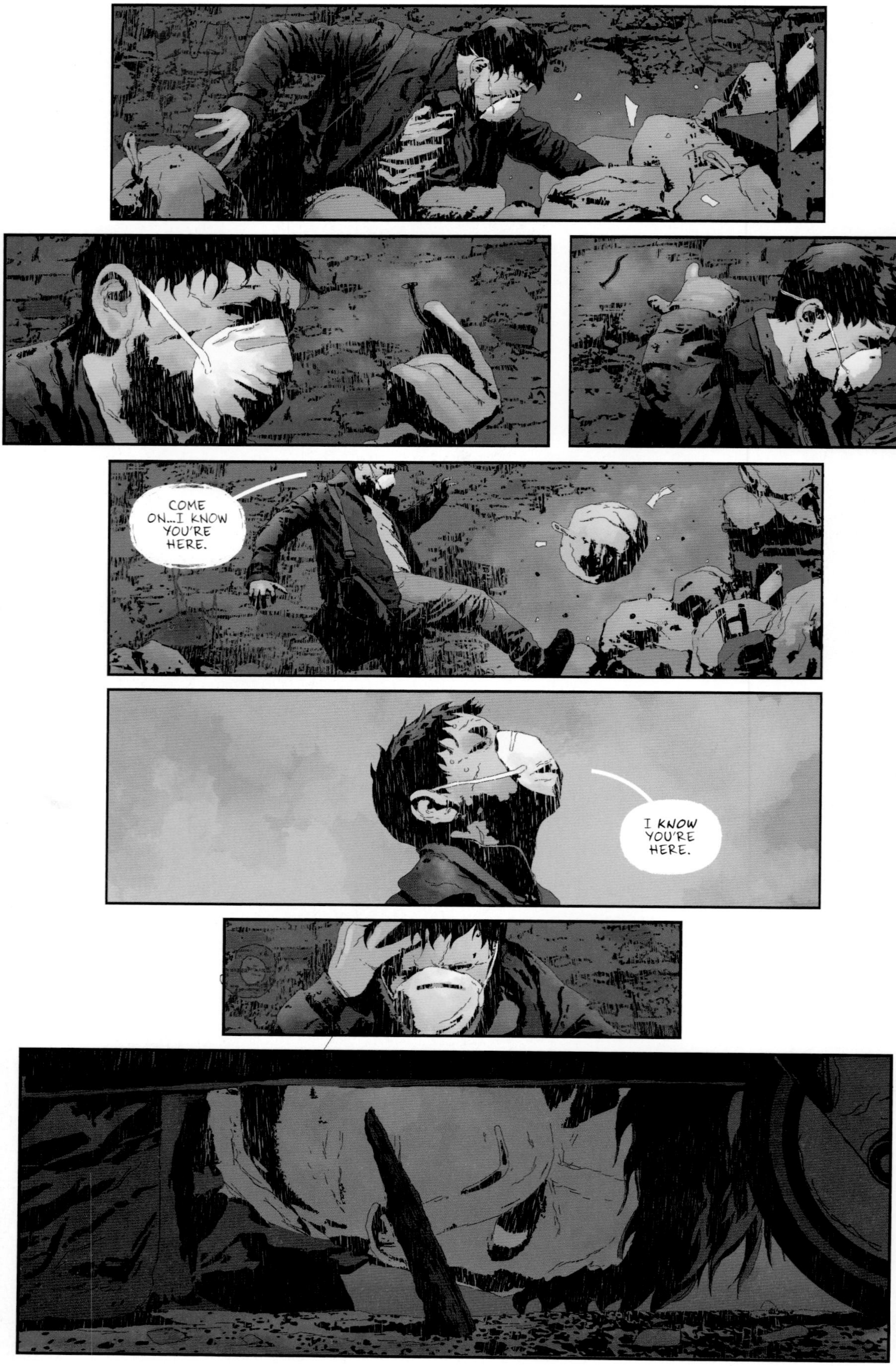
COME ON...I KNOW YOU'RE HERE.
I KNOW YOU'RE HERE.

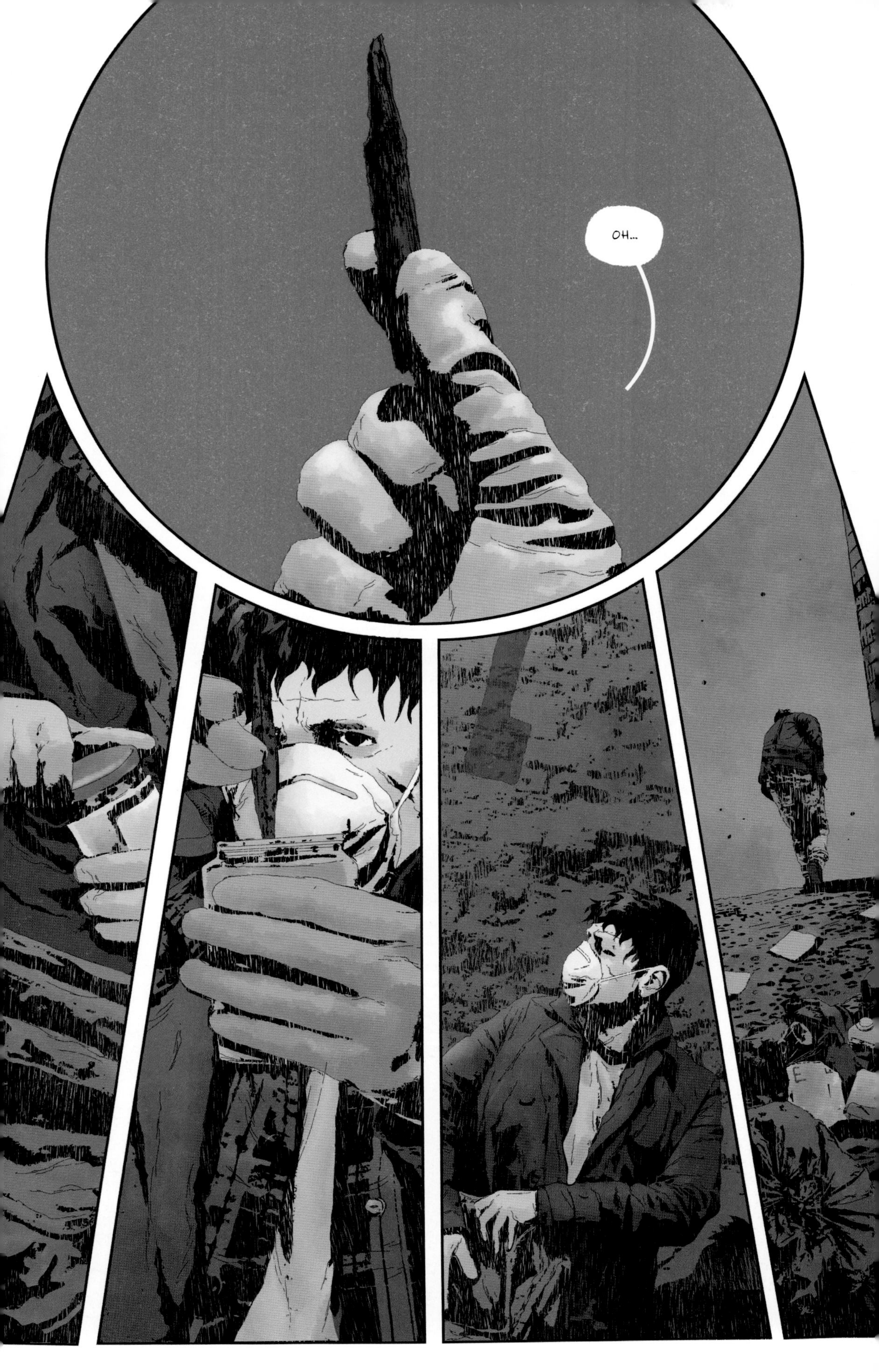
OH...

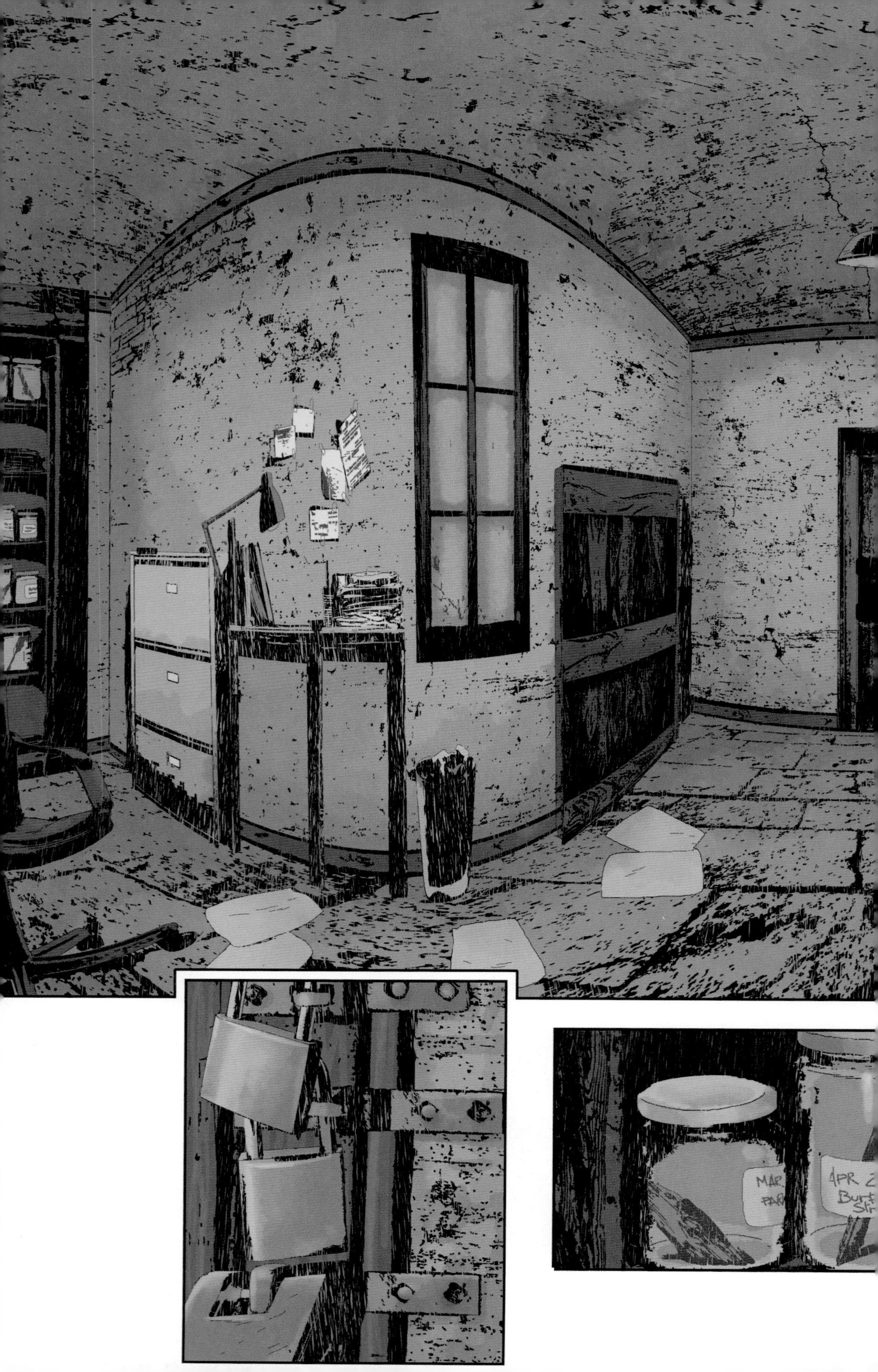

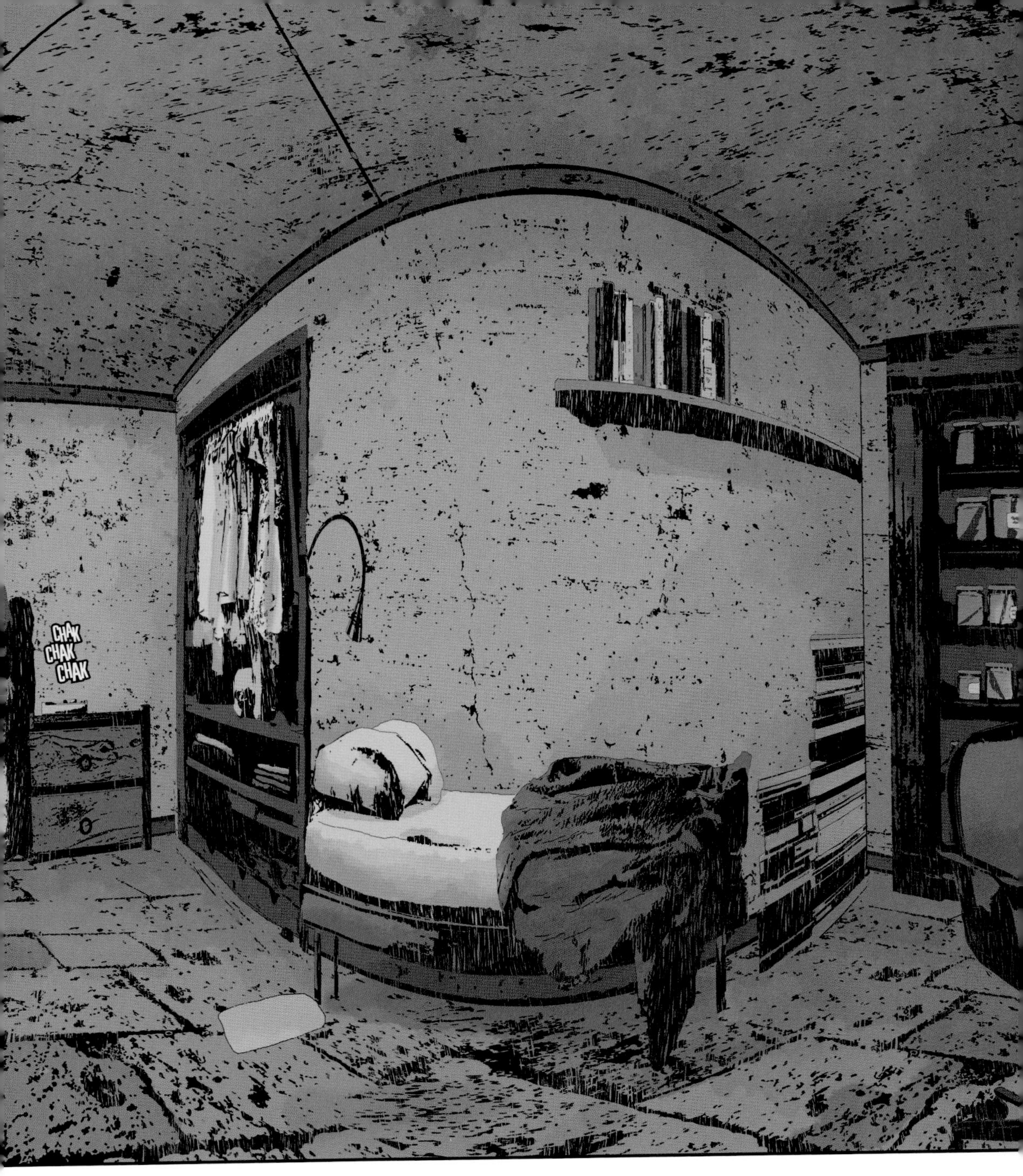
CHAK
CHAK
CHAK

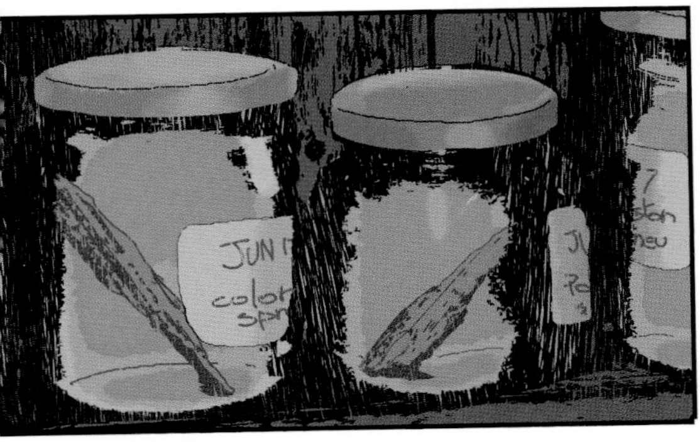

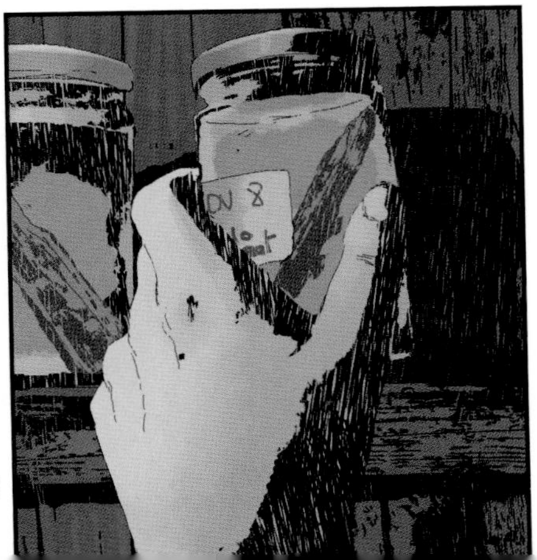

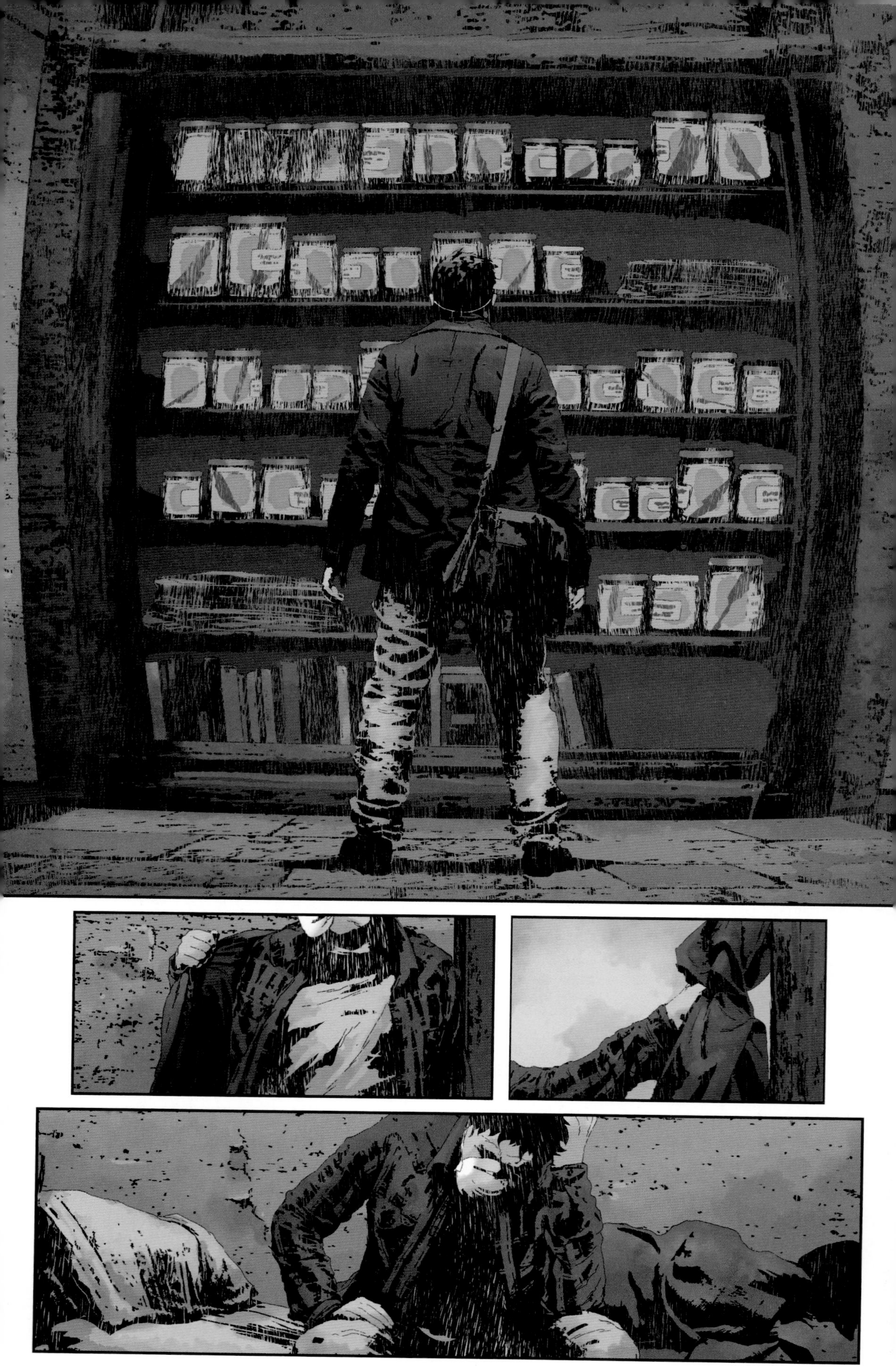

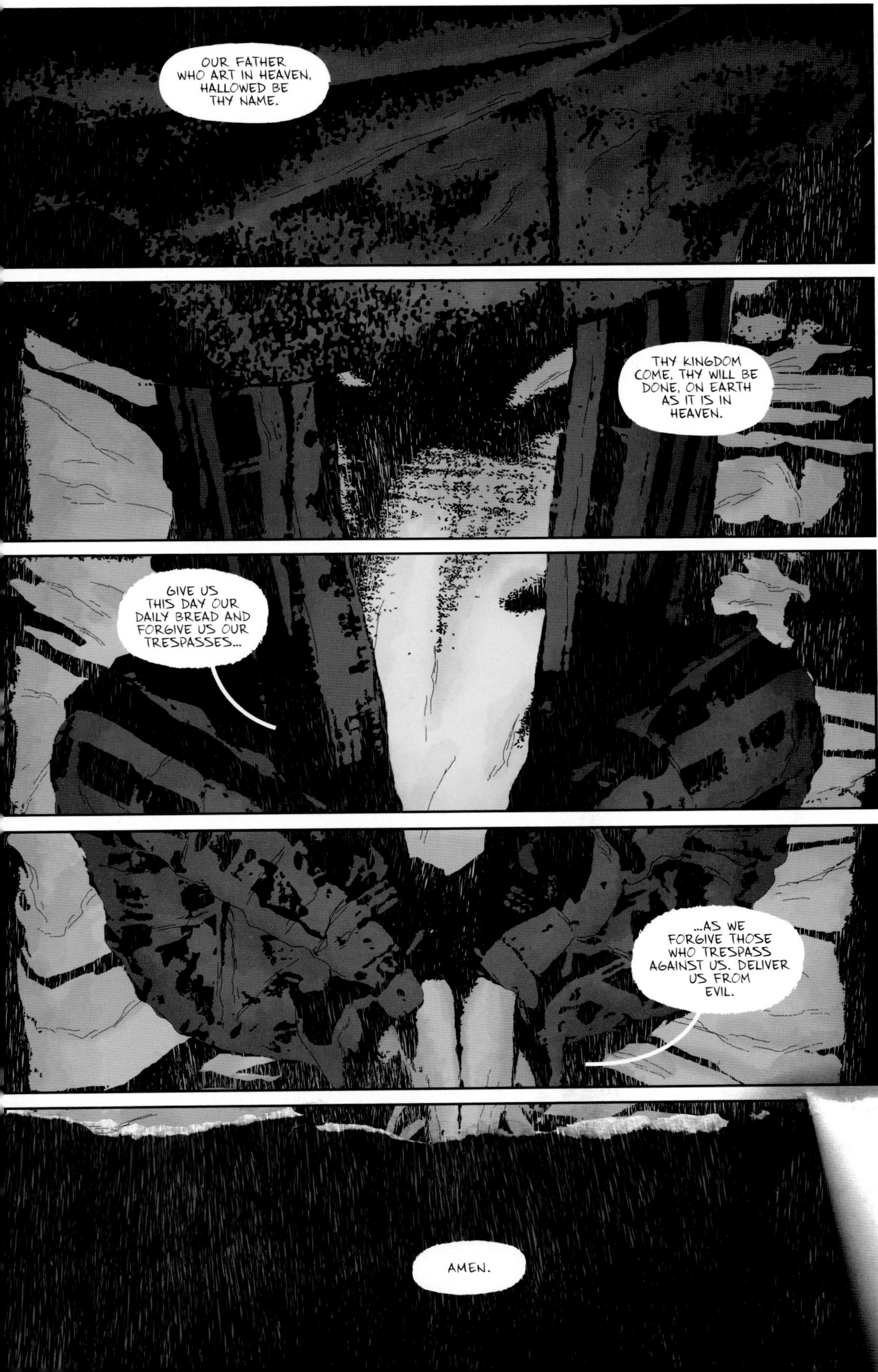
OUR FATHER WHO ART IN HEAVEN, HALLOWED BE THY NAME.
THY KINGDOM COME, THY WILL BE DONE, ON EARTH AS IT IS IN HEAVEN.
GIVE US THIS DAY OUR DAILY BREAD AND FORGIVE US OUR TRESPASSES...
...AS WE FORGIVE THOSE WHO TRESPASS AGAINST US. DELIVER US FROM EVIL.
AMEN.

Jeff Lemire
Andrea Sorrentino

with colors by:
Dave Stewart

lettering and design by:
Steve Wands

and edited by:
Will Dennis

GIDEON
FALLS

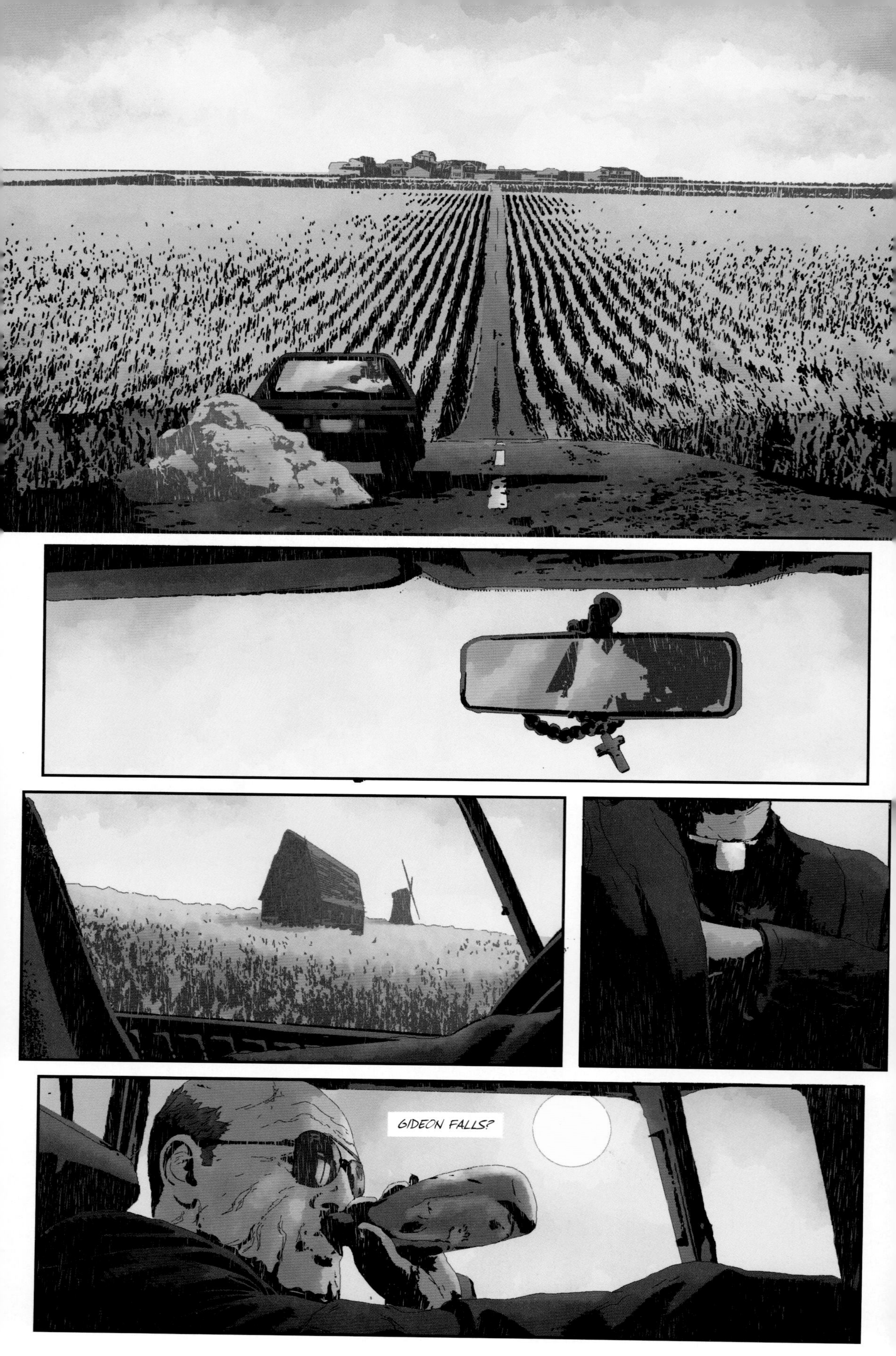
GIDEON FALLS?

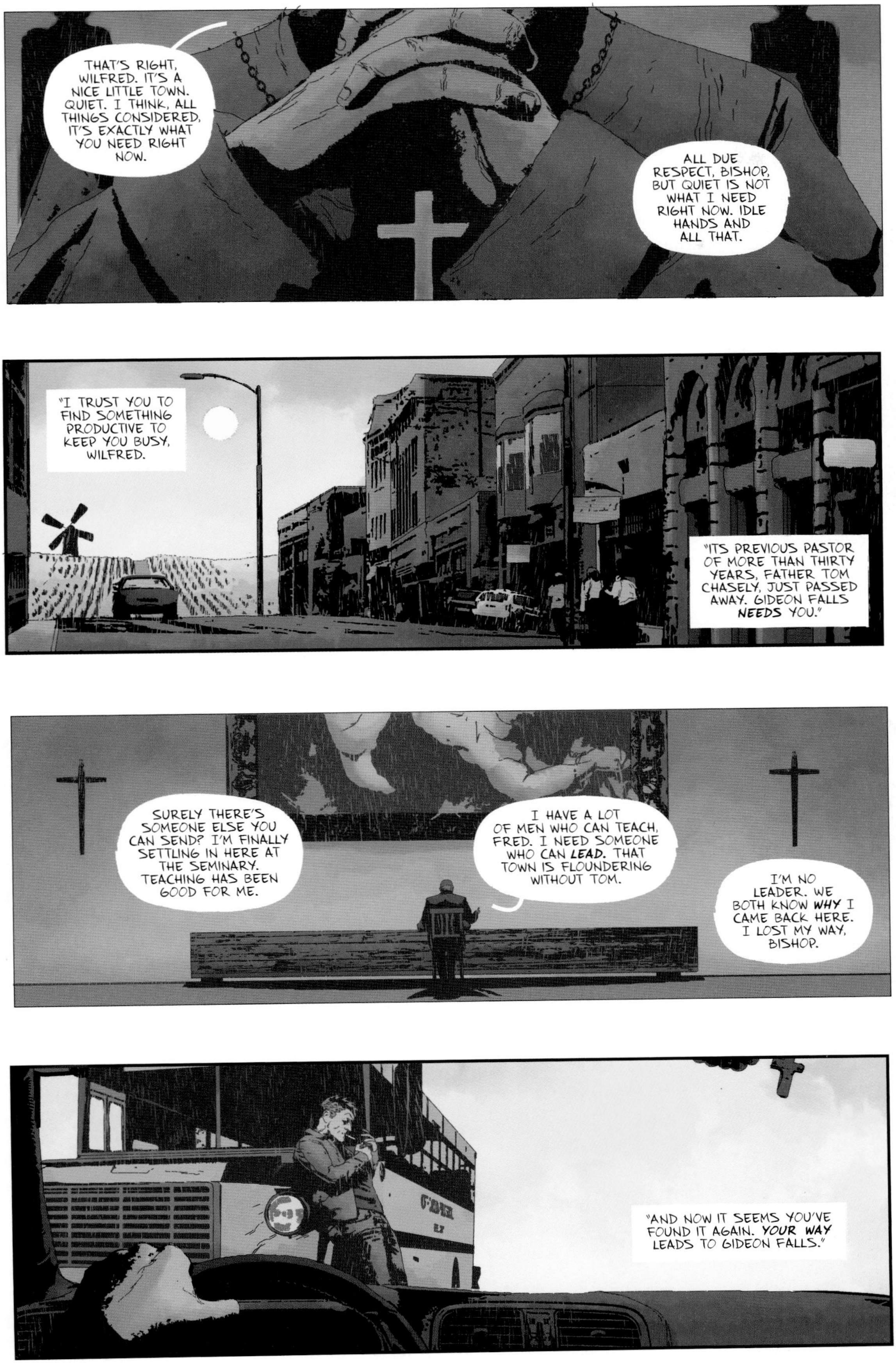
THAT'S RIGHT, WILFRED. IT'S A NICE LITTLE TOWN. QUIET. I THINK, ALL THINGS CONSIDERED, IT'S EXACTLY WHAT YOU NEED RIGHT NOW.
ALL DUE RESPECT, BISHOP, BUT QUIET IS NOT WHAT I NEED RIGHT NOW. IDLE HANDS AND ALL THAT.
"I TRUST YOU TO FIND SOMETHING PRODUCTIVE TO KEEP YOU BUSY, WILFRED.
"ITS PREVIOUS PASTOR OF MORE THAN THIRTY YEARS, FATHER TOM CHASELY, JUST PASSED AWAY. GIDEON FALLS NEEDS YOU."
SURELY THERE'S SOMEONE ELSE YOU CAN SEND? I'M FINALLY SETTLING IN HERE AT THE SEMINARY. TEACHING HAS BEEN GOOD FOR ME.
I HAVE A LOT OF MEN WHO CAN TEACH, FRED. I NEED SOMEONE WHO CAN LEAD. THAT TOWN IS FLOUNDERING WITHOUT TOM.
I'M NO LEADER. WE BOTH KNOW WHY I CAME BACK HERE. I LOST MY WAY, BISHOP.
"AND NOW IT SEEMS YOU'VE FOUND IT AGAIN. YOUR WAY LEADS TO GIDEON FALLS."

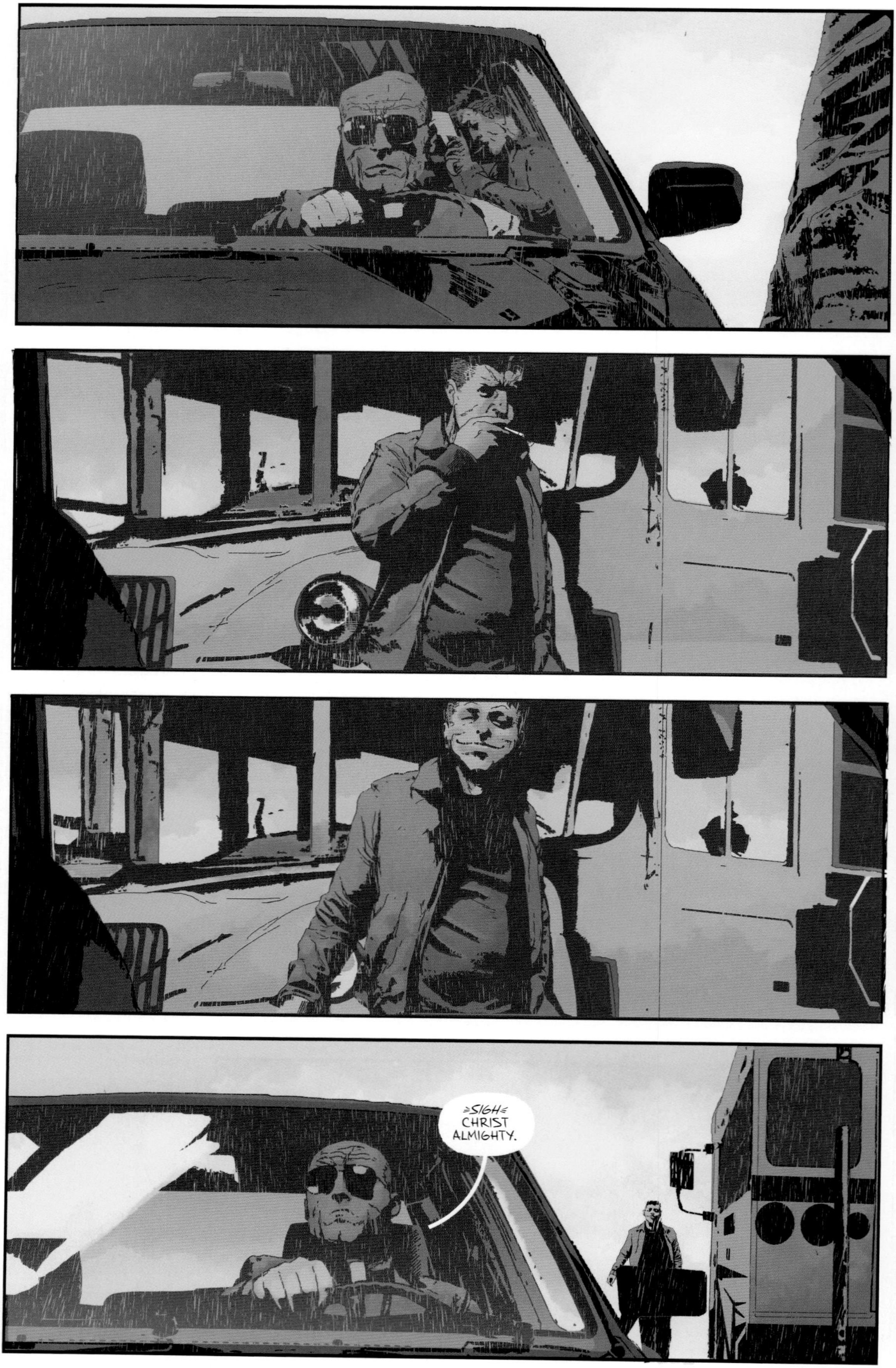
SIGH
CHRIST ALMIGHTY.

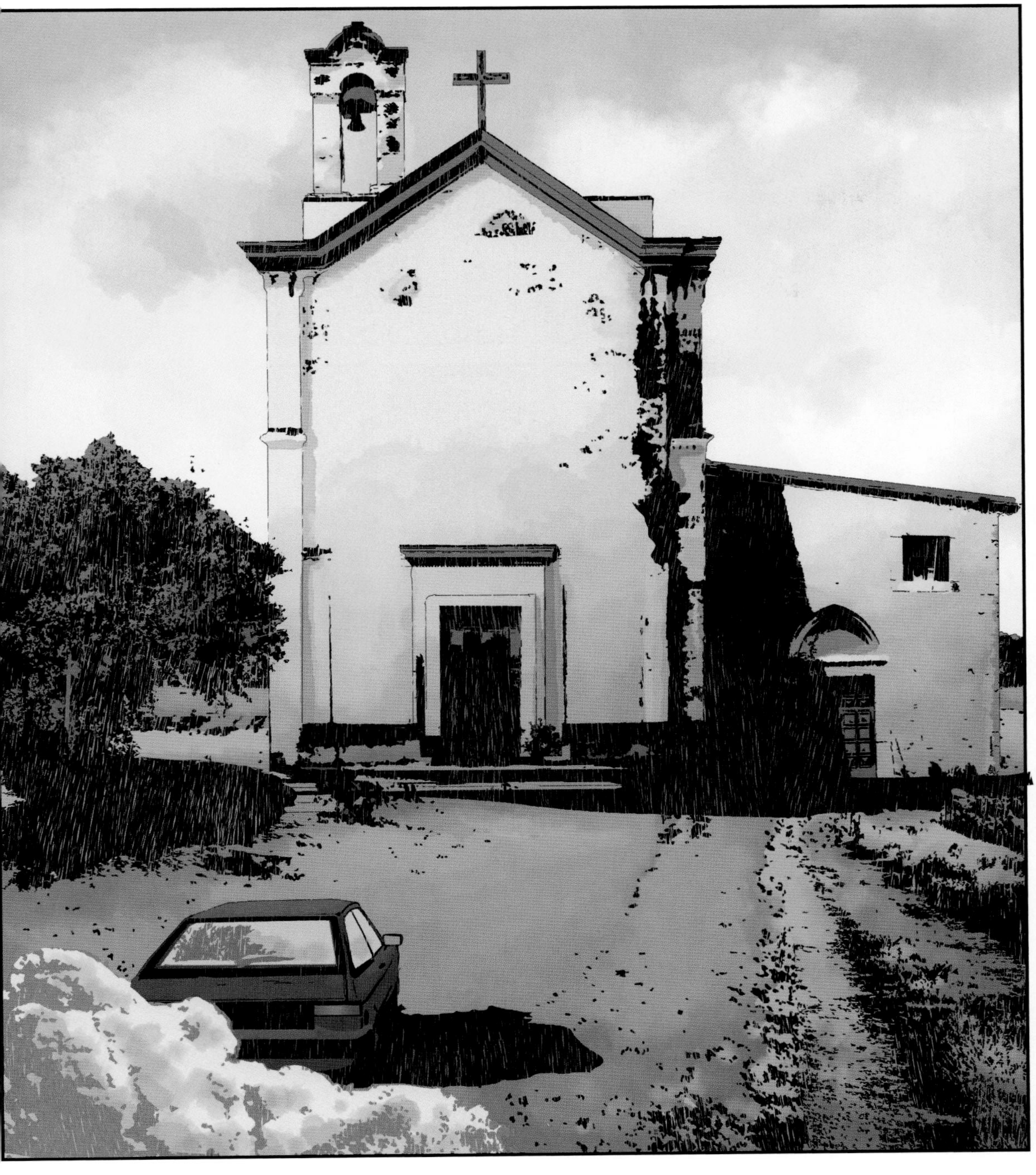

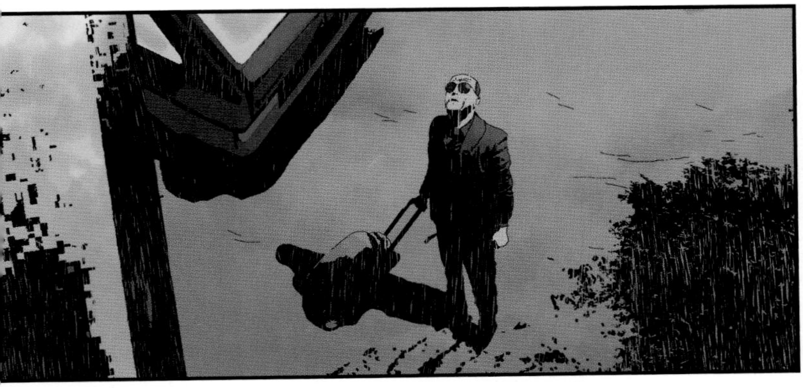

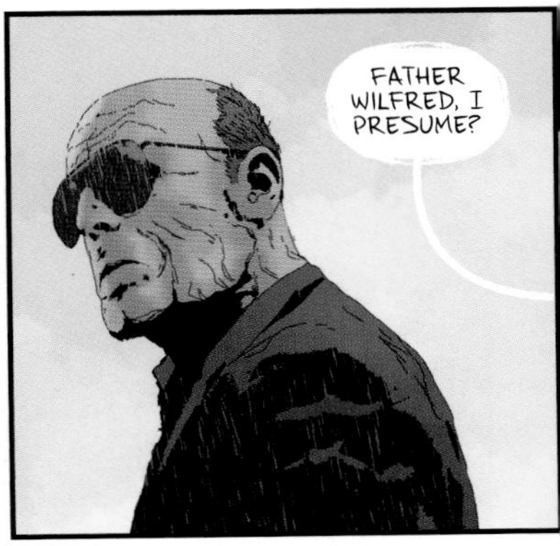
FATHER WILFRED, I PRESUME?

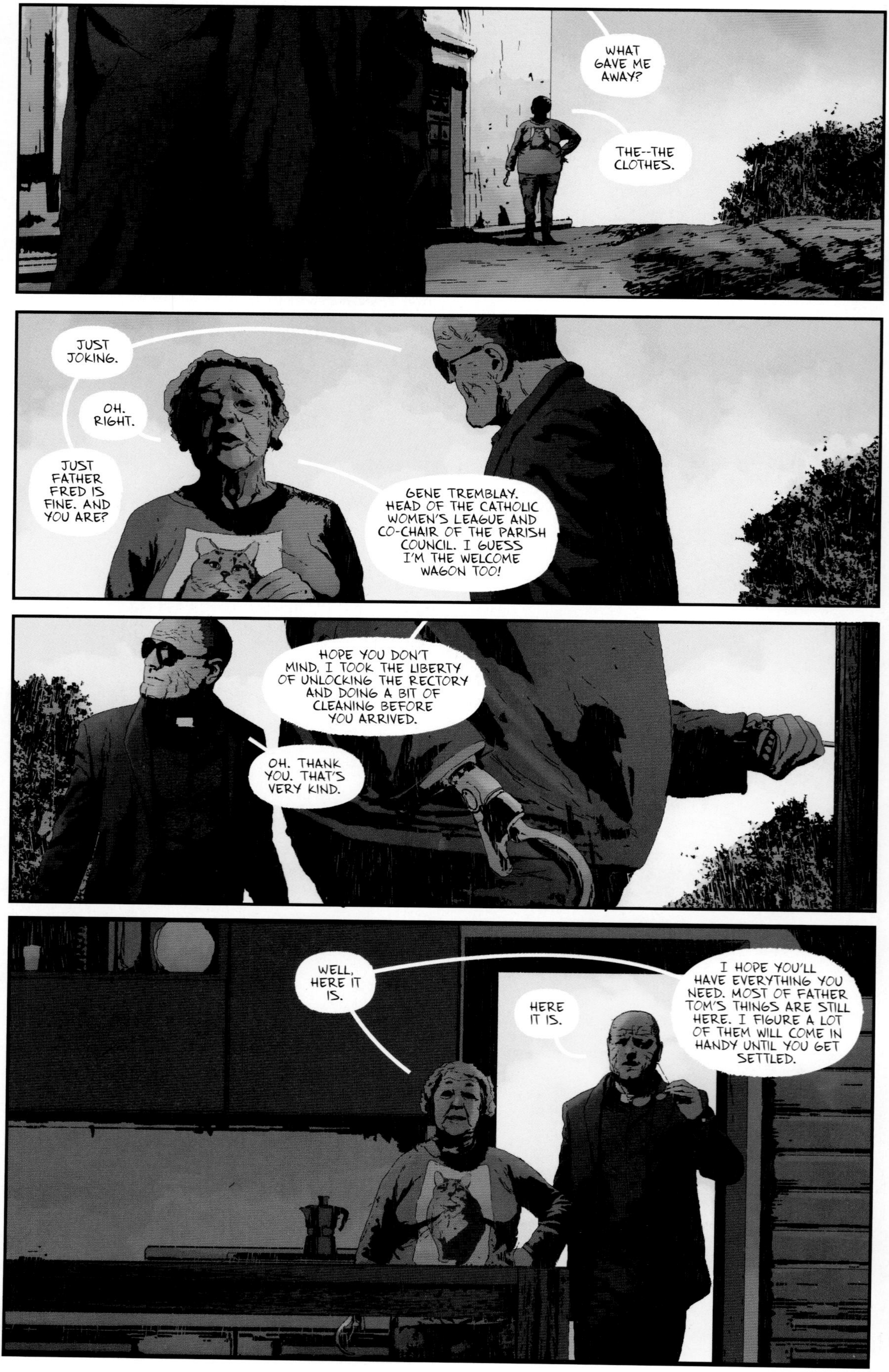
WHAT GAVE ME AWAY?
THE--THE CLOTHES.
JUST JOKING.
OH. RIGHT.
JUST FATHER FRED IS FINE. AND YOU ARE?
GENE TREMBLAY. HEAD OF THE CATHOLIC WOMEN'S LEAGUE AND CO-CHAIR OF THE PARISH COUNCIL. I GUESS I'M THE WELCOME WAGON TOO!
HOPE YOU DON'T MIND, I TOOK THE LIBERTY OF UNLOCKING THE RECTORY AND DOING A BIT OF CLEANING BEFORE YOU ARRIVED.
OH. THANK YOU. THAT'S VERY KIND.
WELL, HERE IT IS.
I HOPE YOU'LL HAVE EVERYTHING YOU NEED. MOST OF FATHER TOM'S THINGS ARE STILL HERE. I FIGURE A LOT OF THEM WILL COME IN HANDY UNTIL YOU GET SETTLED.
HERE IT IS.

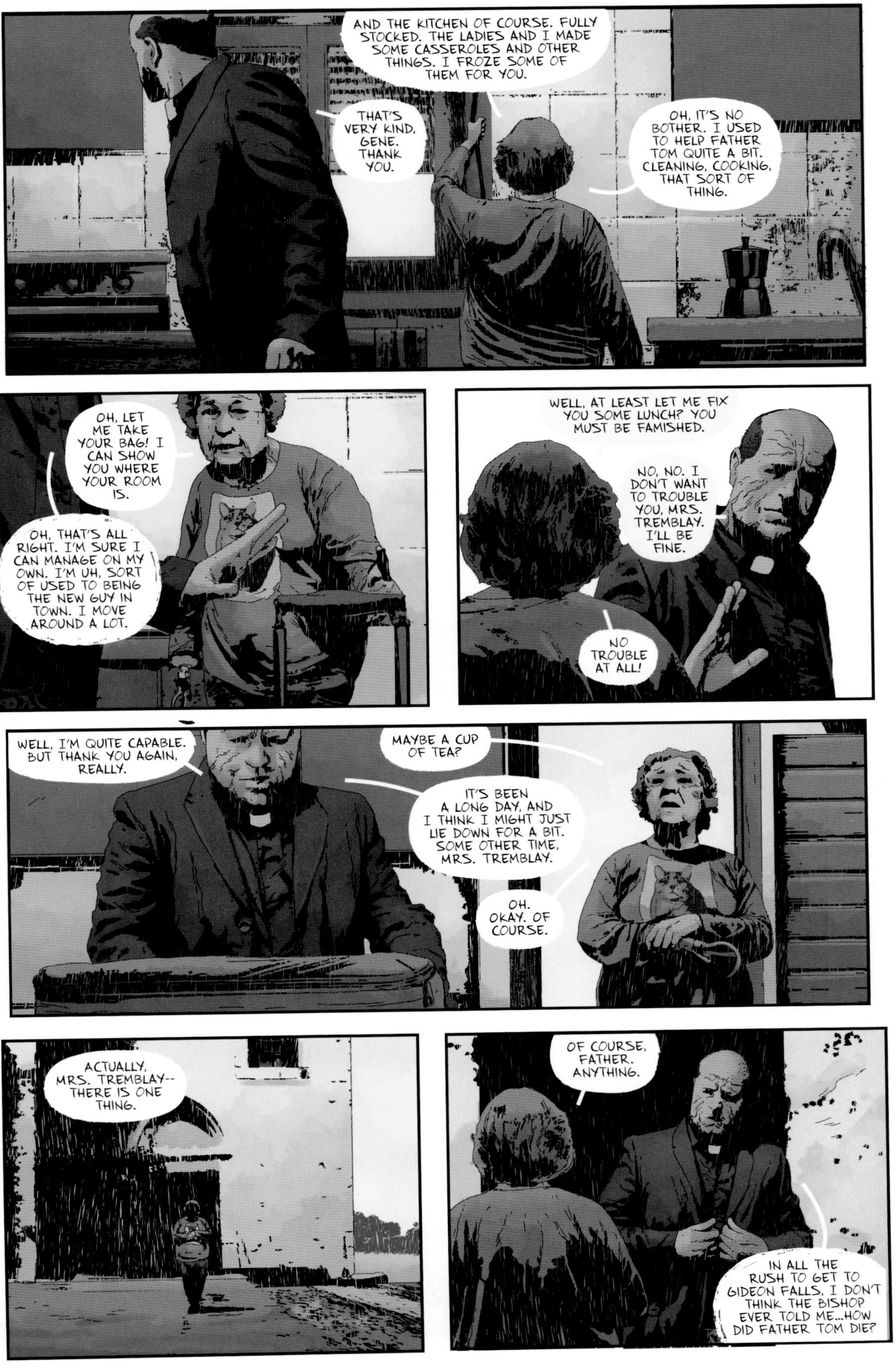
AND THE KITCHEN OF COURSE. FULLY STOCKED. THE LADIES AND I MADE SOME CASSEROLES AND OTHER THINGS. I FROZE SOME OF THEM FOR YOU.
THAT'S VERY KIND, GENE. THANK YOU.
OH, IT'S NO BOTHER. I USED TO HELP FATHER TOM QUITE A BIT. CLEANING, COOKING, THAT SORT OF THING.
OH, LET ME TAKE YOUR BAG! I CAN SHOW YOU WHERE YOUR ROOM IS.
OH, THAT'S ALL RIGHT. I'M SURE I CAN MANAGE ON MY OWN. I'M UH, SORT OF USED TO BEING THE NEW GUY IN TOWN. I MOVE AROUND A LOT.
WELL, AT LEAST LET ME FIX YOU SOME LUNCH? YOU MUST BE FAMISHED.
NO, NO. I DON'T WANT TO TROUBLE YOU, MRS. TREMBLAY. I'LL BE FINE.
NO TROUBLE AT ALL!
WELL, I'M QUITE CAPABLE. BUT THANK YOU AGAIN, REALLY.
MAYBE A CUP OF TEA?
IT'S BEEN A LONG DAY, AND I THINK I MIGHT JUST LIE DOWN FOR A BIT. SOME OTHER TIME, MRS. TREMBLAY.
OH. OKAY. OF COURSE.
ACTUALLY, MRS. TREMBLAY-- THERE IS ONE THING.
OF COURSE, FATHER. ANYTHING.
IN ALL THE RUSH TO GET TO GIDEON FALLS, I DON'T THINK THE BISHOP EVER TOLD ME...HOW DID FATHER TOM DIE?

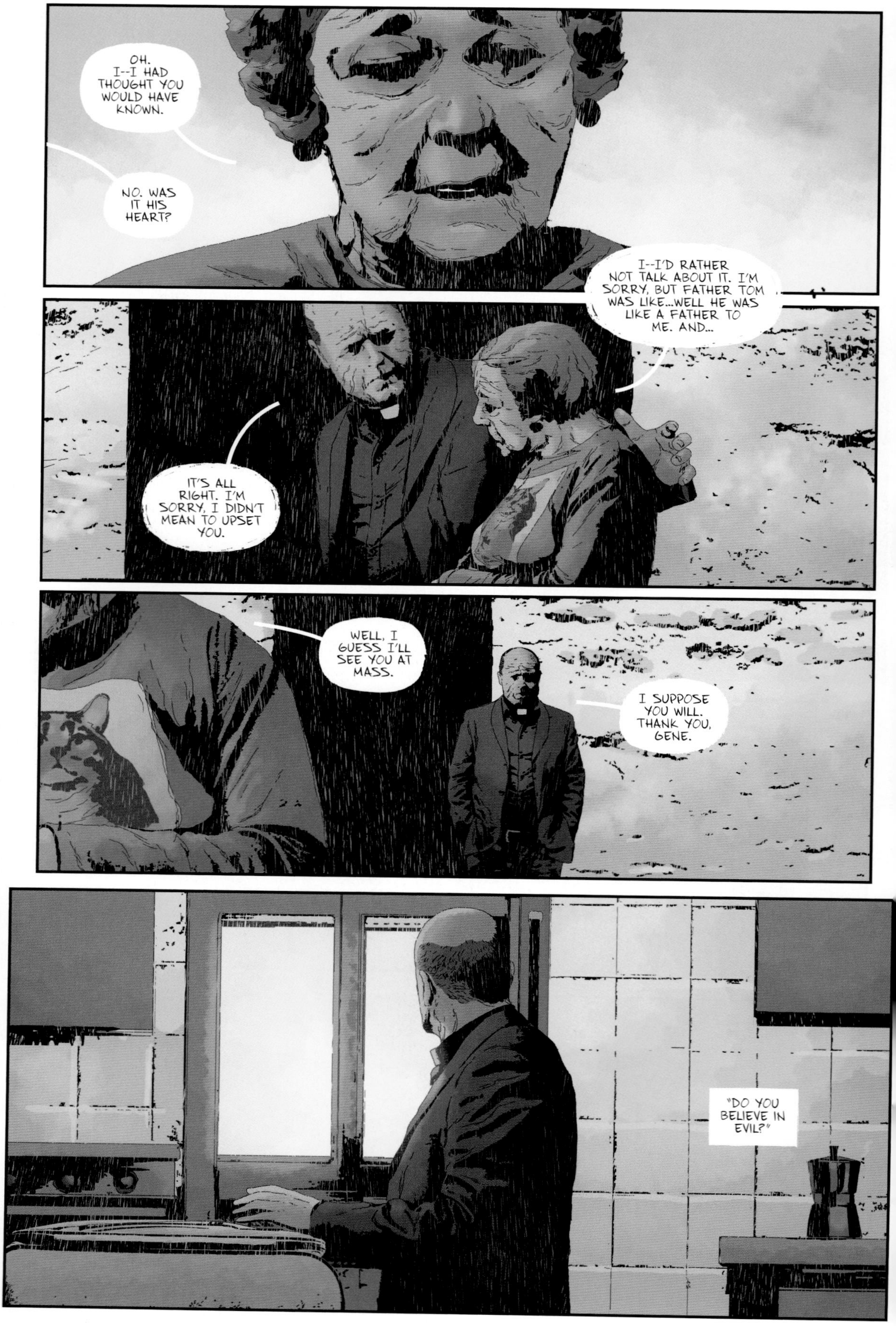

OH. I--I HAD THOUGHT YOU WOULD HAVE KNOWN.
NO. WAS IT HIS HEART?
I--I'D RATHER NOT TALK ABOUT IT. I'M SORRY, BUT FATHER TOM WAS LIKE...WELL HE WAS LIKE A FATHER TO ME. AND...
IT'S ALL RIGHT. I'M SORRY, I DIDN'T MEAN TO UPSET YOU.
WELL, I GUESS I'LL SEE YOU AT MASS.
I SUPPOSE YOU WILL. THANK YOU, GENE.
"DO YOU BELIEVE IN EVIL?"

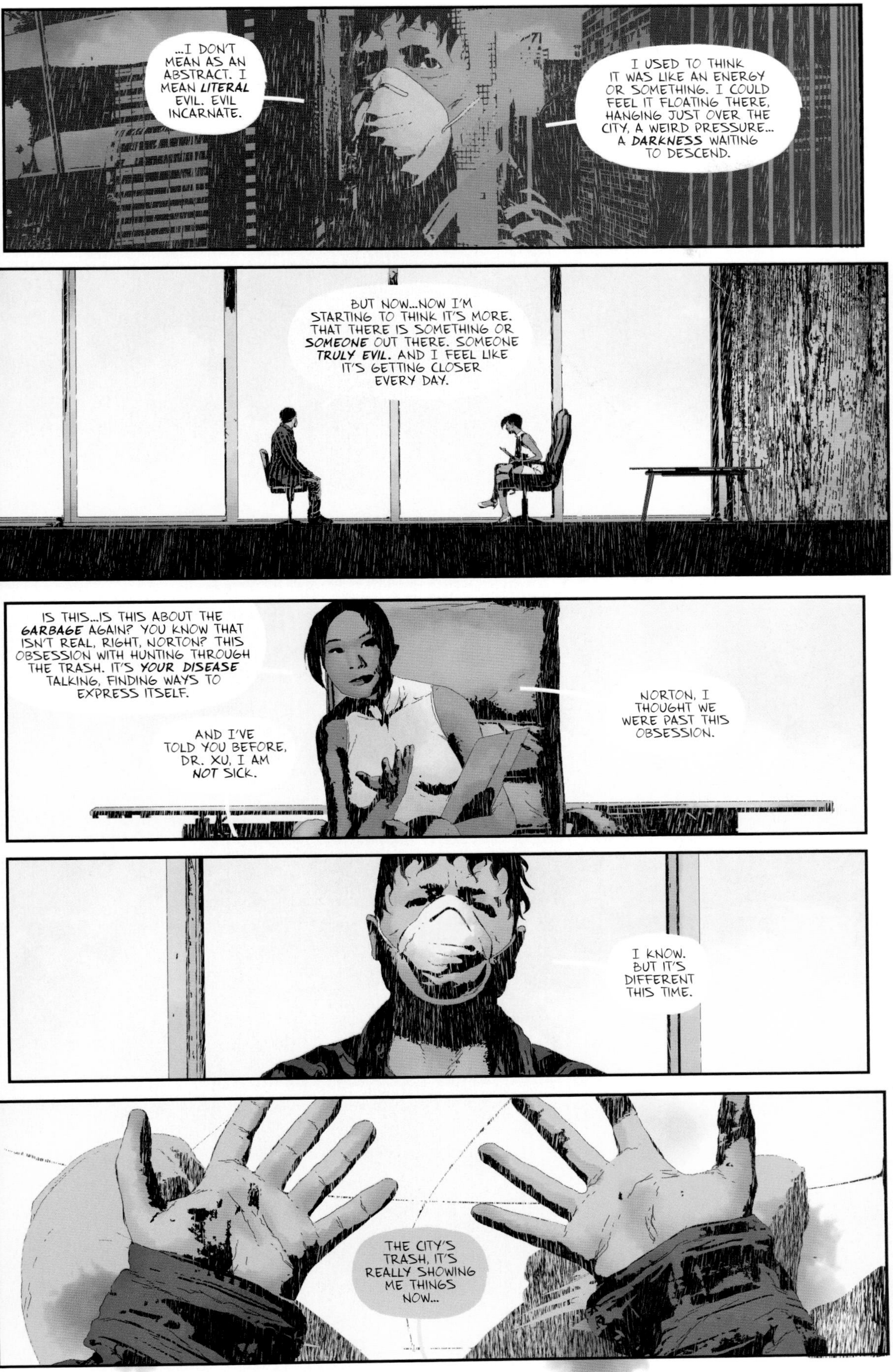
...I DON'T MEAN AS AN ABSTRACT. I MEAN LITERAL EVIL. EVIL INCARNATE.
I USED TO THINK IT WAS LIKE AN ENERGY OR SOMETHING. I COULD FEEL IT FLOATING THERE, HANGING JUST OVER THE CITY, A WEIRD PRESSURE... A DARKNESS WAITING TO DESCEND.
BUT NOW...NOW I'M STARTING TO THINK IT'S MORE. THAT THERE IS SOMETHING OR SOMEONE OUT THERE. SOMEONE TRULY EVIL. AND I FEEL LIKE IT'S GETTING CLOSER EVERY DAY.
IS THIS...IS THIS ABOUT THE GARBAGE AGAIN? YOU KNOW THAT ISN'T REAL, RIGHT, NORTON? THIS OBSESSION WITH HUNTING THROUGH THE TRASH. IT'S YOUR DISEASE TALKING, FINDING WAYS TO EXPRESS ITSELF.
AND I'VE TOLD YOU BEFORE, DR. XU, I AM NOT SICK.
NORTON, I THOUGHT WE WERE PAST THIS OBSESSION.
I KNOW. BUT IT'S DIFFERENT THIS TIME.
THE CITY'S TRASH, IT'S REALLY SHOWING ME THINGS NOW...

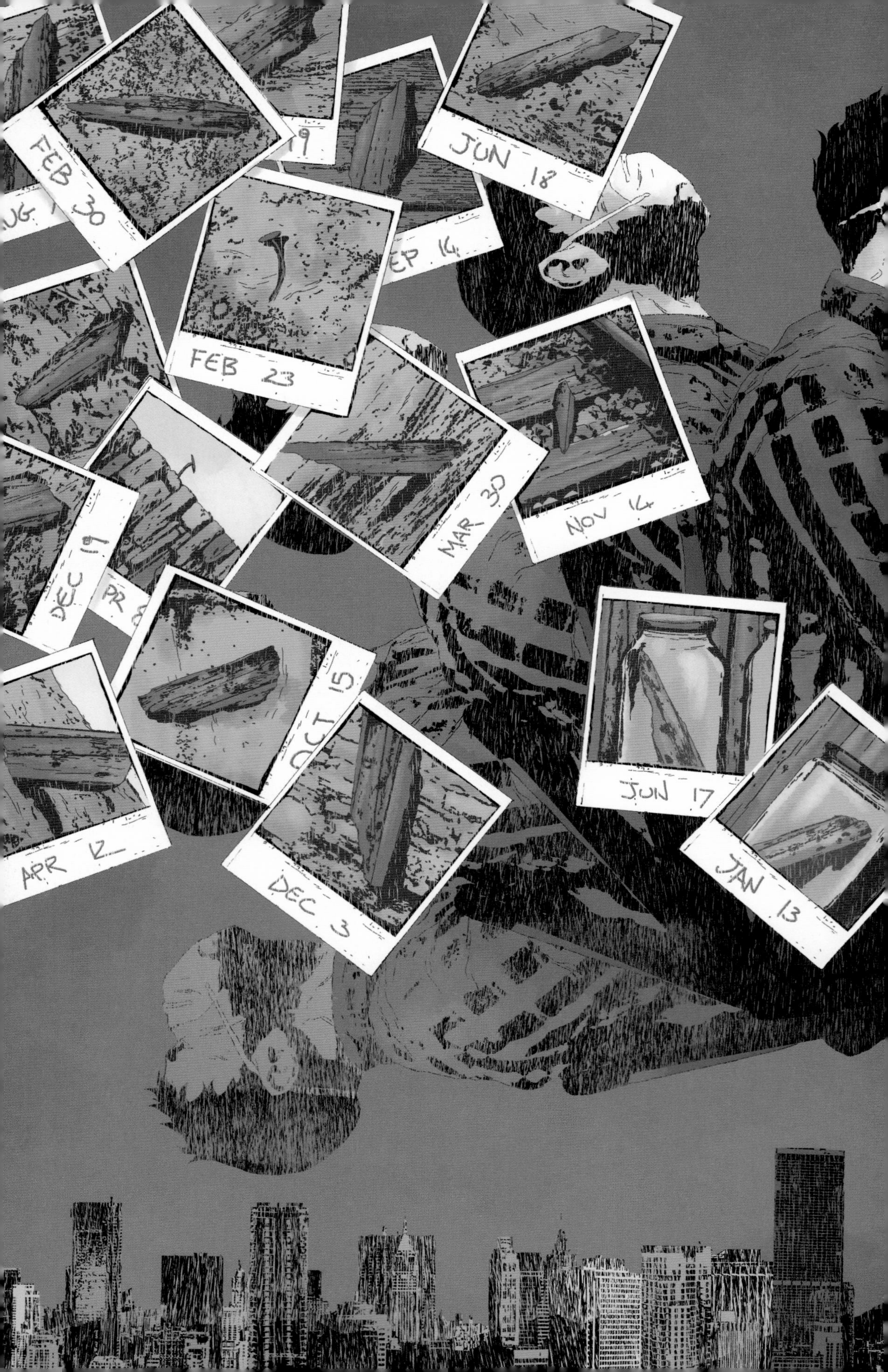
FEB 30
JUN 18
FEB 23
MAR 30
NOV 14
DEC 19
OCT 15
JUN 17
APR 12
DEC 3
JAN 13

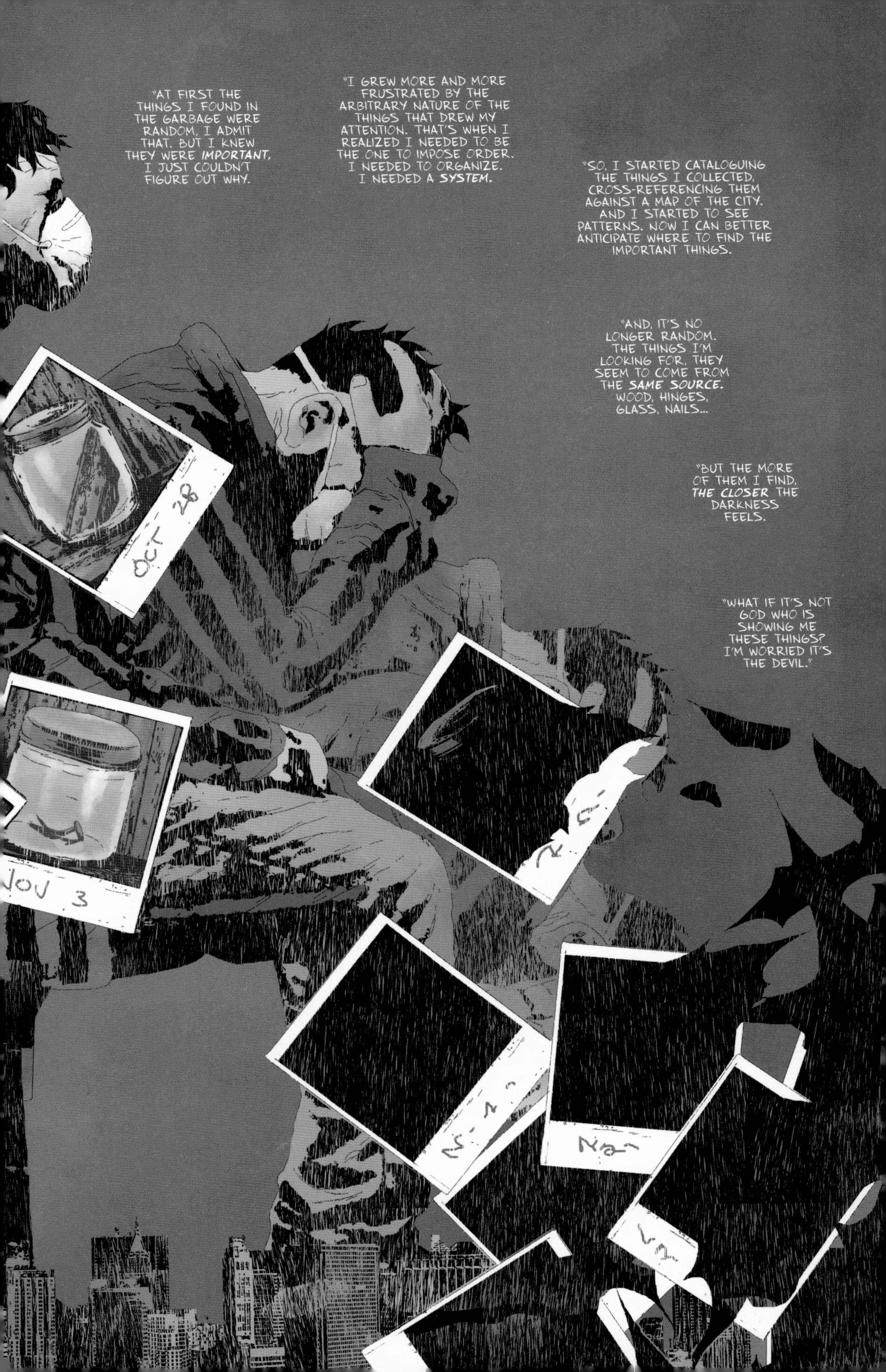
"AT FIRST THE THINGS I FOUND IN THE GARBAGE WERE RANDOM, I ADMIT THAT. BUT I KNEW THEY WERE *IMPORTANT*, I JUST COULDN'T FIGURE OUT WHY.
"I GREW MORE AND MORE FRUSTRATED BY THE ARBITRARY NATURE OF THE THINGS THAT DREW MY ATTENTION. THAT'S WHEN I REALIZED I NEEDED TO BE THE ONE TO IMPOSE ORDER. I NEEDED TO ORGANIZE. I NEEDED A **SYSTEM.**
"SO, I STARTED CATALOGUING THE THINGS I COLLECTED, CROSS-REFERENCING THEM AGAINST A MAP OF THE CITY. AND I STARTED TO SEE PATTERNS. NOW I CAN BETTER ANTICIPATE WHERE TO FIND THE IMPORTANT THINGS.
"AND, IT'S NO LONGER RANDOM. THE THINGS I'M LOOKING FOR, THEY SEEM TO COME FROM THE **SAME SOURCE.** WOOD, HINGES, GLASS, NAILS...
"BUT THE MORE OF THEM I FIND, ***THE CLOSER*** THE DARKNESS FEELS.
"WHAT IF IT'S NOT GOD WHO IS SHOWING ME THESE THINGS? I'M WORRIED IT'S THE DEVIL."
OCT 28
NOV 3

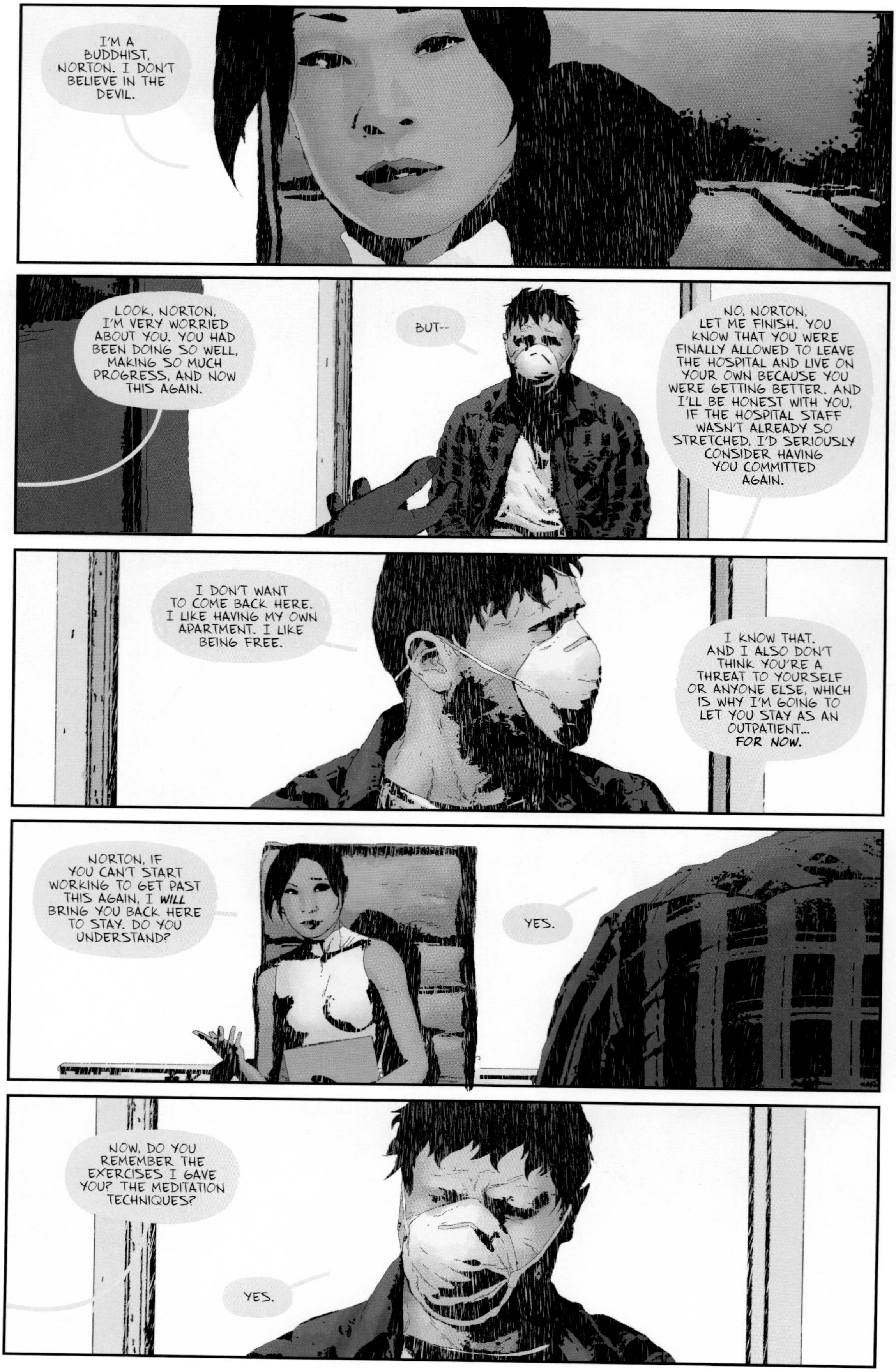
I'M A BUDDHIST, NORTON. I DON'T BELIEVE IN THE DEVIL.
LOOK, NORTON, I'M VERY WORRIED ABOUT YOU. YOU HAD BEEN DOING SO WELL, MAKING SO MUCH PROGRESS, AND NOW THIS AGAIN.
BUT--
NO, NORTON, LET ME FINISH. YOU KNOW THAT YOU WERE FINALLY ALLOWED TO LEAVE THE HOSPITAL AND LIVE ON YOUR OWN BECAUSE YOU WERE GETTING BETTER. AND I'LL BE HONEST WITH YOU, IF THE HOSPITAL STAFF WASN'T ALREADY SO STRETCHED, I'D SERIOUSLY CONSIDER HAVING YOU COMMITTED AGAIN.
I DON'T WANT TO COME BACK HERE. I LIKE HAVING MY OWN APARTMENT. I LIKE BEING FREE.
I KNOW THAT. AND I ALSO DON'T THINK YOU'RE A THREAT TO YOURSELF OR ANYONE ELSE, WHICH IS WHY I'M GOING TO LET YOU STAY AS AN OUTPATIENT... **FOR NOW.**
NORTON, IF YOU CAN'T START WORKING TO GET PAST THIS AGAIN, I **WILL** BRING YOU BACK HERE TO STAY. DO YOU UNDERSTAND?
YES.
NOW, DO YOU REMEMBER THE EXERCISES I GAVE YOU? THE MEDITATION TECHNIQUES?
YES.

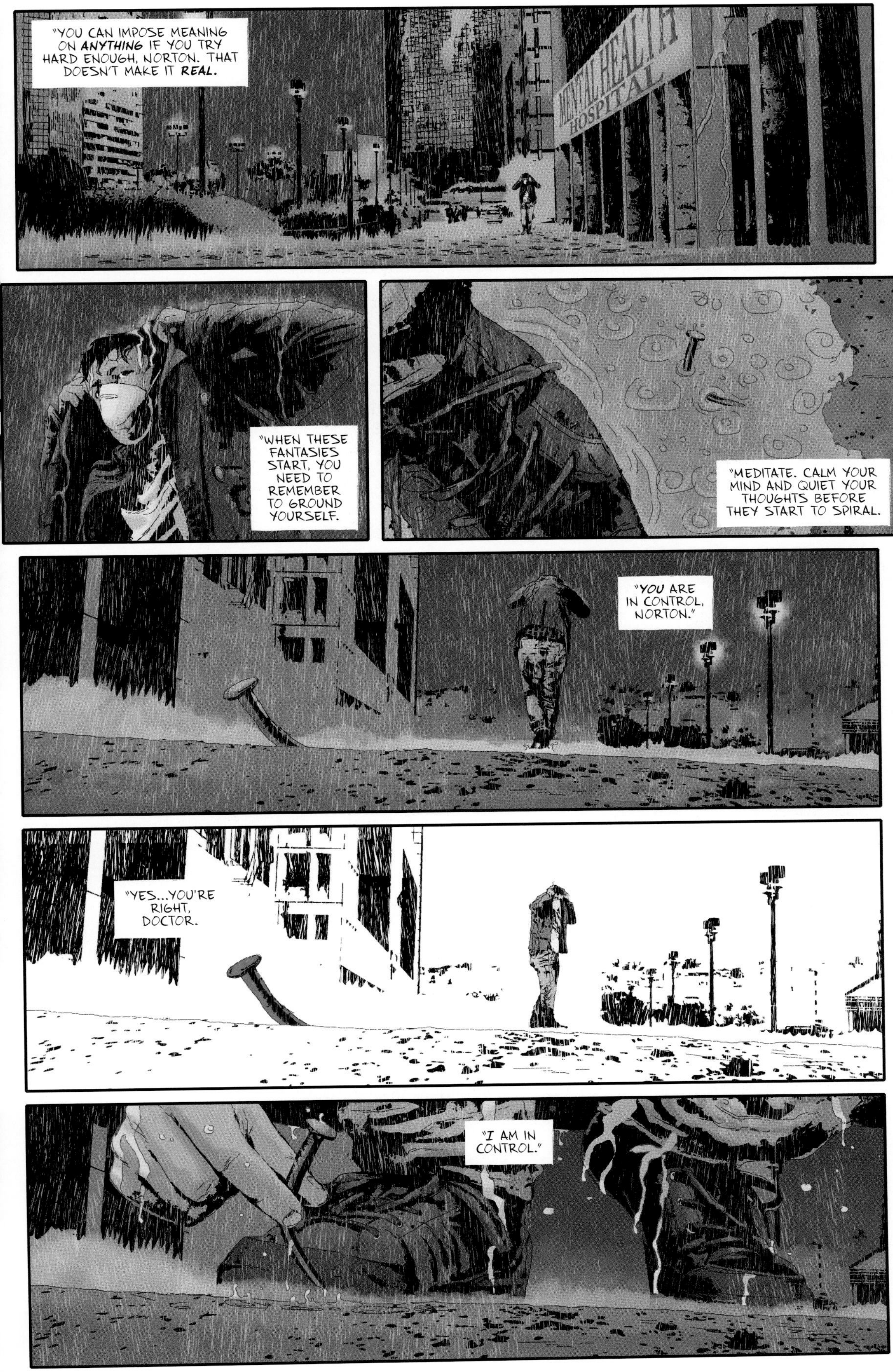

"YOU CAN IMPOSE MEANING ON ANYTHING IF YOU TRY HARD ENOUGH, NORTON. THAT DOESN'T MAKE IT REAL.
MENTAL HEALTH HOSPITAL
"WHEN THESE FANTASIES START, YOU NEED TO REMEMBER TO GROUND YOURSELF.
"MEDITATE. CALM YOUR MIND AND QUIET YOUR THOUGHTS BEFORE THEY START TO SPIRAL.
"YOU ARE IN CONTROL, NORTON."
"YES...YOU'RE RIGHT, DOCTOR.
"I AM IN CONTROL."

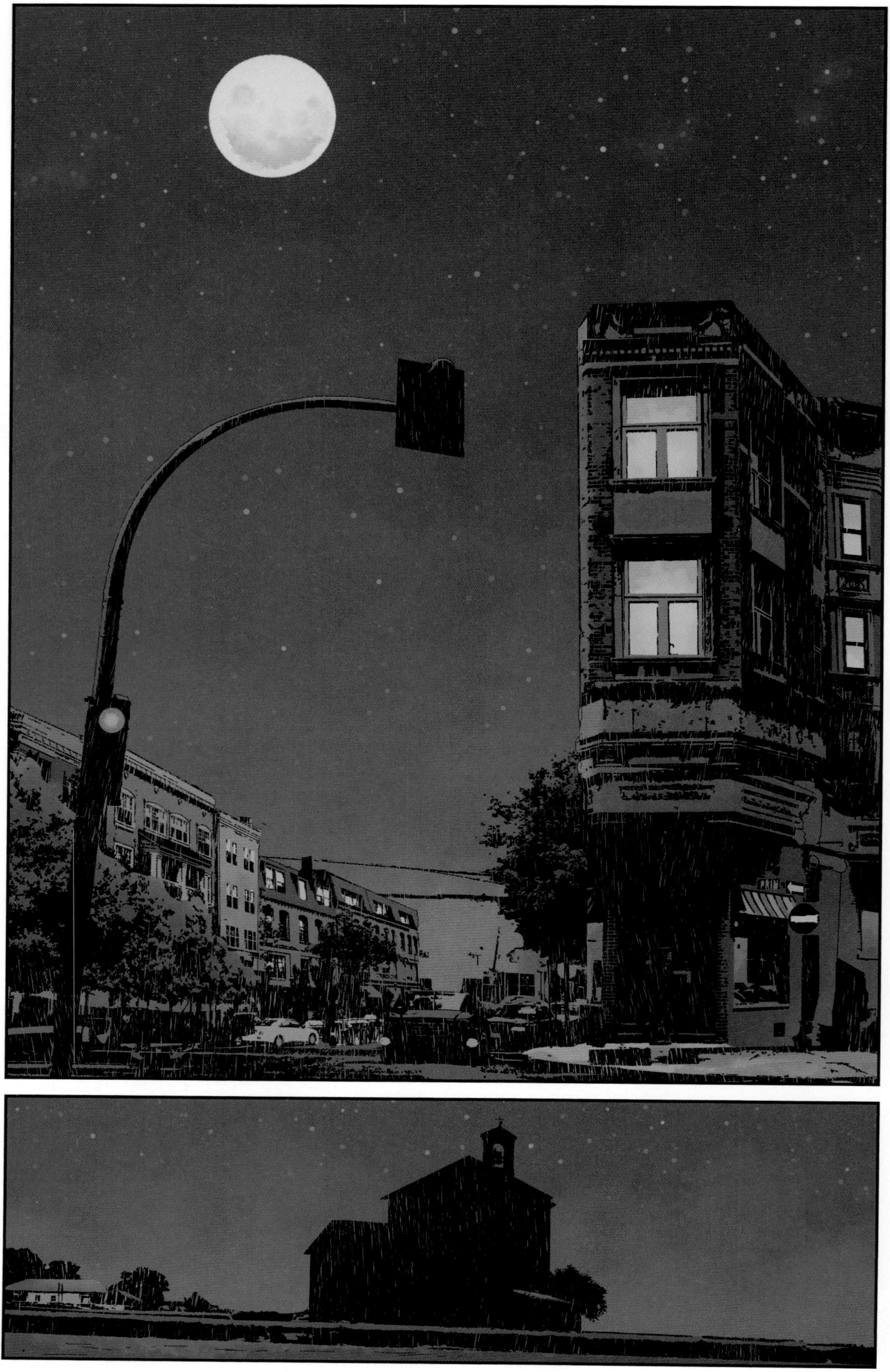

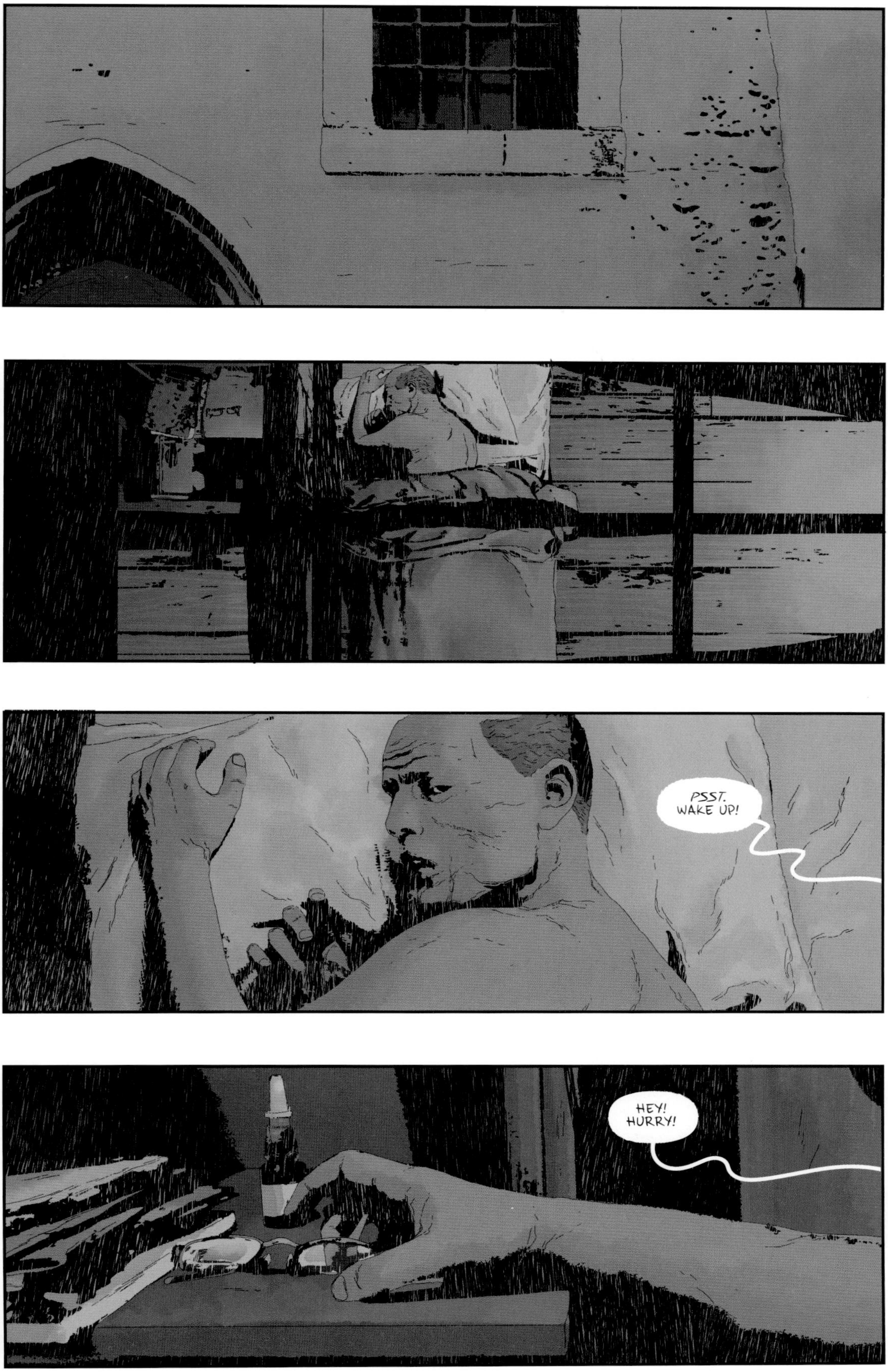
PSST. WAKE UP!
HEY! HURRY!

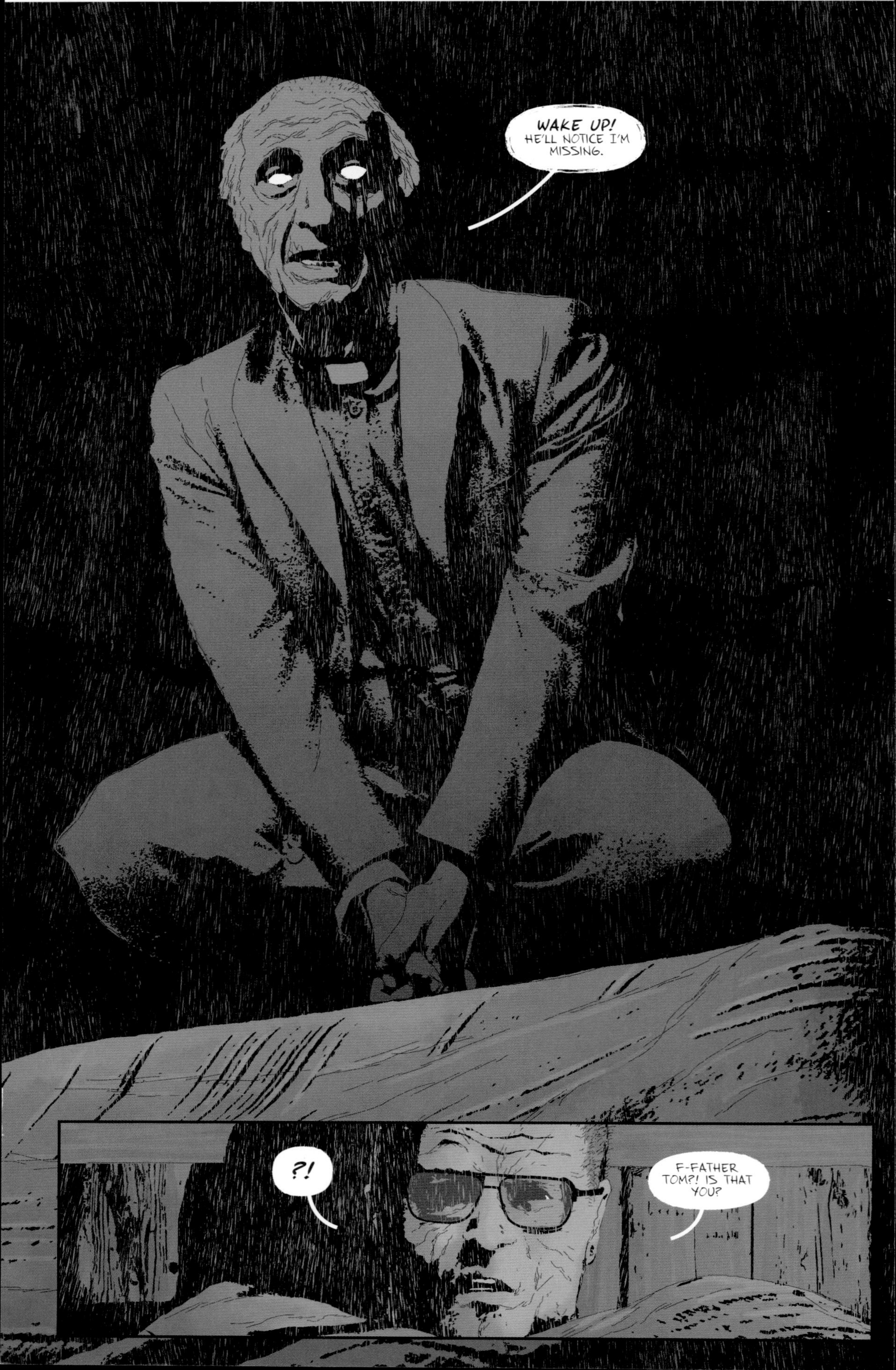
WAKE UP! HE'LL NOTICE I'M MISSING.
?!
F-FATHER TOM?! IS THAT YOU?

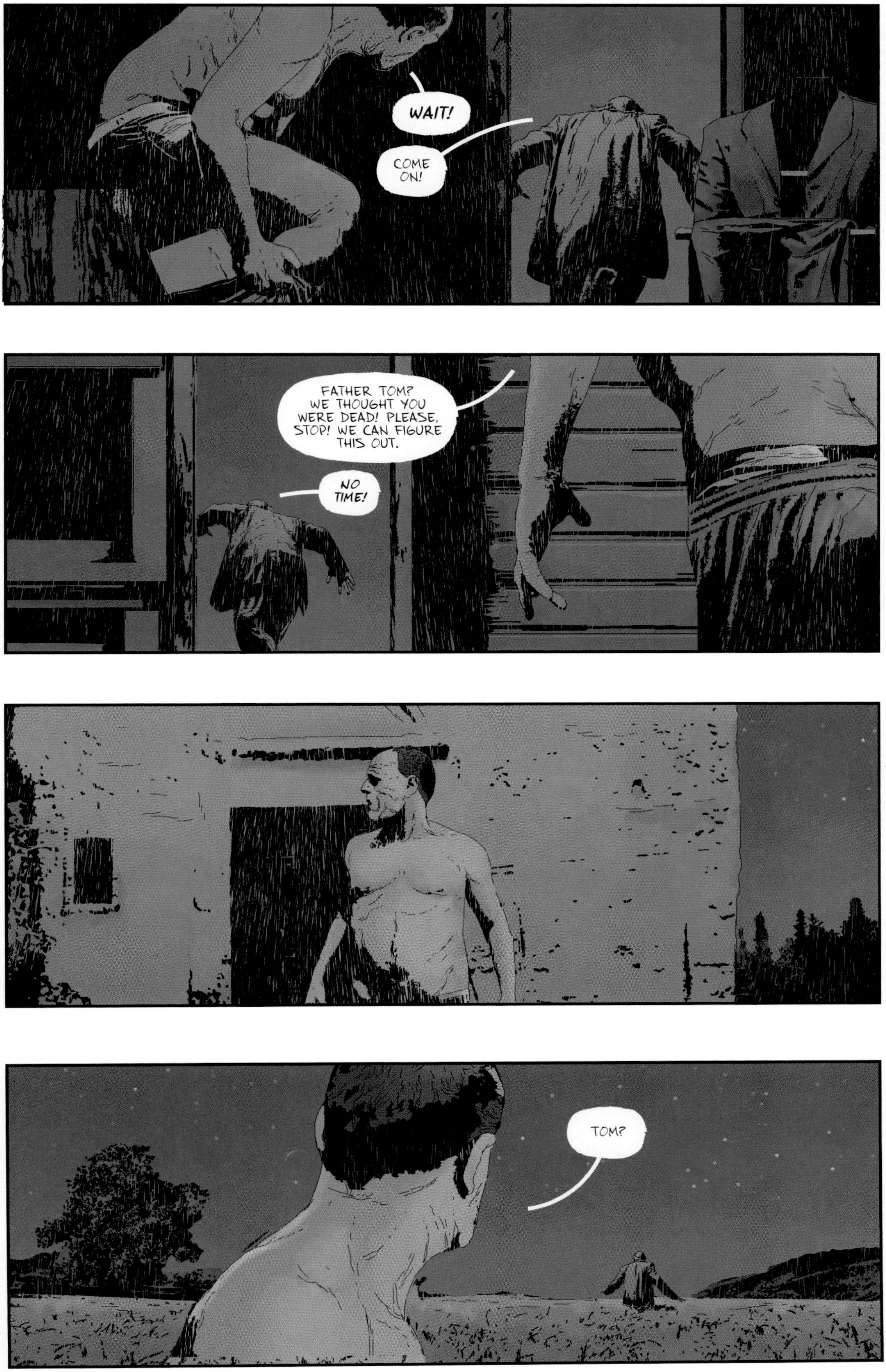
WAIT!
COME ON!
FATHER TOM? WE THOUGHT YOU WERE DEAD! PLEASE, STOP! WE CAN FIGURE THIS OUT.
NO TIME!
TOM?

PERSONAL JOURNAL AUGUST 12:
I SAW DR. XU AGAIN TODAY AND
NOW I'M WORRIED THAT MY WORK
MAY BE IN JEOPARDY...

I KNOW THAT SHE MEANS WELL. I
KNOW THAT SHE THINKS SHE IS
HELPING ME. BUT, I CAN'T GO BACK
TO THE HOSPITAL. I CAN'T.

I'M SO CLOSE NOW. I CAN
FEEL IT. A PART OF ME
WANTED TO TELL DR. XU THE
TRUTH, BUT I'M SCARED THAT
WOULD MAKE HER EVEN MORE
SKEPTICAL OF MY WORK.

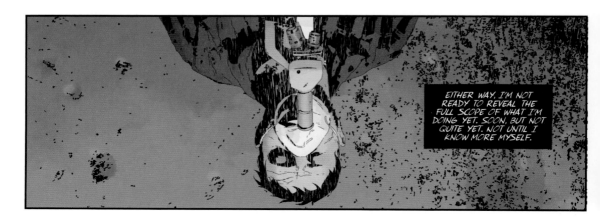

EITHER WAY, I'M NOT
READY TO REVEAL THE
FULL SCOPE OF WHAT I'M
DOING YET. SOON, BUT NOT
QUITE YET. NOT UNTIL I
KNOW MORE MYSELF.

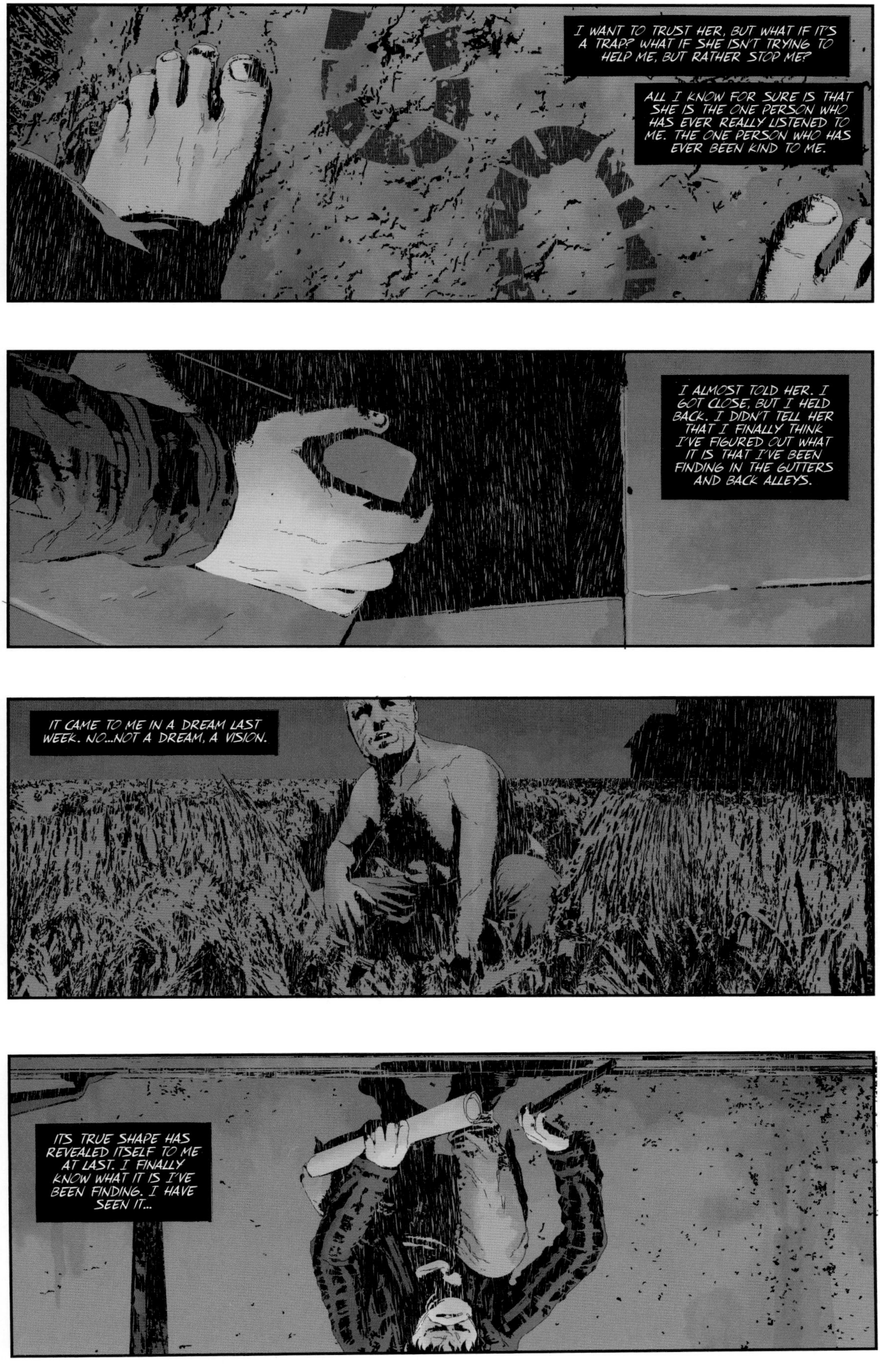
I WANT TO TRUST HER, BUT WHAT IF IT'S A TRAP? WHAT IF SHE ISN'T TRYING TO HELP ME, BUT RATHER STOP ME?
ALL I KNOW FOR SURE IS THAT SHE IS THE ONE PERSON WHO HAS EVER REALLY LISTENED TO ME. THE ONE PERSON WHO HAS EVER BEEN KIND TO ME.
I ALMOST TOLD HER. I GOT CLOSE, BUT I HELD BACK. I DIDN'T TELL HER THAT I FINALLY THINK I'VE FIGURED OUT WHAT IT IS THAT I'VE BEEN FINDING IN THE GUTTERS AND BACK ALLEYS.
IT CAME TO ME IN A DREAM LAST WEEK. NO...NOT A DREAM, A VISION.
ITS TRUE SHAPE HAS REVEALED ITSELF TO ME AT LAST. I FINALLY KNOW WHAT IT IS I'VE BEEN FINDING. I HAVE SEEN IT...

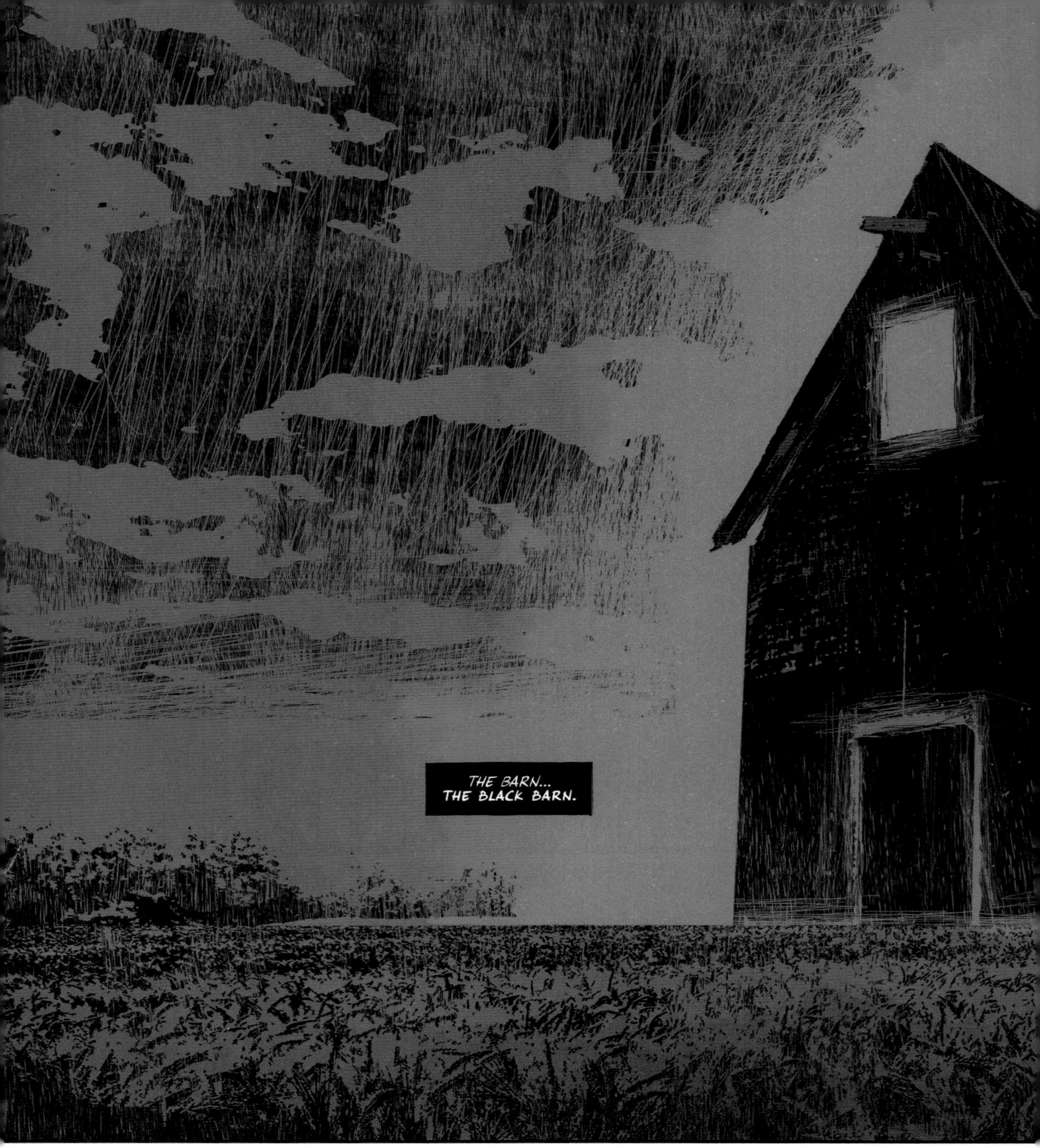
THE BARN...
THE BLACK BARN.

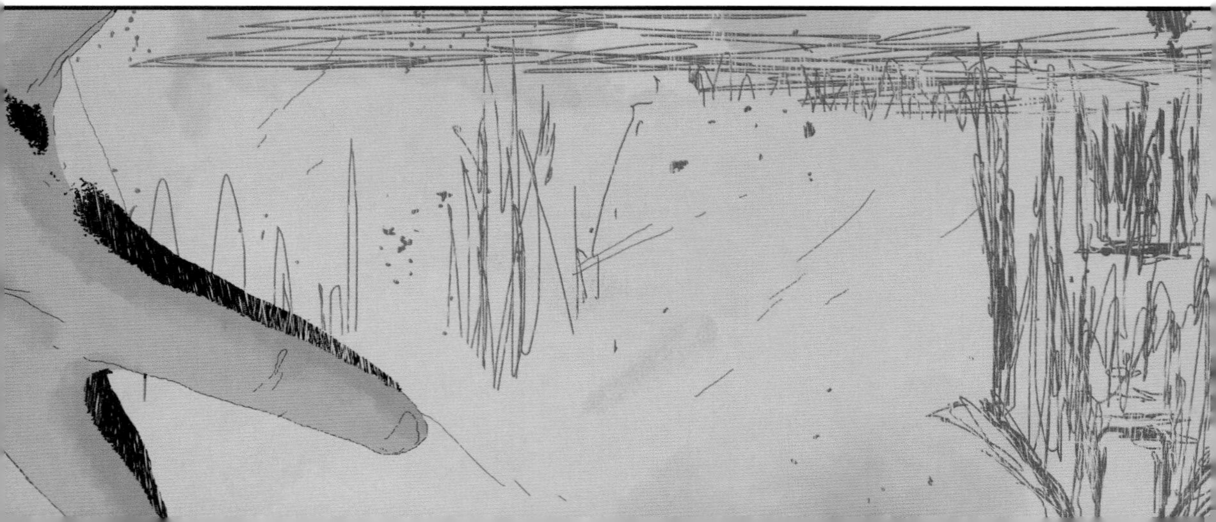

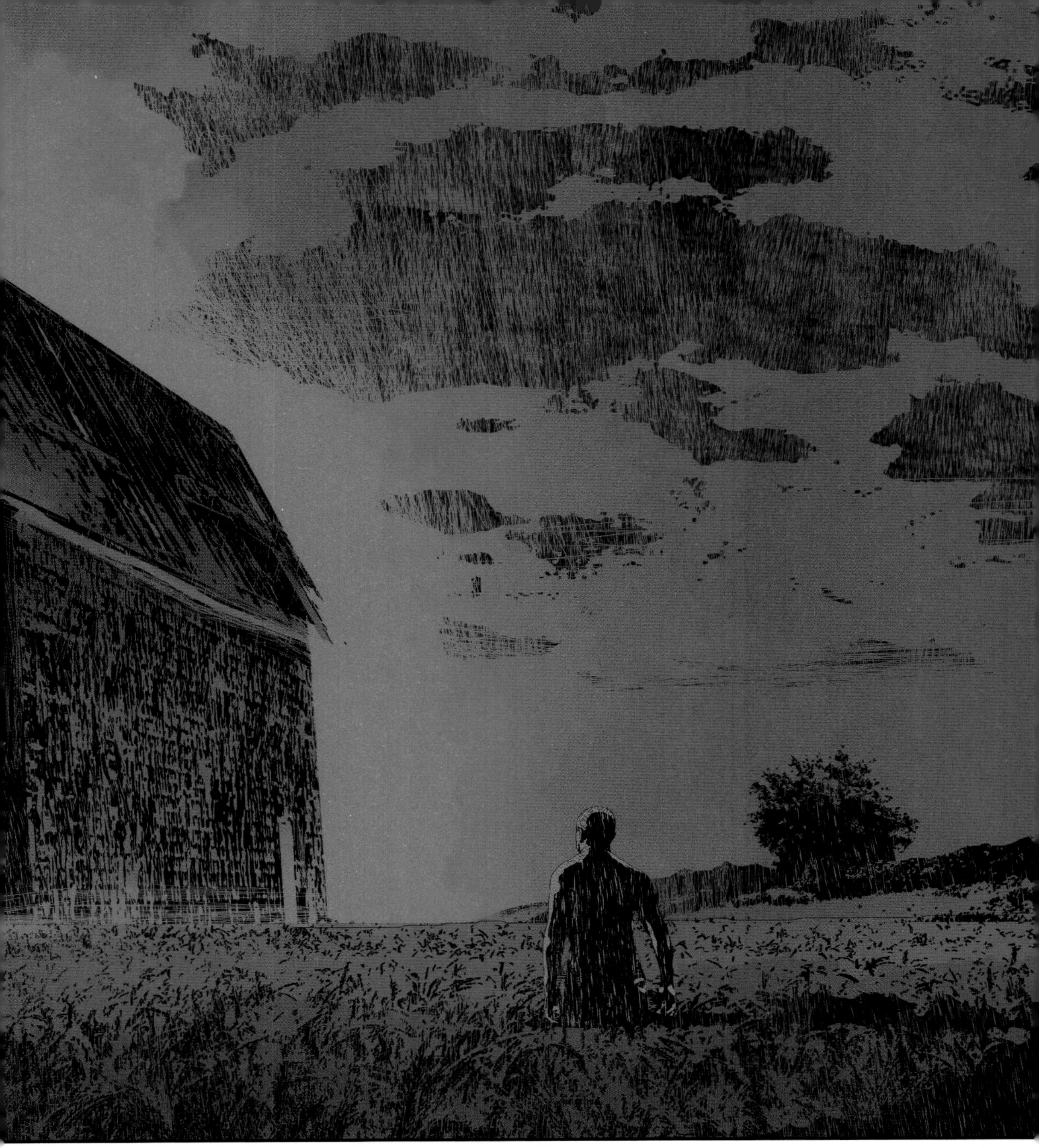

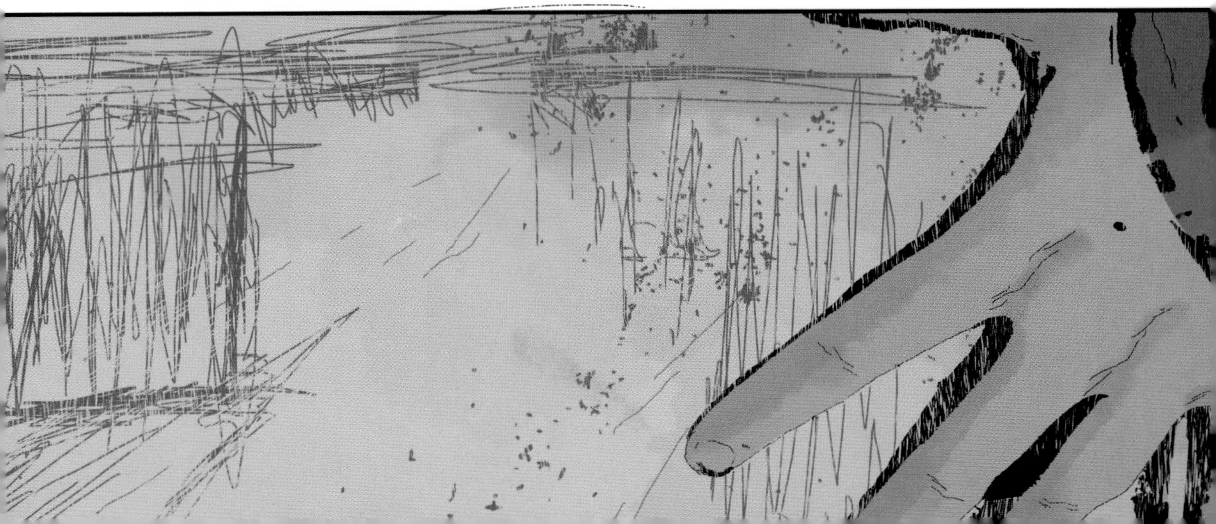

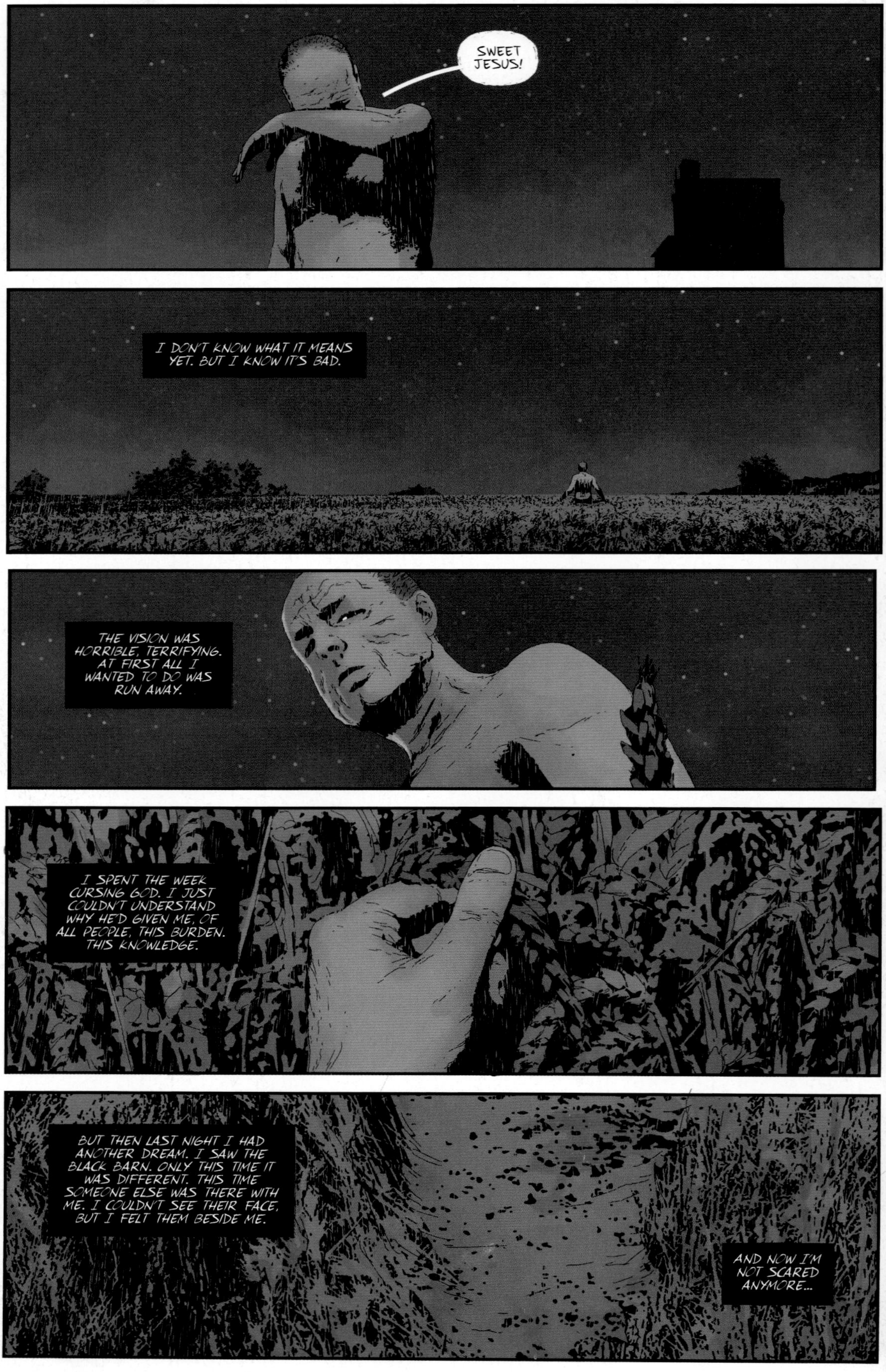
SWEET JESUS!
I DON'T KNOW WHAT IT MEANS YET. BUT I KNOW IT'S BAD.
THE VISION WAS HORRIBLE, TERRIFYING. AT FIRST ALL I WANTED TO DO WAS RUN AWAY.
I SPENT THE WEEK CURSING GOD. I JUST COULDN'T UNDERSTAND WHY HE'D GIVEN ME, OF ALL PEOPLE, THIS BURDEN. THIS KNOWLEDGE.
BUT THEN LAST NIGHT I HAD ANOTHER DREAM. I SAW THE BLACK BARN. ONLY THIS TIME IT WAS DIFFERENT. THIS TIME SOMEONE ELSE WAS THERE WITH ME. I COULDN'T SEE THEIR FACE, BUT I FELT THEM BESIDE ME.
AND NOW I'M NOT SCARED ANYMORE...

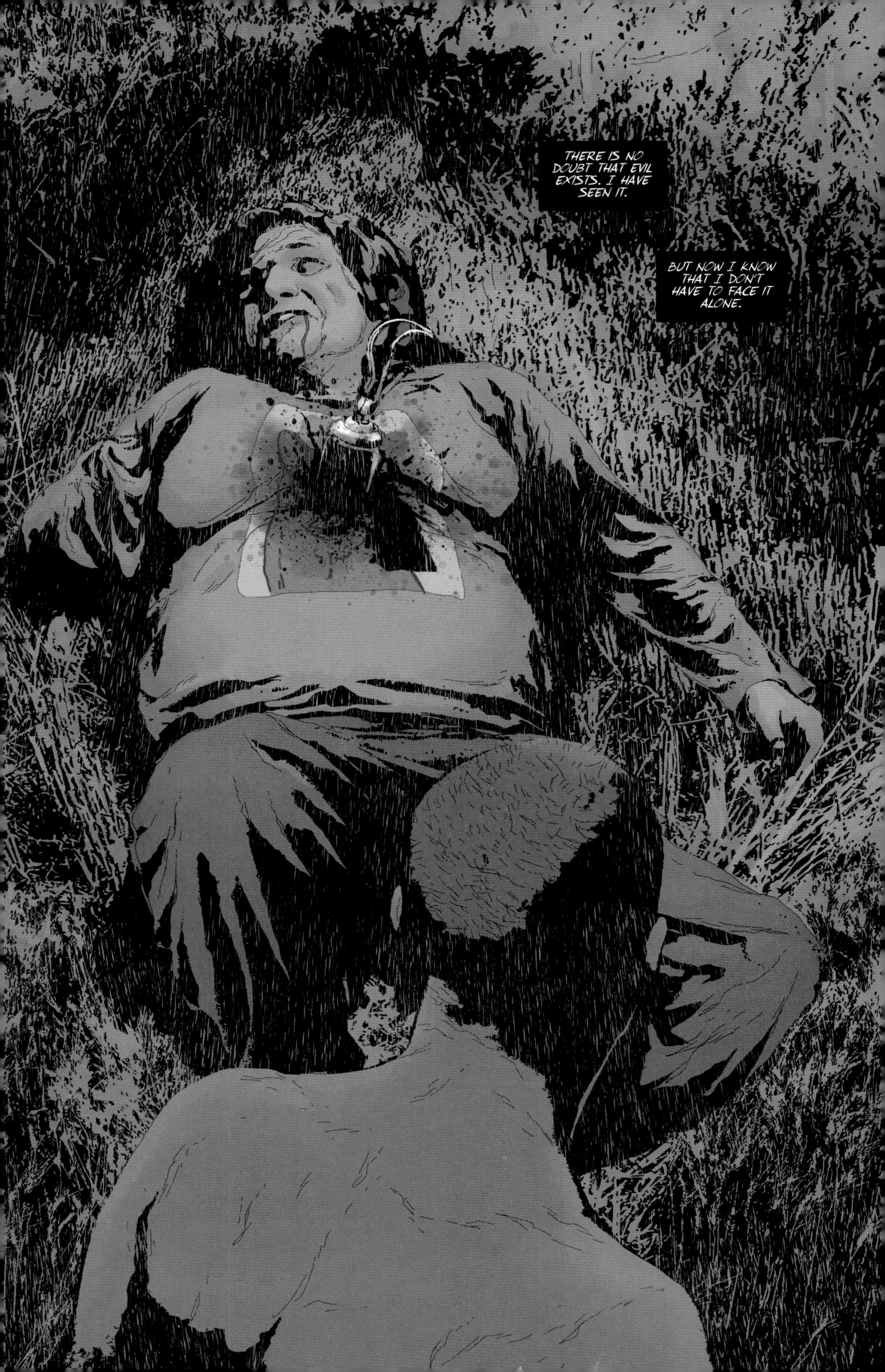
THERE IS NO DOUBT THAT EVIL EXISTS. I HAVE SEEN IT.
BUT NOW I KNOW THAT I DON'T HAVE TO FACE IT ALONE.

Two

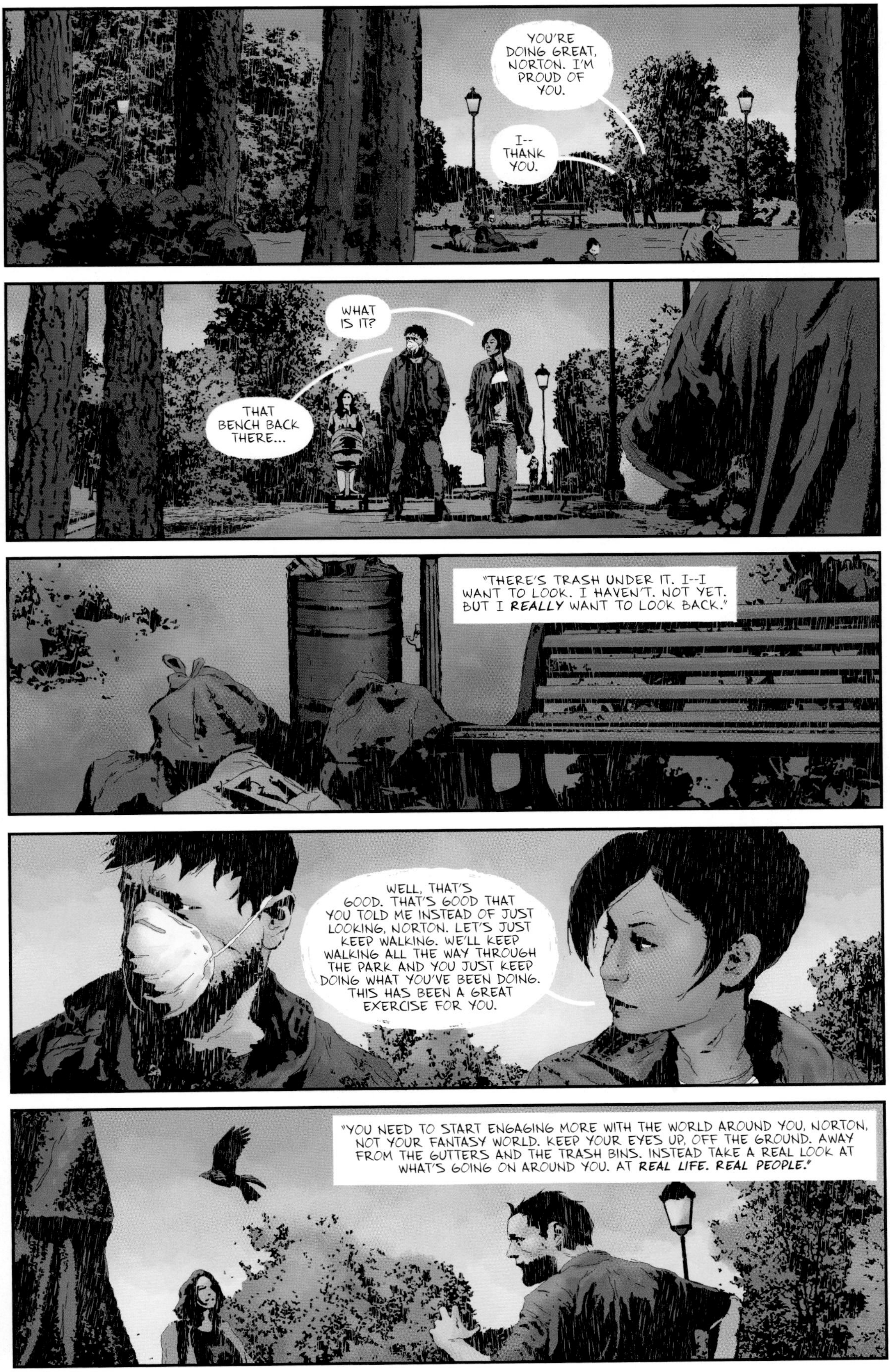
YOU'RE DOING GREAT, NORTON. I'M PROUD OF YOU.
I-- THANK YOU.
WHAT IS IT?
THAT BENCH BACK THERE...
"THERE'S TRASH UNDER IT. I--I WANT TO LOOK. I HAVEN'T. NOT YET. BUT I REALLY WANT TO LOOK BACK."
WELL, THAT'S GOOD. THAT'S GOOD THAT YOU TOLD ME INSTEAD OF JUST LOOKING, NORTON. LET'S JUST KEEP WALKING. WE'LL KEEP WALKING ALL THE WAY THROUGH THE PARK AND YOU JUST KEEP DOING WHAT YOU'VE BEEN DOING. THIS HAS BEEN A GREAT EXERCISE FOR YOU.
"YOU NEED TO START ENGAGING MORE WITH THE WORLD AROUND YOU, NORTON, NOT YOUR FANTASY WORLD. KEEP YOUR EYES UP, OFF THE GROUND. AWAY FROM THE GUTTERS AND THE TRASH BINS. INSTEAD TAKE A REAL LOOK AT WHAT'S GOING ON AROUND YOU. AT REAL LIFE. REAL PEOPLE."

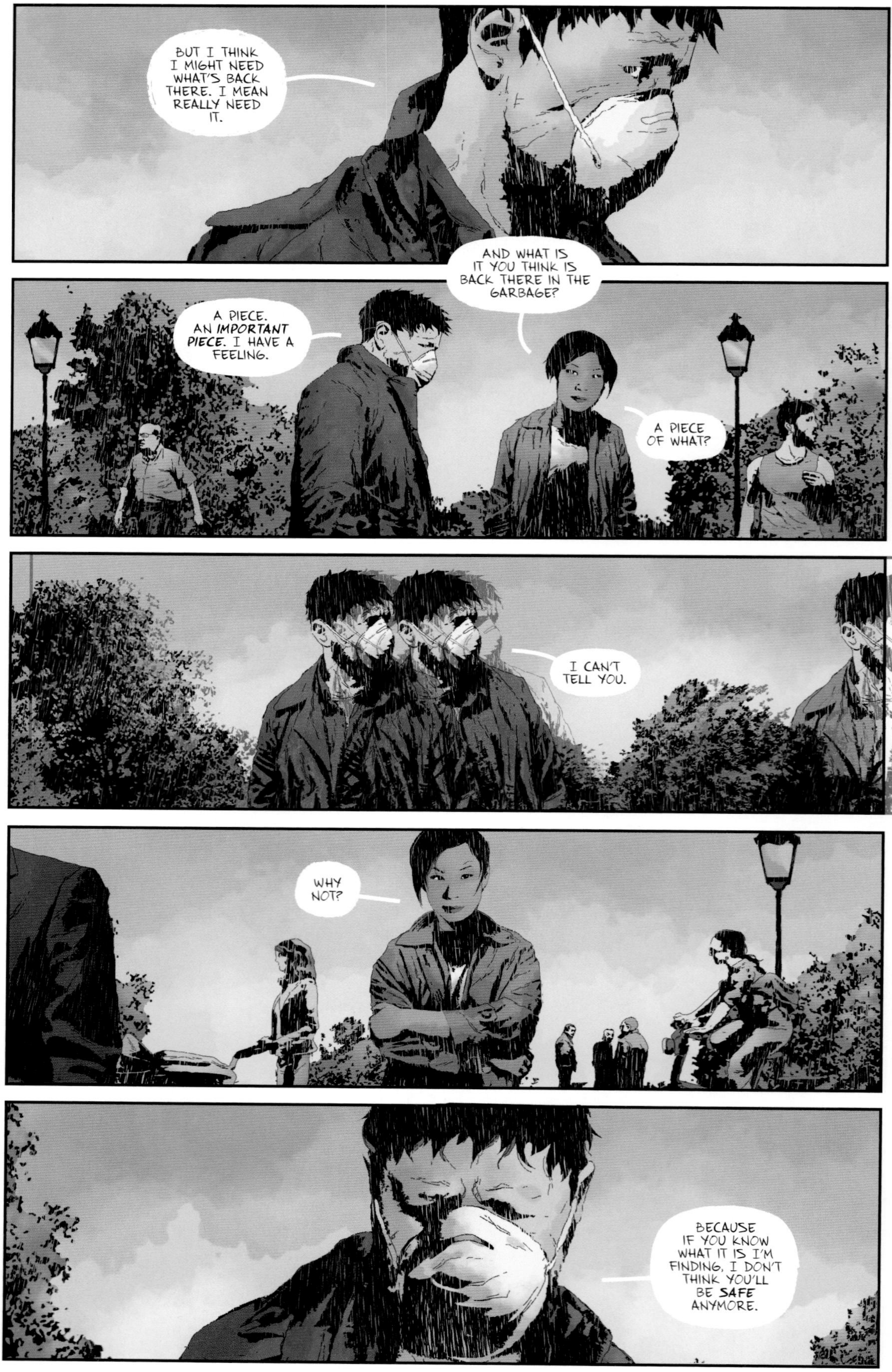
BUT I THINK I MIGHT NEED WHAT'S BACK THERE. I MEAN REALLY NEED IT.
AND WHAT IS IT YOU THINK IS BACK THERE IN THE GARBAGE?
A PIECE. AN IMPORTANT PIECE. I HAVE A FEELING.
A PIECE OF WHAT?
I CAN'T TELL YOU.
WHY NOT?
BECAUSE IF YOU KNOW WHAT IT IS I'M FINDING, I DON'T THINK YOU'LL BE SAFE ANYMORE.

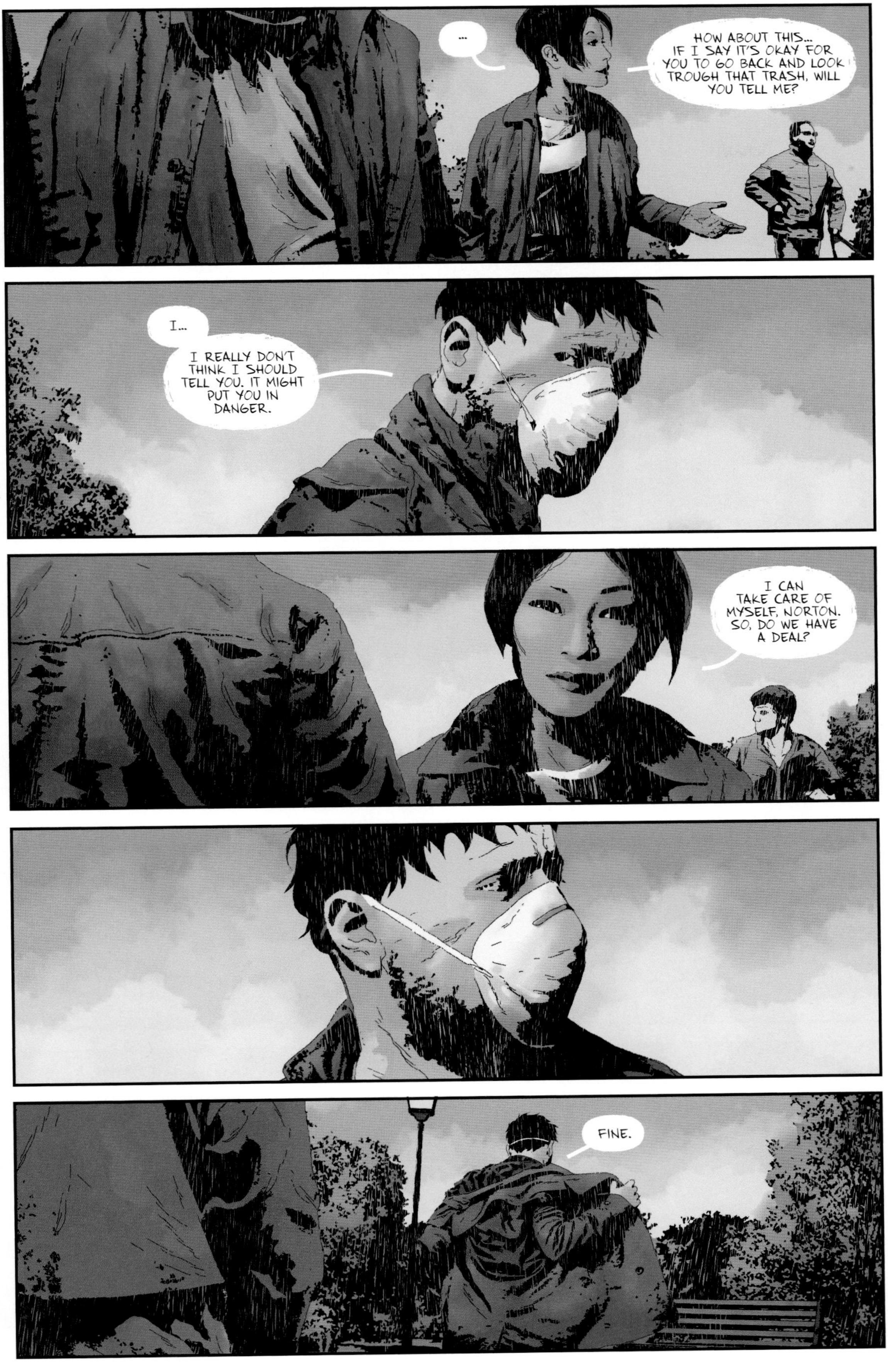
...
HOW ABOUT THIS... IF I SAY IT'S OKAY FOR YOU TO GO BACK AND LOOK TROUGH THAT TRASH, WILL YOU TELL ME?
I...
I REALLY DON'T THINK I SHOULD TELL YOU. IT MIGHT PUT YOU IN DANGER.
I CAN TAKE CARE OF MYSELF, NORTON. SO, DO WE HAVE A DEAL?
FINE.

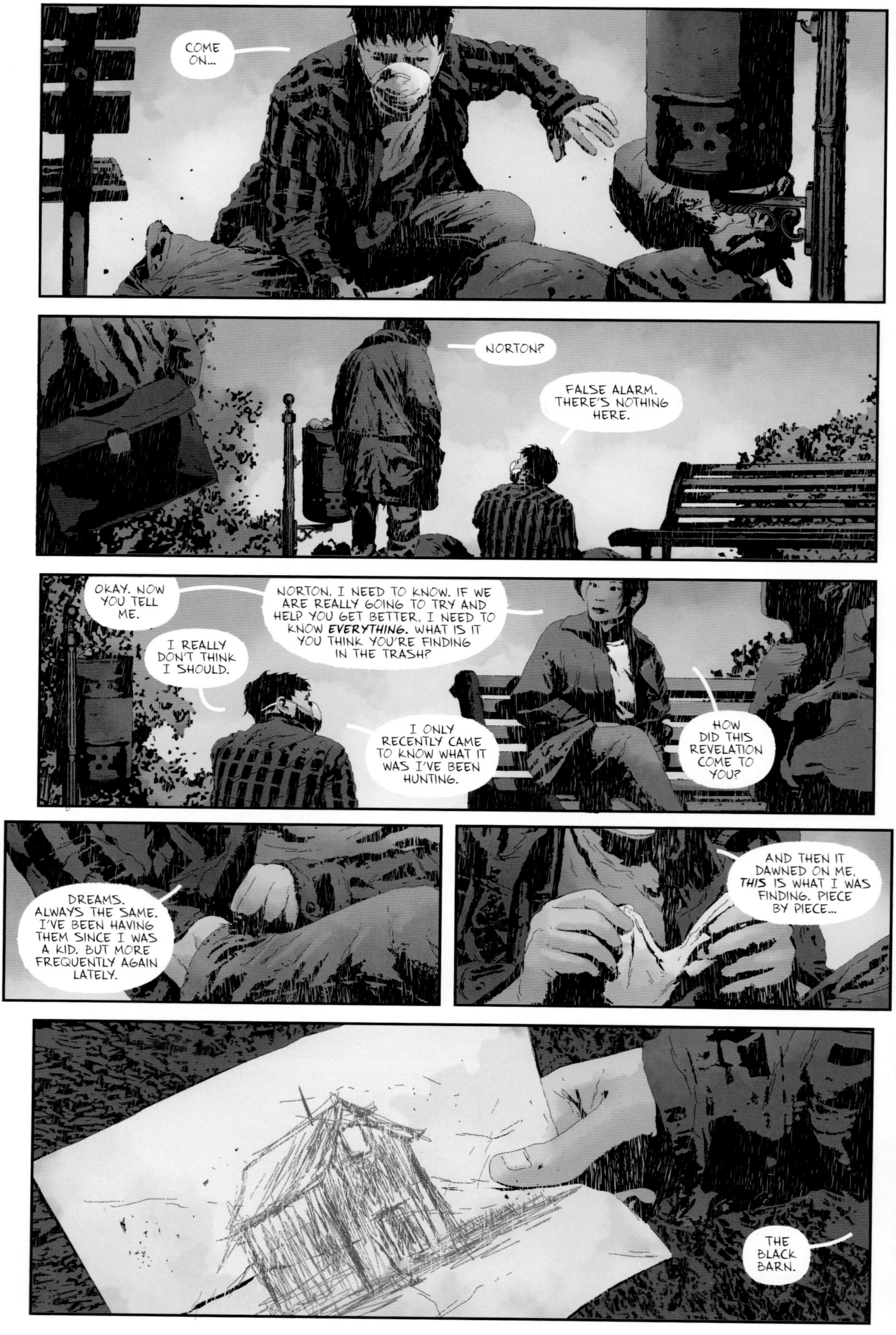
COME ON...
NORTON?
FALSE ALARM. THERE'S NOTHING HERE.
OKAY. NOW YOU TELL ME.
NORTON, I NEED TO KNOW. IF WE ARE REALLY GOING TO TRY AND HELP YOU GET BETTER, I NEED TO KNOW **EVERYTHING**. WHAT IS IT YOU THINK YOU'RE FINDING IN THE TRASH?
I REALLY DON'T THINK I SHOULD.
I ONLY RECENTLY CAME TO KNOW WHAT IT WAS I'VE BEEN HUNTING.
HOW DID THIS REVELATION COME TO YOU?
DREAMS. ALWAYS THE SAME. I'VE BEEN HAVING THEM SINCE I WAS A KID. BUT MORE FREQUENTLY AGAIN LATELY.
AND THEN IT DAWNED ON ME, ***THIS*** IS WHAT I WAS FINDING. PIECE BY PIECE...
THE BLACK BARN.

...THAT'S RIGHT, A *BARN*. AN OLD BARN.

THERE'S NO BARN BACK BEHIND THE REDDING HOUSE. THERE'S NOTHING BACK THERE EXCEPT THE CORNFIELD, FATHER.

WELL, I--I SAW A BARN. MAYBE IT WAS EARLIER, ON MY WAY BACK THERE. I DON'T--IT'S ALL A BIT OF A BLUR NOW. ALL I REALLY REMEMBER CLEARLY IS POOR MRS. TREMBLAY LYING THERE.

YOU HAVE TO BELIEVE ME, SHERIFF. I FOUND HER LIKE THAT. I WOULD NEVER--

IT WAS SO HORRIBLE.

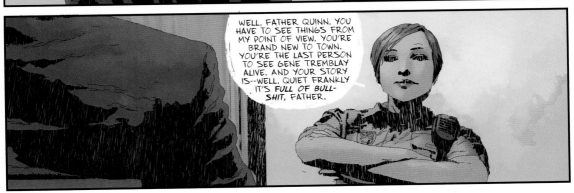

WELL, FATHER QUINN, YOU HAVE TO SEE THINGS FROM MY POINT OF VIEW. YOU'RE BRAND NEW TO TOWN. YOU'RE THE LAST PERSON TO SEE GENE TREMBLAY ALIVE. AND YOUR STORY IS--WELL, QUIET FRANKLY, IT'S *FULL OF BULL-SHIT*, FATHER.

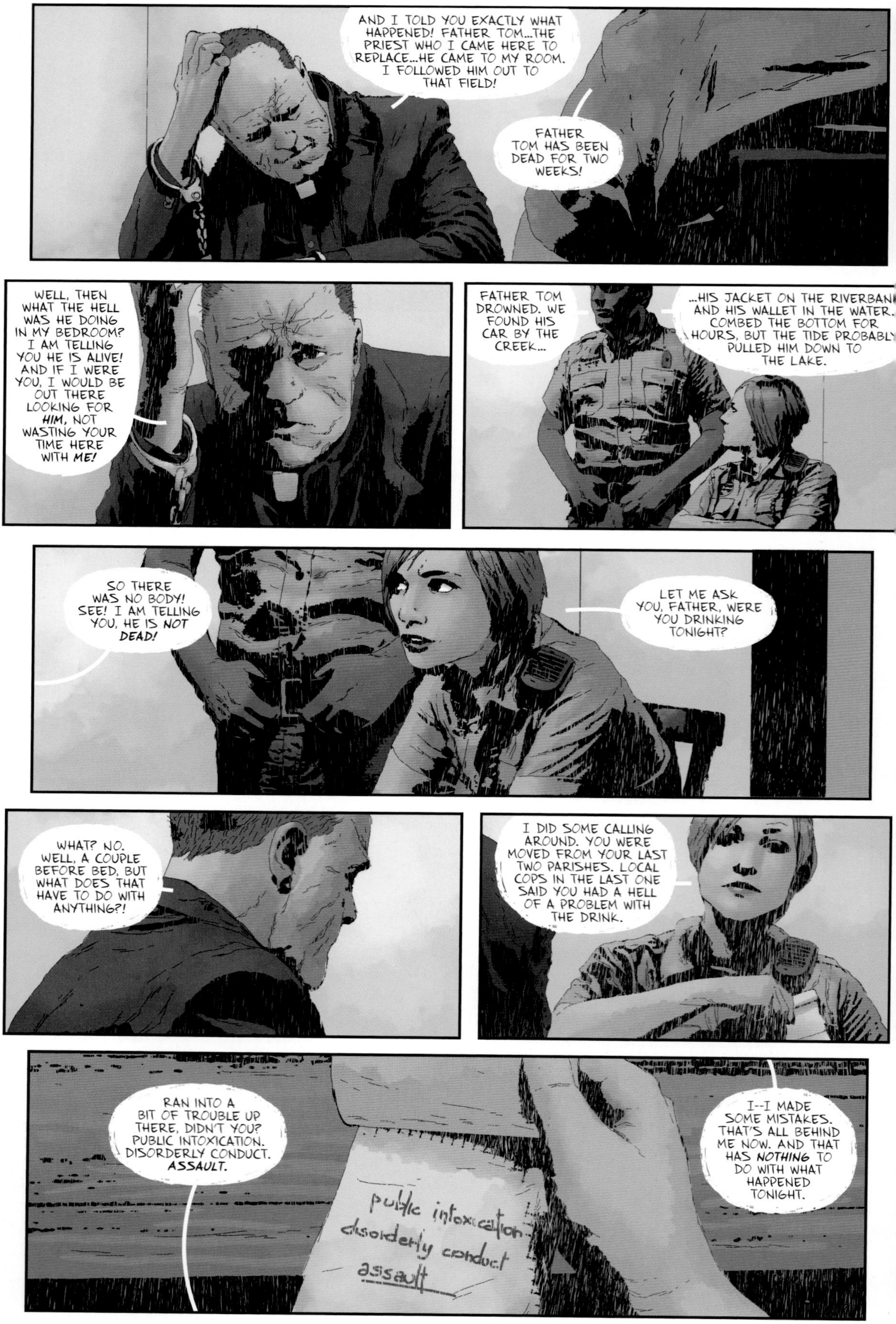
AND I TOLD YOU EXACTLY WHAT HAPPENED! FATHER TOM...THE PRIEST WHO I CAME HERE TO REPLACE...HE CAME TO MY ROOM. I FOLLOWED HIM OUT TO THAT FIELD!
FATHER TOM HAS BEEN DEAD FOR TWO WEEKS!
WELL, THEN WHAT THE HELL WAS HE DOING IN MY BEDROOM? I AM TELLING YOU HE IS ALIVE! AND IF I WERE YOU, I WOULD BE OUT THERE LOOKING FOR HIM, NOT WASTING YOUR TIME HERE WITH ME!
FATHER TOM DROWNED. WE FOUND HIS CAR BY THE CREEK...
...HIS JACKET ON THE RIVERBAN AND HIS WALLET IN THE WATER. COMBED THE BOTTOM FOR HOURS, BUT THE TIDE PROBABL PULLED HIM DOWN TO THE LAKE.
SO THERE WAS NO BODY! SEE! I AM TELLING YOU, HE IS NOT DEAD!
LET ME ASK YOU, FATHER, WERE YOU DRINKING TONIGHT?
WHAT? NO. WELL, A COUPLE BEFORE BED, BUT WHAT DOES THAT HAVE TO DO WITH ANYTHING?!
I DID SOME CALLING AROUND. YOU WERE MOVED FROM YOUR LAST TWO PARISHES. LOCAL COPS IN THE LAST ONE SAID YOU HAD A HELL OF A PROBLEM WITH THE DRINK.
RAN INTO A BIT OF TROUBLE UP THERE, DIDN'T YOU? PUBLIC INTOXICATION. DISORDERLY CONDUCT. ASSAULT.
public intoxication
disorderly conduct
assault
I--I MADE SOME MISTAKES. THAT'S ALL BEHIND ME NOW. AND THAT HAS NOTHING TO DO WITH WHAT HAPPENED TONIGHT.

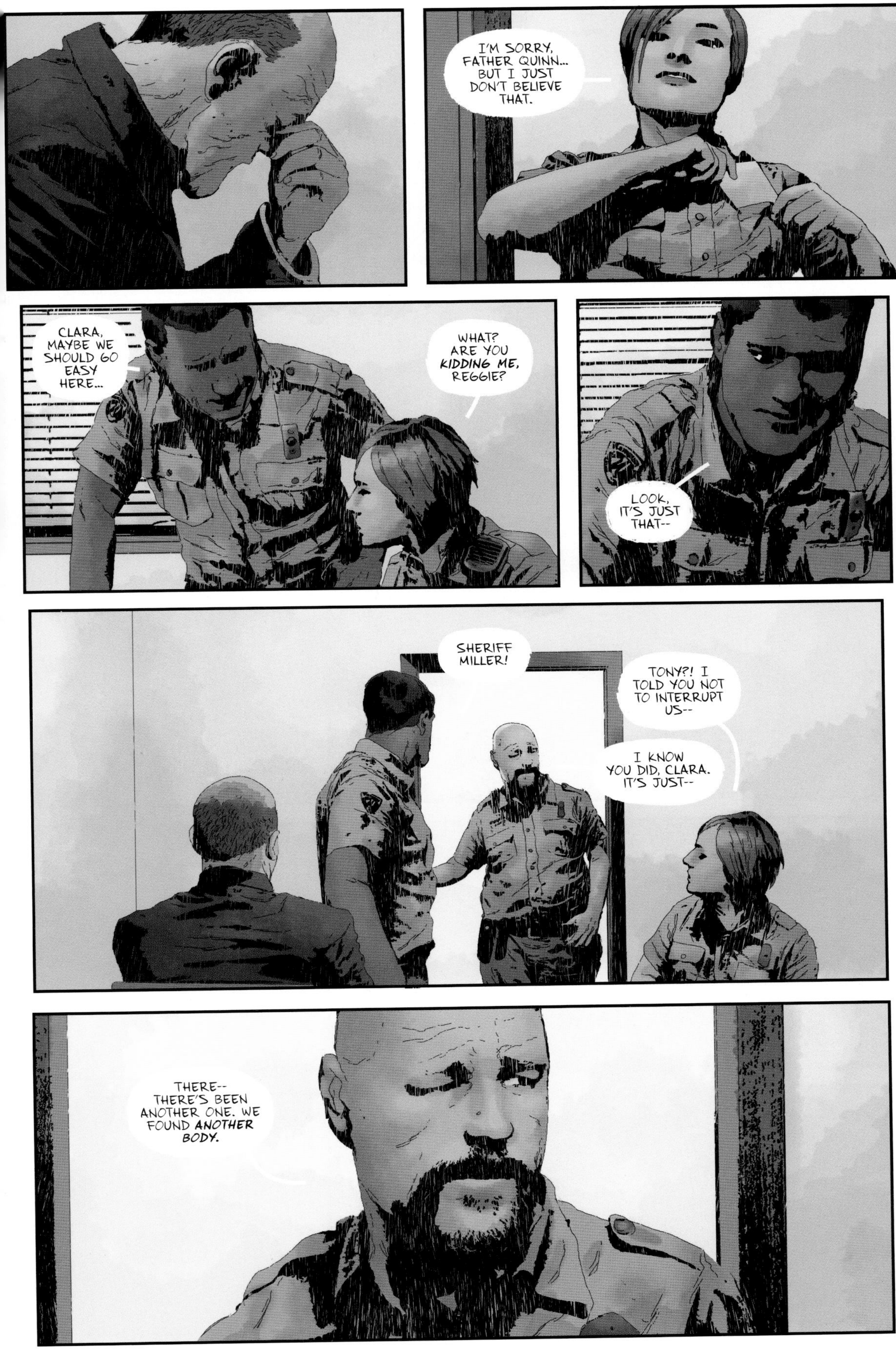
I'M SORRY, FATHER QUINN... BUT I JUST DON'T BELIEVE THAT.
CLARA, MAYBE WE SHOULD GO EASY HERE...
WHAT? ARE YOU **KIDDING ME,** REGGIE?
LOOK, IT'S JUST THAT--
SHERIFF MILLER!
TONY?! I TOLD YOU NOT TO INTERRUPT US--
I KNOW YOU DID, CLARA. IT'S JUST--
THERE-- THERE'S BEEN ANOTHER ONE. WE FOUND **ANOTHER BODY.**

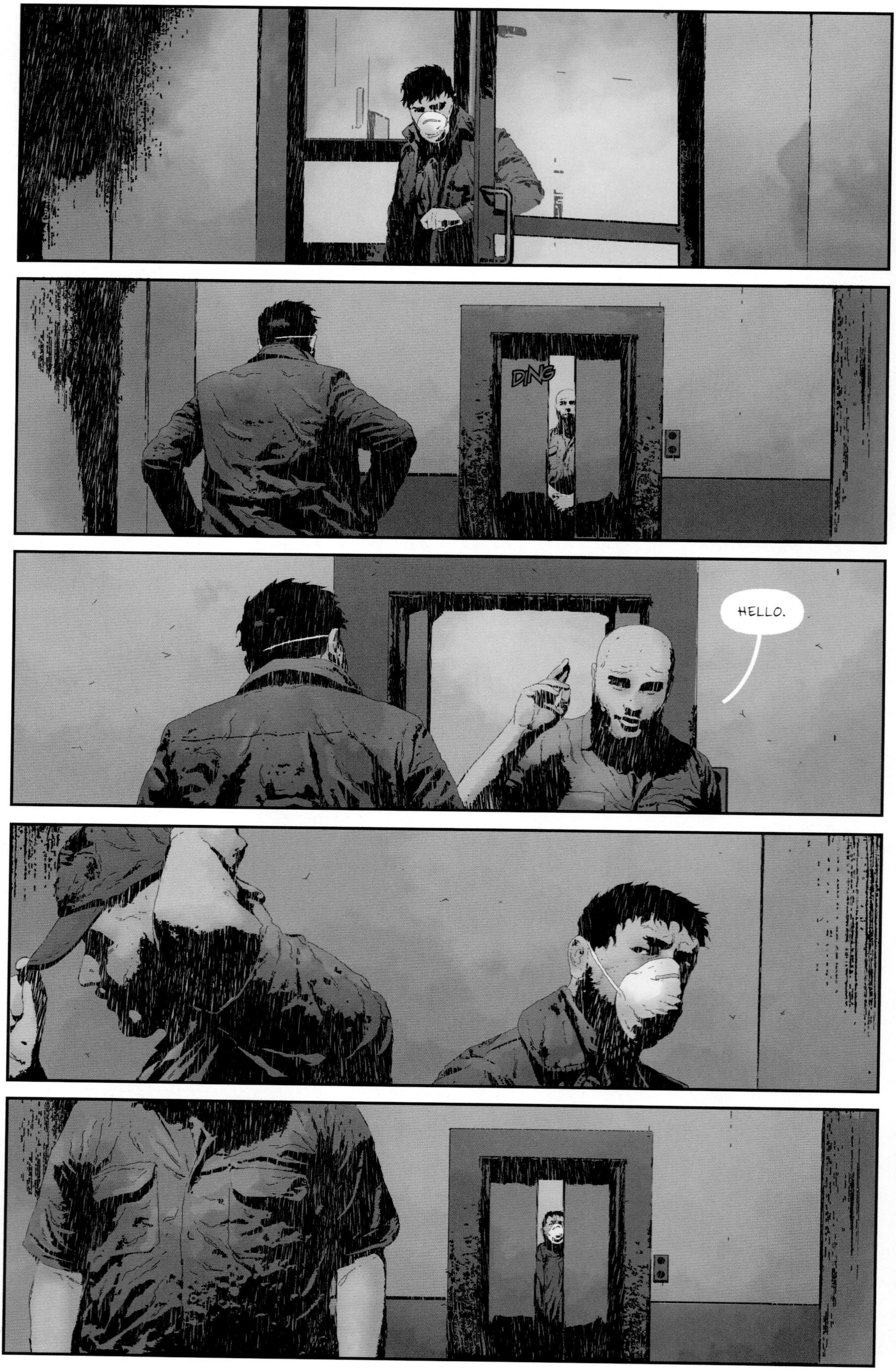
DING
HELLO.

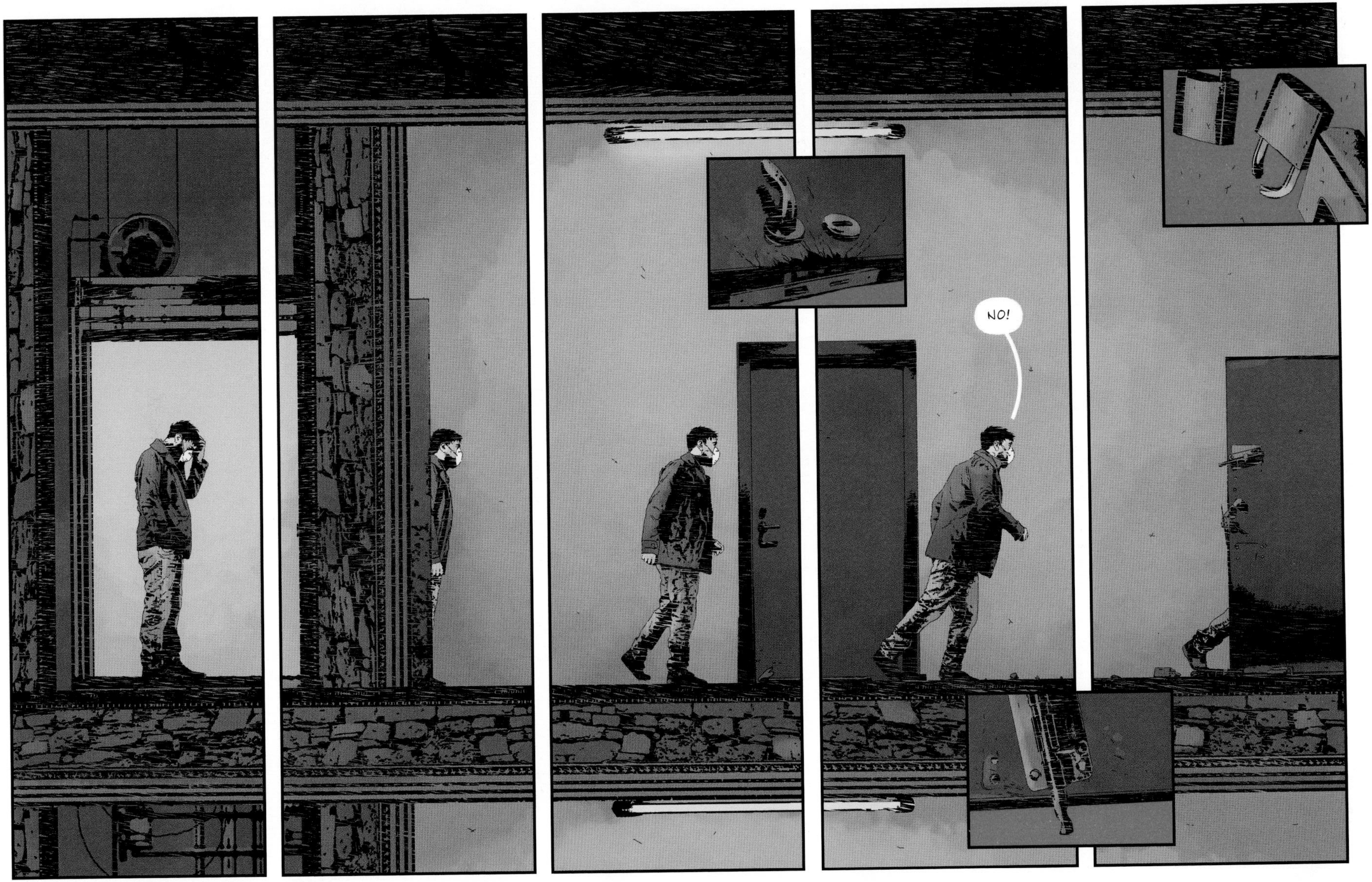
NO!

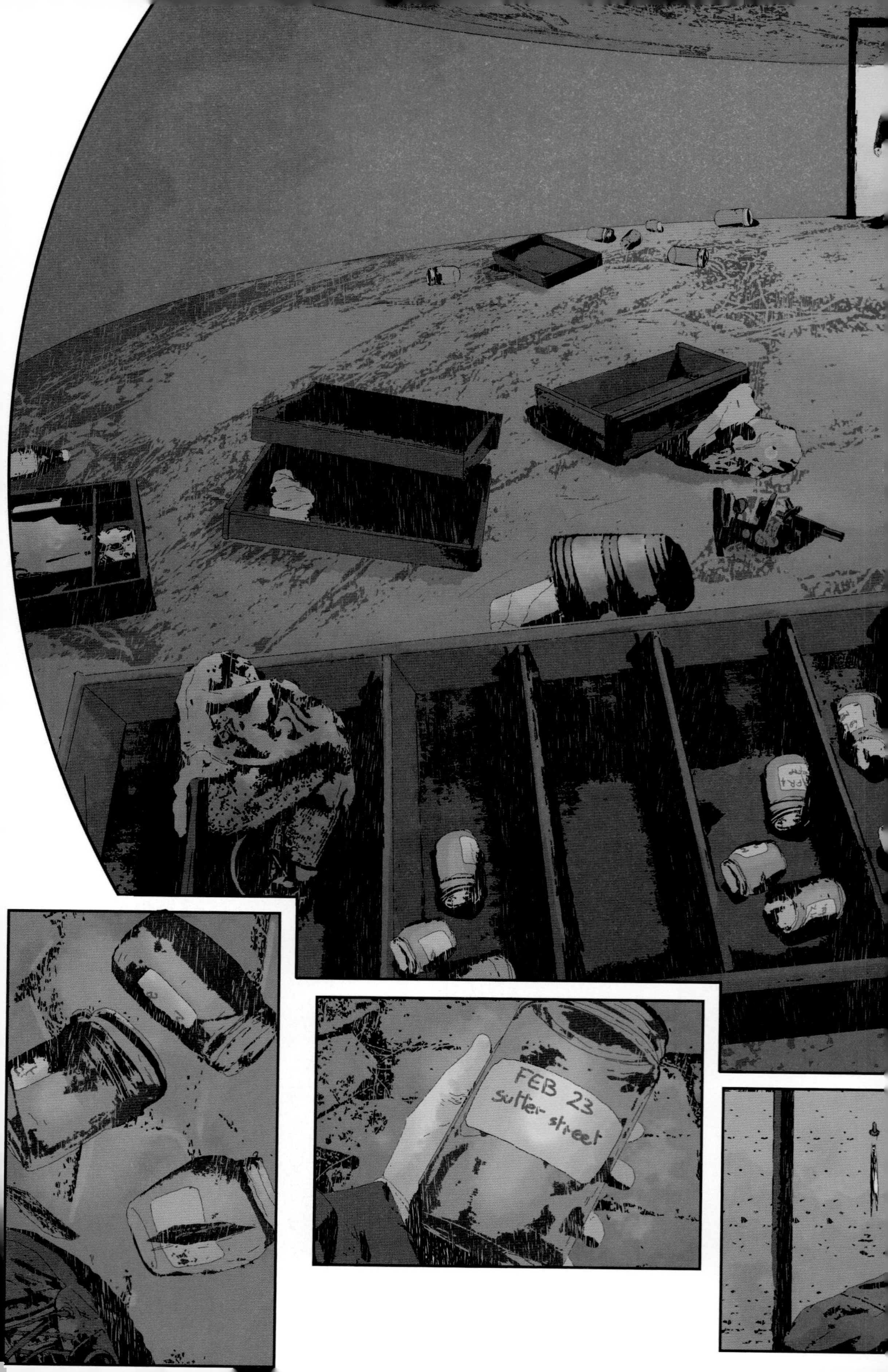
FEB 23
sutter street

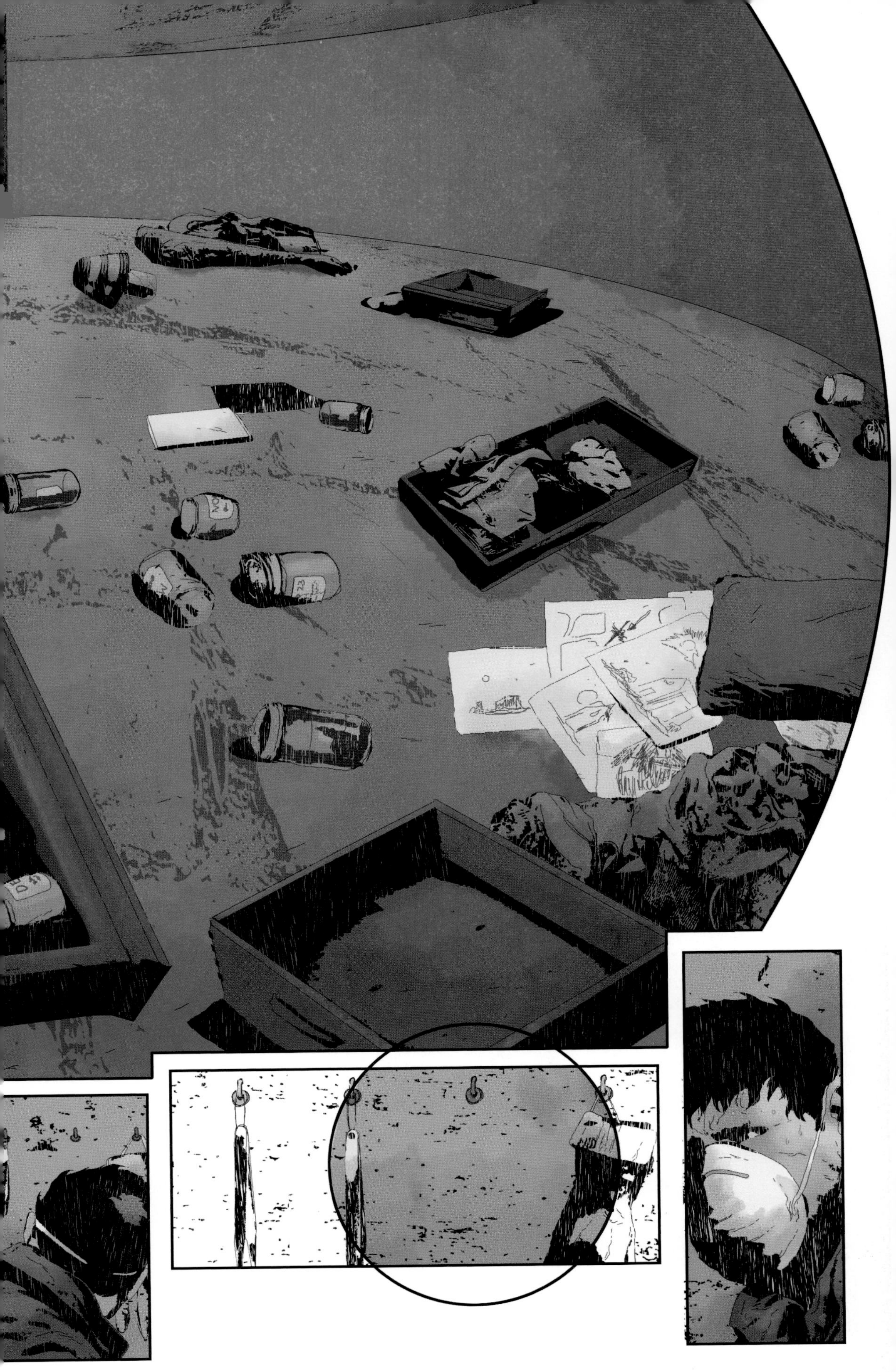

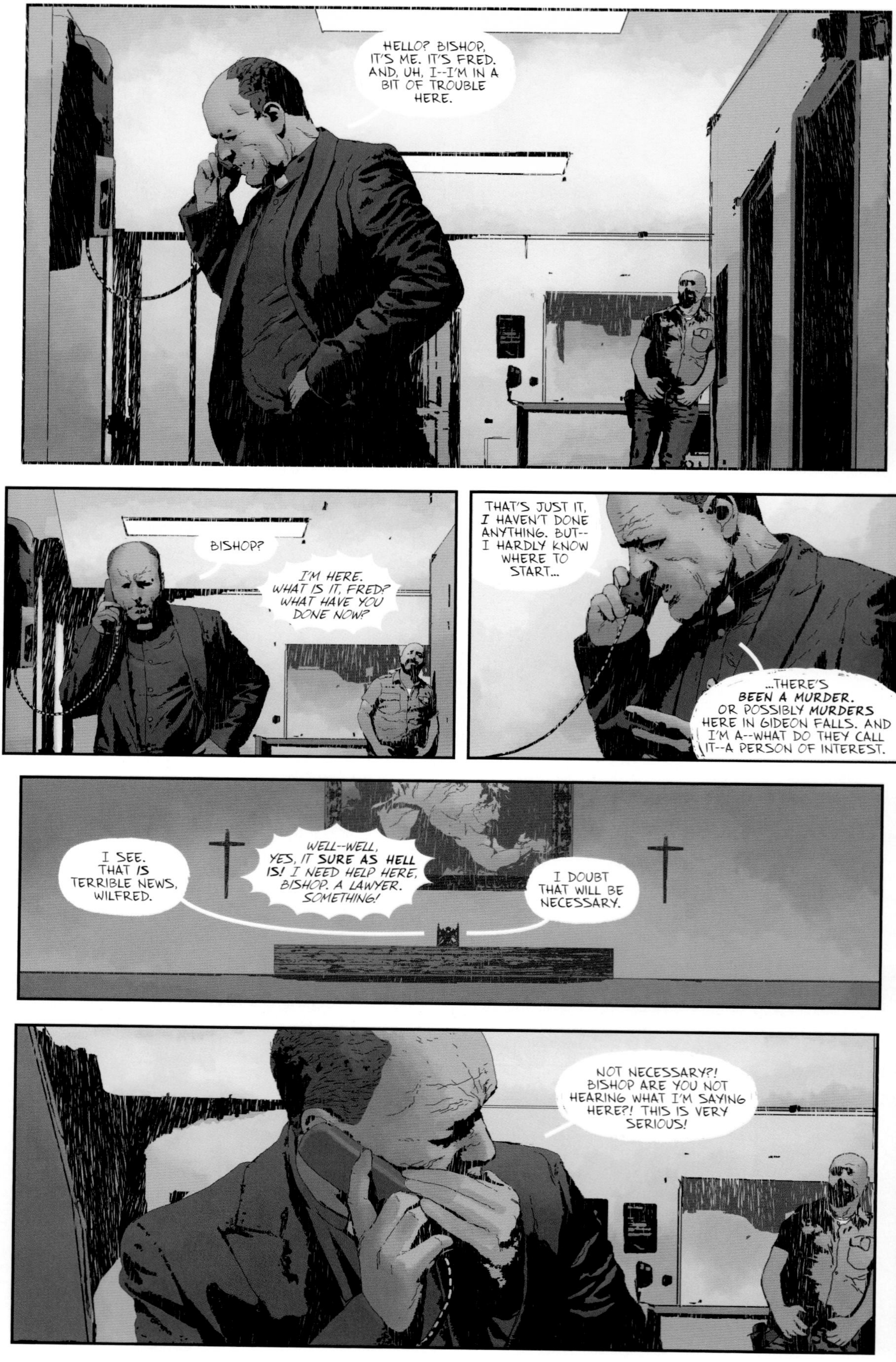
HELLO? BISHOP, IT'S ME. IT'S FRED. AND, UH, I--I'M IN A BIT OF TROUBLE HERE.
BISHOP?
I'M HERE. WHAT IS IT, FRED? WHAT HAVE YOU DONE NOW?
THAT'S JUST IT, I HAVEN'T DONE ANYTHING. BUT-- I HARDLY KNOW WHERE TO START...
...THERE'S BEEN A MURDER. OR POSSIBLY MURDERS HERE IN GIDEON FALLS. AND I'M A--WHAT DO THEY CALL IT--A PERSON OF INTEREST.
I SEE. THAT IS TERRIBLE NEWS, WILFRED.
WELL--WELL, YES, IT SURE AS HELL IS! I NEED HELP HERE, BISHOP. A LAWYER. SOMETHING!
I DOUBT THAT WILL BE NECESSARY.
NOT NECESSARY?! BISHOP ARE YOU NOT HEARING WHAT I'M SAYING HERE?! THIS IS VERY SERIOUS!

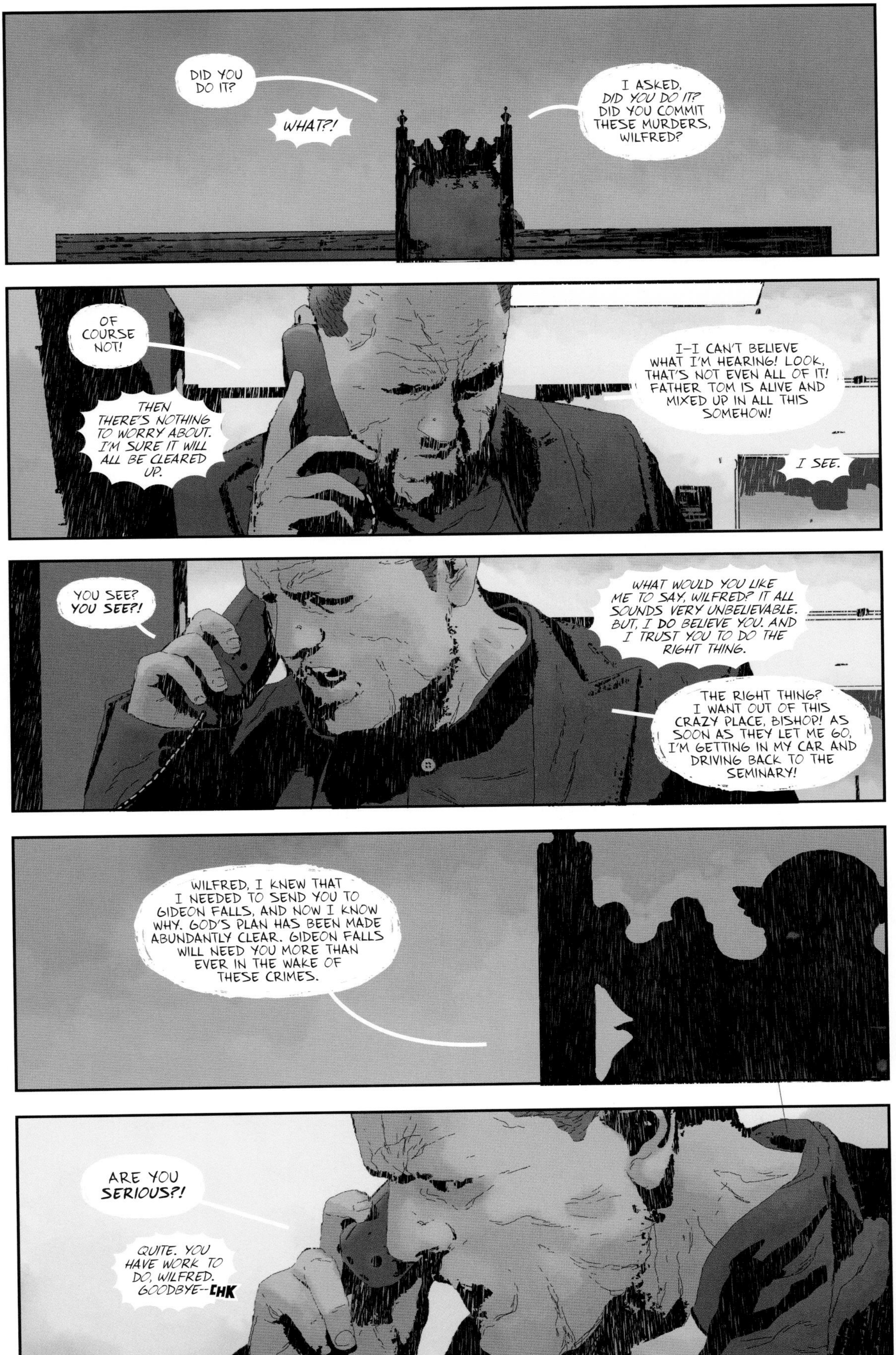
DID YOU DO IT?
WHAT?!
I ASKED, DID YOU DO IT? DID YOU COMMIT THESE MURDERS, WILFRED?
OF COURSE NOT!
THEN THERE'S NOTHING TO WORRY ABOUT. I'M SURE IT WILL ALL BE CLEARED UP.
I—I CAN'T BELIEVE WHAT I'M HEARING! LOOK, THAT'S NOT EVEN ALL OF IT! FATHER TOM IS ALIVE AND MIXED UP IN ALL THIS SOMEHOW!
I SEE.
YOU SEE? YOU SEE?!
WHAT WOULD YOU LIKE ME TO SAY, WILFRED? IT ALL SOUNDS VERY UNBELIEVABLE. BUT, I DO BELIEVE YOU. AND I TRUST YOU TO DO THE RIGHT THING.
THE RIGHT THING? I WANT OUT OF THIS CRAZY PLACE, BISHOP! AS SOON AS THEY LET ME GO, I'M GETTING IN MY CAR AND DRIVING BACK TO THE SEMINARY!
WILFRED, I KNEW THAT I NEEDED TO SEND YOU TO GIDEON FALLS, AND NOW I KNOW WHY. GOD'S PLAN HAS BEEN MADE ABUNDANTLY CLEAR. GIDEON FALLS WILL NEED YOU MORE THAN EVER IN THE WAKE OF THESE CRIMES.
ARE YOU SERIOUS?!
QUITE. YOU HAVE WORK TO DO, WILFRED. GOODBYE--CHK

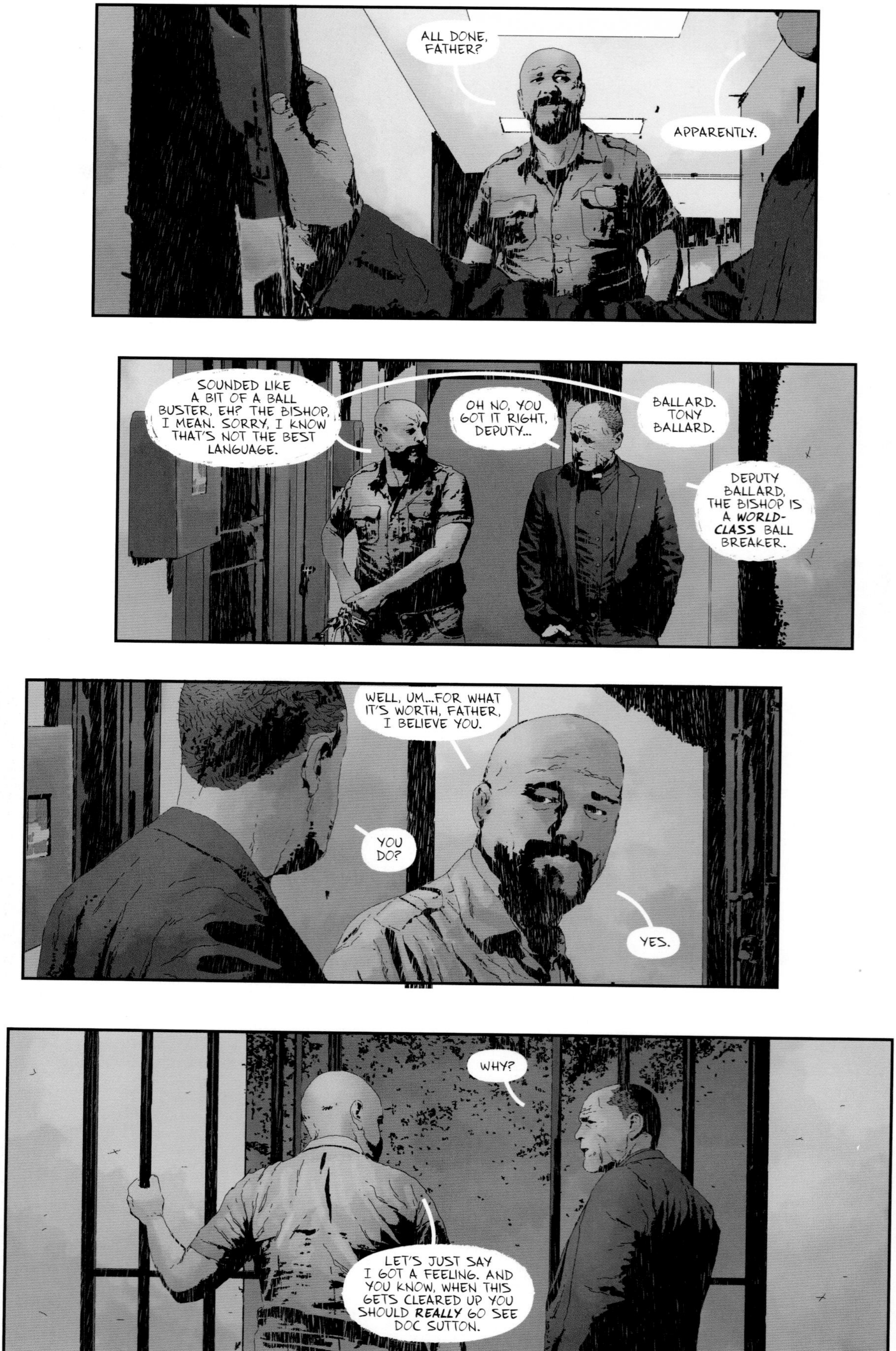
ALL DONE, FATHER?
APPARENTLY.
SOUNDED LIKE A BIT OF A BALL BUSTER, EH? THE BISHOP, I MEAN. SORRY, I KNOW THAT'S NOT THE BEST LANGUAGE.
OH NO, YOU GOT IT RIGHT, DEPUTY...
BALLARD. TONY BALLARD.
DEPUTY BALLARD, THE BISHOP IS A **WORLD-CLASS** BALL BREAKER.
WELL, UM...FOR WHAT IT'S WORTH, FATHER, I BELIEVE YOU.
YOU DO?
YES.
WHY?
LET'S JUST SAY I GOT A FEELING. AND YOU KNOW, WHEN THIS GETS CLEARED UP YOU SHOULD **REALLY** GO SEE DOC SUTTON.

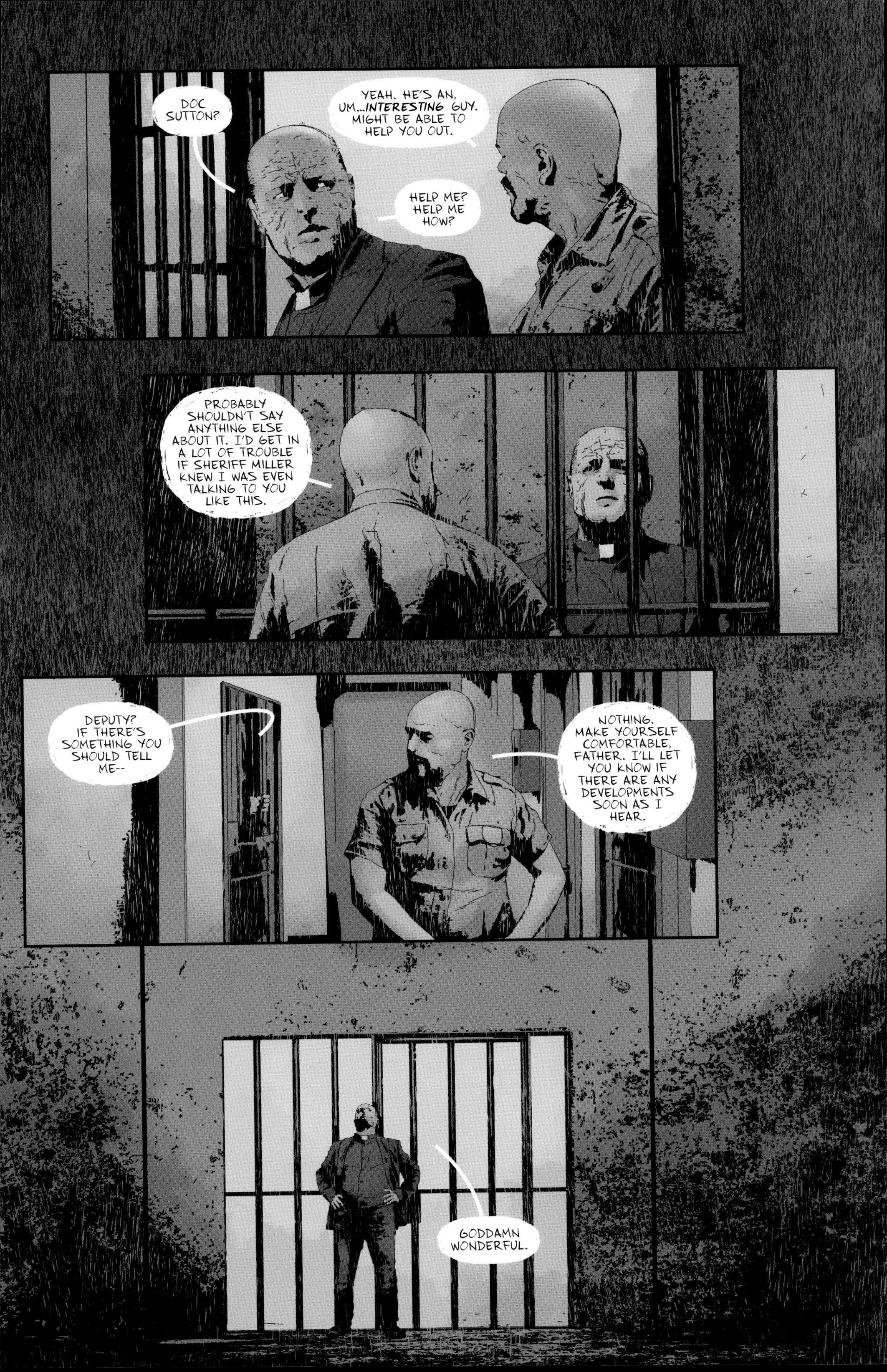
DOC SUTTON?
YEAH. HE'S AN, UM...INTERESTING GUY. MIGHT BE ABLE TO HELP YOU OUT.
HELP ME? HELP ME HOW?
PROBABLY SHOULDN'T SAY ANYTHING ELSE ABOUT IT. I'D GET IN A LOT OF TROUBLE IF SHERIFF MILLER KNEW I WAS EVEN TALKING TO YOU LIKE THIS.
DEPUTY? IF THERE'S SOMETHING YOU SHOULD TELL ME--
NOTHING. MAKE YOURSELF COMFORTABLE, FATHER. I'LL LET YOU KNOW IF THERE ARE ANY DEVELOPMENTS SOON AS I HEAR.
GODDAMN WONDERFUL.

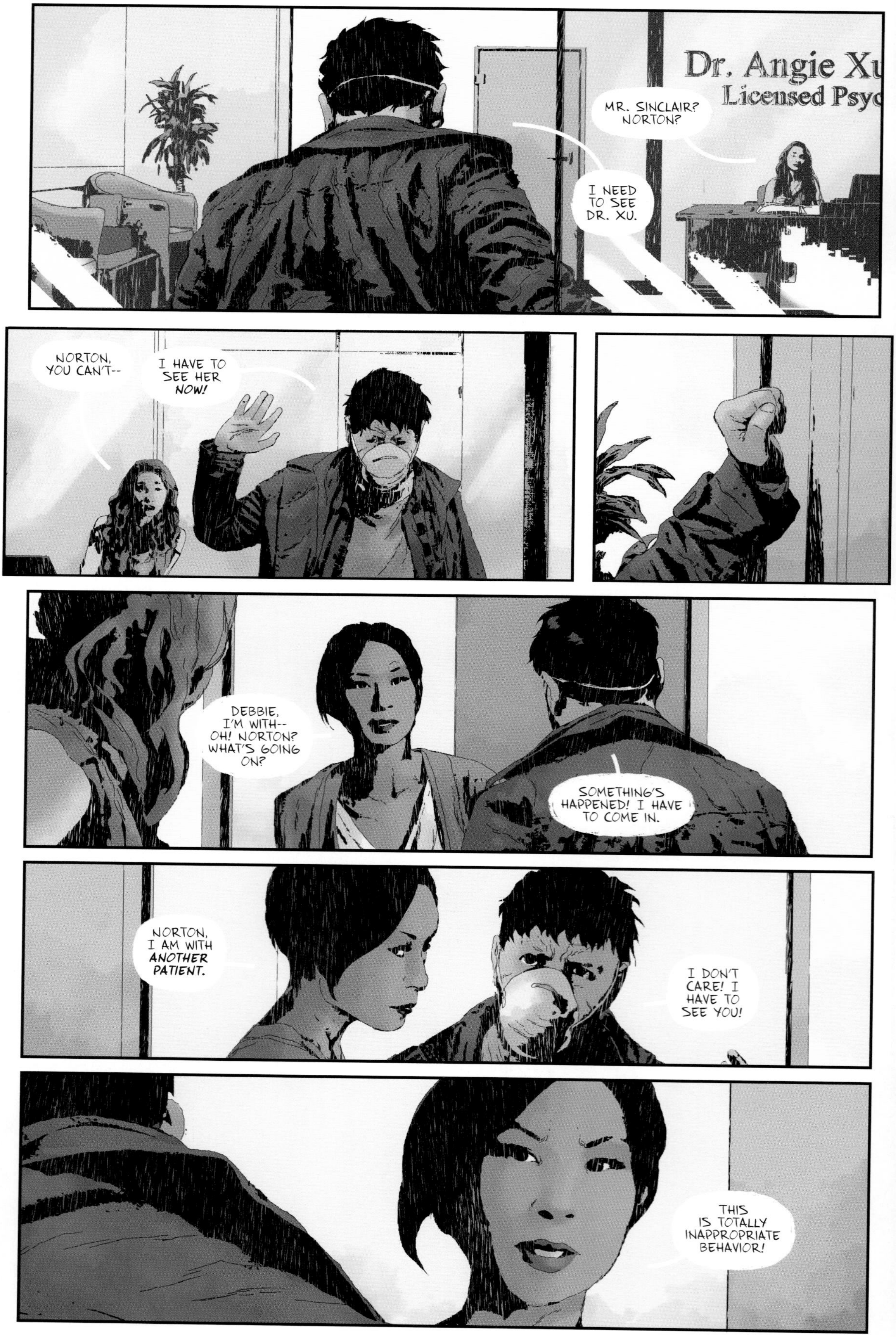
Dr. Angie Xu
Licensed Psyc
MR. SINCLAIR? NORTON?
I NEED TO SEE DR. XU.
NORTON, YOU CAN'T--
I HAVE TO SEE HER NOW!
DEBBIE, I'M WITH-- OH! NORTON? WHAT'S GOING ON?
SOMETHING'S HAPPENED! I HAVE TO COME IN.
NORTON, I AM WITH ANOTHER PATIENT.
I DON'T CARE! I HAVE TO SEE YOU!
THIS IS TOTALLY INAPPROPRIATE BEHAVIOR!

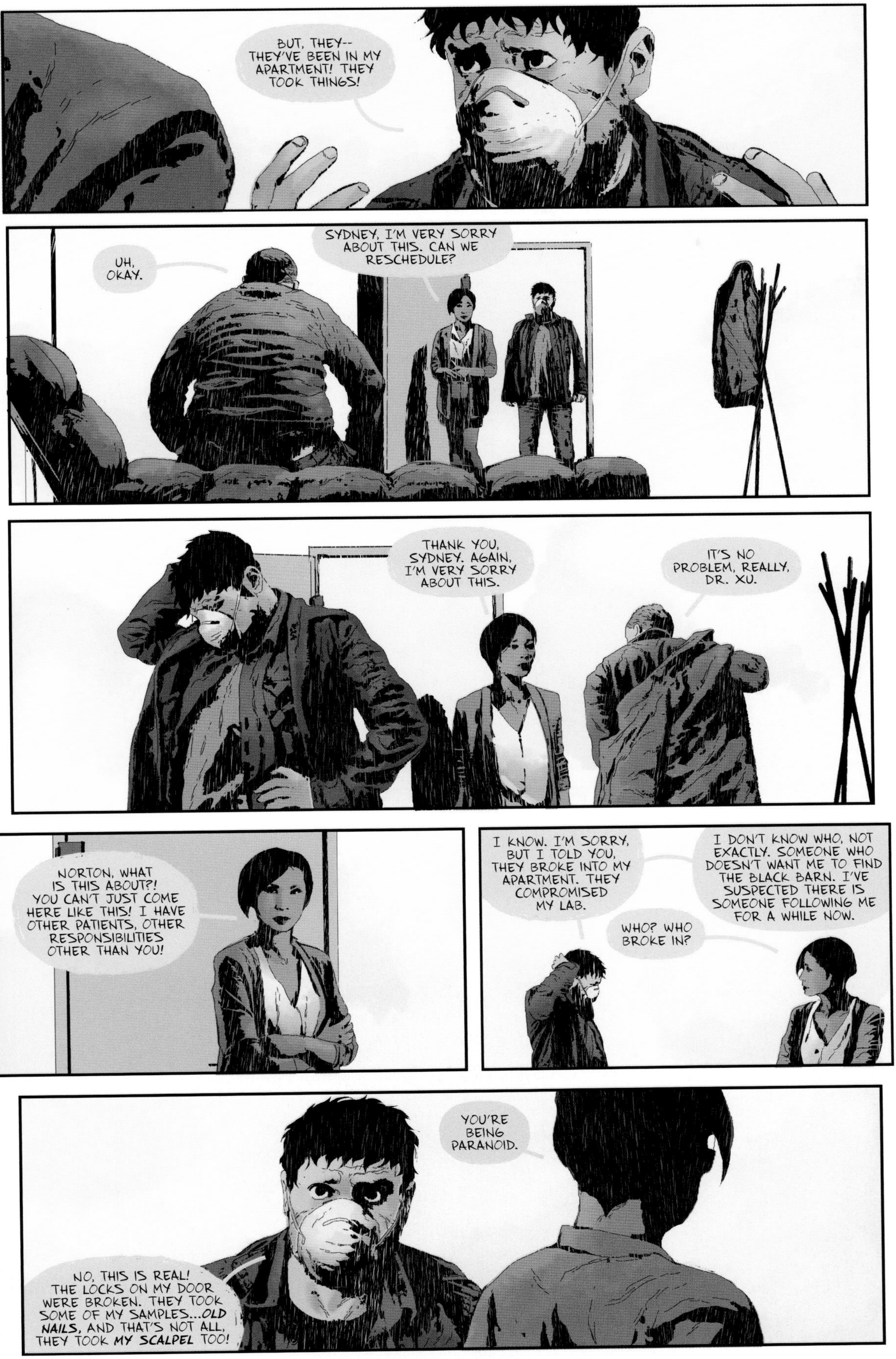
BUT, THEY-- THEY'VE BEEN IN MY APARTMENT! THEY TOOK THINGS!
SYDNEY, I'M VERY SORRY ABOUT THIS. CAN WE RESCHEDULE?
UH, OKAY.
THANK YOU, SYDNEY. AGAIN, I'M VERY SORRY ABOUT THIS.
IT'S NO PROBLEM, REALLY, DR. XU.
NORTON, WHAT IS THIS ABOUT?! YOU CAN'T JUST COME HERE LIKE THIS! I HAVE OTHER PATIENTS, OTHER RESPONSIBILITIES OTHER THAN YOU!
I KNOW. I'M SORRY, BUT I TOLD YOU, THEY BROKE INTO MY APARTMENT. THEY COMPROMISED MY LAB.
WHO? WHO BROKE IN?
I DON'T KNOW WHO, NOT EXACTLY. SOMEONE WHO DOESN'T WANT ME TO FIND THE BLACK BARN. I'VE SUSPECTED THERE IS SOMEONE FOLLOWING ME FOR A WHILE NOW.
YOU'RE BEING PARANOID.
NO, THIS IS REAL! THE LOCKS ON MY DOOR WERE BROKEN. THEY TOOK SOME OF MY SAMPLES...OLD NAILS, AND THAT'S NOT ALL, THEY TOOK MY SCALPEL TOO!

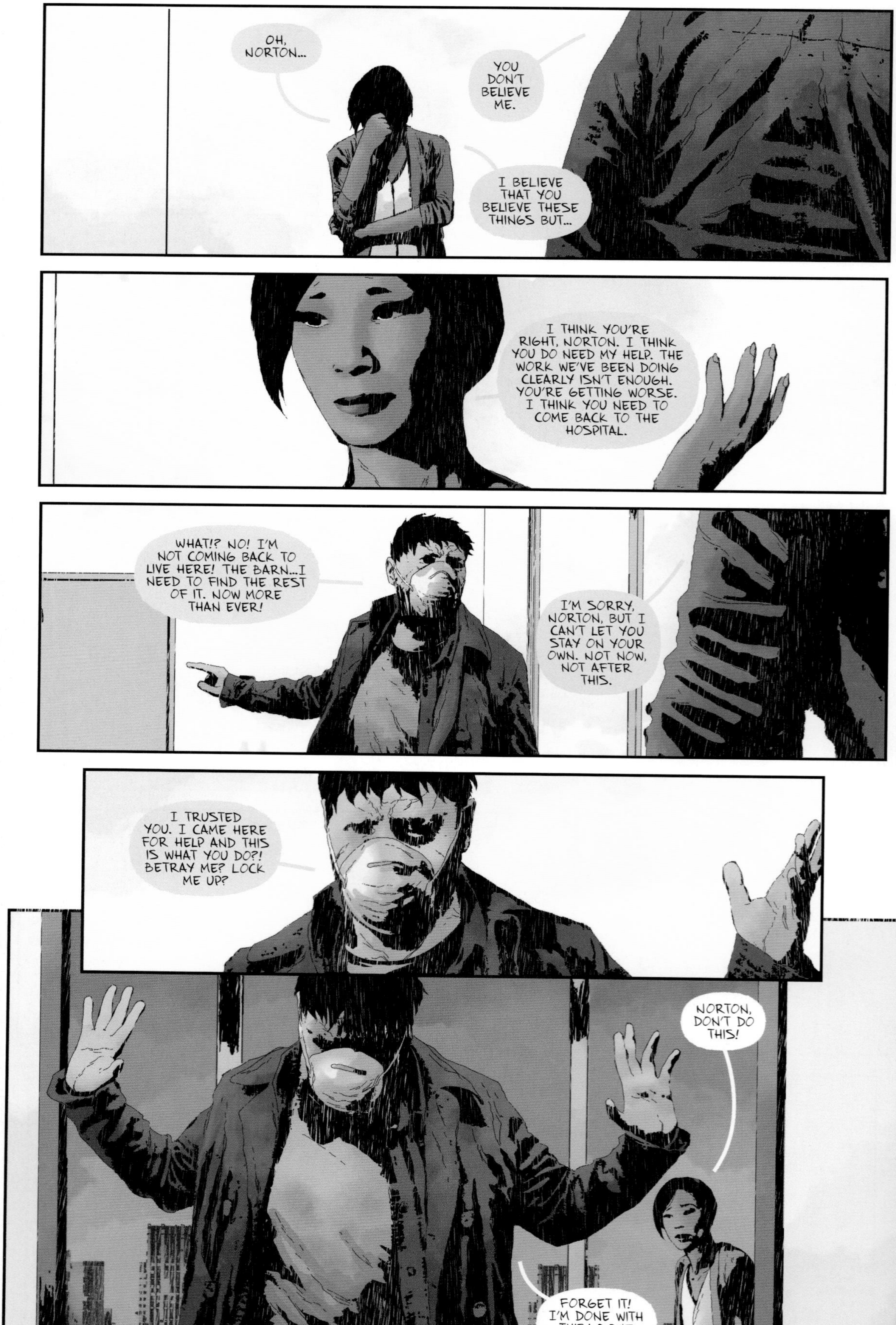
OH, NORTON...
YOU DON'T BELIEVE ME.
I BELIEVE THAT YOU BELIEVE THESE THINGS BUT...
I THINK YOU'RE RIGHT, NORTON. I THINK YOU DO NEED MY HELP. THE WORK WE'VE BEEN DOING CLEARLY ISN'T ENOUGH. YOU'RE GETTING WORSE. I THINK YOU NEED TO COME BACK TO THE HOSPITAL.
WHAT!? NO! I'M NOT COMING BACK TO LIVE HERE! THE BARN...I NEED TO FIND THE REST OF IT. NOW MORE THAN EVER!
I'M SORRY, NORTON, BUT I CAN'T LET YOU STAY ON YOUR OWN. NOT NOW, NOT AFTER THIS.
I TRUSTED YOU. I CAME HERE FOR HELP AND THIS IS WHAT YOU DO?! BETRAY ME? LOCK ME UP?
NORTON, DON'T DO THIS!
FORGET IT! I'M DONE WITH THIS! DONE WITH YOU!

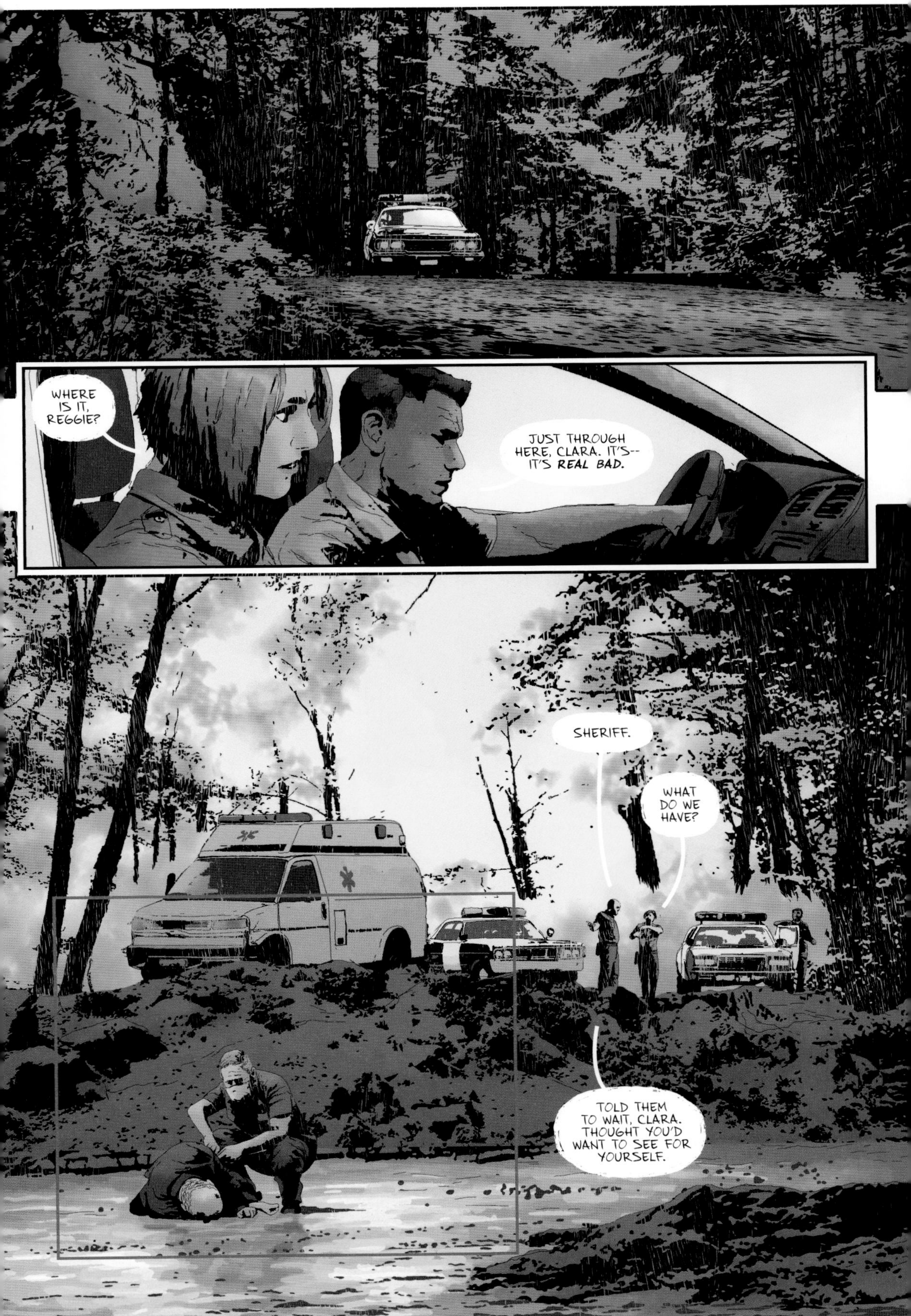
WHERE IS IT, REGGIE?
JUST THROUGH HERE, CLARA. IT'S-- IT'S REAL BAD.
SHERIFF.
WHAT DO WE HAVE?
TOLD THEM TO WAIT, CLARA. THOUGHT YOU'D WANT TO SEE FOR YOURSELF.

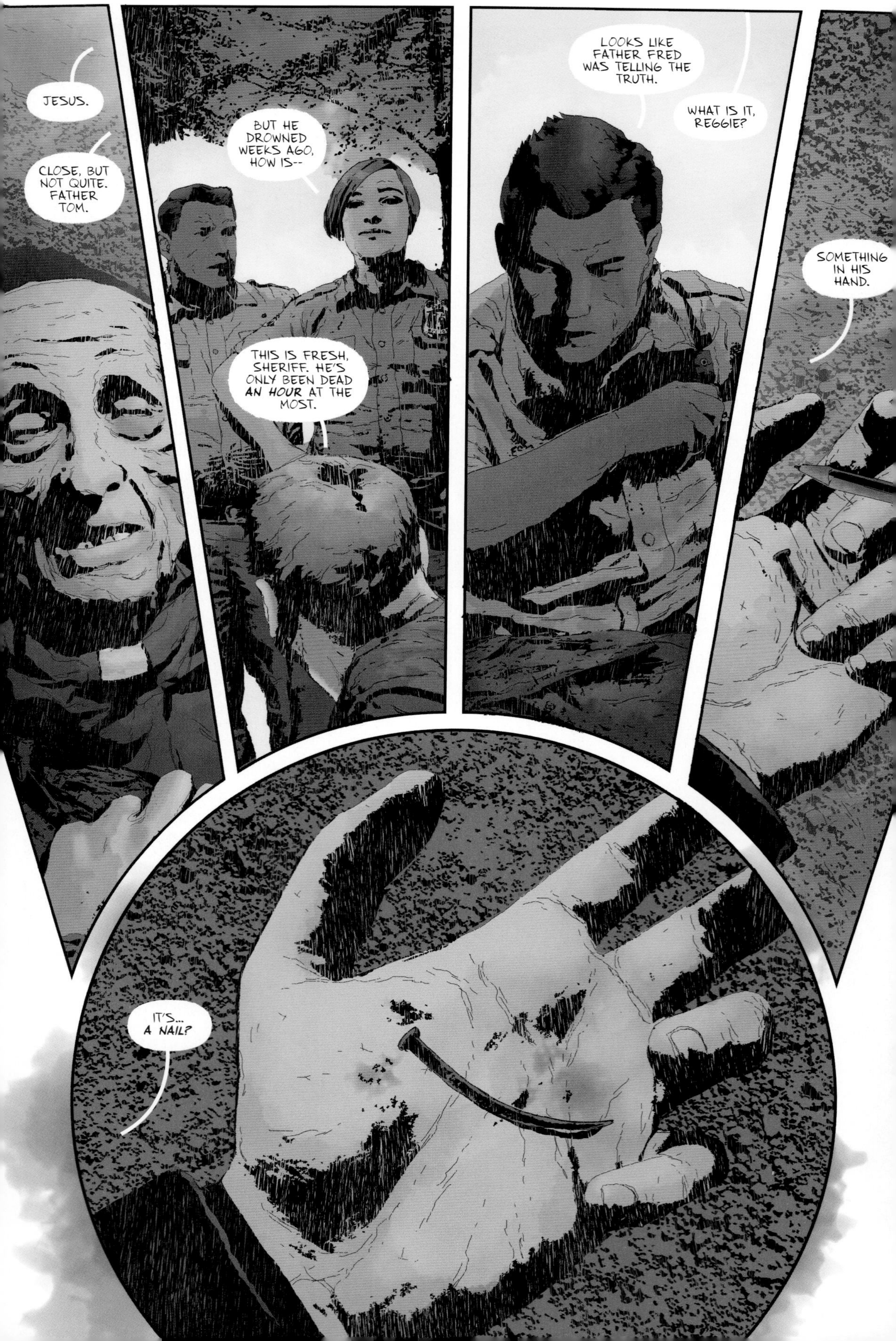

JESUS.
CLOSE, BUT NOT QUITE. FATHER TOM.
BUT HE DROWNED WEEKS AGO, HOW IS--
THIS IS FRESH, SHERIFF. HE'S ONLY BEEN DEAD AN HOUR AT THE MOST.
LOOKS LIKE FATHER FRED WAS TELLING THE TRUTH.
WHAT IS IT, REGGIE?
SOMETHING IN HIS HAND.
IT'S... A NAIL?

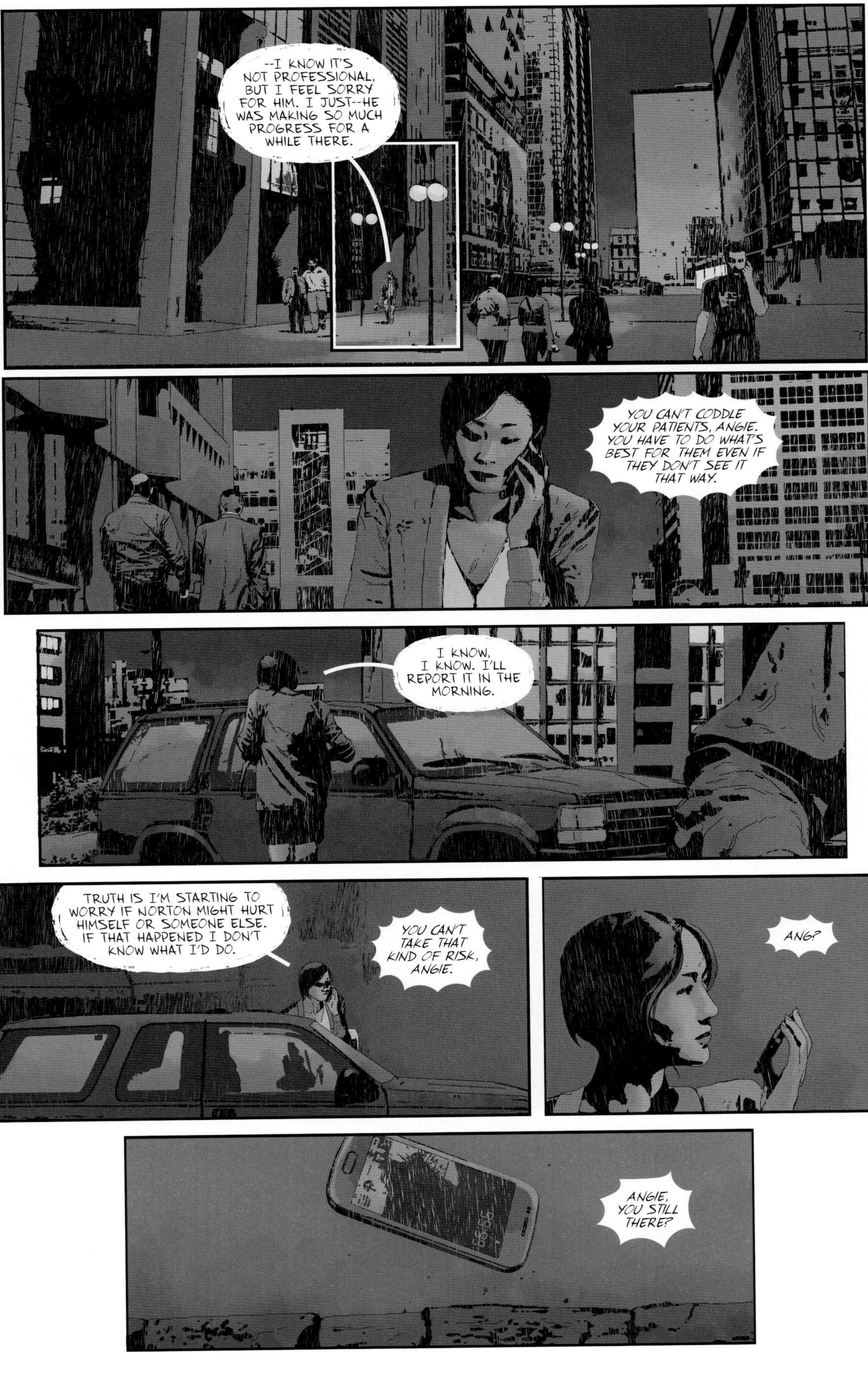
--I KNOW IT'S NOT PROFESSIONAL, BUT I FEEL SORRY FOR HIM. I JUST--HE WAS MAKING SO MUCH PROGRESS FOR A WHILE THERE.
YOU CAN'T CODDLE YOUR PATIENTS, ANGIE. YOU HAVE TO DO WHAT'S BEST FOR THEM EVEN IF THEY DON'T SEE IT THAT WAY.
I KNOW, I KNOW. I'LL REPORT IT IN THE MORNING.
TRUTH IS I'M STARTING TO WORRY IF NORTON MIGHT HURT HIMSELF OR SOMEONE ELSE. IF THAT HAPPENED I DON'T KNOW WHAT I'D DO.
YOU CAN'T TAKE THAT KIND OF RISK, ANGIE.
ANG?
ANGIE, YOU STILL THERE?

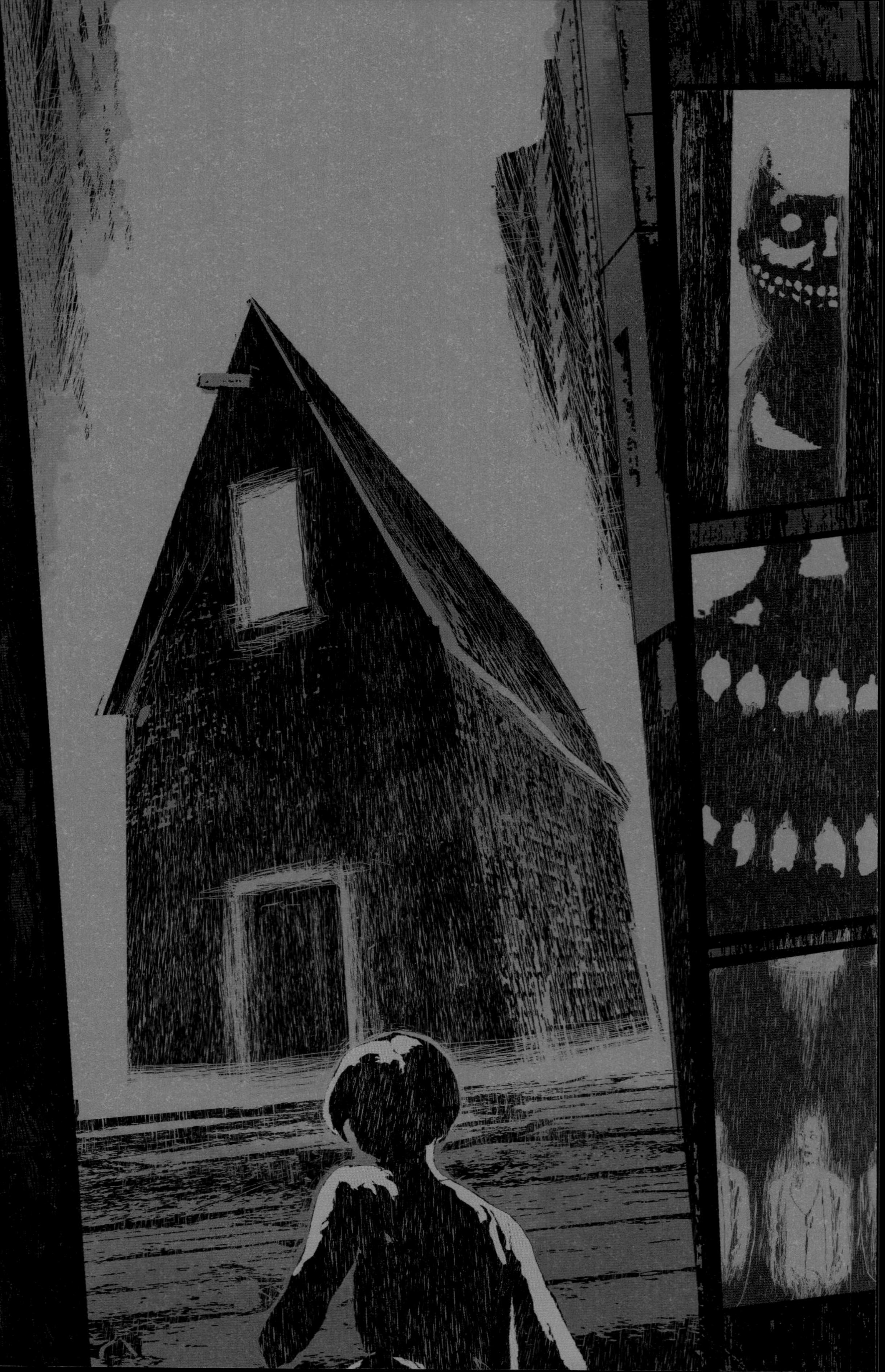

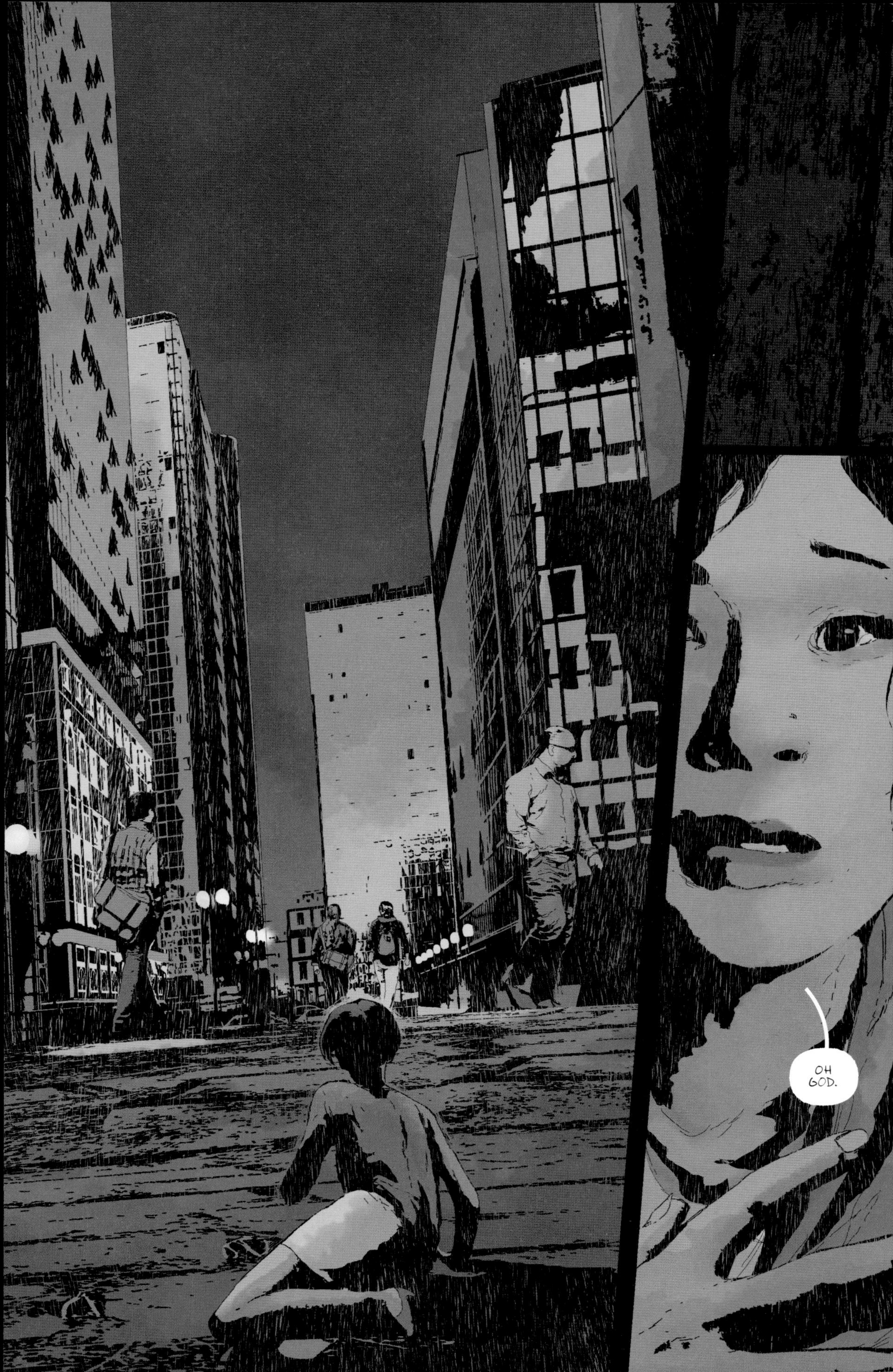
OH GOD.

Three

HOLY BIBLE
WHISKY
KNOCK KNOCK

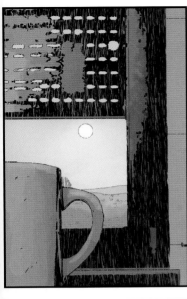

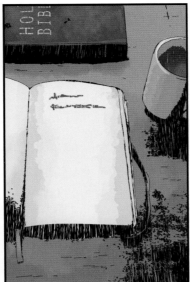

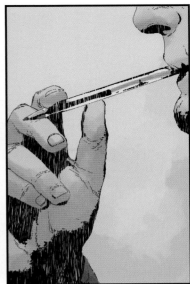

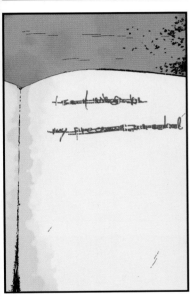

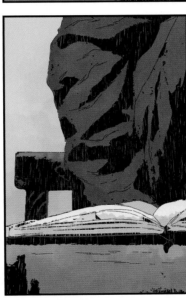

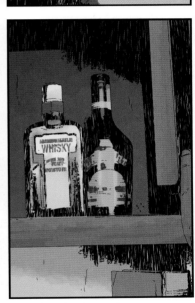

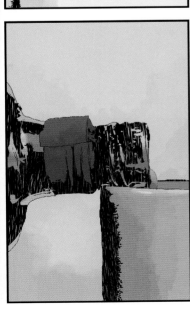

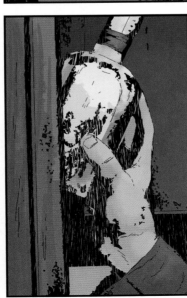

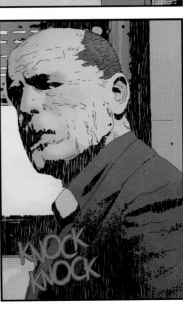

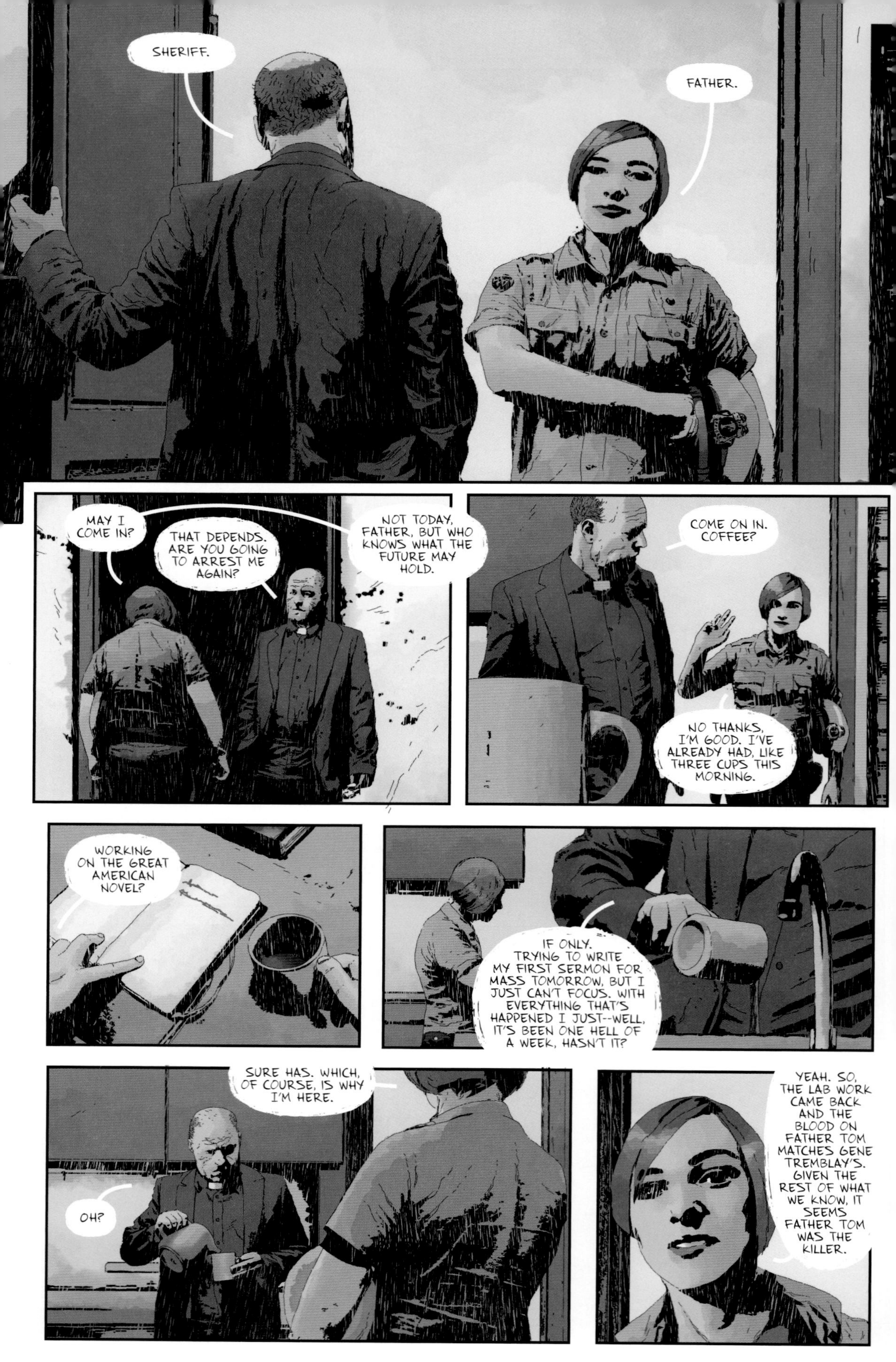
SHERIFF.
FATHER.
MAY I COME IN?
THAT DEPENDS. ARE YOU GOING TO ARREST ME AGAIN?
NOT TODAY, FATHER, BUT WHO KNOWS WHAT THE FUTURE MAY HOLD.
COME ON IN. COFFEE?
NO THANKS, I'M GOOD. I'VE ALREADY HAD, LIKE THREE CUPS THIS MORNING.
WORKING ON THE GREAT AMERICAN NOVEL?
IF ONLY. TRYING TO WRITE MY FIRST SERMON FOR MASS TOMORROW, BUT I JUST CAN'T FOCUS. WITH EVERYTHING THAT'S HAPPENED I JUST--WELL, IT'S BEEN ONE HELL OF A WEEK, HASN'T IT?
SURE HAS. WHICH, OF COURSE, IS WHY I'M HERE.
OH?
YEAH. SO, THE LAB WORK CAME BACK AND THE BLOOD ON FATHER TOM MATCHES GENE TREMBLAY'S. GIVEN THE REST OF WHAT WE KNOW, IT SEEMS FATHER TOM WAS THE KILLER.

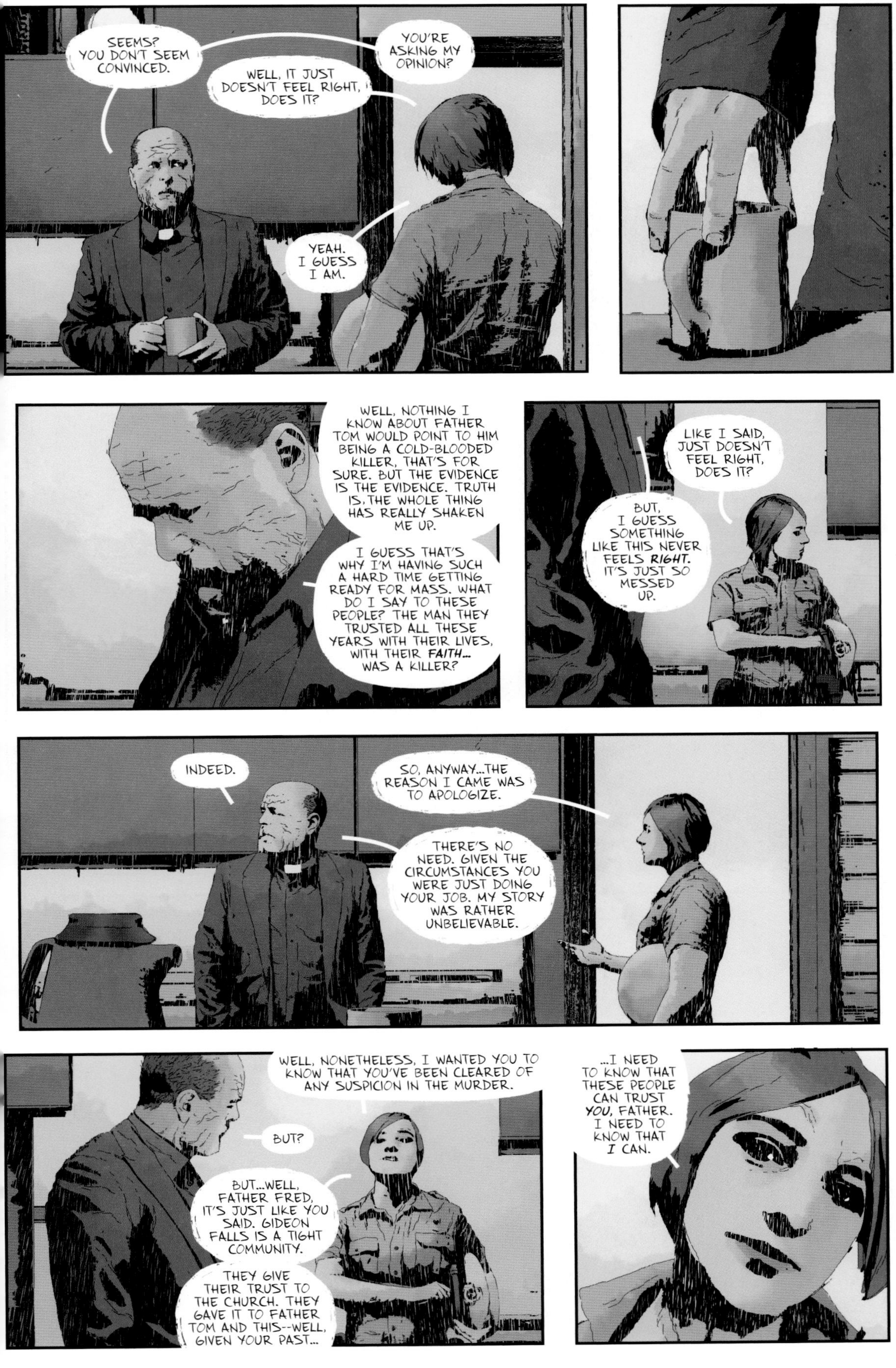
SEEMS? YOU DON'T SEEM CONVINCED.
YOU'RE ASKING MY OPINION?
WELL, IT JUST DOESN'T FEEL RIGHT, DOES IT?
YEAH. I GUESS I AM.
WELL, NOTHING I KNOW ABOUT FATHER TOM WOULD POINT TO HIM BEING A COLD-BLOODED KILLER, THAT'S FOR SURE. BUT THE EVIDENCE IS THE EVIDENCE. TRUTH IS, THE WHOLE THING HAS REALLY SHAKEN ME UP.
I GUESS THAT'S WHY I'M HAVING SUCH A HARD TIME GETTING READY FOR MASS. WHAT DO I SAY TO THESE PEOPLE? THE MAN THEY TRUSTED ALL THESE YEARS WITH THEIR LIVES, WITH THEIR FAITH... WAS A KILLER?
LIKE I SAID, JUST DOESN'T FEEL RIGHT, DOES IT?
BUT, I GUESS SOMETHING LIKE THIS NEVER FEELS RIGHT. IT'S JUST SO MESSED UP.
INDEED.
SO, ANYWAY...THE REASON I CAME WAS TO APOLOGIZE.
THERE'S NO NEED. GIVEN THE CIRCUMSTANCES YOU WERE JUST DOING YOUR JOB. MY STORY WAS RATHER UNBELIEVABLE.
WELL, NONETHELESS, I WANTED YOU TO KNOW THAT YOU'VE BEEN CLEARED OF ANY SUSPICION IN THE MURDER.
BUT?
BUT...WELL, FATHER FRED, IT'S JUST LIKE YOU SAID. GIDEON FALLS IS A TIGHT COMMUNITY.
THEY GIVE THEIR TRUST TO THE CHURCH. THEY GAVE IT TO FATHER TOM AND THIS--WELL, GIVEN YOUR PAST...
...I NEED TO KNOW THAT THESE PEOPLE CAN TRUST YOU, FATHER. I NEED TO KNOW THAT I CAN.

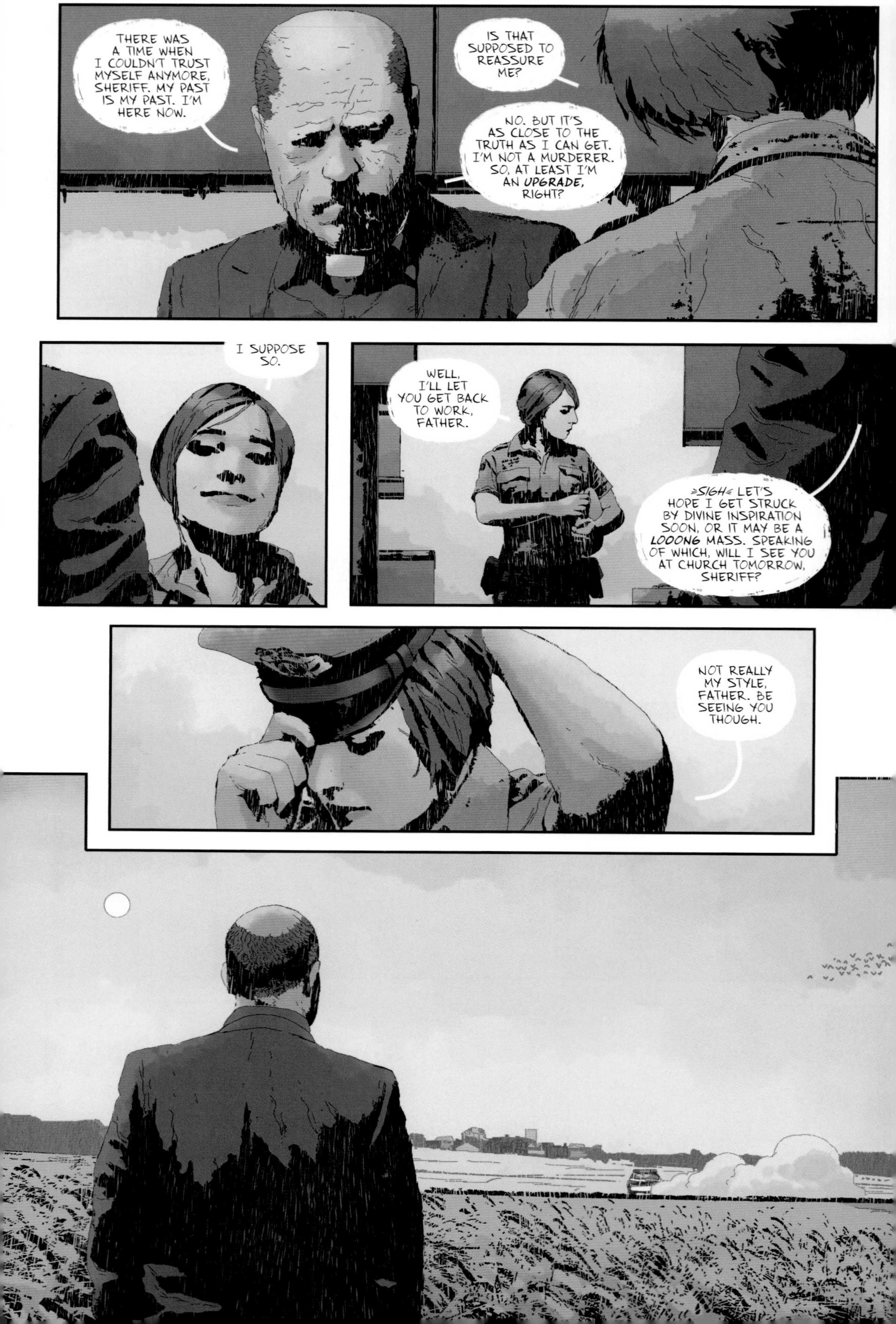
THERE WAS A TIME WHEN I COULDN'T TRUST MYSELF ANYMORE, SHERIFF. MY PAST IS MY PAST. I'M HERE NOW.
IS THAT SUPPOSED TO REASSURE ME?
NO. BUT IT'S AS CLOSE TO THE TRUTH AS I CAN GET. I'M NOT A MURDERER. SO, AT LEAST I'M AN UPGRADE, RIGHT?
I SUPPOSE SO.
WELL, I'LL LET YOU GET BACK TO WORK, FATHER.
SIGH LET'S HOPE I GET STRUCK BY DIVINE INSPIRATION SOON, OR IT MAY BE A LOOONG MASS. SPEAKING OF WHICH, WILL I SEE YOU AT CHURCH TOMORROW, SHERIFF?
NOT REALLY MY STYLE, FATHER. BE SEEING YOU THOUGH.

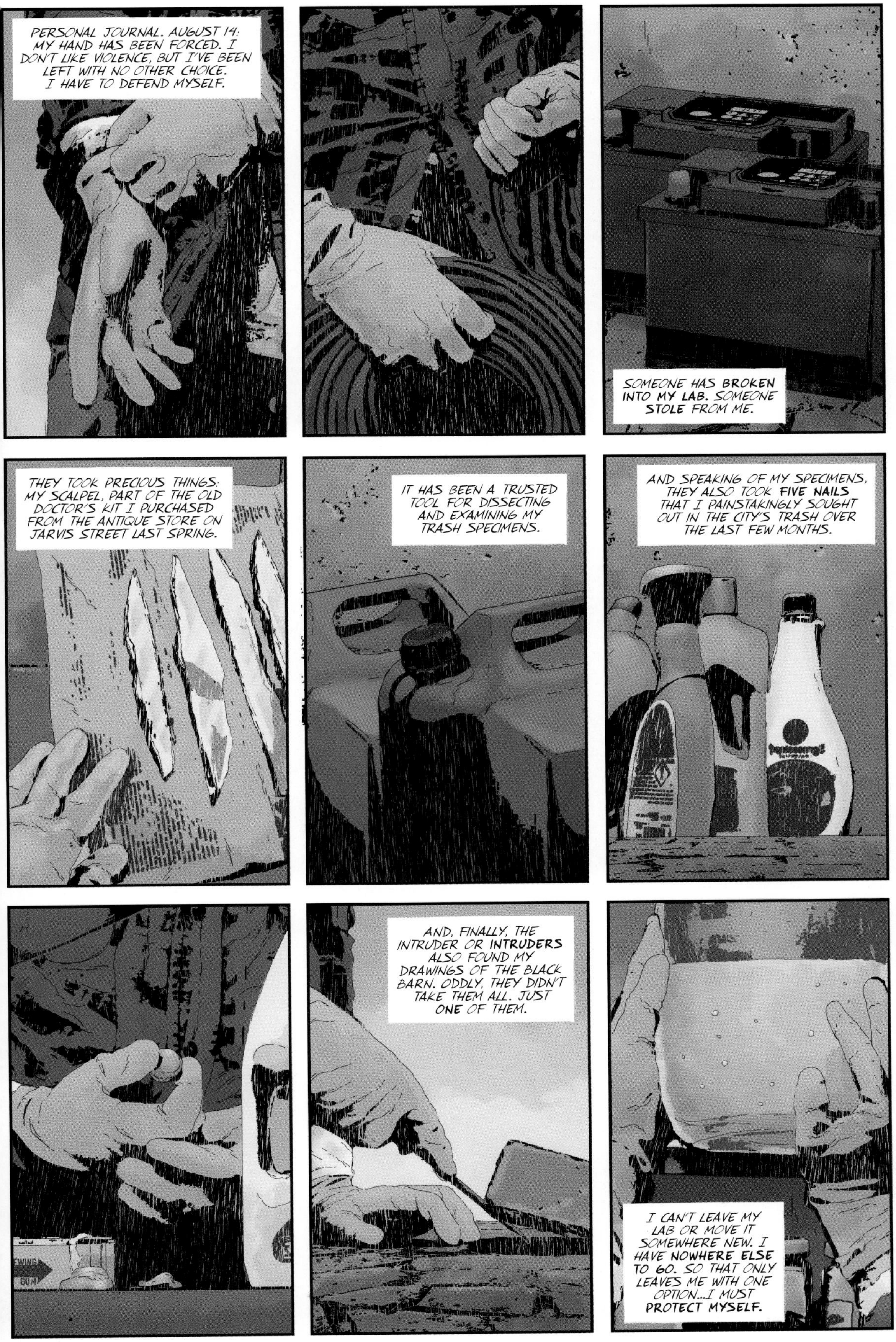
PERSONAL JOURNAL. AUGUST 14: MY HAND HAS BEEN FORCED. I DON'T LIKE VIOLENCE, BUT I'VE BEEN LEFT WITH NO OTHER CHOICE. I HAVE TO DEFEND MYSELF.
SOMEONE HAS BROKEN INTO MY LAB. SOMEONE STOLE FROM ME.
THEY TOOK PRECIOUS THINGS: MY SCALPEL, PART OF THE OLD DOCTOR'S KIT I PURCHASED FROM THE ANTIQUE STORE ON JARVIS STREET LAST SPRING.
IT HAS BEEN A TRUSTED TOOL FOR DISSECTING AND EXAMINING MY TRASH SPECIMENS.
AND SPEAKING OF MY SPECIMENS, THEY ALSO TOOK FIVE NAILS THAT I PAINSTAKINGLY SOUGHT OUT IN THE CITY'S TRASH OVER THE LAST FEW MONTHS.
CHEWING GUM
AND, FINALLY, THE INTRUDER OR INTRUDERS ALSO FOUND MY DRAWINGS OF THE BLACK BARN. ODDLY, THEY DIDN'T TAKE THEM ALL. JUST ONE OF THEM.
I CAN'T LEAVE MY LAB OR MOVE IT SOMEWHERE NEW. I HAVE NOWHERE ELSE TO GO. SO THAT ONLY LEAVES ME WITH ONE OPTION...I MUST PROTECT MYSELF.

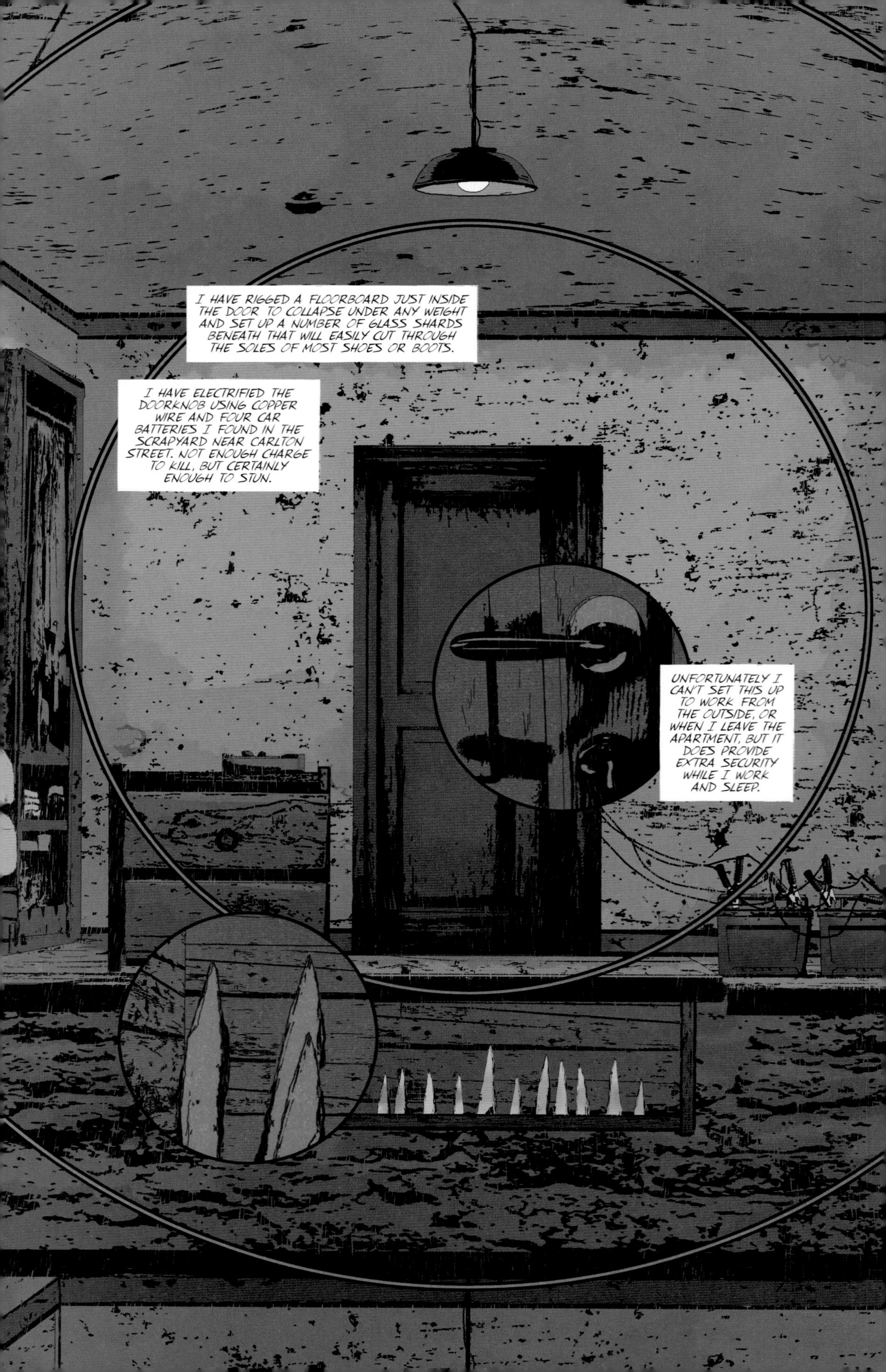
I HAVE RIGGED A FLOORBOARD JUST INSIDE THE DOOR TO COLLAPSE UNDER ANY WEIGHT AND SET UP A NUMBER OF GLASS SHARDS BENEATH THAT WILL EASILY CUT THROUGH THE SOLES OF MOST SHOES OR BOOTS.
I HAVE ELECTRIFIED THE DOORKNOB USING COPPER WIRE AND FOUR CAR BATTERIES I FOUND IN THE SCRAPYARD NEAR CARLTON STREET. NOT ENOUGH CHARGE TO KILL, BUT CERTAINLY ENOUGH TO STUN.
UNFORTUNATELY I CAN'T SET THIS UP TO WORK FROM THE OUTSIDE, OR WHEN I LEAVE THE APARTMENT, BUT IT DOES PROVIDE EXTRA SECURITY WHILE I WORK AND SLEEP.

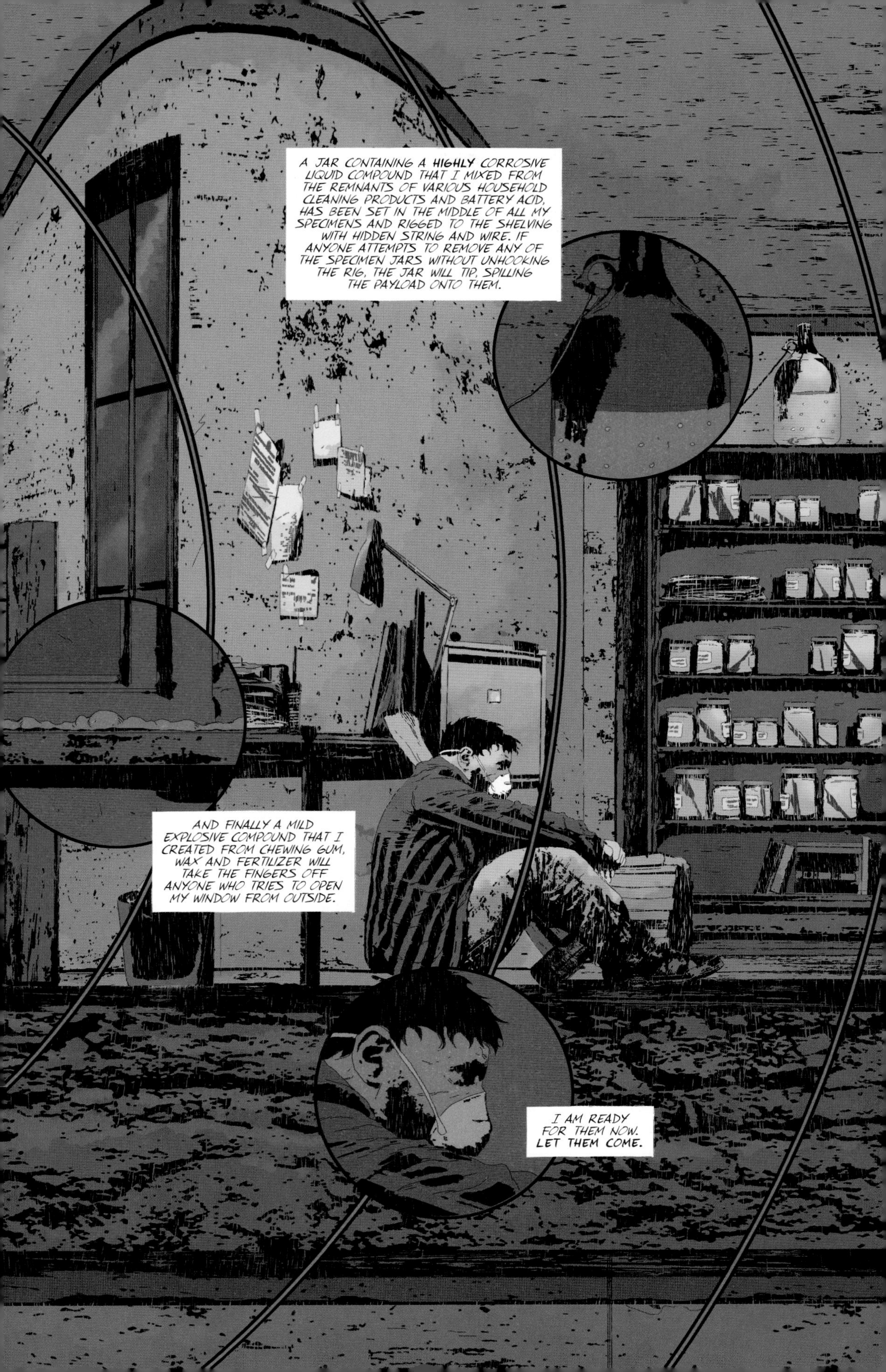
A JAR CONTAINING A **HIGHLY** CORROSIVE LIQUID COMPOUND THAT I MIXED FROM THE REMNANTS OF VARIOUS HOUSEHOLD CLEANING PRODUCTS AND BATTERY ACID, HAS BEEN SET IN THE MIDDLE OF ALL MY SPECIMENS AND RIGGED TO THE SHELVING WITH HIDDEN STRING AND WIRE. IF ANYONE ATTEMPTS TO REMOVE ANY OF THE SPECIMEN JARS WITHOUT UNHOOKING THE RIG, THE JAR WILL TIP, SPILLING THE PAYLOAD ONTO THEM.
AND FINALLY A MILD EXPLOSIVE COMPOUND THAT I CREATED FROM CHEWING GUM, WAX AND FERTILIZER WILL TAKE THE FINGERS OFF ANYONE WHO TRIES TO OPEN MY WINDOW FROM OUTSIDE.
I AM READY FOR THEM NOW. **LET THEM COME.**

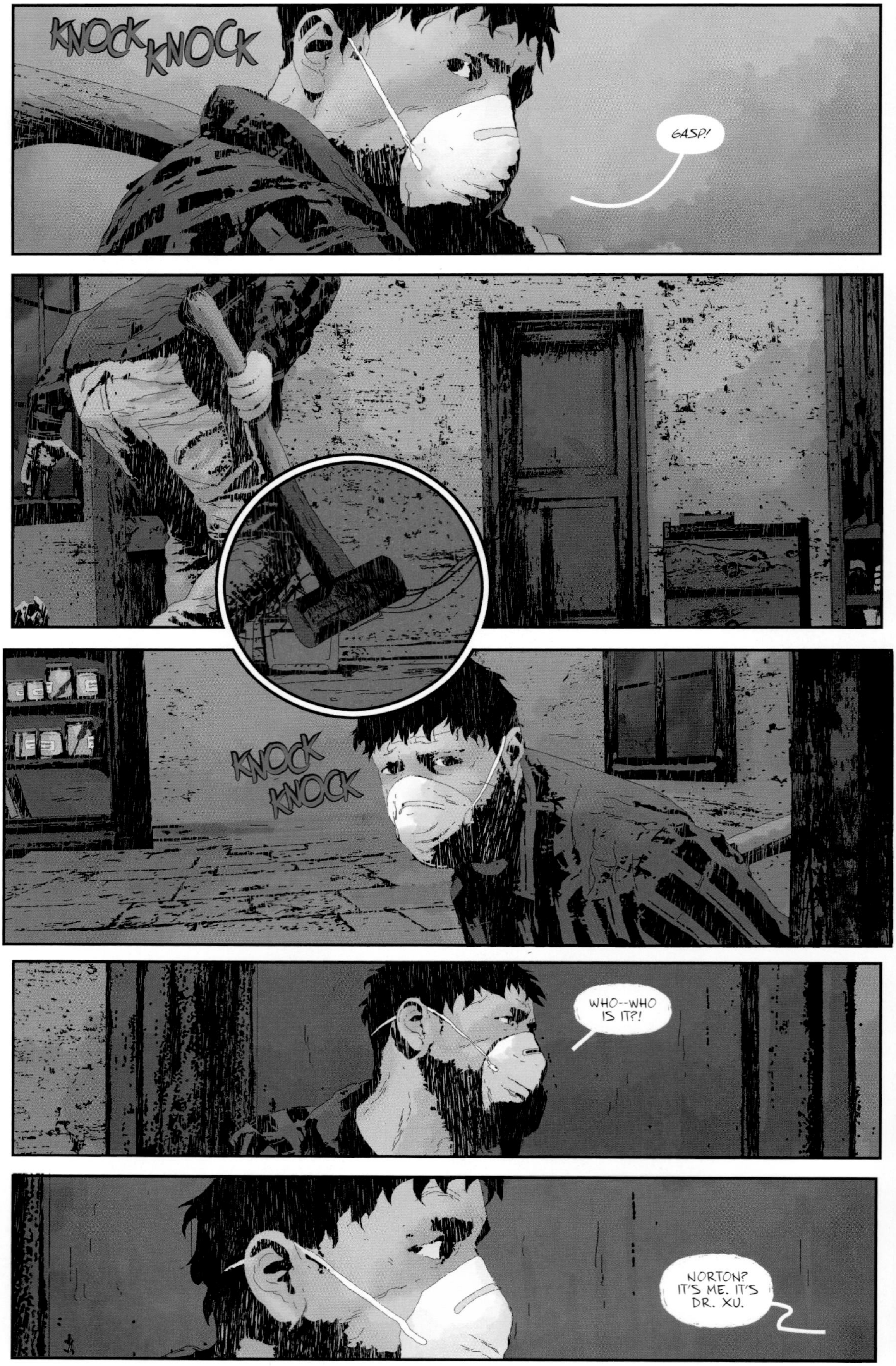
KNOCK KNOCK
GASP!
KNOCK KNOCK
WHO--WHO IS IT?!
NORTON? IT'S ME. IT'S DR. XU.

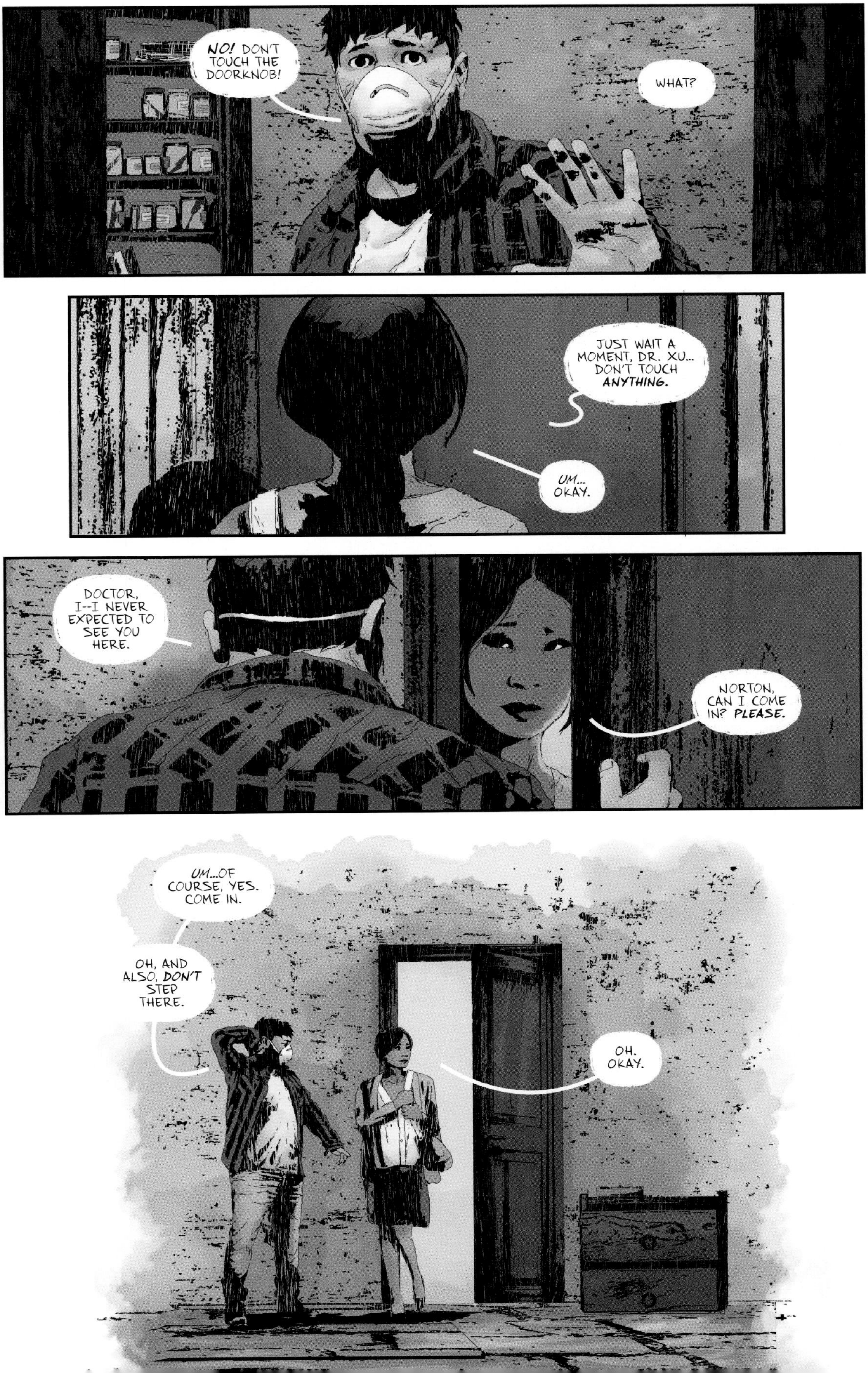
NO! DON'T TOUCH THE DOORKNOB!
WHAT?
JUST WAIT A MOMENT, DR. XU... DON'T TOUCH ANYTHING.
UM... OKAY.
DOCTOR, I--I NEVER EXPECTED TO SEE YOU HERE.
NORTON, CAN I COME IN? PLEASE.
UM...OF COURSE, YES. COME IN.
OH, AND ALSO, DON'T STEP THERE.
OH. OKAY.

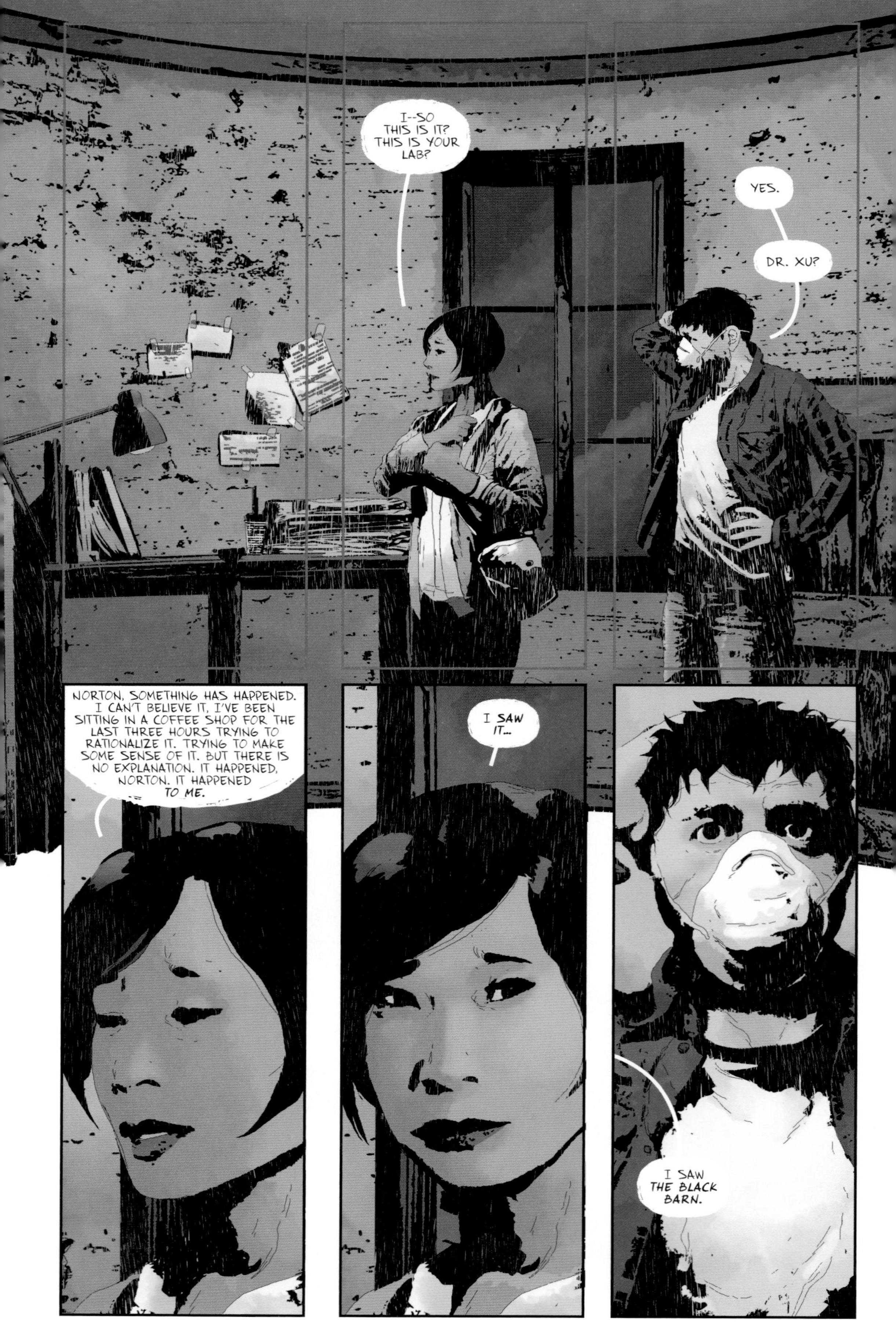
I--SO THIS IS IT? THIS IS YOUR LAB?
YES.
DR. XU?
NORTON, SOMETHING HAS HAPPENED. I CAN'T BELIEVE IT, I'VE BEEN SITTING IN A COFFEE SHOP FOR THE LAST THREE HOURS TRYING TO RATIONALIZE IT. TRYING TO MAKE SOME SENSE OF IT. BUT THERE IS NO EXPLANATION. IT HAPPENED, NORTON. IT HAPPENED TO ME.
I SAW IT...
I SAW THE BLACK BARN.

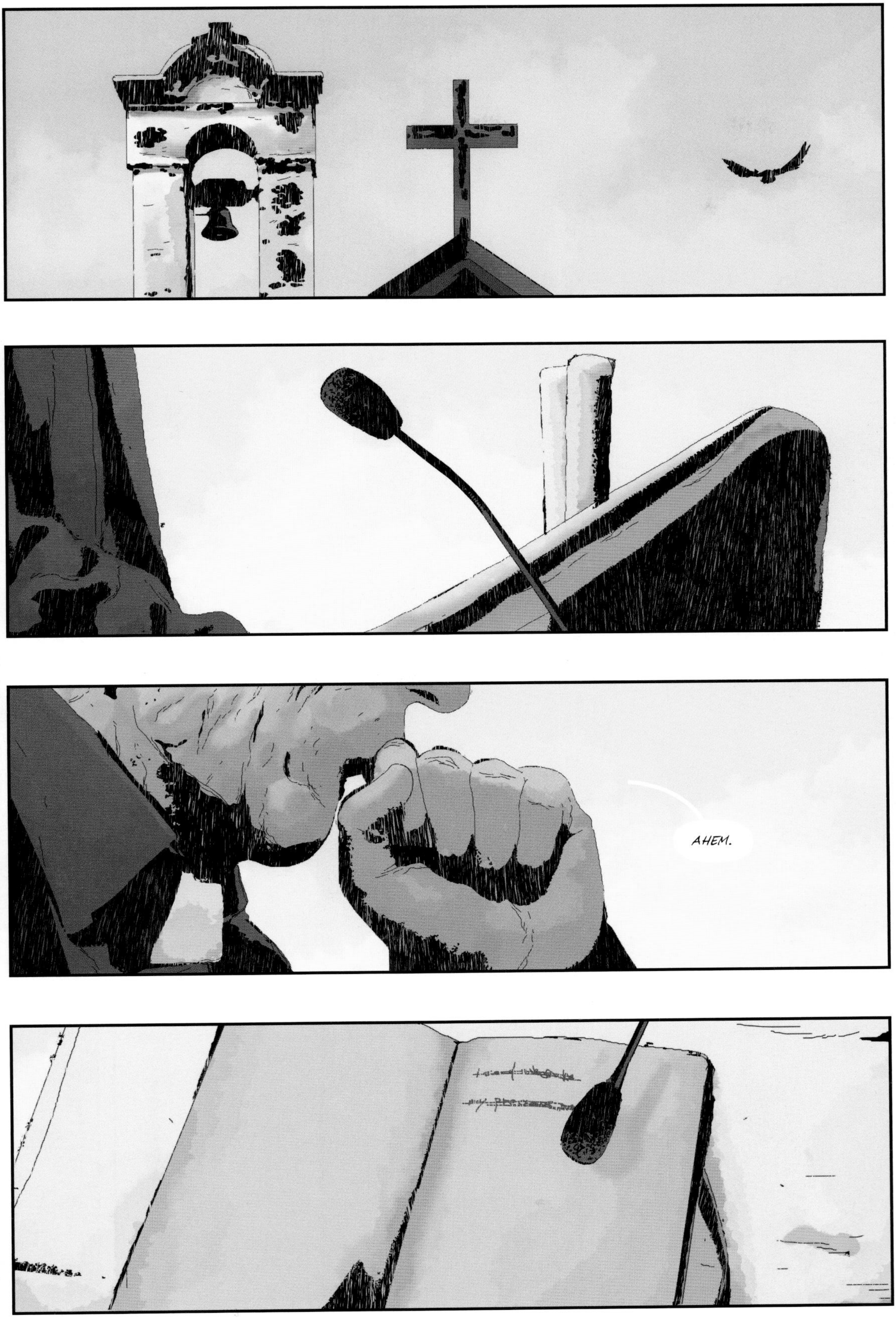
AHEM.

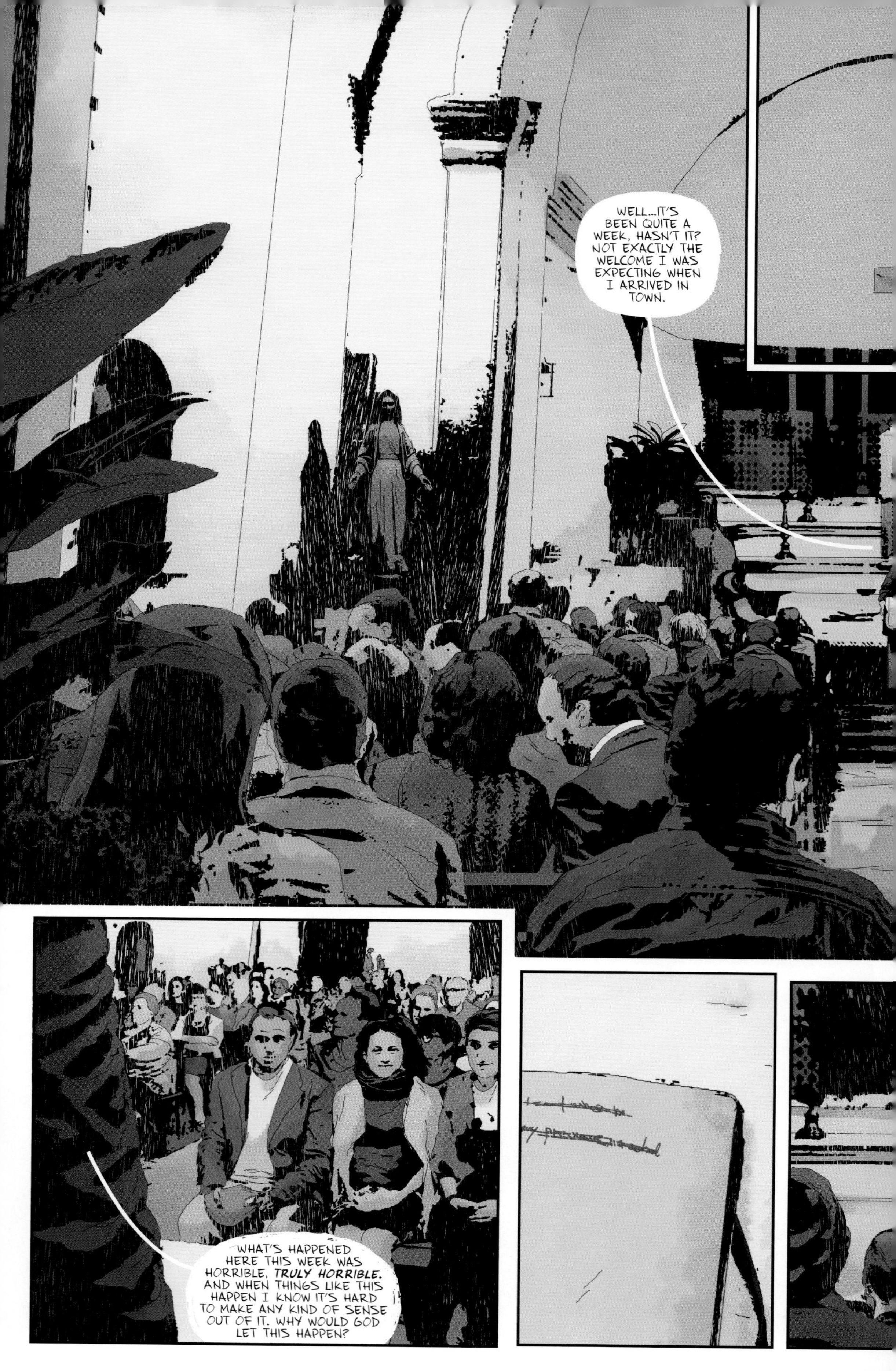
WELL...IT'S BEEN QUITE A WEEK, HASN'T IT? NOT EXACTLY THE WELCOME I WAS EXPECTING WHEN I ARRIVED IN TOWN.
WHAT'S HAPPENED HERE THIS WEEK WAS HORRIBLE, *TRULY HORRIBLE.* AND WHEN THINGS LIKE THIS HAPPEN I KNOW IT'S HARD TO MAKE ANY KIND OF SENSE OUT OF IT. WHY WOULD GOD LET THIS HAPPEN?

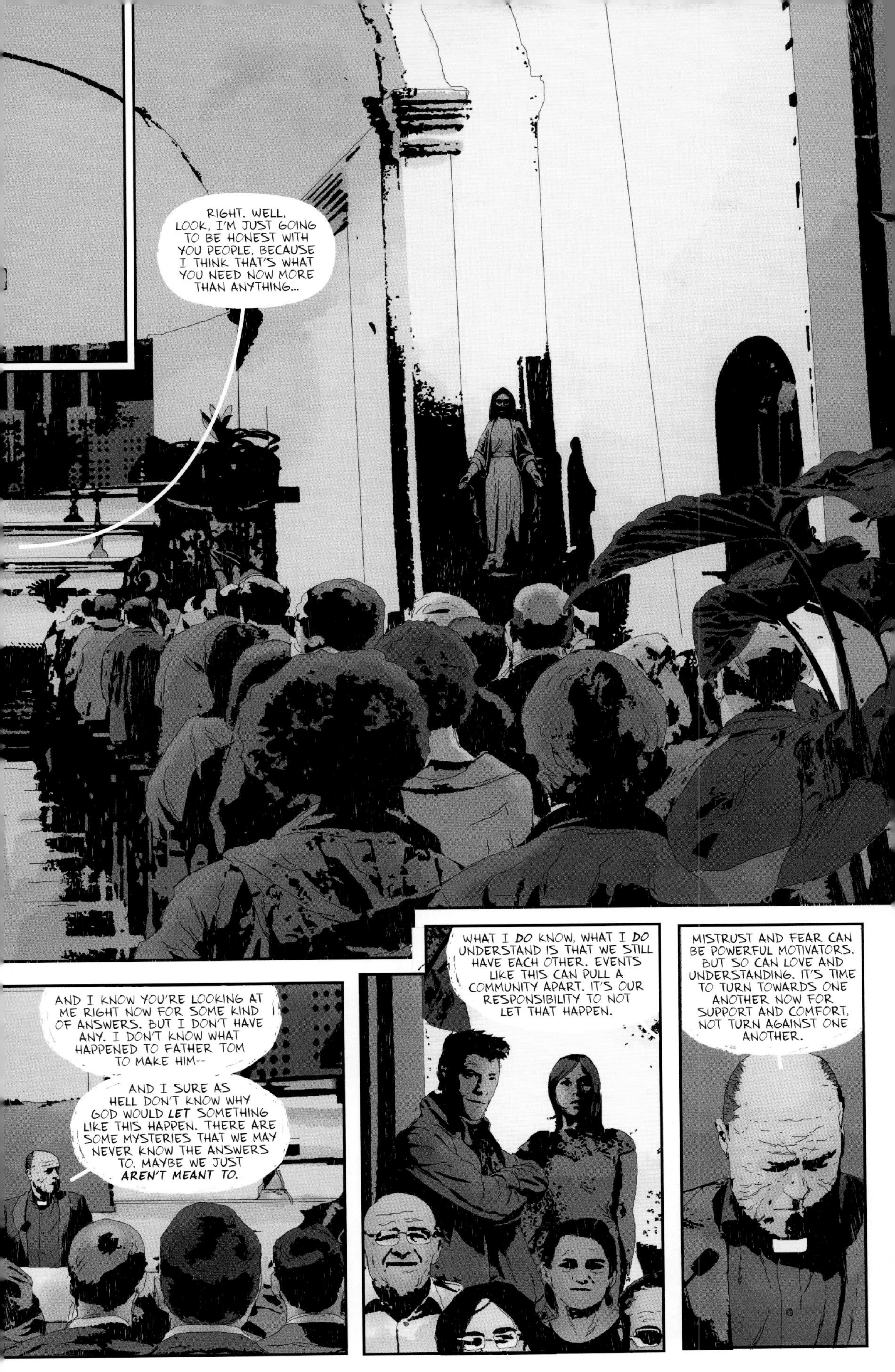
RIGHT. WELL, LOOK, I'M JUST GOING TO BE HONEST WITH YOU PEOPLE, BECAUSE I THINK THAT'S WHAT YOU NEED NOW MORE THAN ANYTHING...
AND I KNOW YOU'RE LOOKING AT ME RIGHT NOW FOR SOME KIND OF ANSWERS. BUT I DON'T HAVE ANY. I DON'T KNOW WHAT HAPPENED TO FATHER TOM TO MAKE HIM--
AND I SURE AS HELL DON'T KNOW WHY GOD WOULD **LET** SOMETHING LIKE THIS HAPPEN. THERE ARE SOME MYSTERIES THAT WE MAY NEVER KNOW THE ANSWERS TO. MAYBE WE JUST **AREN'T MEANT TO.**
WHAT I ***DO*** KNOW, WHAT I ***DO*** UNDERSTAND IS THAT WE STILL HAVE EACH OTHER. EVENTS LIKE THIS CAN PULL A COMMUNITY APART. IT'S OUR RESPONSIBILITY TO NOT LET THAT HAPPEN.
MISTRUST AND FEAR CAN BE POWERFUL MOTIVATORS. BUT SO CAN LOVE AND UNDERSTANDING. IT'S TIME TO TURN TOWARDS ONE ANOTHER NOW FOR SUPPORT AND COMFORT, NOT TURN AGAINST ONE ANOTHER.

--VERY NICE TO MEET YOU TOO, MRS. BROMLEY.

GOD BLESS YOU, FATHER WILFRED.

FRED, PLEASE. CALL ME FRED.

I ENJOYED THE MASS VERY MUCH, FATHER. I FOUND YOUR HONESTY...REFRESHING.

OH, THANK YOU. I, UH, I THINK I SAW YOU ON MY WAY INTO TOWN? YOU DRIVE THE SCHOOL BUS?

THAT'S RIGHT. FOR TWENTY YEARS NOW. JOE REDDY. THIS IS MY WIFE, JANET.

VERY NICE TO MEET YOU, JOE, JANET.

SO, WHERE ARE YOU COMING TO US FROM, FATHER?

WELL, I'M UP RIGHT FROM THE SEMINARY OUTSIDE OF THE CITY ACTUALLY. BUT BEFORE THAT, I'VE TRAVELLED AROUND A LOT. BIT OF A VAGABOND.

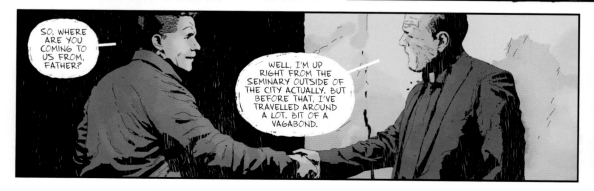

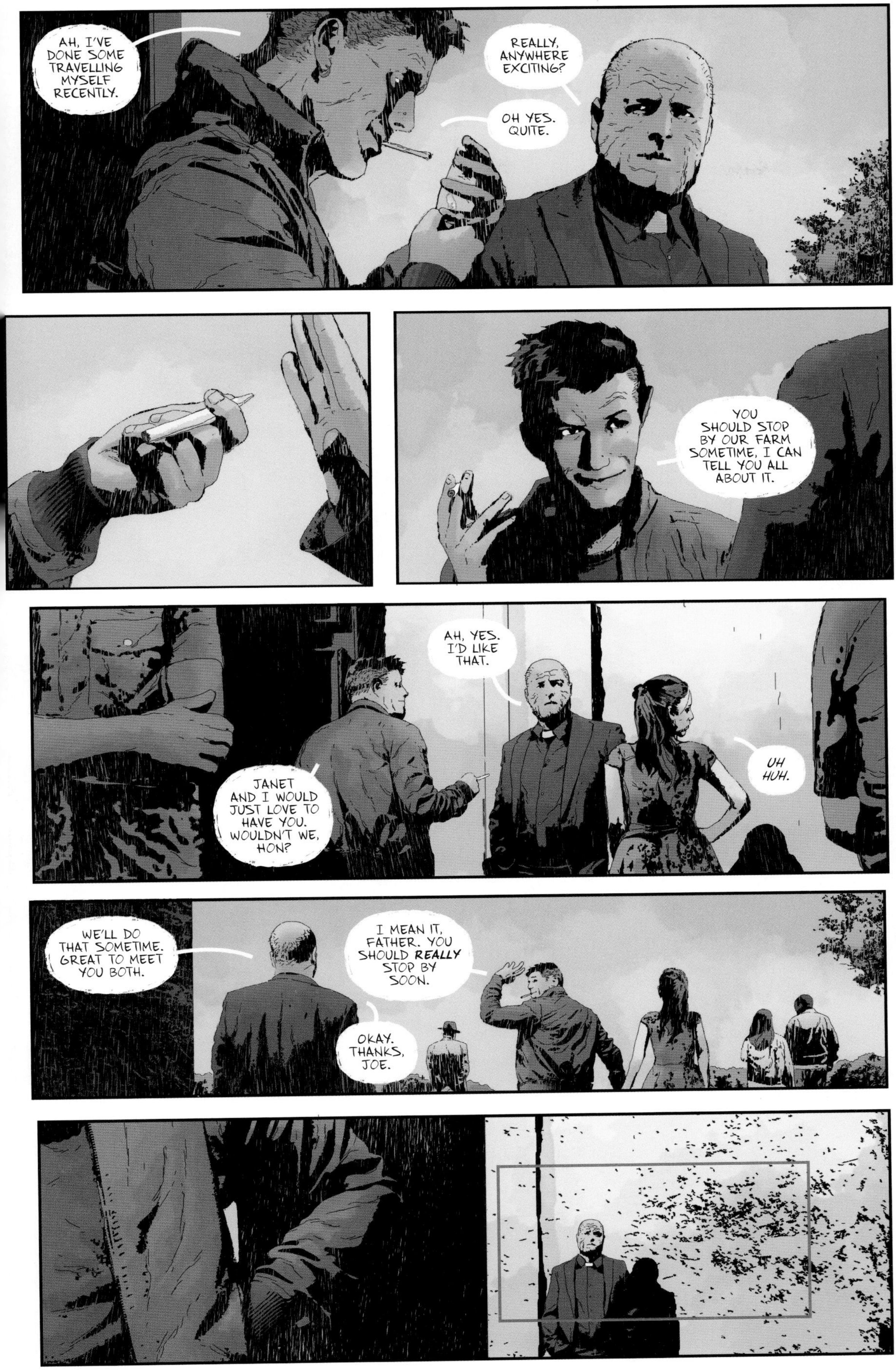
AH, I'VE DONE SOME TRAVELLING MYSELF RECENTLY.
REALLY, ANYWHERE EXCITING?
OH YES. QUITE.
YOU SHOULD STOP BY OUR FARM SOMETIME, I CAN TELL YOU ALL ABOUT IT.
AH, YES. I'D LIKE THAT.
JANET AND I WOULD JUST LOVE TO HAVE YOU. WOULDN'T WE, HON?
UH HUH.
WE'LL DO THAT SOMETIME. GREAT TO MEET YOU BOTH.
I MEAN IT, FATHER. YOU SHOULD **REALLY** STOP BY SOON.
OKAY. THANKS, JOE.

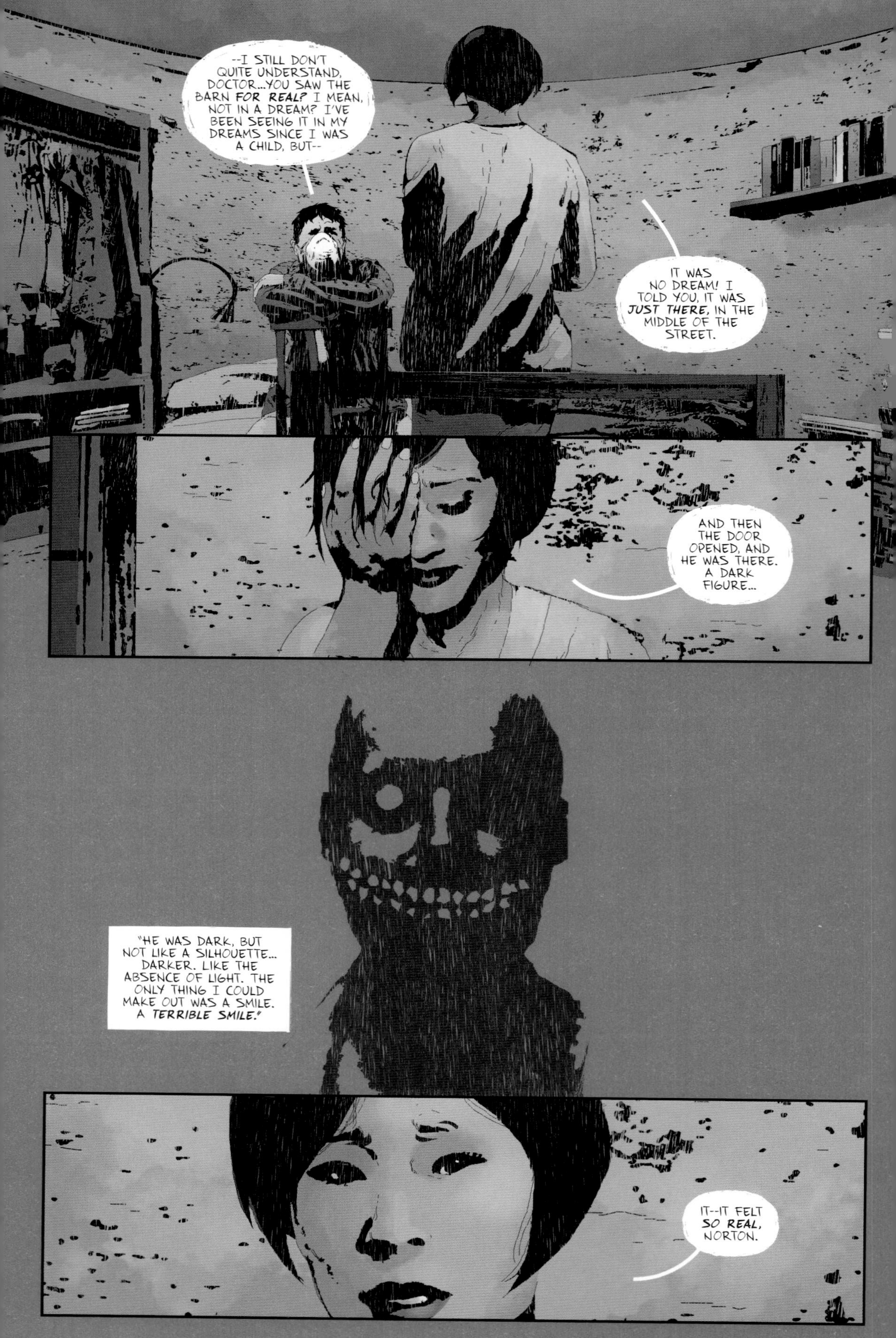
--I STILL DON'T QUITE UNDERSTAND, DOCTOR...YOU SAW THE BARN FOR REAL? I MEAN, NOT IN A DREAM? I'VE BEEN SEEING IT IN MY DREAMS SINCE I WAS A CHILD, BUT--
IT WAS NO DREAM! I TOLD YOU, IT WAS JUST THERE, IN THE MIDDLE OF THE STREET.
AND THEN THE DOOR OPENED, AND HE WAS THERE. A DARK FIGURE...
"HE WAS DARK, BUT NOT LIKE A SILHOUETTE... DARKER. LIKE THE ABSENCE OF LIGHT. THE ONLY THING I COULD MAKE OUT WAS A SMILE. A TERRIBLE SMILE."
IT--IT FELT SO REAL, NORTON.

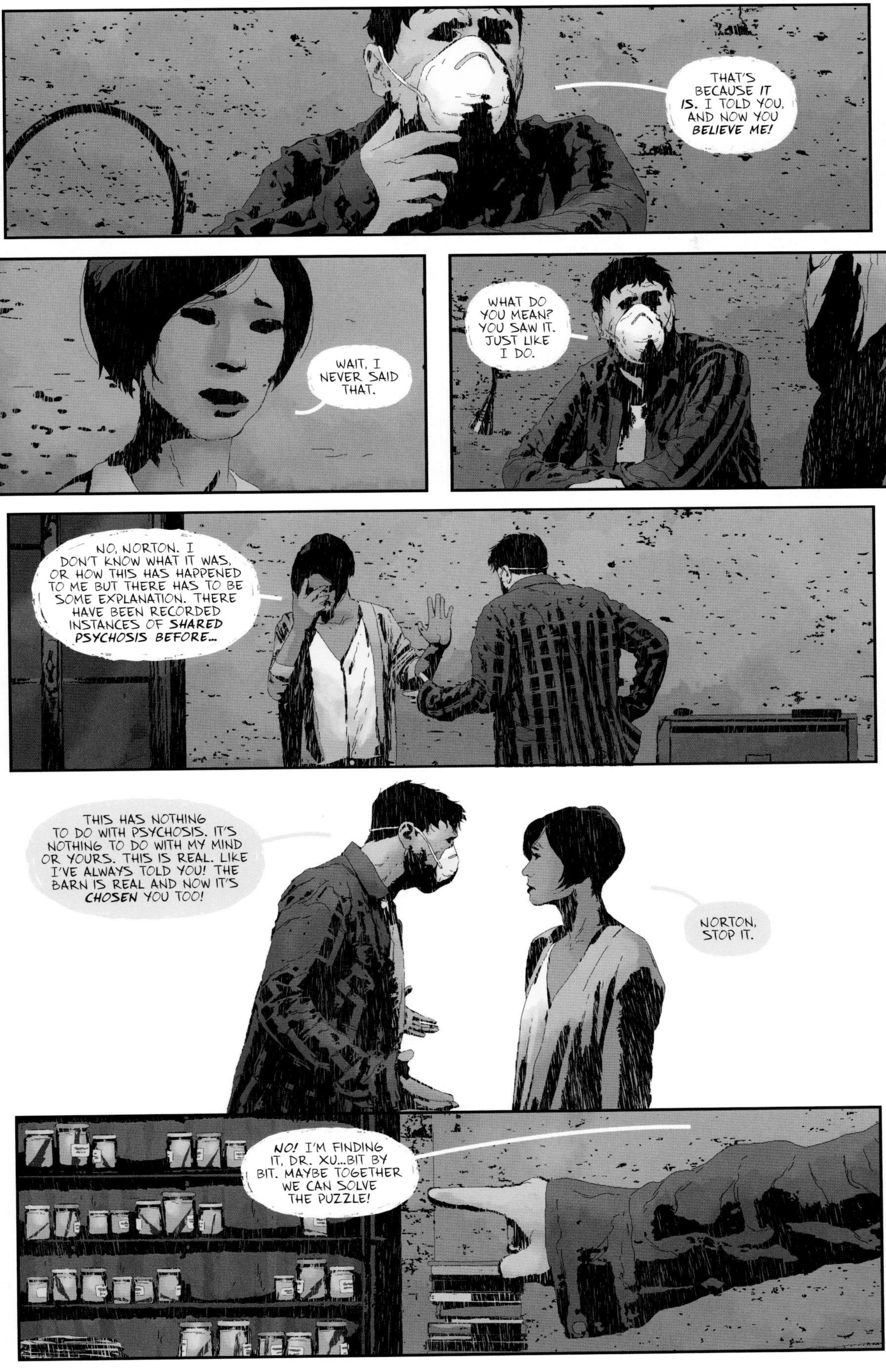
THAT'S BECAUSE IT IS. I TOLD YOU, AND NOW YOU BELIEVE ME!
WAIT, I NEVER SAID THAT.
WHAT DO YOU MEAN? YOU SAW IT. JUST LIKE I DO.
NO, NORTON. I DON'T KNOW WHAT IT WAS, OR HOW THIS HAS HAPPENED TO ME BUT THERE HAS TO BE SOME EXPLANATION. THERE HAVE BEEN RECORDED INSTANCES OF SHARED PSYCHOSIS BEFORE...
THIS HAS NOTHING TO DO WITH PSYCHOSIS. IT'S NOTHING TO DO WITH MY MIND OR YOURS. THIS IS REAL. LIKE I'VE ALWAYS TOLD YOU! THE BARN IS REAL AND NOW IT'S CHOSEN YOU TOO!
NORTON, STOP IT.
NO! I'M FINDING IT, DR. XU...BIT BY BIT. MAYBE TOGETHER WE CAN SOLVE THE PUZZLE!

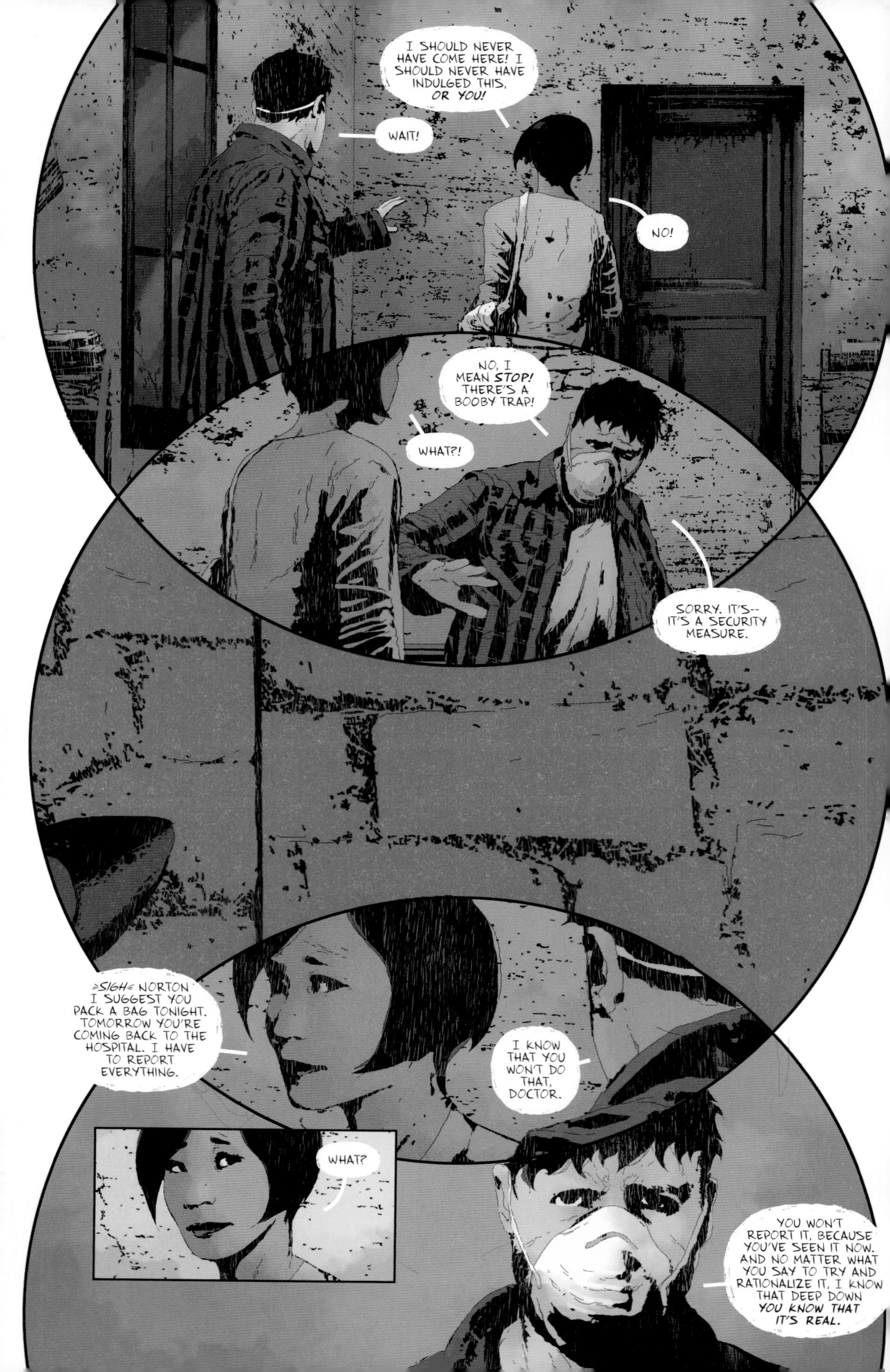
I SHOULD NEVER HAVE COME HERE! I SHOULD NEVER HAVE INDULGED THIS, OR YOU!
WAIT!
NO!
NO, I MEAN STOP! THERE'S A BOOBY TRAP!
WHAT?!
SORRY. IT'S-- IT'S A SECURITY MEASURE.
SIGH NORTON I SUGGEST YOU PACK A BAG TONIGHT. TOMORROW YOU'RE COMING BACK TO THE HOSPITAL. I HAVE TO REPORT EVERYTHING.
I KNOW THAT YOU WON'T DO THAT, DOCTOR.
WHAT?
YOU WON'T REPORT IT, BECAUSE YOU'VE SEEN IT NOW. AND NO MATTER WHAT YOU SAY TO TRY AND RATIONALIZE IT, I KNOW THAT DEEP DOWN YOU KNOW THAT IT'S REAL.

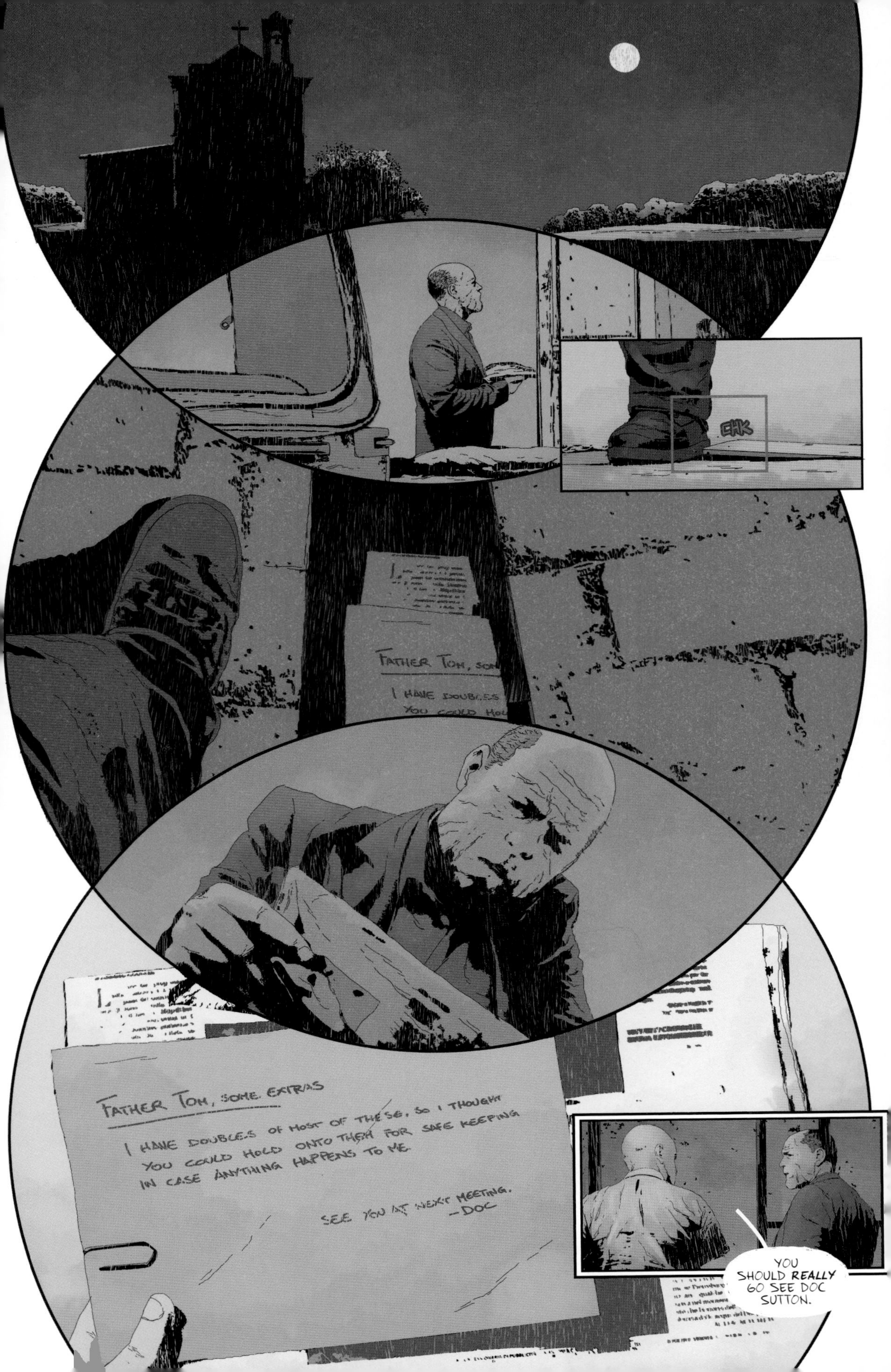
EHK
FATHER TOM, SOME EXTRAS
I HAVE DOUBLES
YOU COULD HOL
FATHER TOM, SOME EXTRAS
I HAVE DOUBLES OF MOST OF THESE, SO I THOUGHT YOU COULD HOLD ONTO THEM FOR SAFE KEEPING IN CASE ANYTHING HAPPENS TO ME.
SEE YOU AT NEXT MEETING.
-DOC
YOU SHOULD REALLY GO SEE DOC SUTTON.

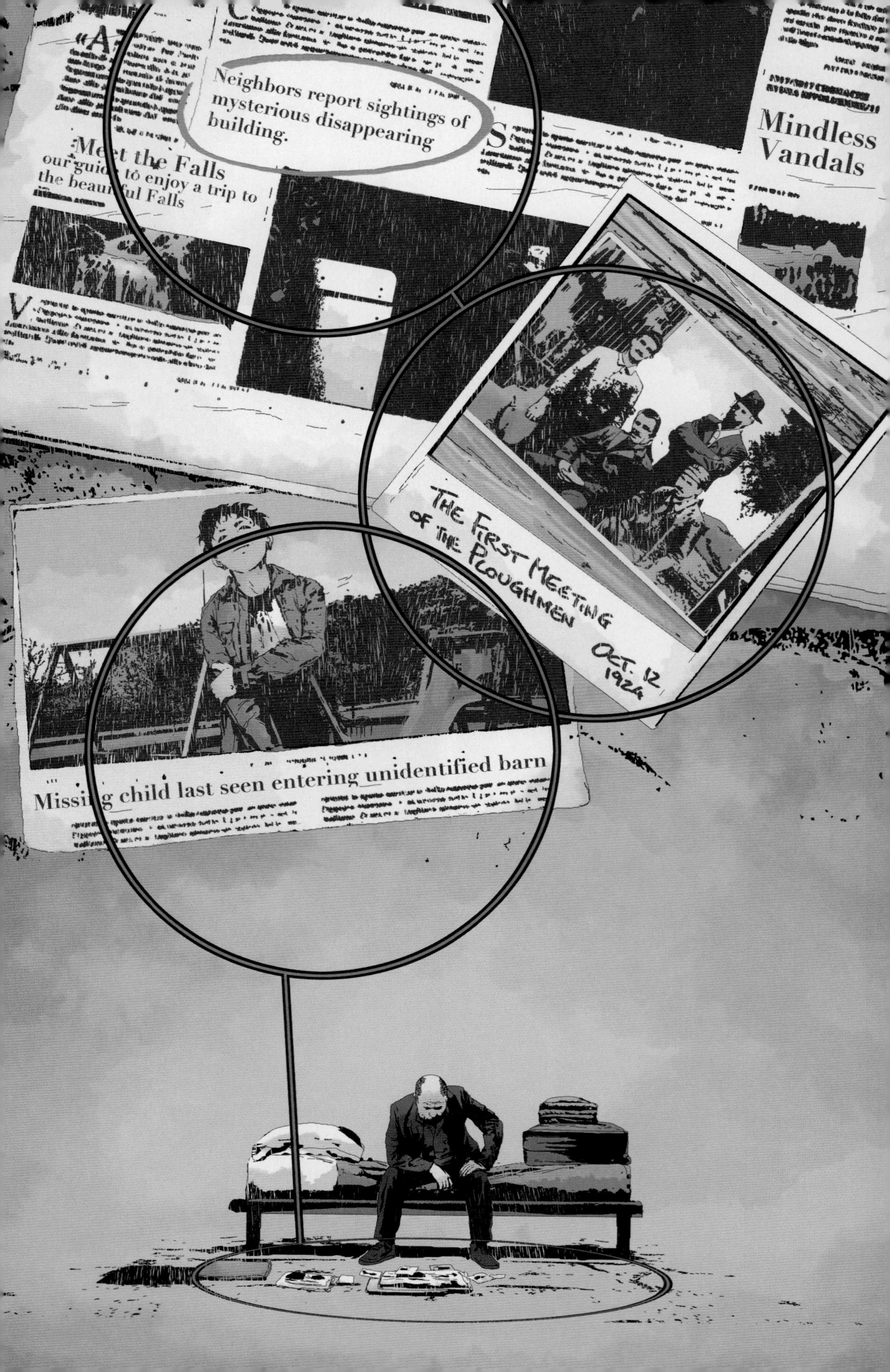

Neighbors report sightings of mysterious disappearing building.
Meet the Falls
our guide to enjoy a trip to the beautiful Falls
Mindless Vandals
THE FIRST MEETING OF THE PLOUGHMEN
OCT. 12 1924
Missing child last seen entering unidentified barn

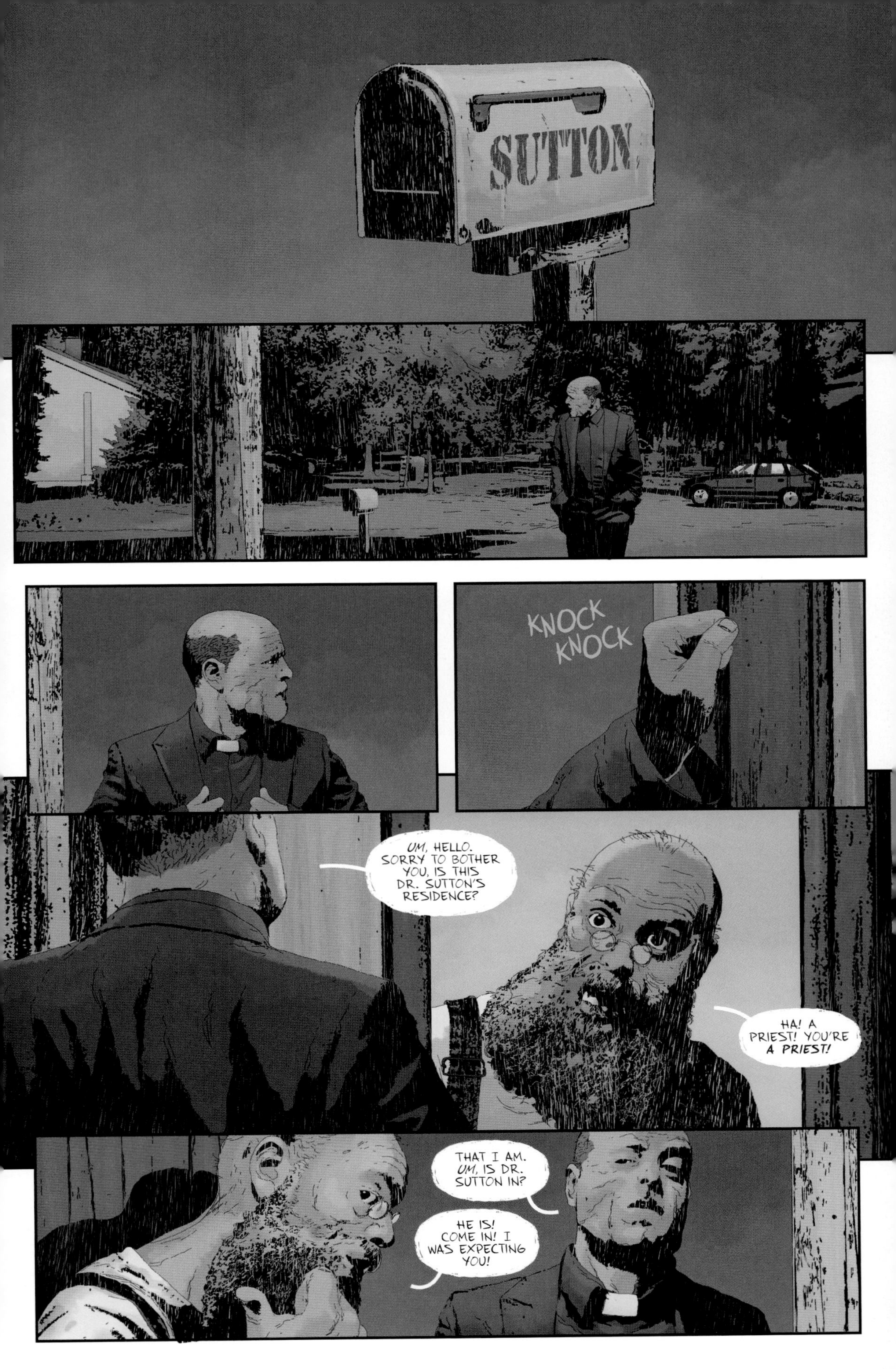
SUTTON
KNOCK KNOCK
UM, HELLO. SORRY TO BOTHER YOU, IS THIS DR. SUTTON'S RESIDENCE?
HA! A PRIEST! YOU'RE A PRIEST!
THAT I AM. UM, IS DR. SUTTON IN?
HE IS! COME IN! I WAS EXPECTING YOU!

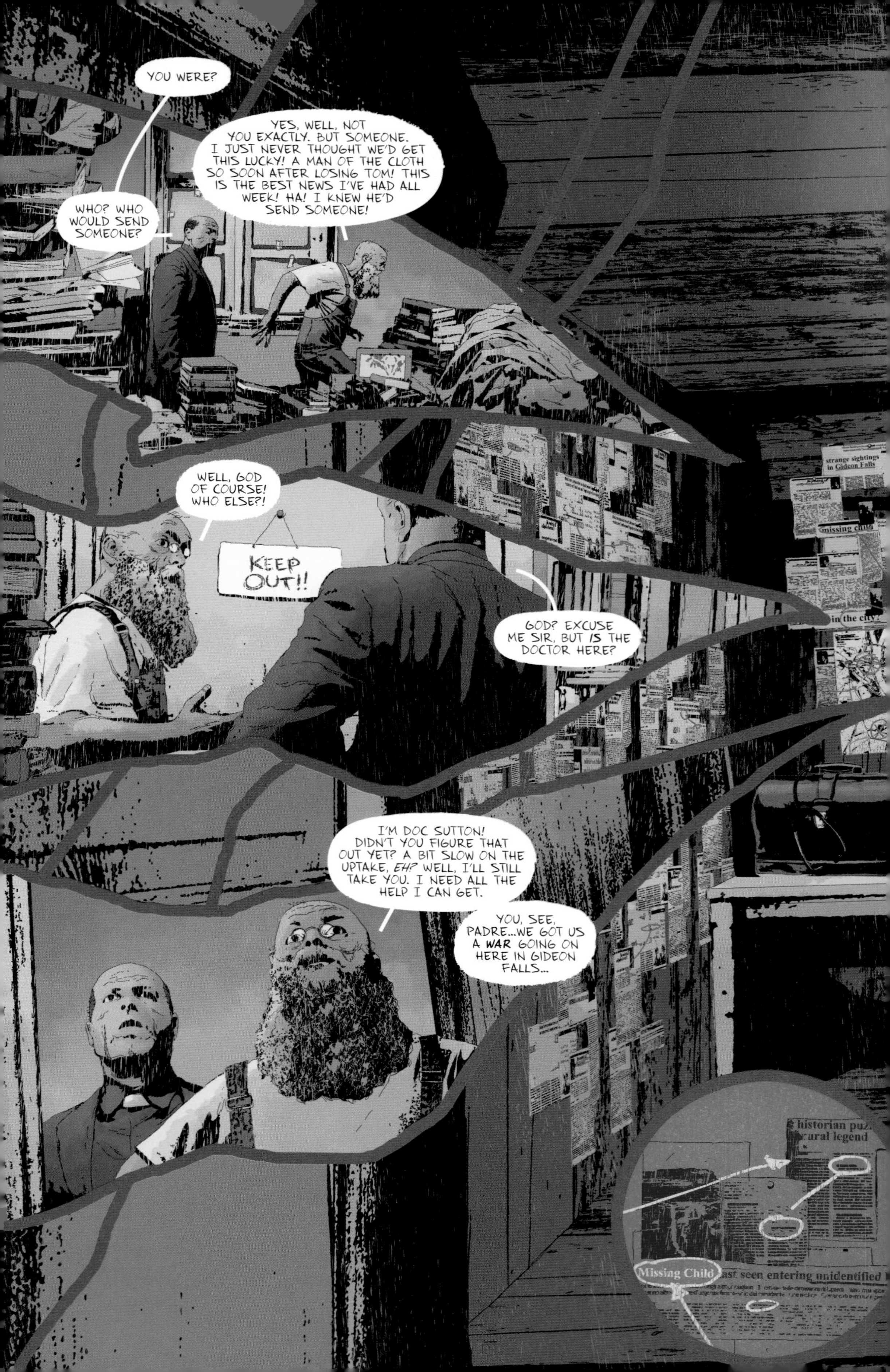
YOU WERE?
YES, WELL, NOT YOU EXACTLY. BUT SOMEONE. I JUST NEVER THOUGHT WE'D GET THIS LUCKY! A MAN OF THE CLOTH SO SOON AFTER LOSING TOM! THIS IS THE BEST NEWS I'VE HAD ALL WEEK! HA! I KNEW HE'D SEND SOMEONE!
WHO? WHO WOULD SEND SOMEONE?
WELL, GOD OF COURSE! WHO ELSE?!
KEEP OUT!!
GOD? EXCUSE ME SIR, BUT IS THE DOCTOR HERE?
strange sightings in Gideon Falls
I'M DOC SUTTON! DIDN'T YOU FIGURE THAT OUT YET? A BIT SLOW ON THE UPTAKE, EH? WELL, I'LL STILL TAKE YOU. I NEED ALL THE HELP I CAN GET.
YOU, SEE, PADRE...WE GOT US A WAR GOING ON HERE IN GIDEON FALLS...
Missing Child

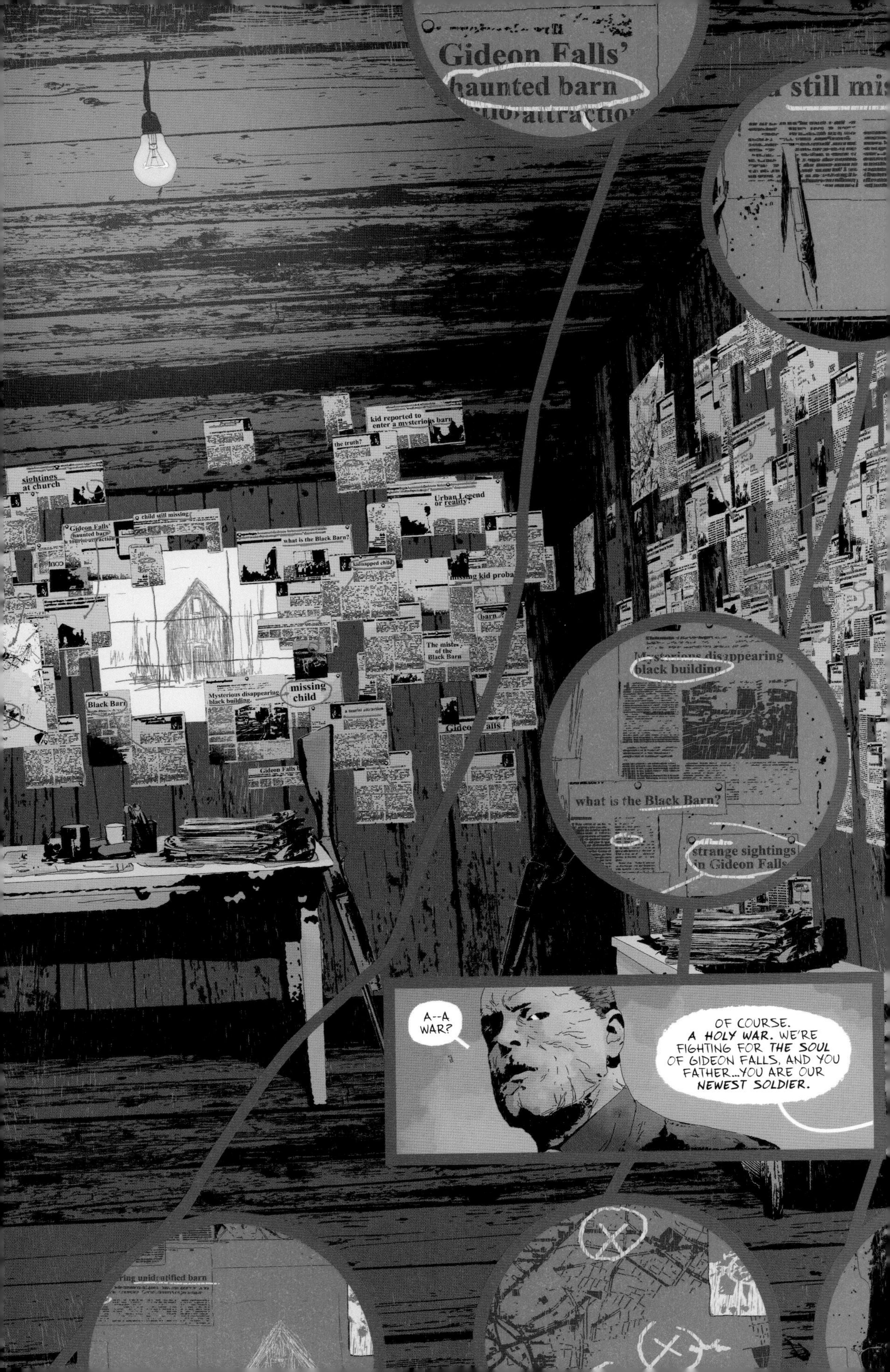
Gideon Falls'
haunted barn
still mis
kid reported to enter a mysterious barn
the truth?
sightings at church
Urban Legend or reality?
child still missing
Gideon Falls' haunted barn
what is the Black Barn
kidnapped child
The mistery of the Black Barn
Mysterious disappearing black building
missing child
Black Barn
a tourist attraction
Gideon Falls
Mysterious disappearing
black building
what is the Black Barn?
strange sightings
in Gideon Falls
A--A WAR?
OF COURSE. A HOLY WAR. WE'RE FIGHTING FOR THE SOUL OF GIDEON FALLS, AND YOU FATHER...YOU ARE OUR NEWEST SOLDIER.

Four

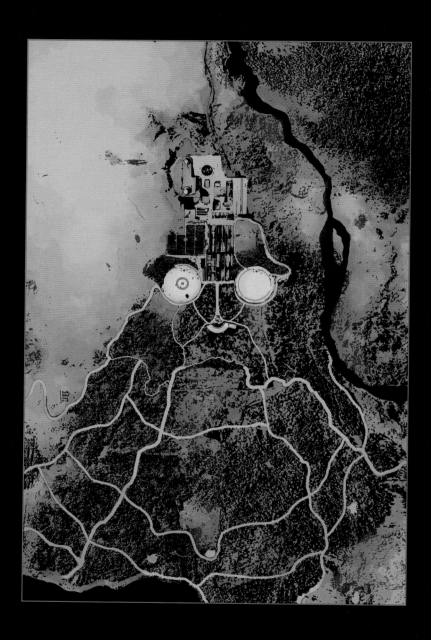

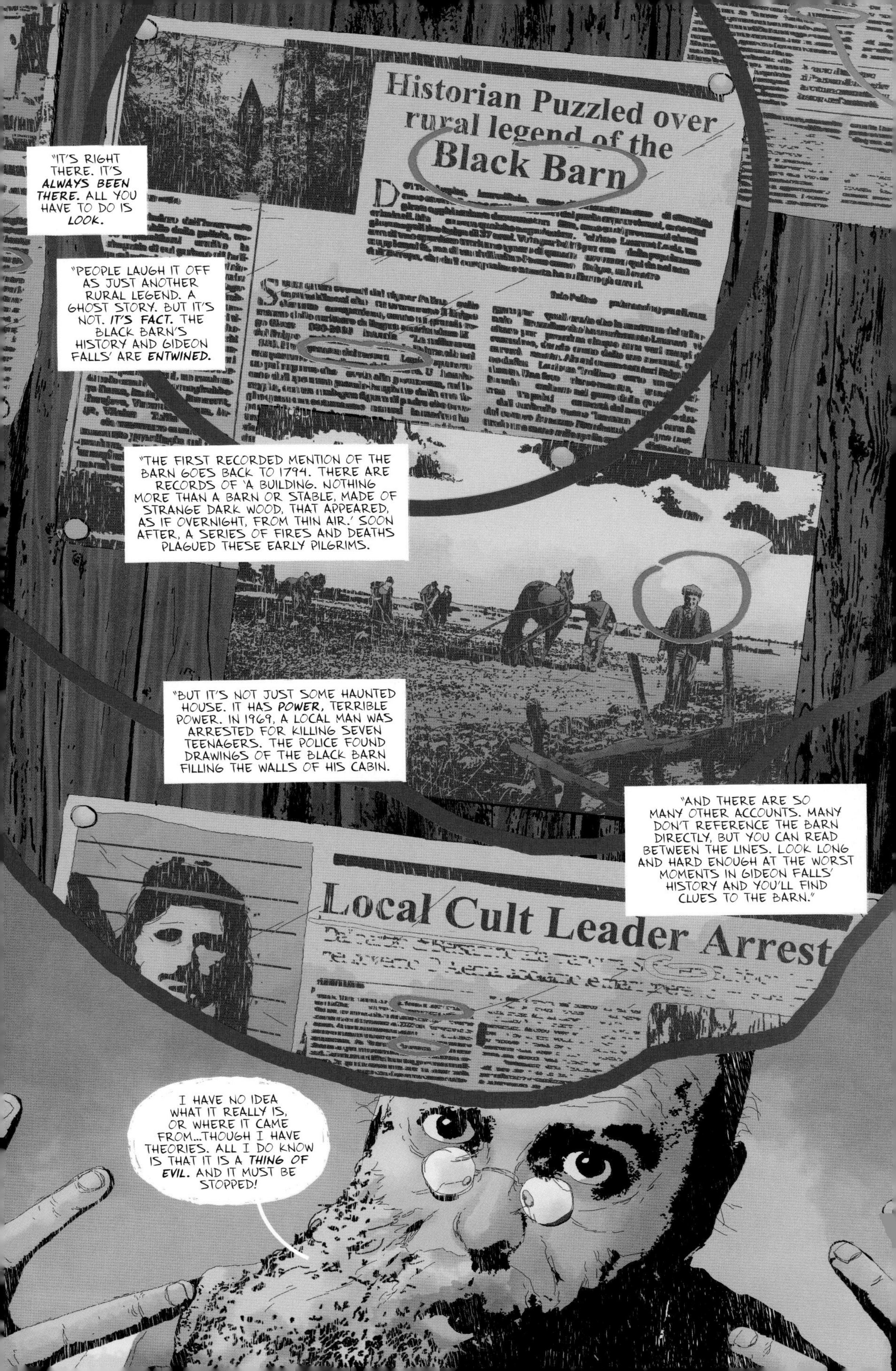
Historian Puzzled over rural legend of the Black Barn
"IT'S RIGHT THERE. IT'S ALWAYS BEEN THERE. ALL YOU HAVE TO DO IS LOOK.
"PEOPLE LAUGH IT OFF AS JUST ANOTHER RURAL LEGEND. A GHOST STORY. BUT IT'S NOT. IT'S FACT. THE BLACK BARN'S HISTORY AND GIDEON FALLS' ARE ENTWINED.
"THE FIRST RECORDED MENTION OF THE BARN GOES BACK TO 1794. THERE ARE RECORDS OF 'A BUILDING. NOTHING MORE THAN A BARN OR STABLE, MADE OF STRANGE DARK WOOD, THAT APPEARED, AS IF OVERNIGHT, FROM THIN AIR.' SOON AFTER, A SERIES OF FIRES AND DEATHS PLAGUED THESE EARLY PILGRIMS.
"BUT IT'S NOT JUST SOME HAUNTED HOUSE. IT HAS POWER. TERRIBLE POWER. IN 1969, A LOCAL MAN WAS ARRESTED FOR KILLING SEVEN TEENAGERS. THE POLICE FOUND DRAWINGS OF THE BLACK BARN FILLING THE WALLS OF HIS CABIN.
"AND THERE ARE SO MANY OTHER ACCOUNTS. MANY DON'T REFERENCE THE BARN DIRECTLY, BUT YOU CAN READ BETWEEN THE LINES. LOOK LONG AND HARD ENOUGH AT THE WORST MOMENTS IN GIDEON FALLS' HISTORY AND YOU'LL FIND CLUES TO THE BARN."
Local Cult Leader Arrest
I HAVE NO IDEA WHAT IT REALLY IS, OR WHERE IT CAME FROM...THOUGH I HAVE THEORIES. ALL I DO KNOW IS THAT IT IS A THING OF EVIL. AND IT MUST BE STOPPED!

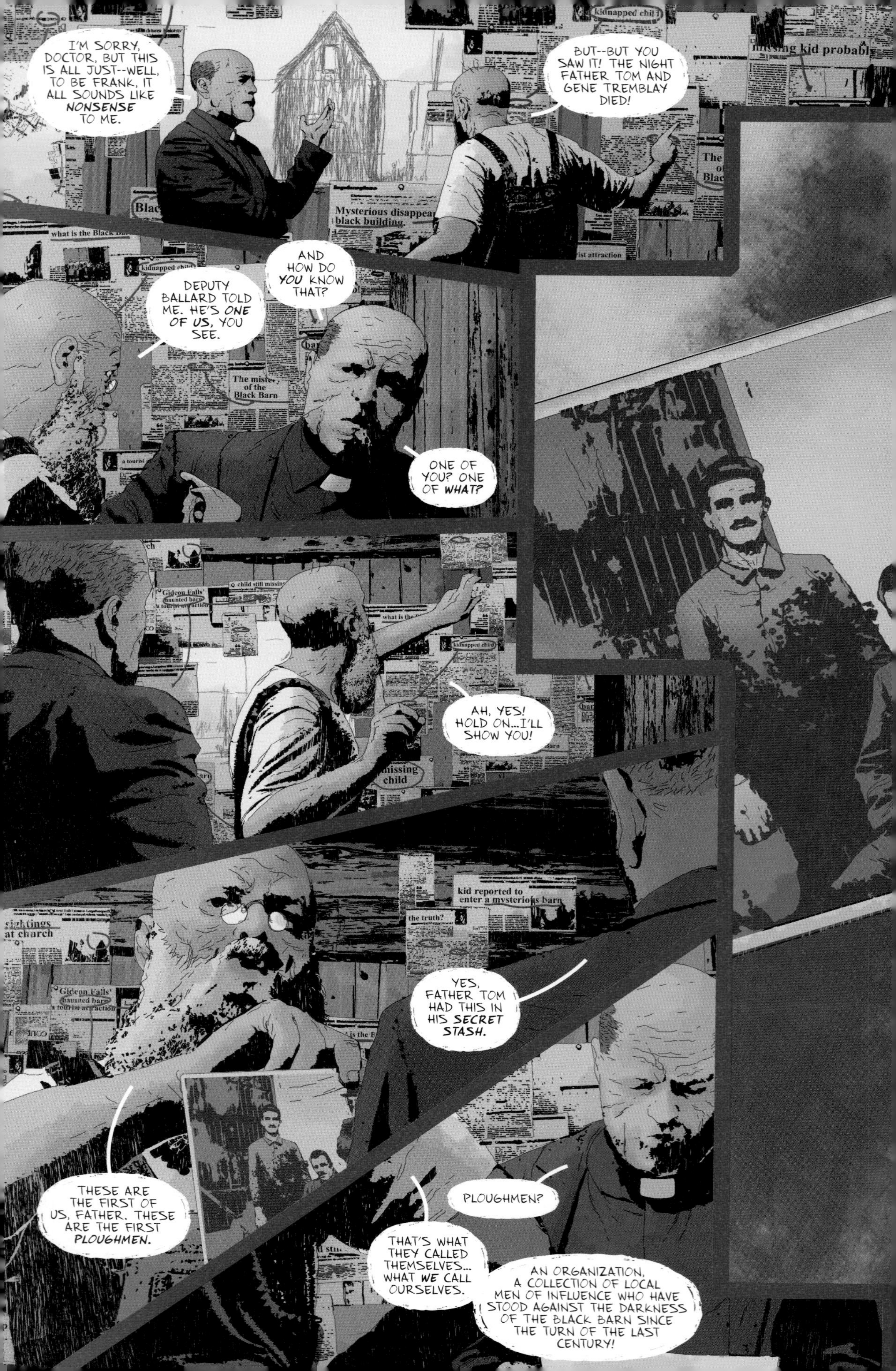
I'M SORRY, DOCTOR, BUT THIS IS ALL JUST--WELL, TO BE FRANK, IT ALL SOUNDS LIKE NONSENSE TO ME.
BUT--BUT YOU SAW IT! THE NIGHT FATHER TOM AND GENE TREMBLAY DIED!
DEPUTY BALLARD TOLD ME. HE'S ONE OF US, YOU SEE.
AND HOW DO YOU KNOW THAT?
ONE OF YOU? ONE OF WHAT?
AH, YES! HOLD ON...I'LL SHOW YOU!
YES, FATHER TOM HAD THIS IN HIS SECRET STASH.
THESE ARE THE FIRST OF US, FATHER. THESE ARE THE FIRST PLOUGHMEN.
PLOUGHMEN?
THAT'S WHAT THEY CALLED THEMSELVES... WHAT WE CALL OURSELVES.
AN ORGANIZATION, A COLLECTION OF LOCAL MEN OF INFLUENCE WHO HAVE STOOD AGAINST THE DARKNESS OF THE BLACK BARN SINCE THE TURN OF THE LAST CENTURY!

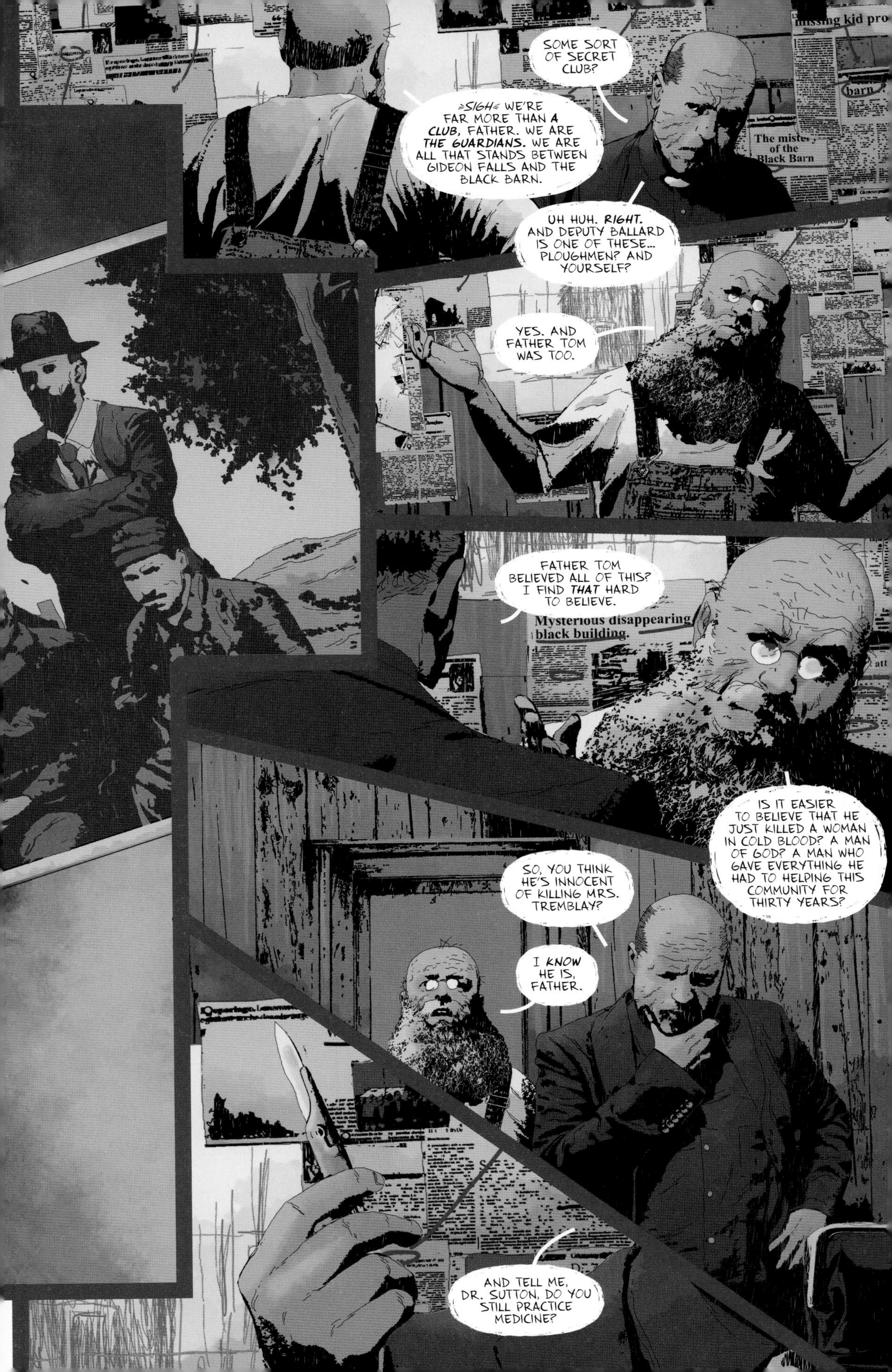

missing kid pro
barn
The mistery of the Black Barn
SOME SORT OF SECRET CLUB?
≷SIGH≶ WE'RE FAR MORE THAN A CLUB, FATHER. WE ARE THE GUARDIANS. WE ARE ALL THAT STANDS BETWEEN GIDEON FALLS AND THE BLACK BARN.
UH HUH. RIGHT. AND DEPUTY BALLARD IS ONE OF THESE... PLOUGHMEN? AND YOURSELF?
YES. AND FATHER TOM WAS TOO.
FATHER TOM BELIEVED ALL OF THIS? I FIND THAT HARD TO BELIEVE.
Mysterious disappearing black building.
IS IT EASIER TO BELIEVE THAT HE JUST KILLED A WOMAN IN COLD BLOOD? A MAN OF GOD? A MAN WHO GAVE EVERYTHING HE HAD TO HELPING THIS COMMUNITY FOR THIRTY YEARS?
SO, YOU THINK HE'S INNOCENT OF KILLING MRS. TREMBLAY?
I KNOW HE IS, FATHER.
AND TELL ME, DR. SUTTON, DO YOU STILL PRACTICE MEDICINE?

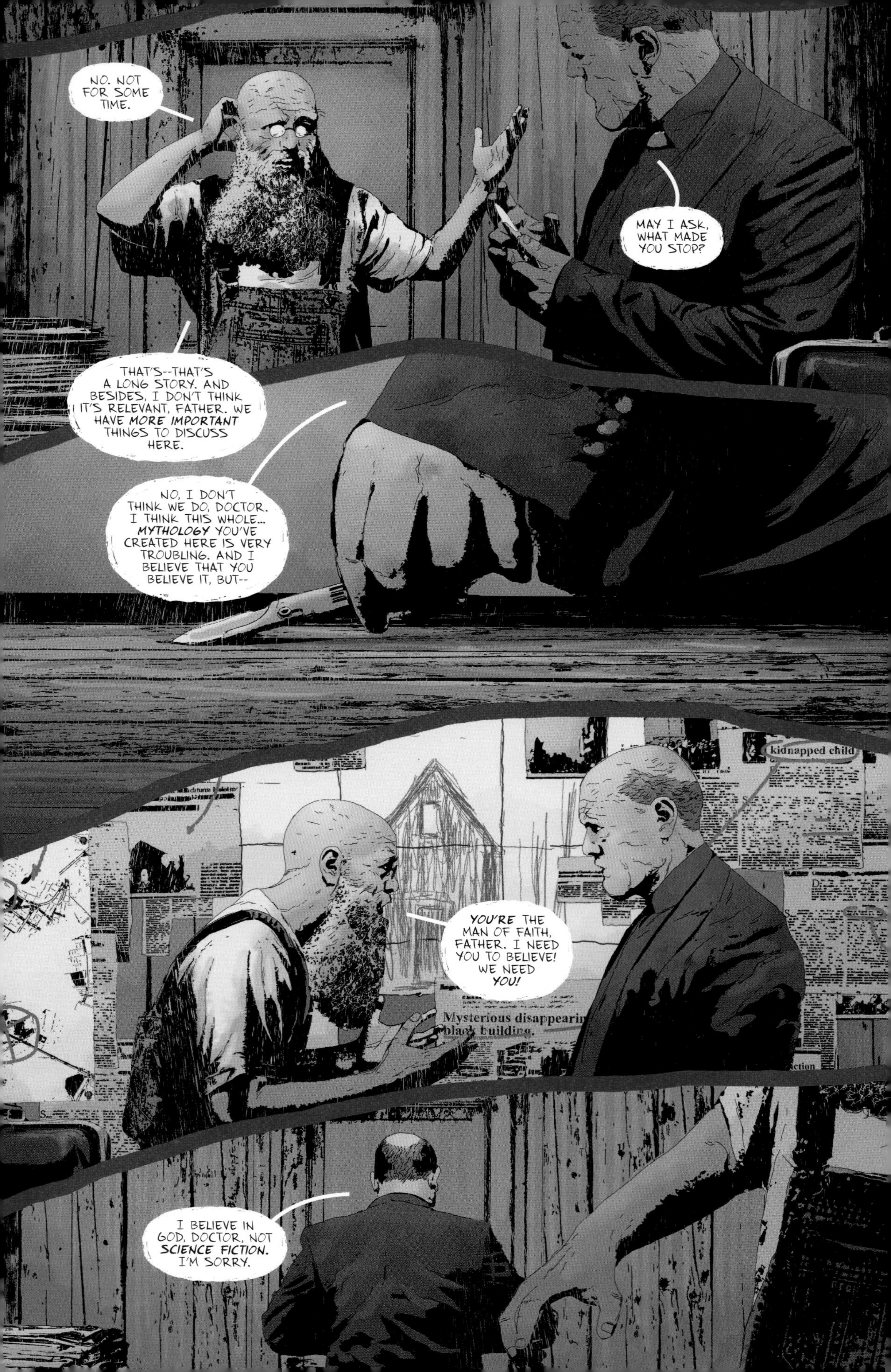
NO. NOT FOR SOME TIME.
MAY I ASK, WHAT MADE YOU STOP?
THAT'S--THAT'S A LONG STORY. AND BESIDES, I DON'T THINK IT'S RELEVANT, FATHER. WE HAVE MORE IMPORTANT THINGS TO DISCUSS HERE.
NO, I DON'T THINK WE DO, DOCTOR. I THINK THIS WHOLE... MYTHOLOGY YOU'VE CREATED HERE IS VERY TROUBLING. AND I BELIEVE THAT YOU BELIEVE IT, BUT--
kidnapped child
YOU'RE THE MAN OF FAITH, FATHER. I NEED YOU TO BELIEVE! WE NEED YOU!
I BELIEVE IN GOD, DOCTOR, NOT SCIENCE FICTION. I'M SORRY.

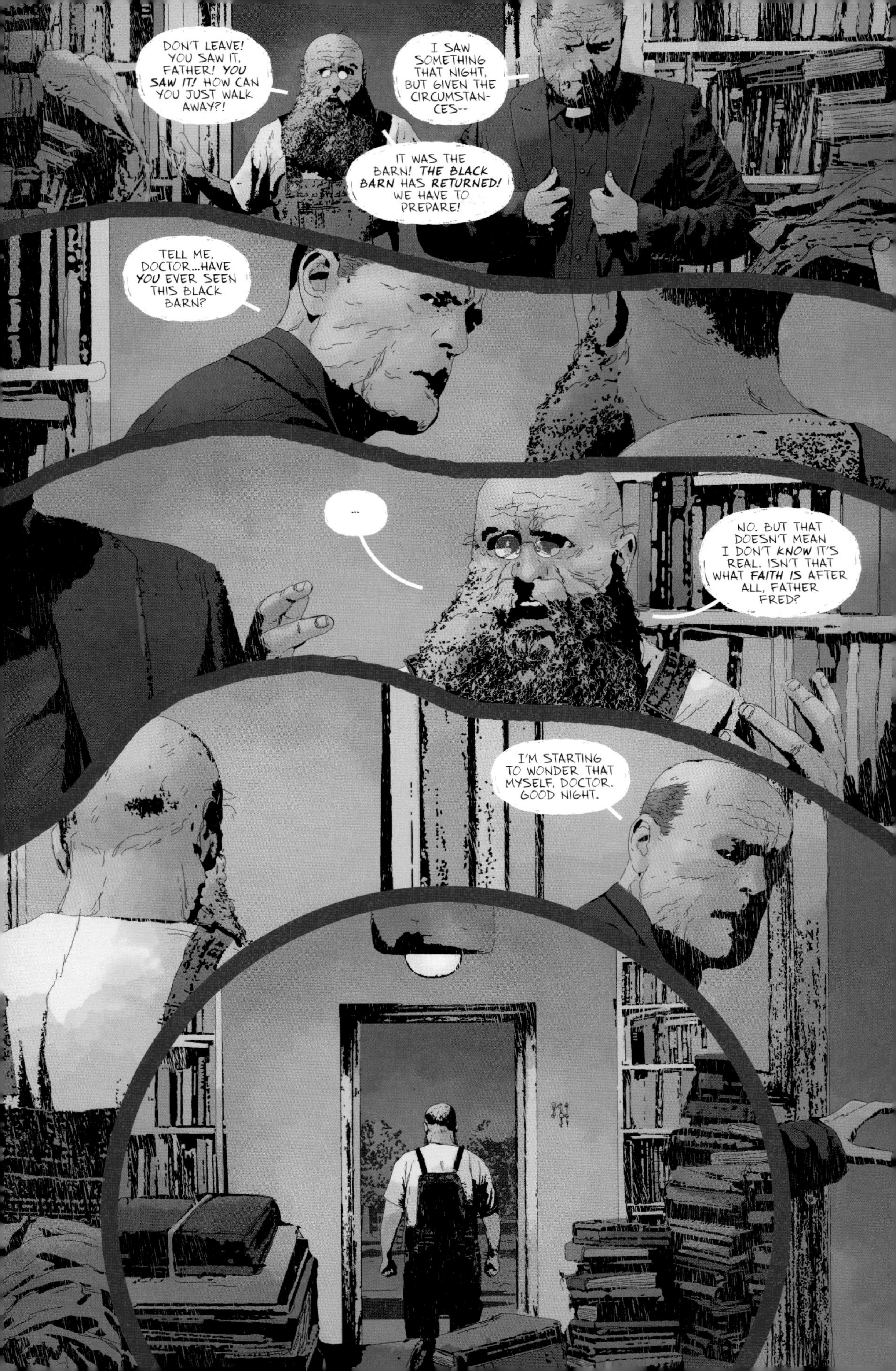
DON'T LEAVE! YOU SAW IT, FATHER! YOU SAW IT! HOW CAN YOU JUST WALK AWAY?!
I SAW SOMETHING THAT NIGHT, BUT GIVEN THE CIRCUMSTANCES--
IT WAS THE BARN! THE BLACK BARN HAS RETURNED! WE HAVE TO PREPARE!
TELL ME, DOCTOR...HAVE YOU EVER SEEN THIS BLACK BARN?
...
NO. BUT THAT DOESN'T MEAN I DON'T KNOW IT'S REAL. ISN'T THAT WHAT FAITH IS AFTER ALL, FATHER FRED?
I'M STARTING TO WONDER THAT MYSELF, DOCTOR. GOOD NIGHT.

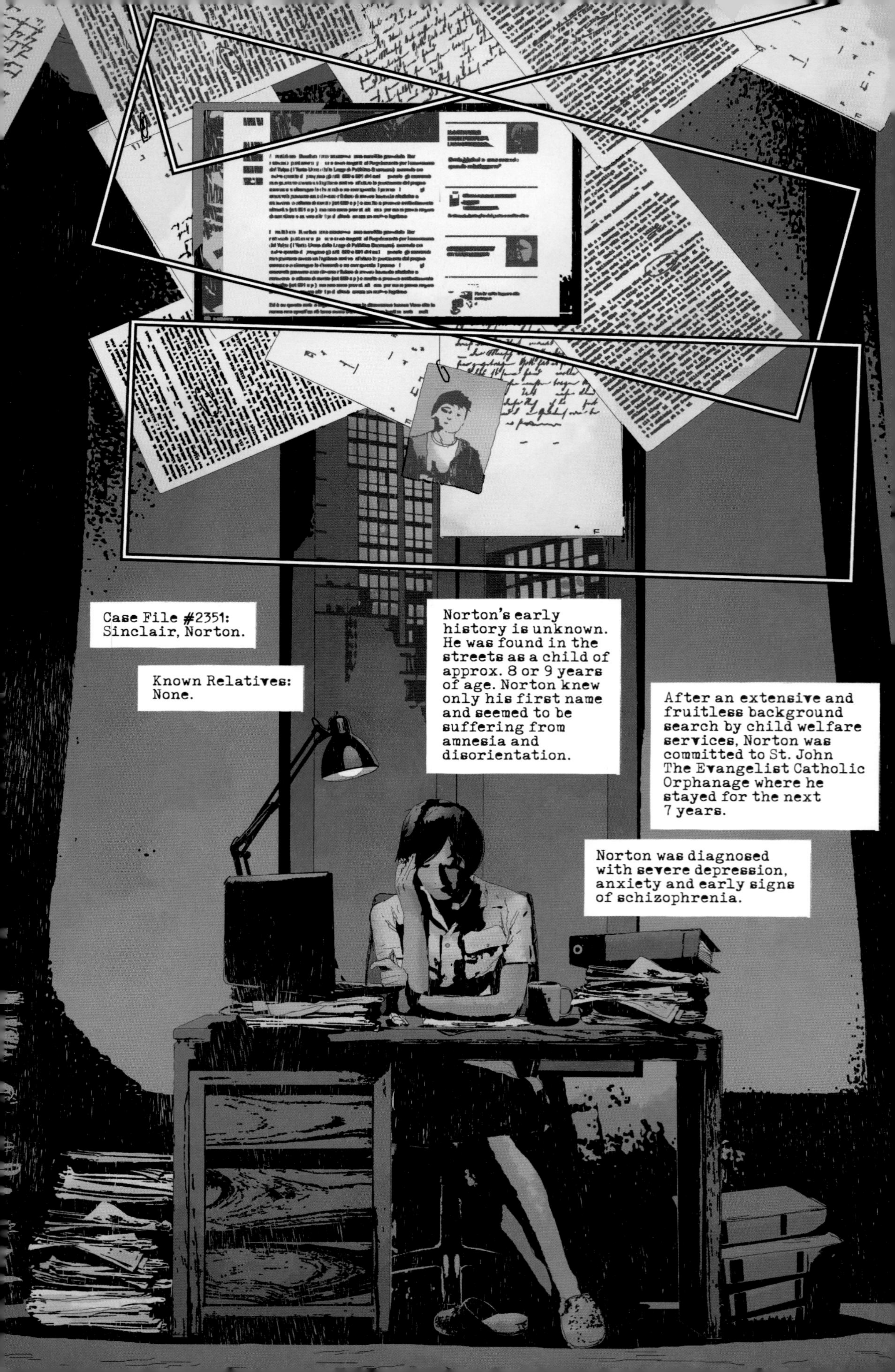
Case File #2351:
Sinclair, Norton.
Known Relatives:
None.
Norton's early history is unknown. He was found in the streets as a child of approx. 8 or 9 years of age. Norton knew only his first name and seemed to be suffering from amnesia and disorientation.
After an extensive and fruitless background search by child welfare services, Norton was committed to St. John The Evangelist Catholic Orphanage where he stayed for the next 7 years.
Norton was diagnosed with severe depression, anxiety and early signs of schizophrenia.

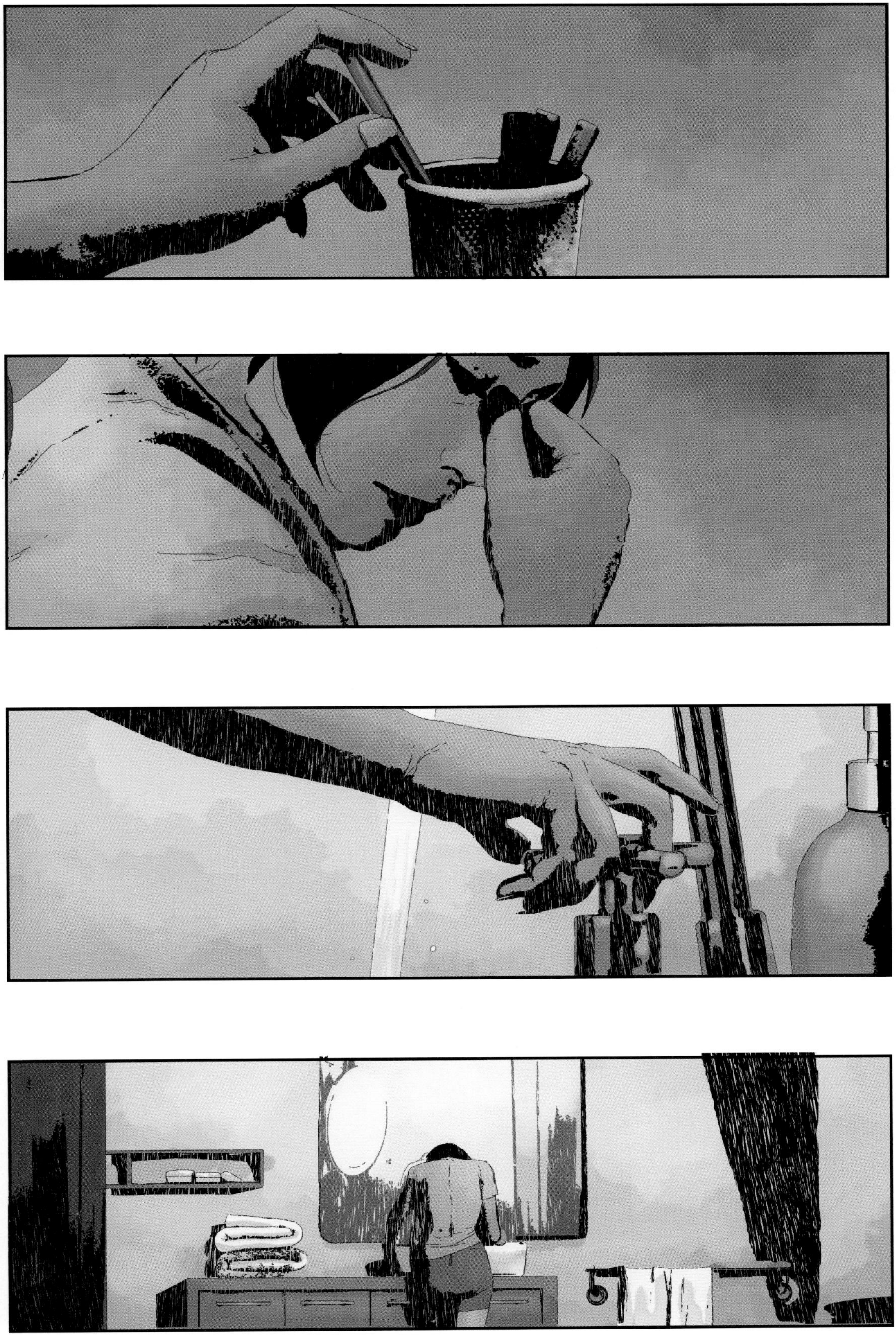

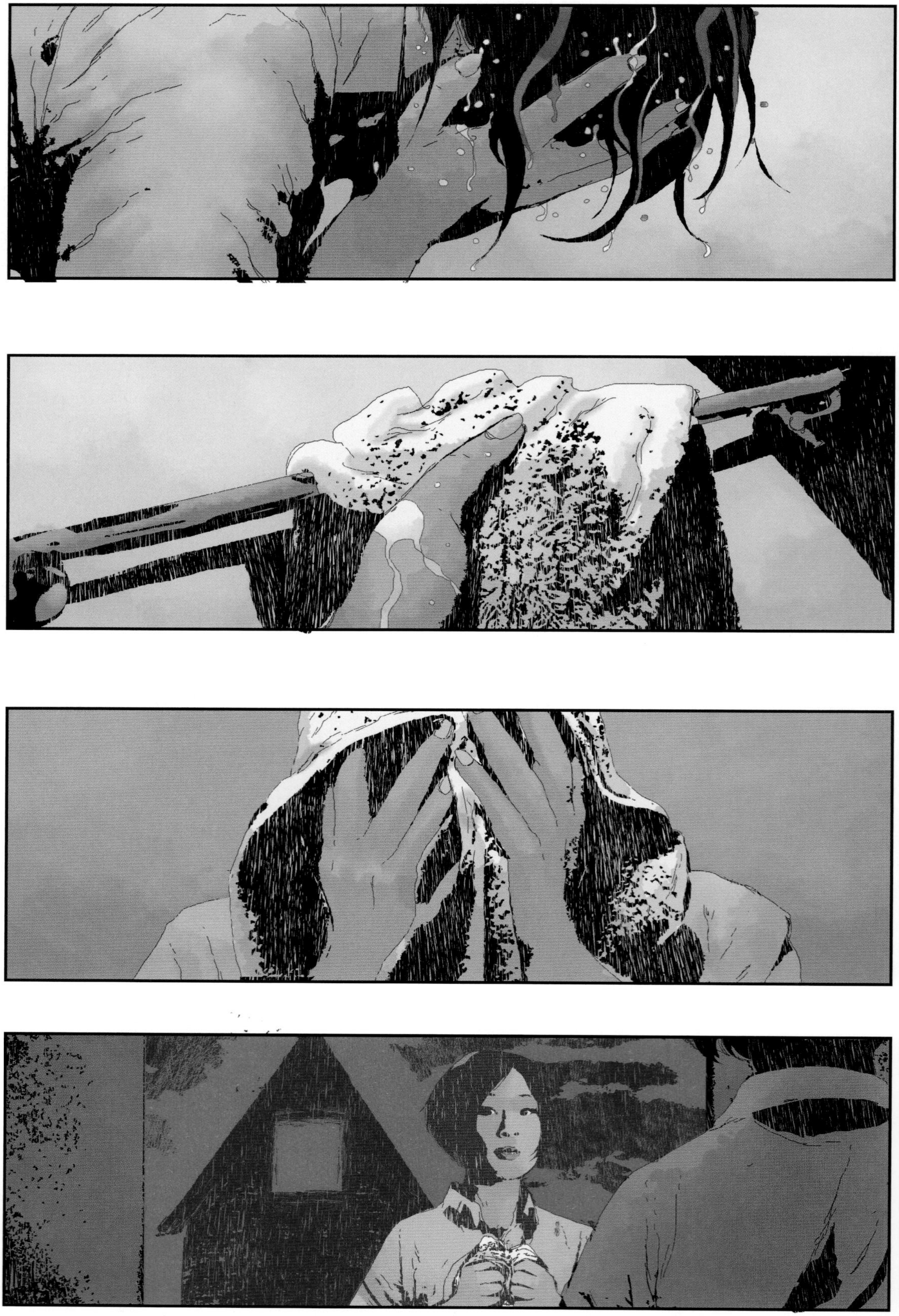

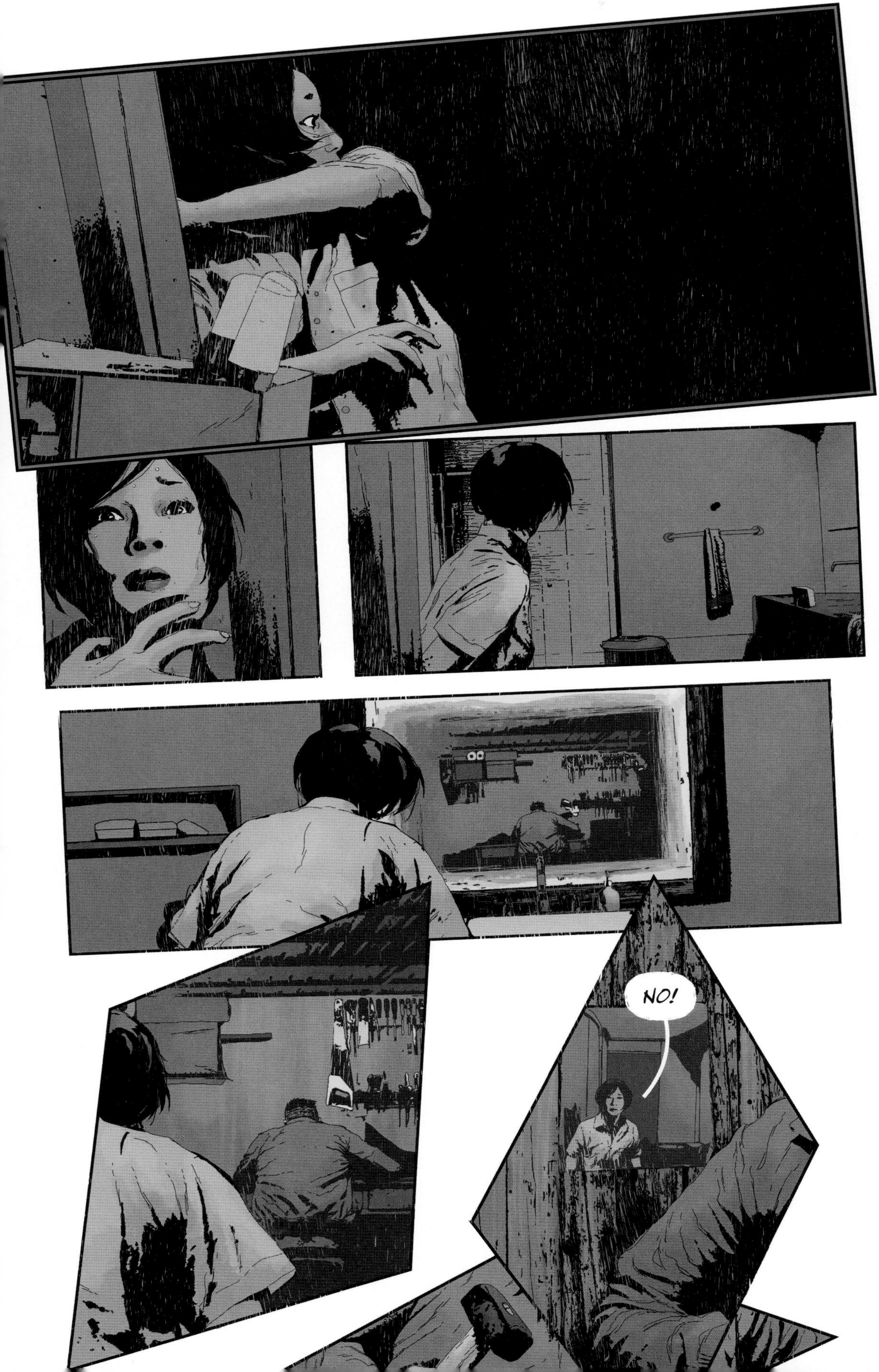
NO!

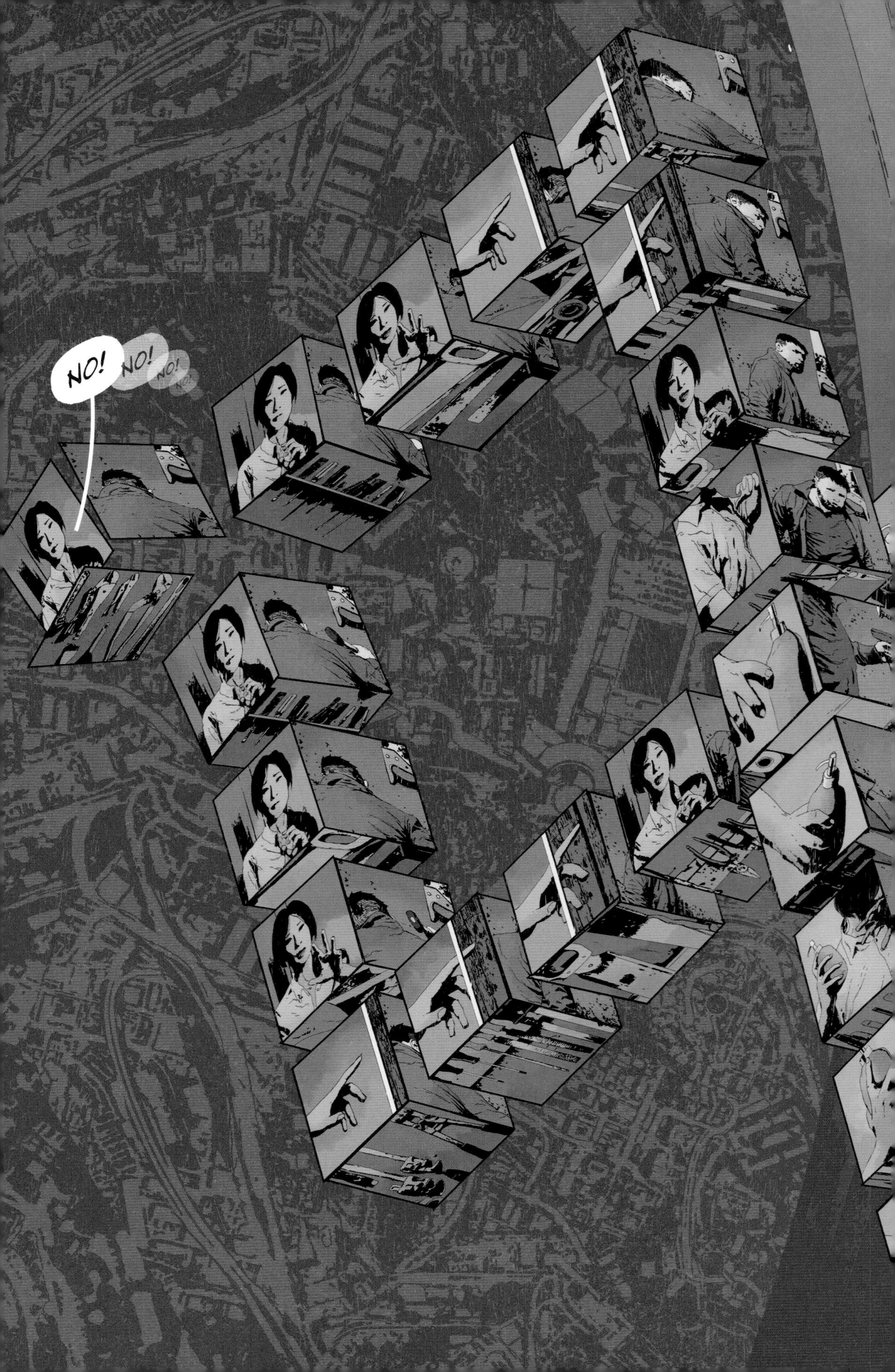
NO!
NO!
NO!
NO!

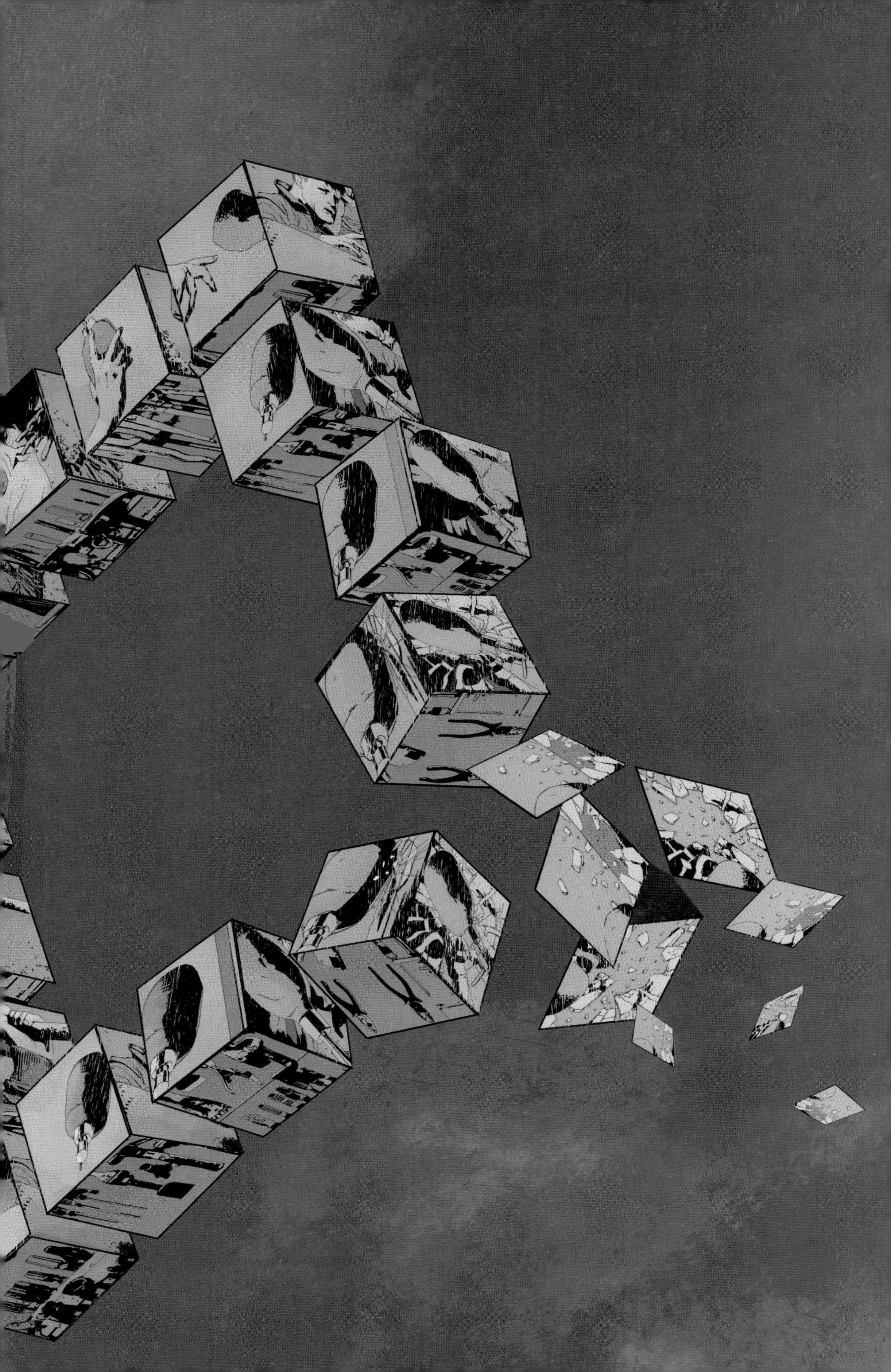

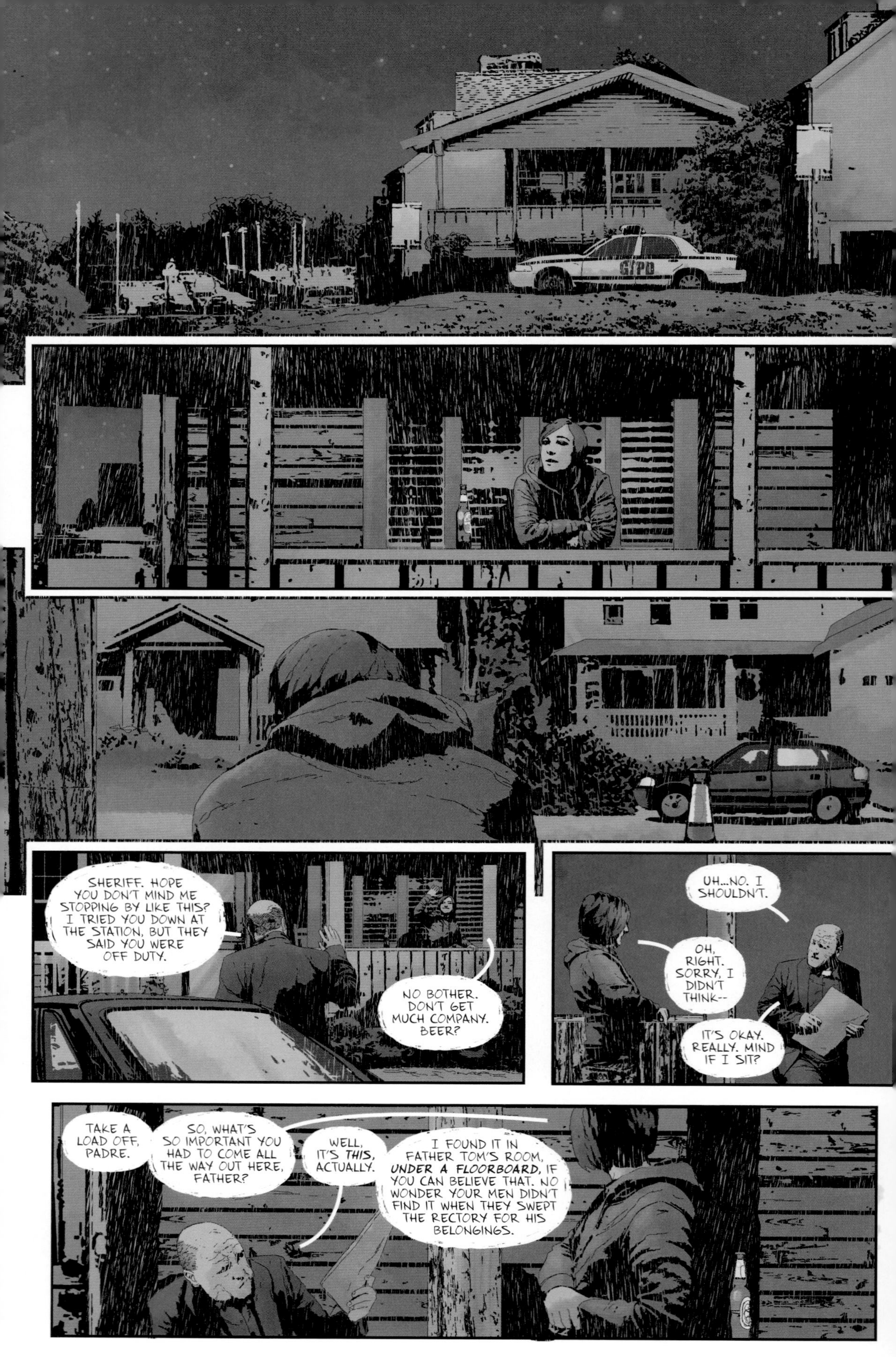
SHERIFF. HOPE YOU DON'T MIND ME STOPPING BY LIKE THIS? I TRIED YOU DOWN AT THE STATION, BUT THEY SAID YOU WERE OFF DUTY.
NO BOTHER. DON'T GET MUCH COMPANY. BEER?
UH...NO. I SHOULDN'T.
OH, RIGHT. SORRY, I DIDN'T THINK--
IT'S OKAY. REALLY. MIND IF I SIT?
TAKE A LOAD OFF, PADRE.
SO, WHAT'S SO IMPORTANT YOU HAD TO COME ALL THE WAY OUT HERE, FATHER?
WELL, IT'S *THIS,* ACTUALLY.
I FOUND IT IN FATHER TOM'S ROOM, ***UNDER A FLOORBOARD,*** IF YOU CAN BELIEVE THAT. NO WONDER YOUR MEN DIDN'T FIND IT WHEN THEY SWEPT THE RECTORY FOR HIS BELONGINGS.

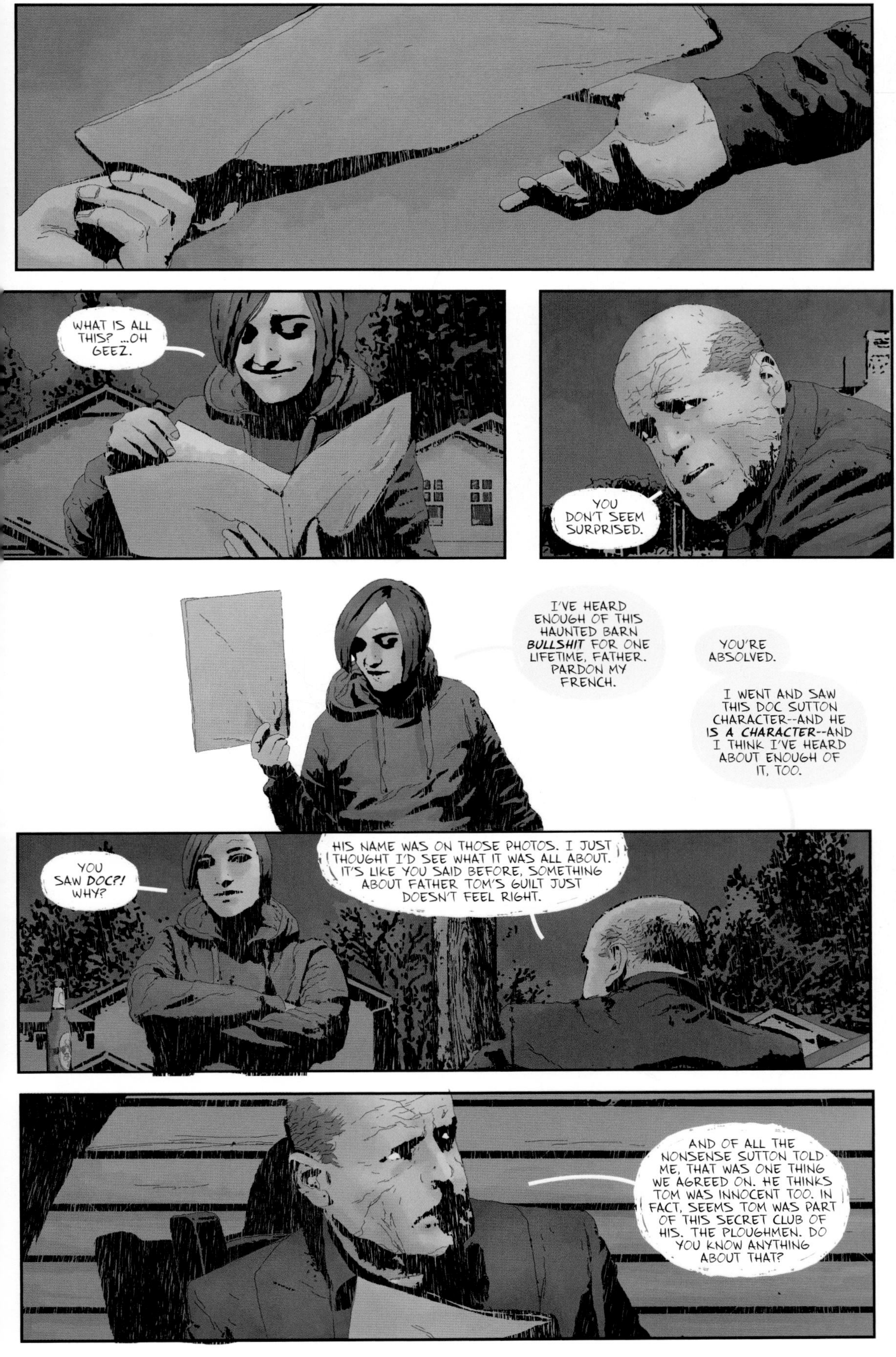
WHAT IS ALL THIS? ...OH GEEZ.
YOU DON'T SEEM SURPRISED.
I'VE HEARD ENOUGH OF THIS HAUNTED BARN **BULLSHIT** FOR ONE LIFETIME, FATHER. PARDON MY FRENCH.
YOU'RE ABSOLVED.
I WENT AND SAW THIS DOC SUTTON CHARACTER--AND HE **IS A CHARACTER**--AND I THINK I'VE HEARD ABOUT ENOUGH OF IT, TOO.
YOU SAW ***DOC?!*** WHY?
HIS NAME WAS ON THOSE PHOTOS. I JUST THOUGHT I'D SEE WHAT IT WAS ALL ABOUT. IT'S LIKE YOU SAID BEFORE, SOMETHING ABOUT FATHER TOM'S GUILT JUST DOESN'T FEEL RIGHT.
AND OF ALL THE NONSENSE SUTTON TOLD ME, THAT WAS ONE THING WE AGREED ON. HE THINKS TOM WAS INNOCENT TOO. IN FACT, SEEMS TOM WAS PART OF THIS SECRET CLUB OF HIS. THE PLOUGHMEN. DO YOU KNOW ANYTHING ABOUT THAT?

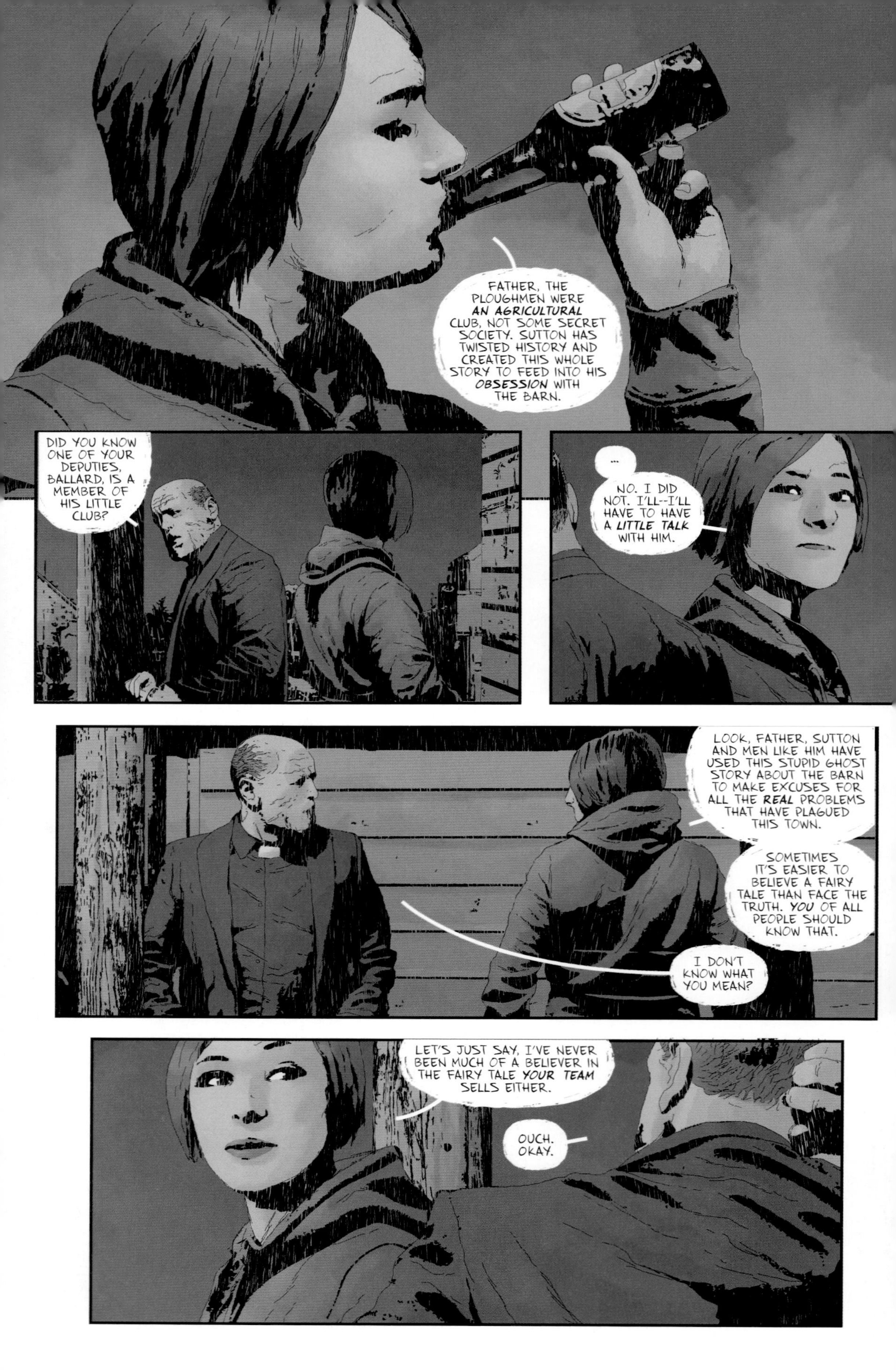
FATHER, THE PLOUGHMEN WERE **AN AGRICULTURAL** CLUB, NOT SOME SECRET SOCIETY. SUTTON HAS TWISTED HISTORY AND CREATED THIS WHOLE STORY TO FEED INTO HIS *OBSESSION* WITH THE BARN.
DID YOU KNOW ONE OF YOUR DEPUTIES, BALLARD, IS A MEMBER OF HIS LITTLE CLUB?
...
NO. I DID NOT. I'LL--I'LL HAVE TO HAVE A *LITTLE TALK* WITH HIM.
LOOK, FATHER, SUTTON AND MEN LIKE HIM HAVE USED THIS STUPID GHOST STORY ABOUT THE BARN TO MAKE EXCUSES FOR ALL THE **REAL** PROBLEMS THAT HAVE PLAGUED THIS TOWN.
SOMETIMES IT'S EASIER TO BELIEVE A FAIRY TALE THAN FACE THE TRUTH. ***YOU*** OF ALL PEOPLE SHOULD KNOW THAT.
I DON'T KNOW WHAT YOU MEAN?
LET'S JUST SAY, I'VE NEVER BEEN MUCH OF A BELIEVER IN THE FAIRY TALE ***YOUR TEAM*** SELLS EITHER.
OUCH. OKAY.

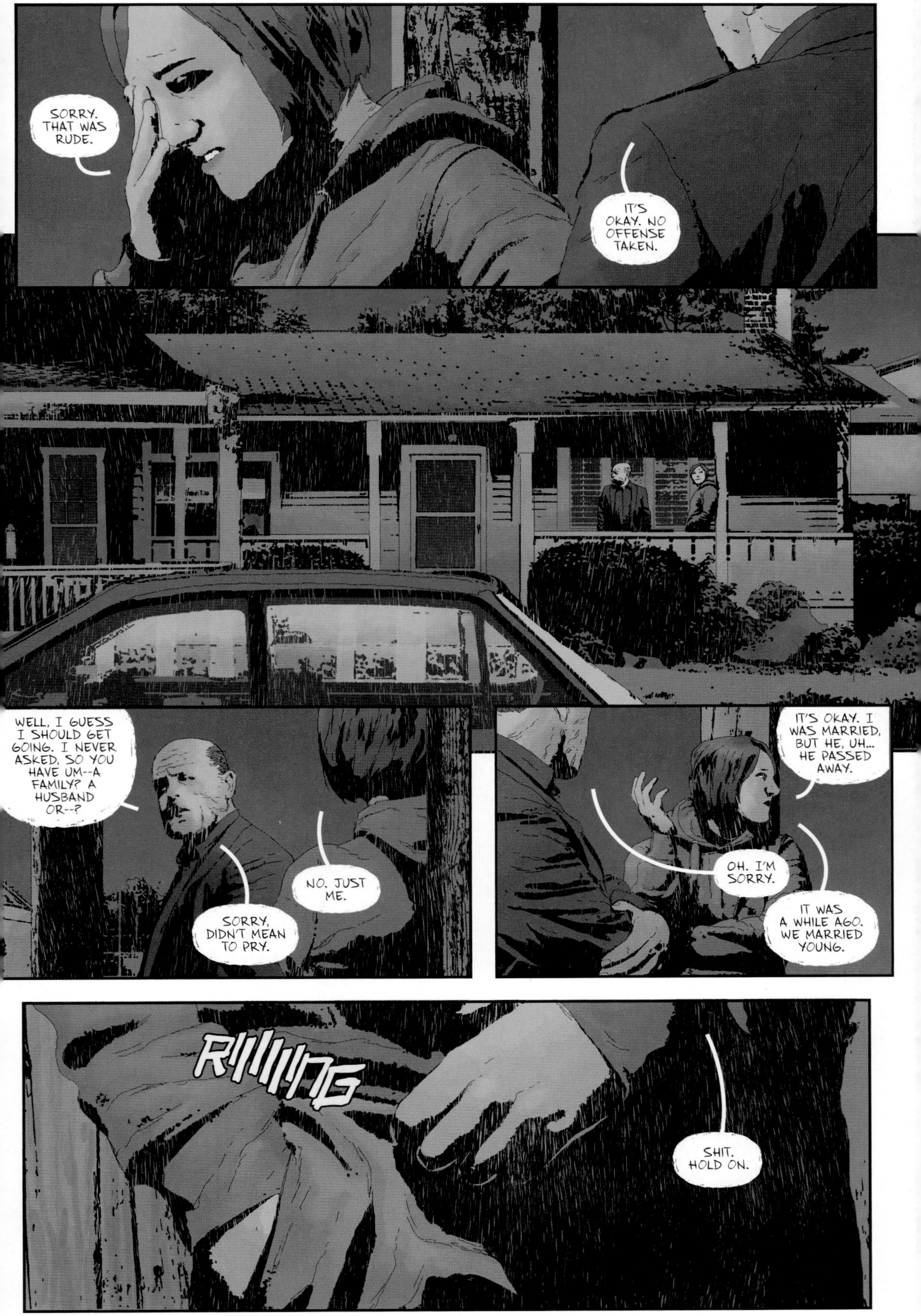
SORRY. THAT WAS RUDE.
IT'S OKAY. NO OFFENSE TAKEN.
WELL, I GUESS I SHOULD GET GOING. I NEVER ASKED, SO YOU HAVE UM--A FAMILY? A HUSBAND OR--?
NO. JUST ME.
SORRY, DIDN'T MEAN TO PRY.
IT'S OKAY. I WAS MARRIED, BUT HE, UH... HE PASSED AWAY.
OH. I'M SORRY.
IT WAS A WHILE AGO. WE MARRIED YOUNG.
RIIIING
SHIT. HOLD ON.

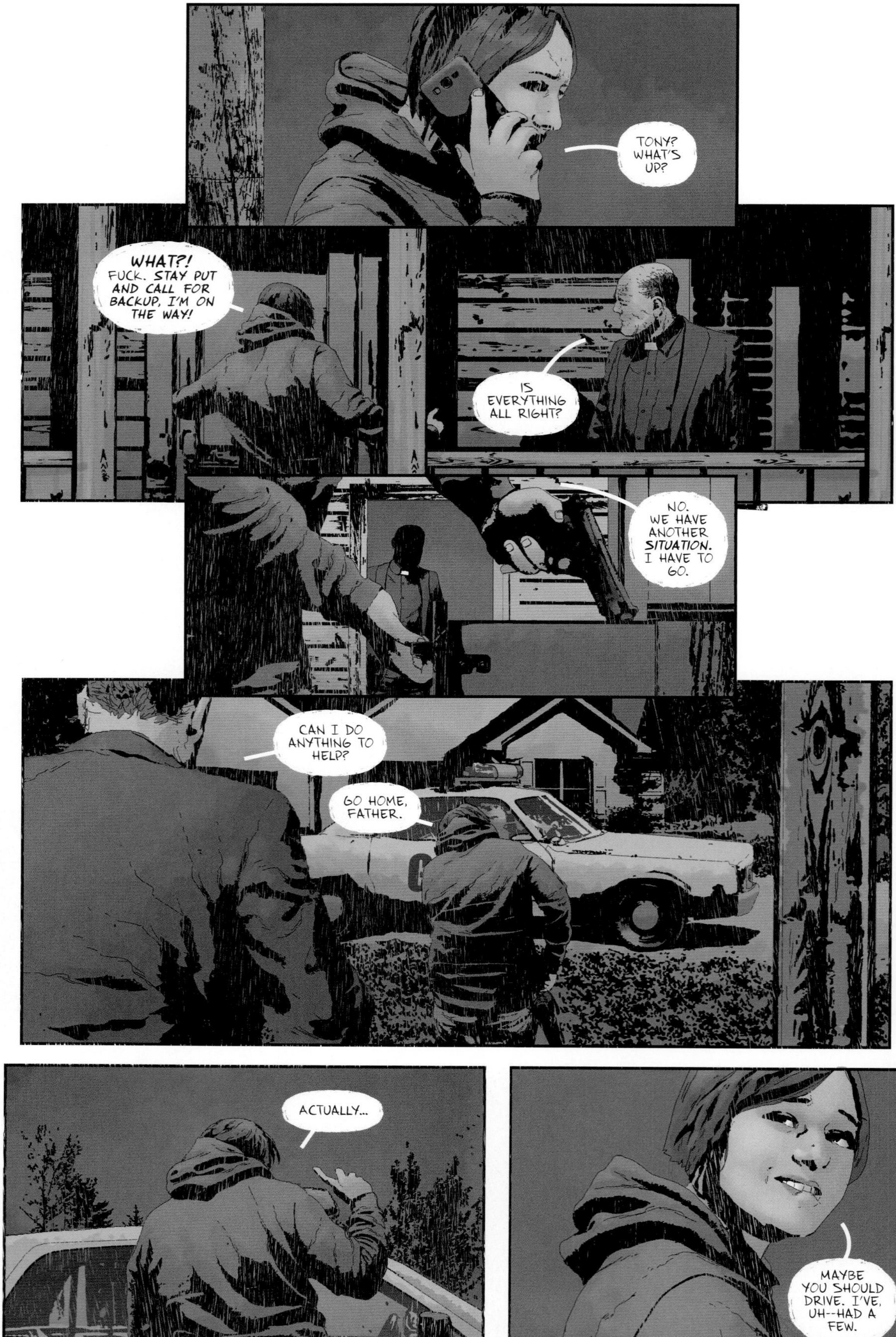

TONY? WHAT'S UP?
WHAT?! FUCK. STAY PUT AND CALL FOR BACKUP, I'M ON THE WAY!
IS EVERYTHING ALL RIGHT?
NO. WE HAVE ANOTHER SITUATION. I HAVE TO GO.
CAN I DO ANYTHING TO HELP?
GO HOME, FATHER.
ACTUALLY...
MAYBE YOU SHOULD DRIVE. I'VE, UH--HAD A FEW.

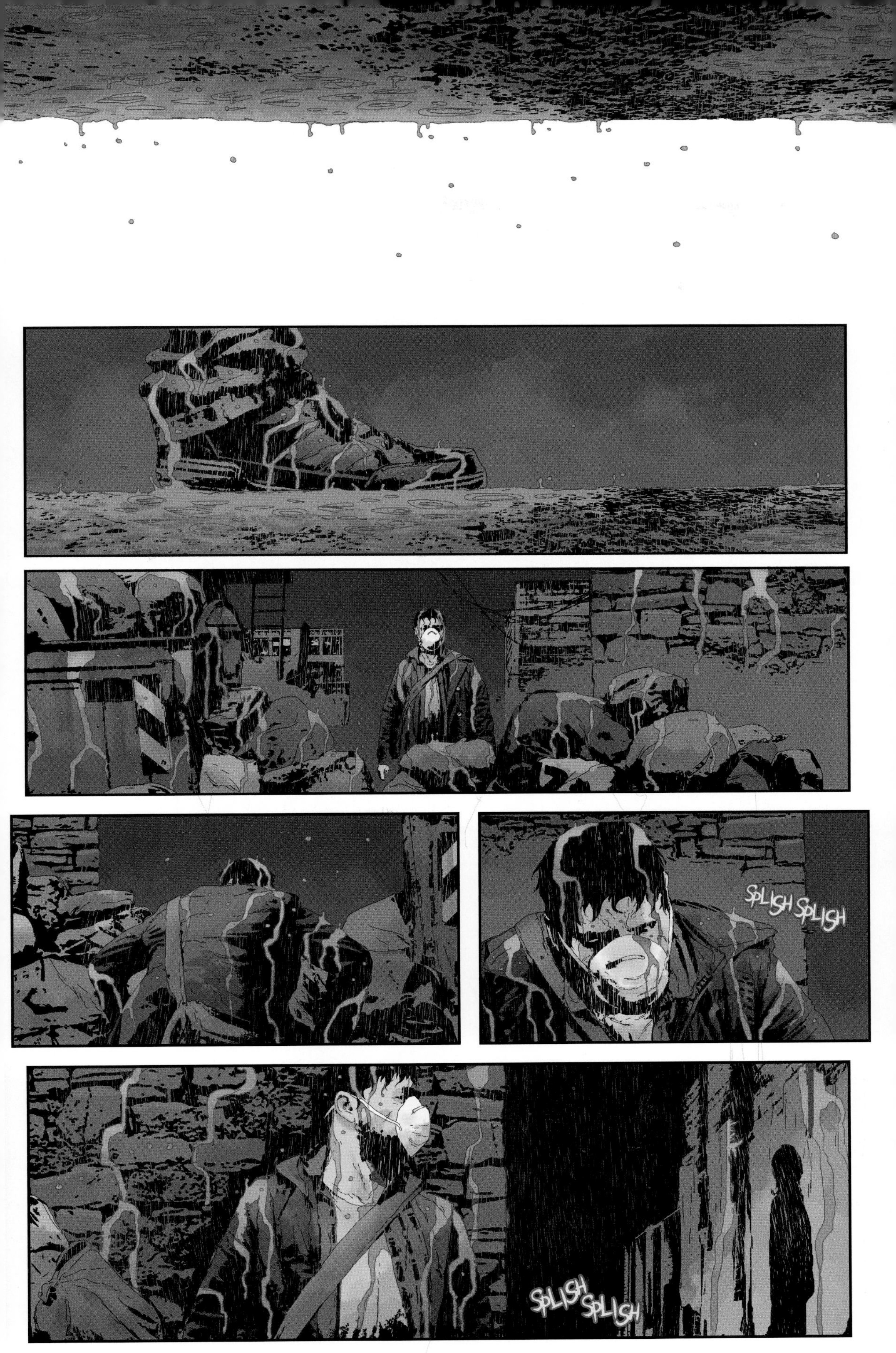
SPLISH SPLISH
SPLISH SPLISH

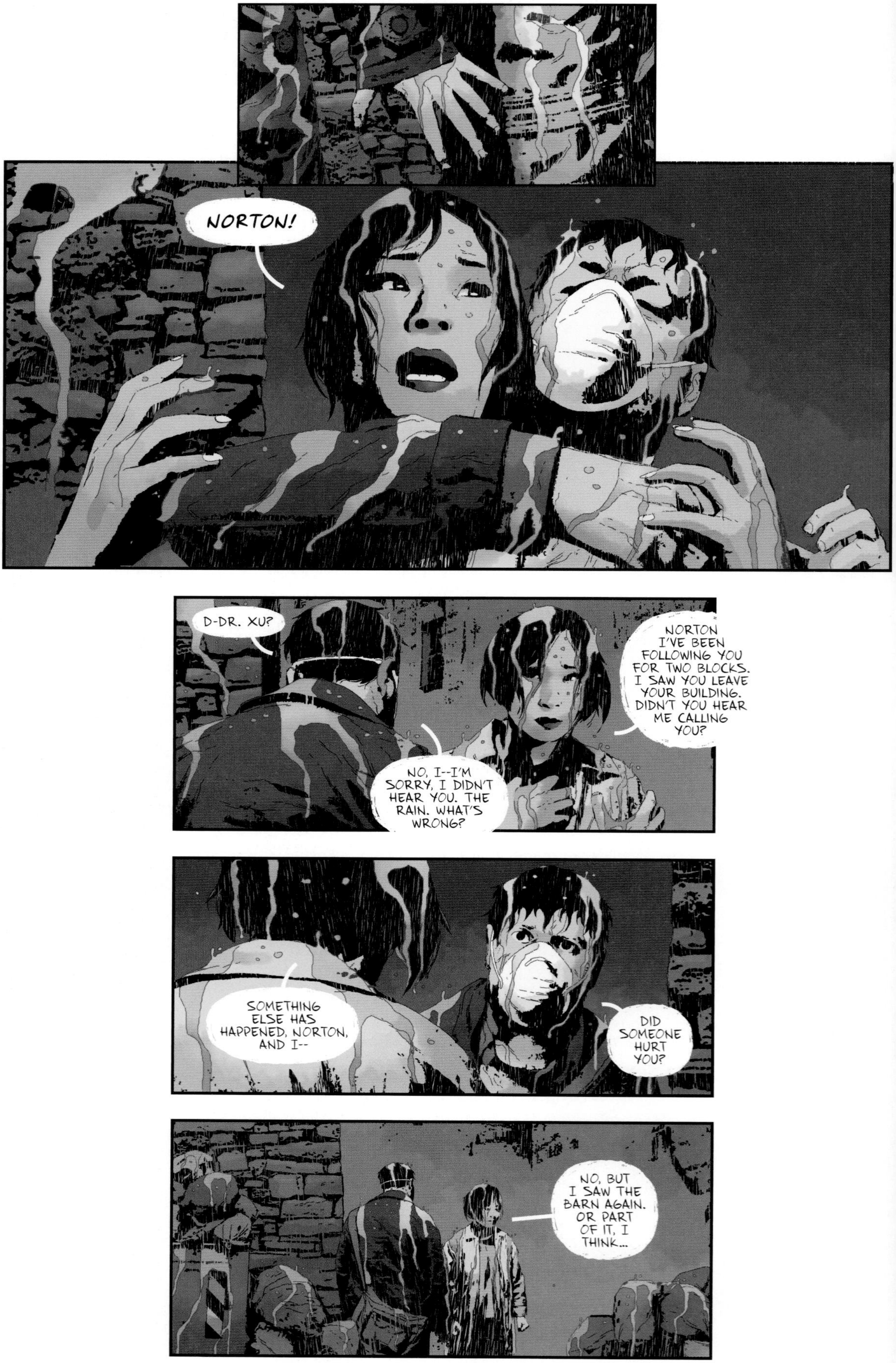
NORTON!
D-DR. XU?
NORTON I'VE BEEN FOLLOWING YOU FOR TWO BLOCKS. I SAW YOU LEAVE YOUR BUILDING. DIDN'T YOU HEAR ME CALLING YOU?
NO, I--I'M SORRY, I DIDN'T HEAR YOU. THE RAIN. WHAT'S WRONG?
SOMETHING ELSE HAS HAPPENED, NORTON, AND I--
DID SOMEONE HURT YOU?
NO, BUT I SAW THE BARN AGAIN. OR PART OF IT, I THINK...

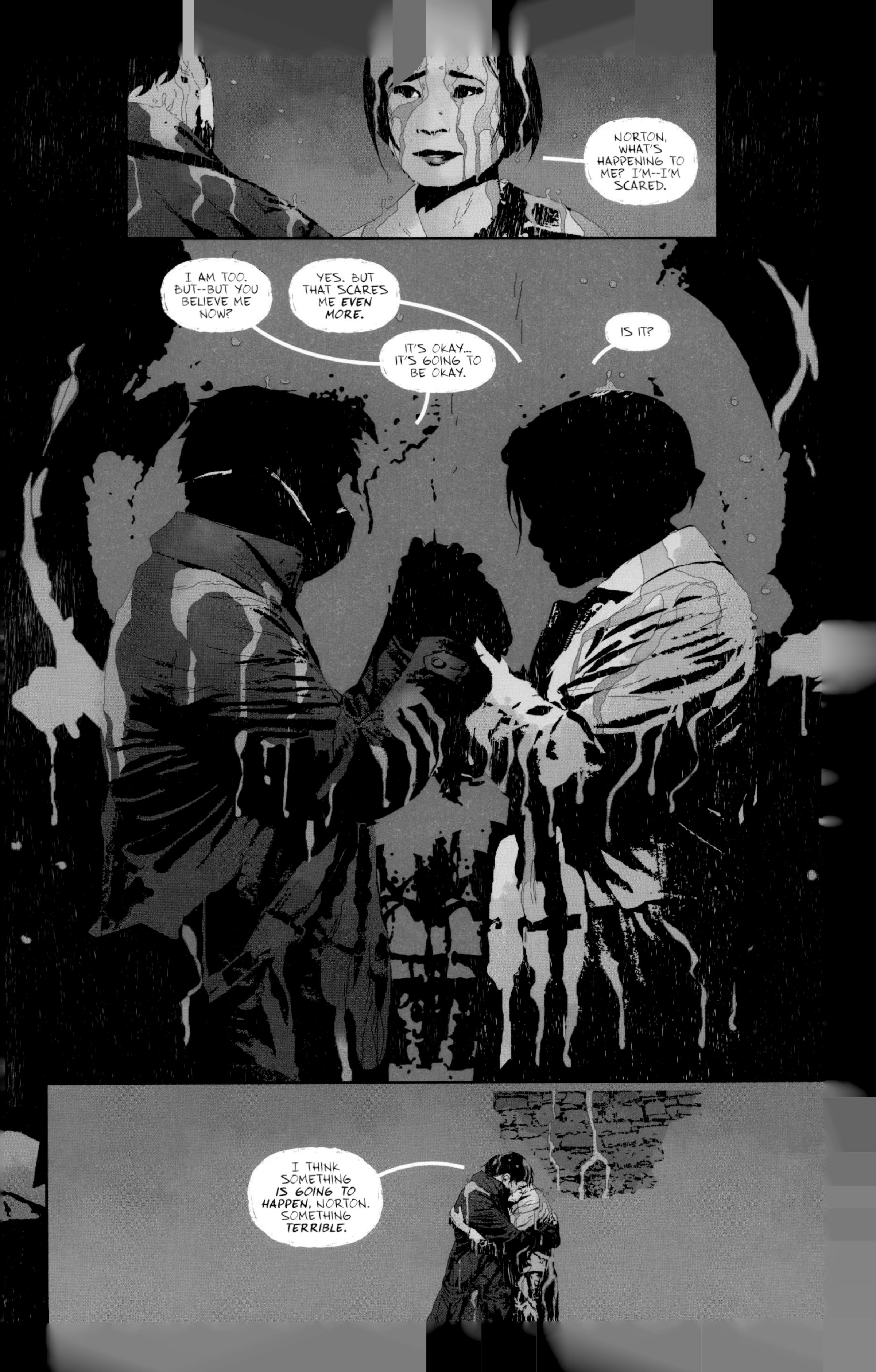
NORTON, WHAT'S HAPPENING TO ME? I'M--I'M SCARED.
I AM TOO. BUT--BUT YOU BELIEVE ME NOW?
YES. BUT THAT SCARES ME **EVEN MORE.**
IT'S OKAY... IT'S GOING TO BE OKAY.
IS IT?
I THINK SOMETHING **IS GOING TO HAPPEN,** NORTON. SOMETHING **TERRIBLE.**

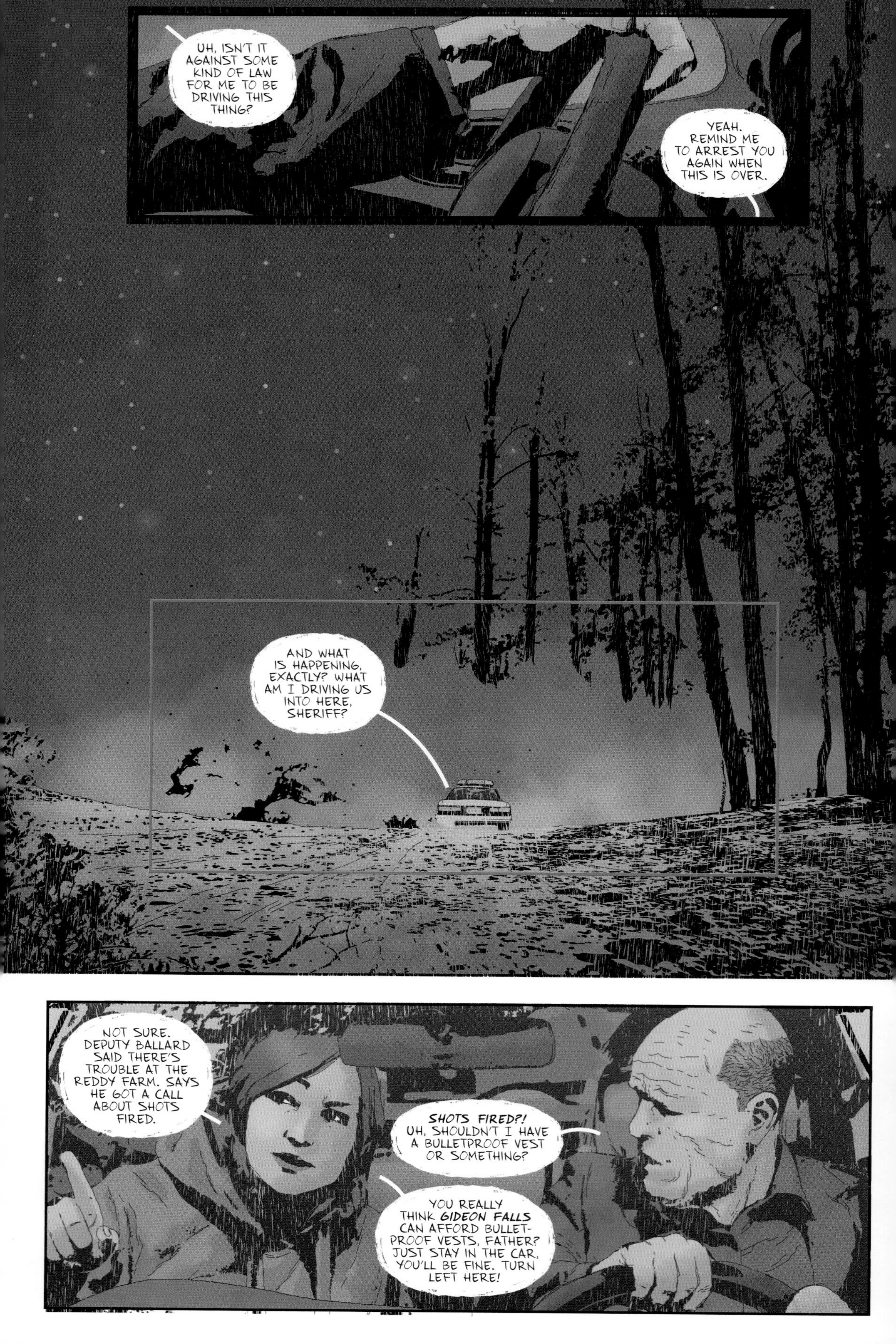
UH, ISN'T IT AGAINST SOME KIND OF LAW FOR ME TO BE DRIVING THIS THING?
YEAH. REMIND ME TO ARREST YOU AGAIN WHEN THIS IS OVER.
AND WHAT IS HAPPENING, EXACTLY? WHAT AM I DRIVING US INTO HERE, SHERIFF?
NOT SURE. DEPUTY BALLARD SAID THERE'S TROUBLE AT THE REDDY FARM. SAYS HE GOT A CALL ABOUT SHOTS FIRED.
SHOTS FIRED?! UH, SHOULDN'T I HAVE A BULLETPROOF VEST OR SOMETHING?
YOU REALLY THINK *GIDEON FALLS* CAN AFFORD BULLET-PROOF VESTS, FATHER? JUST STAY IN THE CAR, YOU'LL BE FINE. TURN LEFT HERE!

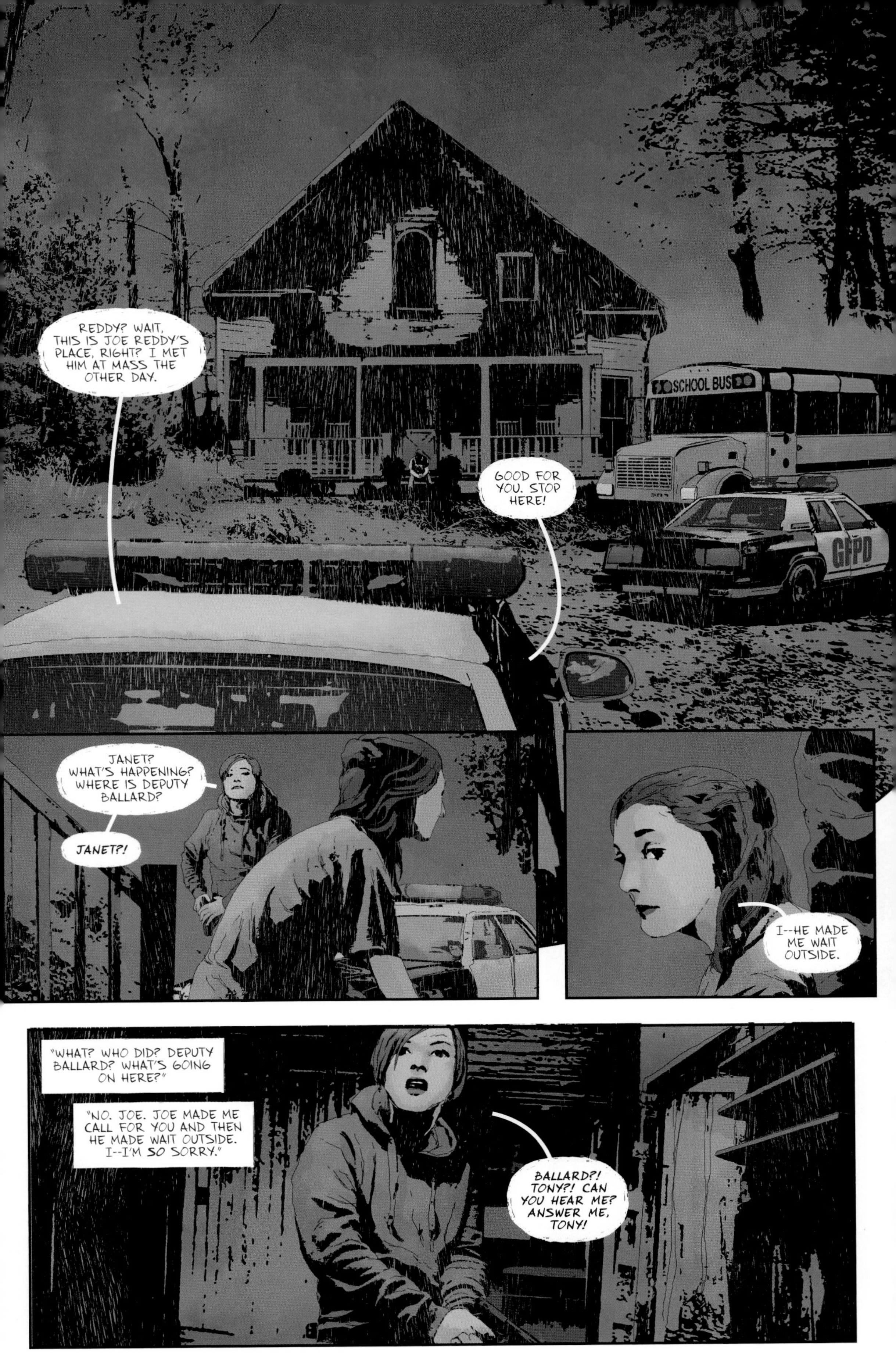
REDDY? WAIT, THIS IS JOE REDDY'S PLACE, RIGHT? I MET HIM AT MASS THE OTHER DAY.
SCHOOL BUS
GOOD FOR YOU. STOP HERE!
GFPD
JANET? WHAT'S HAPPENING? WHERE IS DEPUTY BALLARD?
JANET?!
I--HE MADE ME WAIT OUTSIDE.
"WHAT? WHO DID? DEPUTY BALLARD? WHAT'S GOING ON HERE?"
"NO. JOE. JOE MADE ME CALL FOR YOU AND THEN HE MADE WAIT OUTSIDE. I--I'M SO SORRY."
BALLARD?! TONY?! CAN YOU HEAR ME? ANSWER ME, TONY!

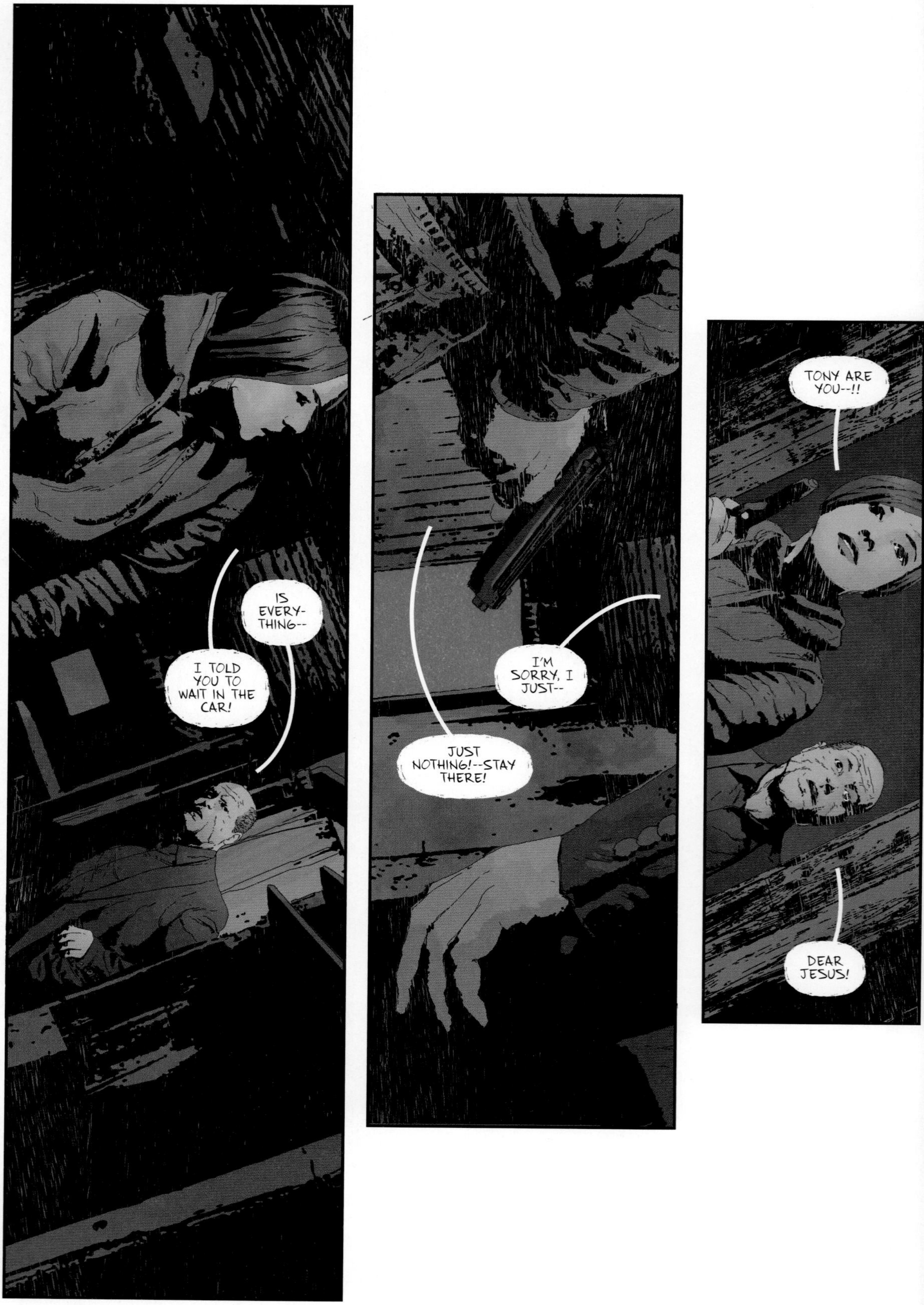
IS EVERY-THING--
I TOLD YOU TO WAIT IN THE CAR!
I'M SORRY, I JUST--
JUST NOTHING!--STAY THERE!
TONY ARE YOU--!!
DEAR JESUS!

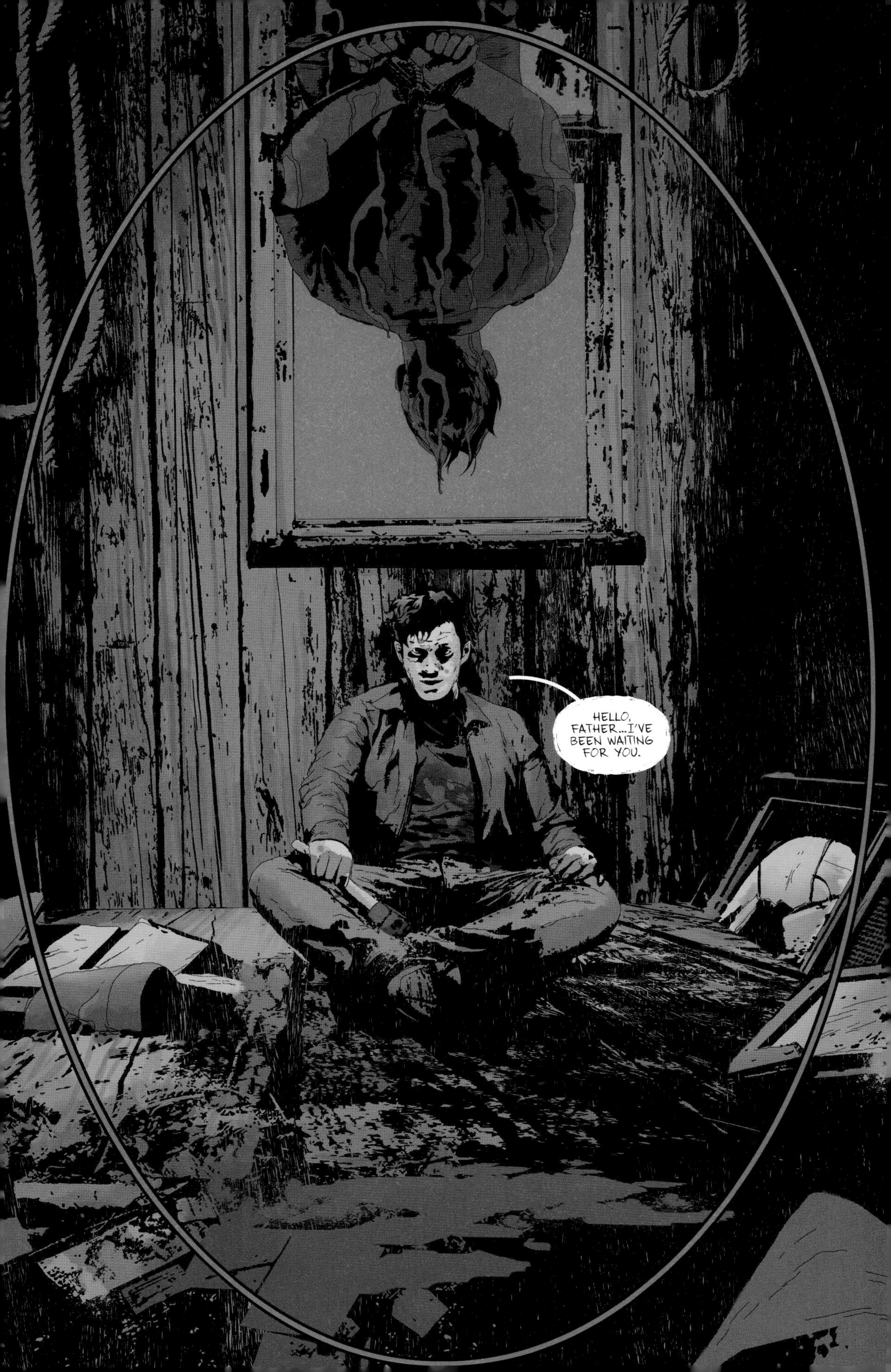
HELLO, FATHER...I'VE BEEN WAITING FOR YOU.

Five

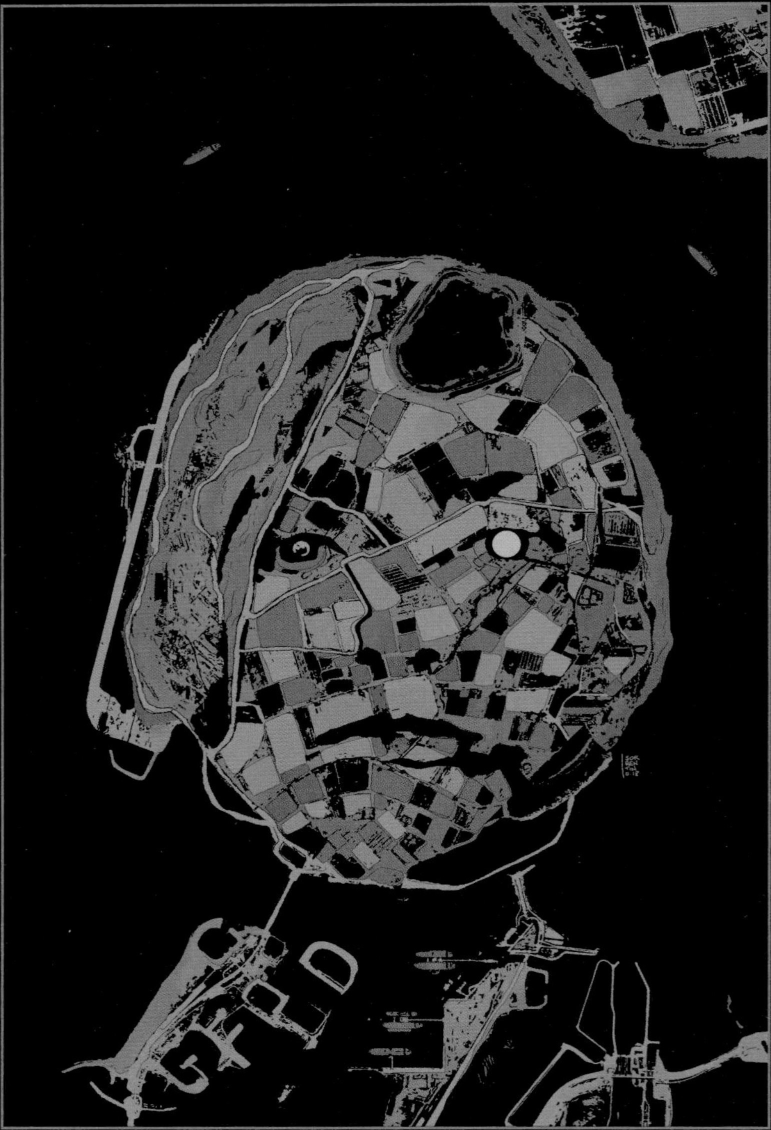

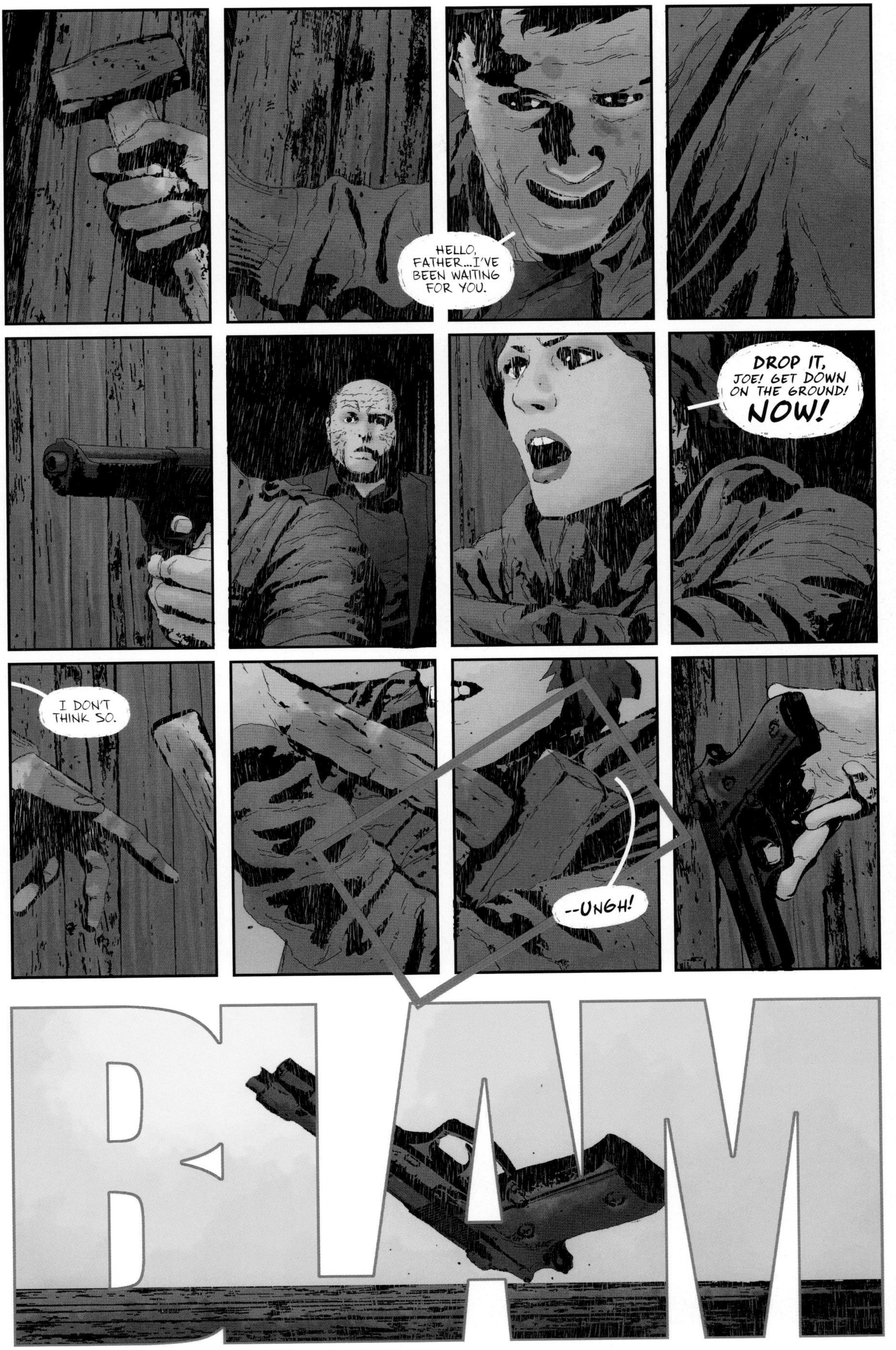
HELLO, FATHER...I'VE BEEN WAITING FOR YOU.
DROP IT, JOE! GET DOWN ON THE GROUND! NOW!
I DON'T THINK SO.
--UNGH!
BLAM

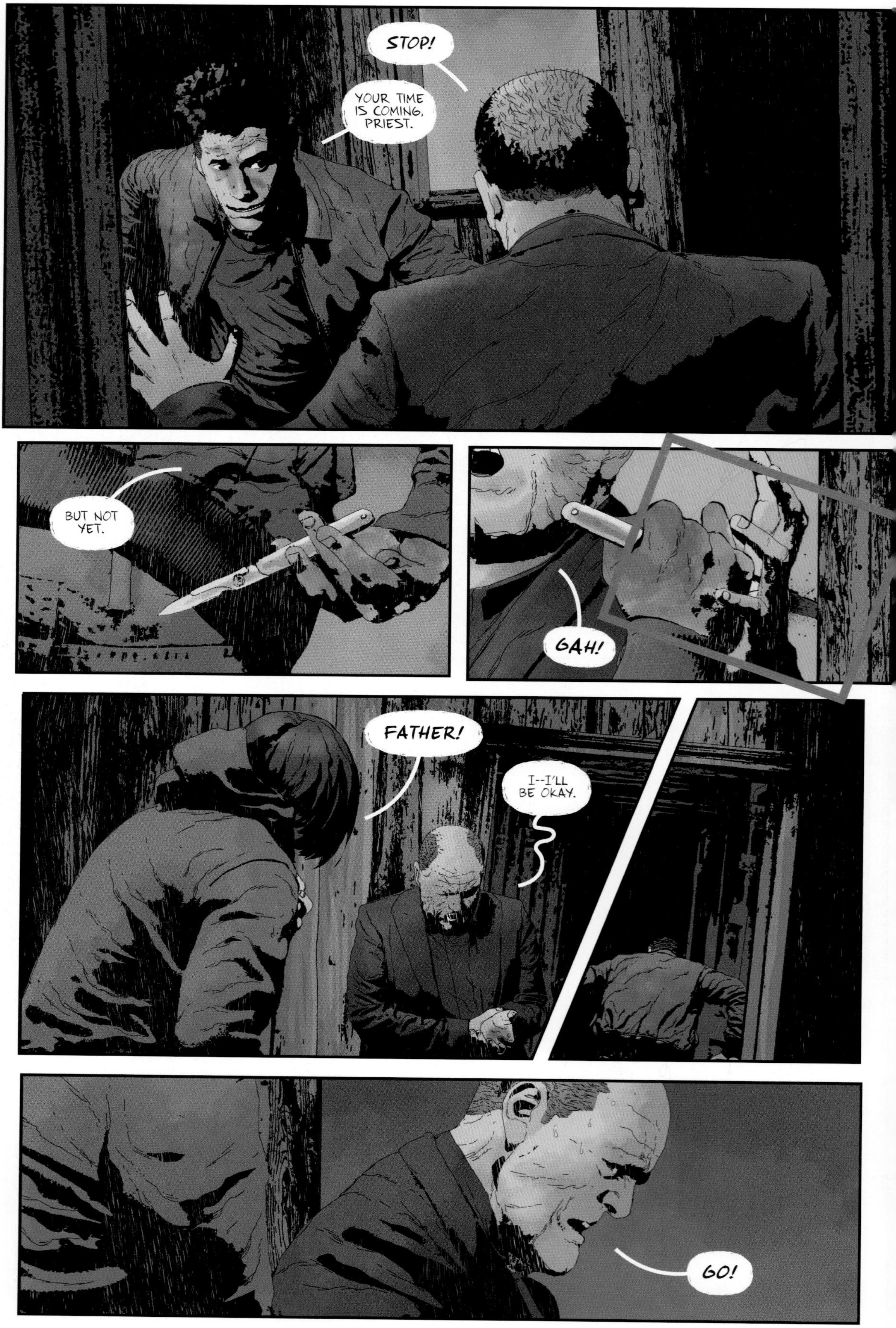
STOP!
YOUR TIME IS COMING, PRIEST.
BUT NOT YET.
GAH!
FATHER!
I--I'LL BE OKAY.
GO!

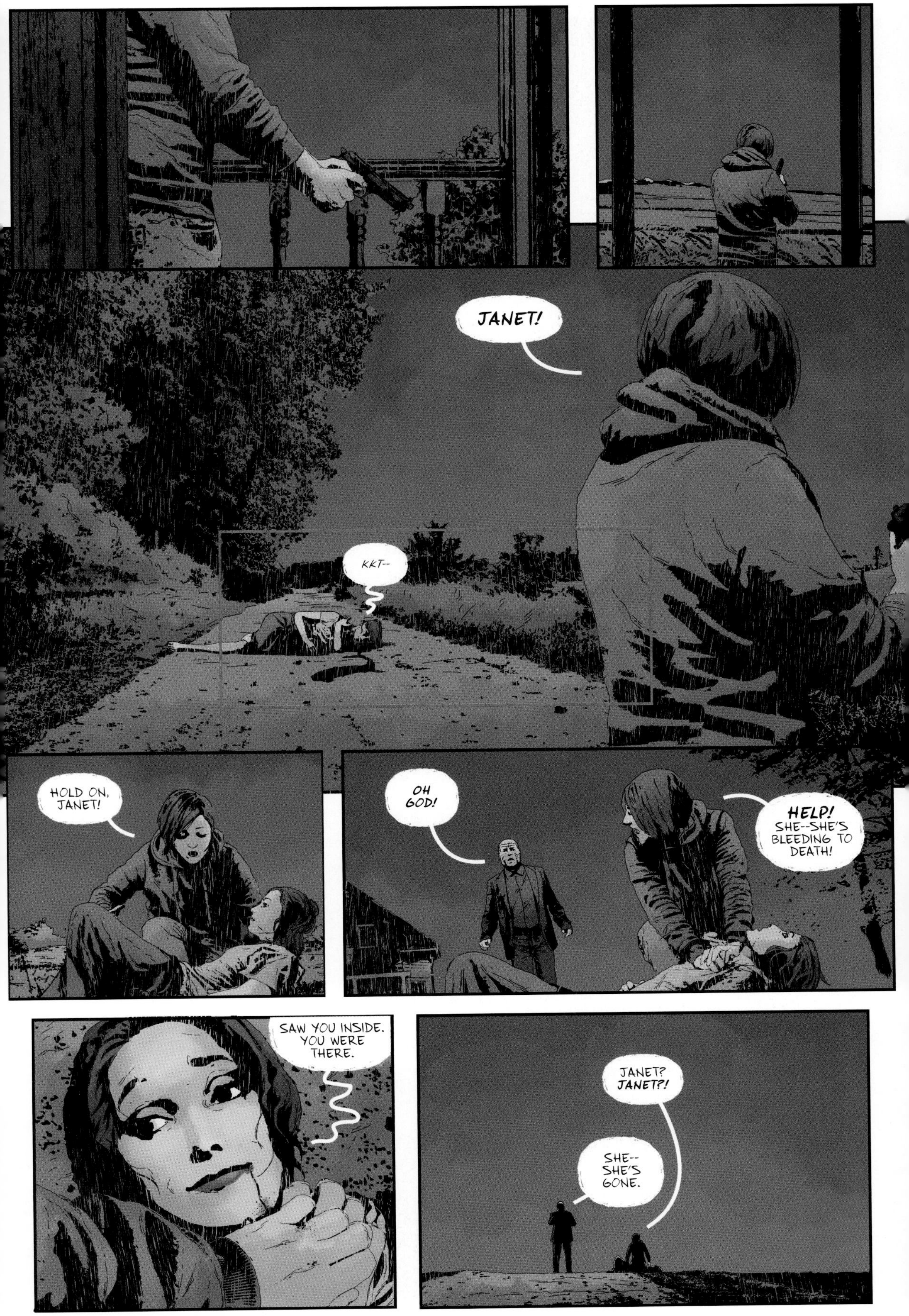
JANET!
KKT--
HOLD ON, JANET!
OH GOD!
HELP! SHE--SHE'S BLEEDING TO DEATH!
SAW YOU INSIDE. YOU WERE THERE.
JANET? JANET?!
SHE-- SHE'S GONE.

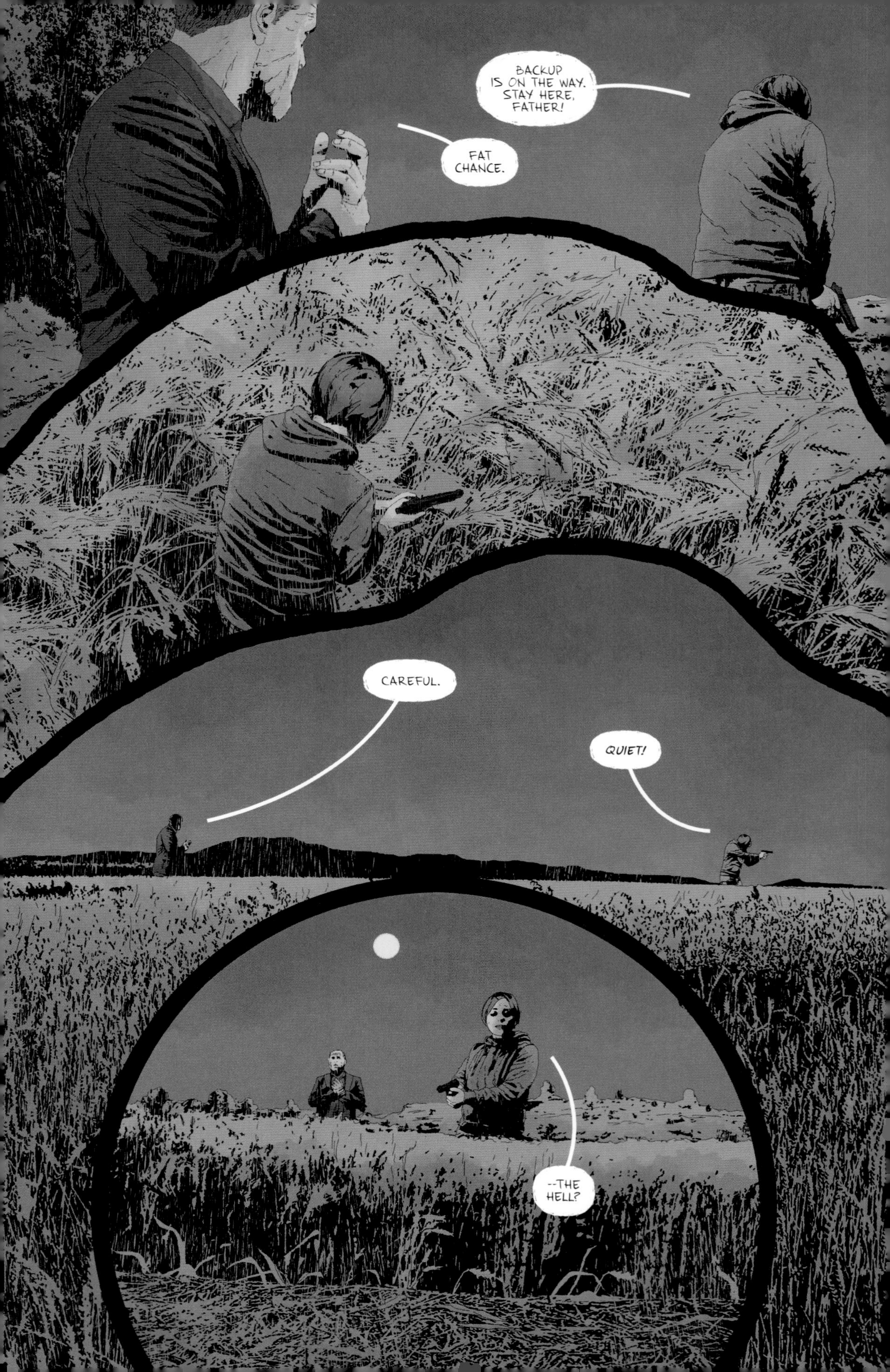
BACKUP IS ON THE WAY. STAY HERE, FATHER!
FAT CHANCE.
CAREFUL.
QUIET!
--THE HELL?

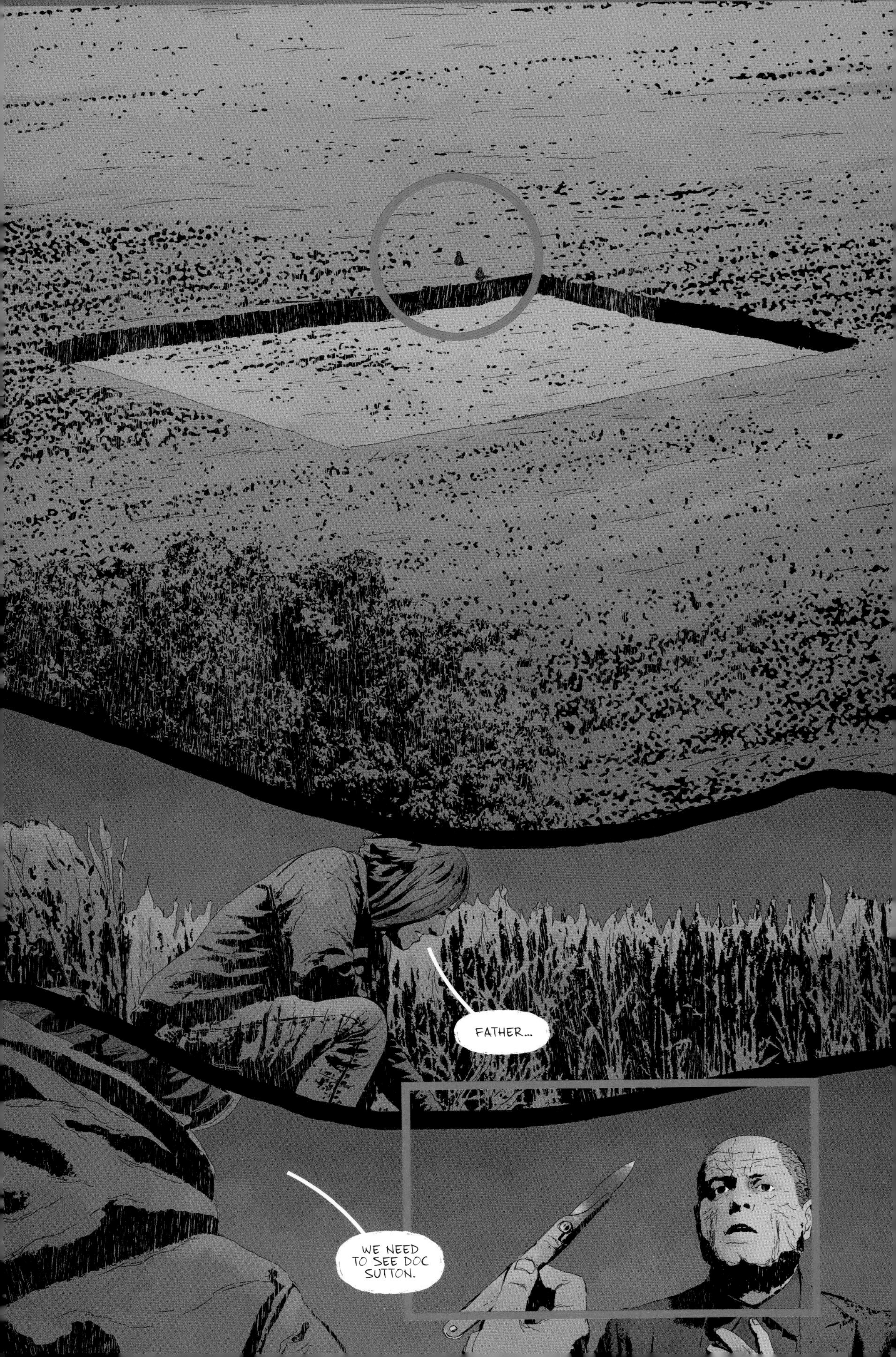
FATHER...
WE NEED TO SEE DOC SUTTON.

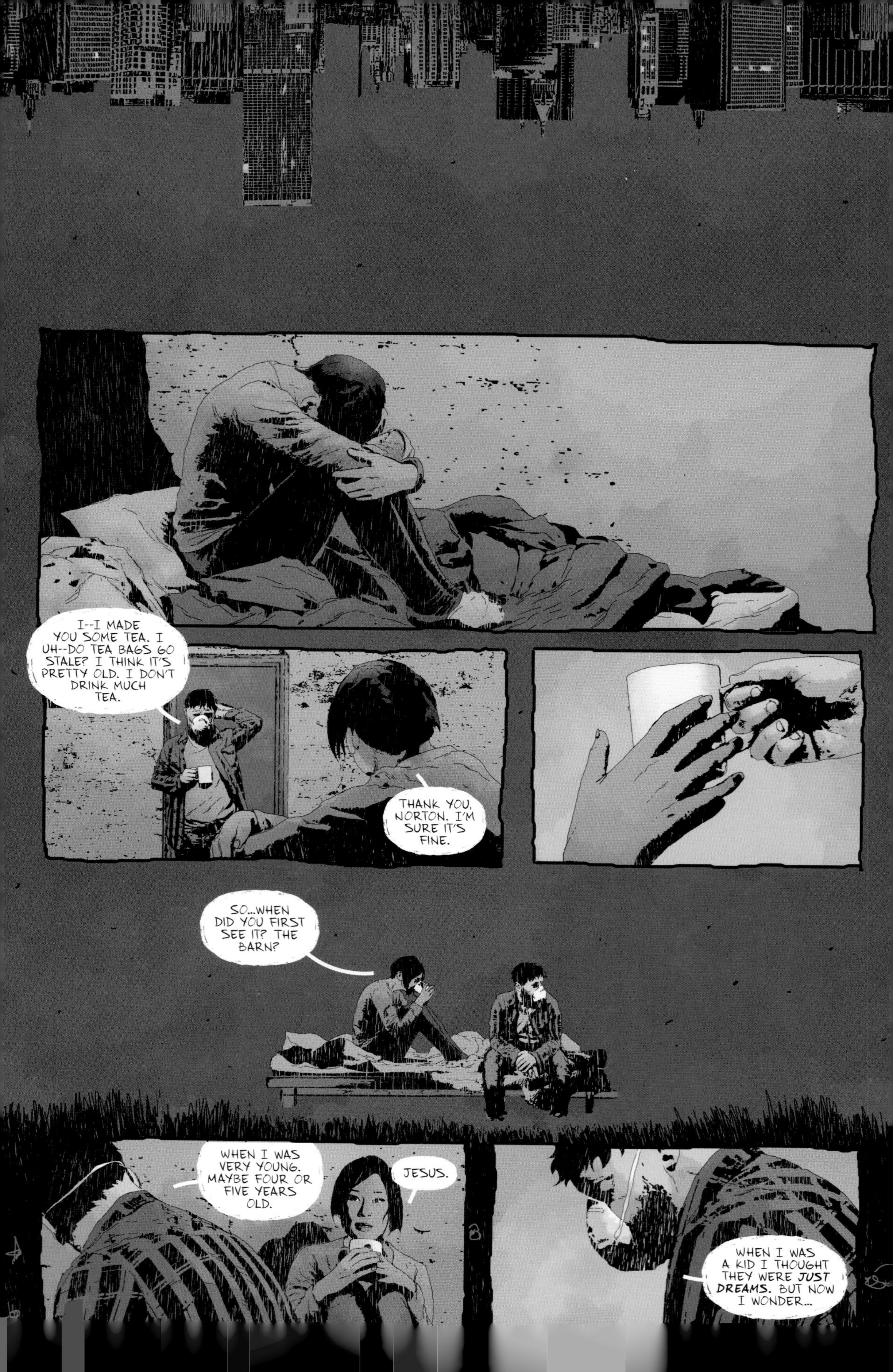
I--I MADE YOU SOME TEA. I UH--DO TEA BAGS GO STALE? I THINK IT'S PRETTY OLD. I DON'T DRINK MUCH TEA.
THANK YOU, NORTON. I'M SURE IT'S FINE.
SO...WHEN DID YOU FIRST SEE IT? THE BARN?
WHEN I WAS VERY YOUNG. MAYBE FOUR OR FIVE YEARS OLD.
JESUS.
WHEN I WAS A KID I THOUGHT THEY WERE *JUST DREAMS.* BUT NOW I WONDER...

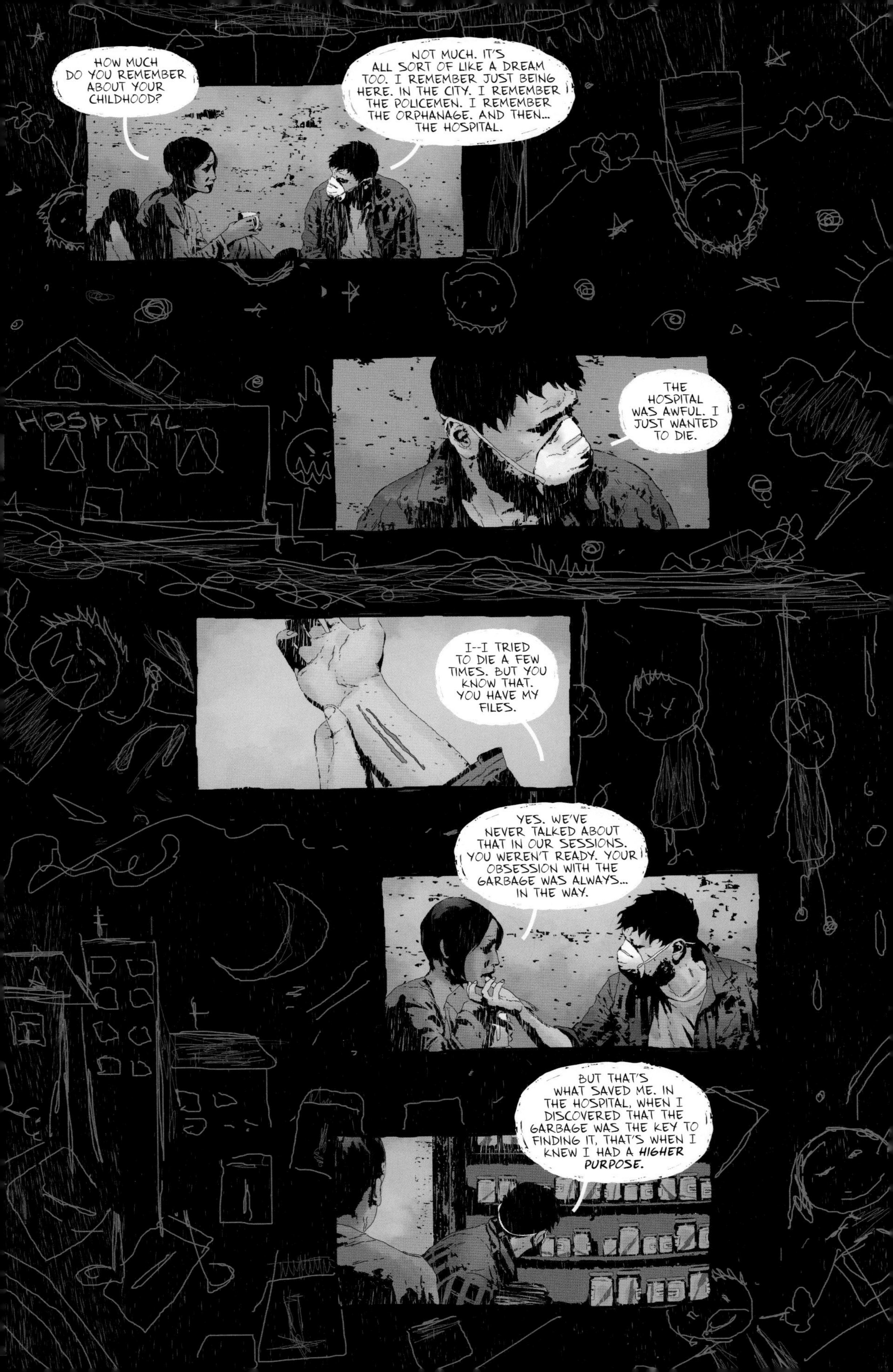
HOW MUCH DO YOU REMEMBER ABOUT YOUR CHILDHOOD?
NOT MUCH. IT'S ALL SORT OF LIKE A DREAM TOO. I REMEMBER JUST BEING HERE. IN THE CITY. I REMEMBER THE POLICEMEN. I REMEMBER THE ORPHANAGE. AND THEN... THE HOSPITAL.
HOSPITAL
THE HOSPITAL WAS AWFUL. I JUST WANTED TO DIE.
I--I TRIED TO DIE A FEW TIMES. BUT YOU KNOW THAT. YOU HAVE MY FILES.
YES. WE'VE NEVER TALKED ABOUT THAT IN OUR SESSIONS. YOU WEREN'T READY. YOUR OBSESSION WITH THE GARBAGE WAS ALWAYS... IN THE WAY.
BUT THAT'S WHAT SAVED ME. IN THE HOSPITAL, WHEN I DISCOVERED THAT THE GARBAGE WAS THE KEY TO FINDING IT, THAT'S WHEN I KNEW I HAD A ***HIGHER PURPOSE.***

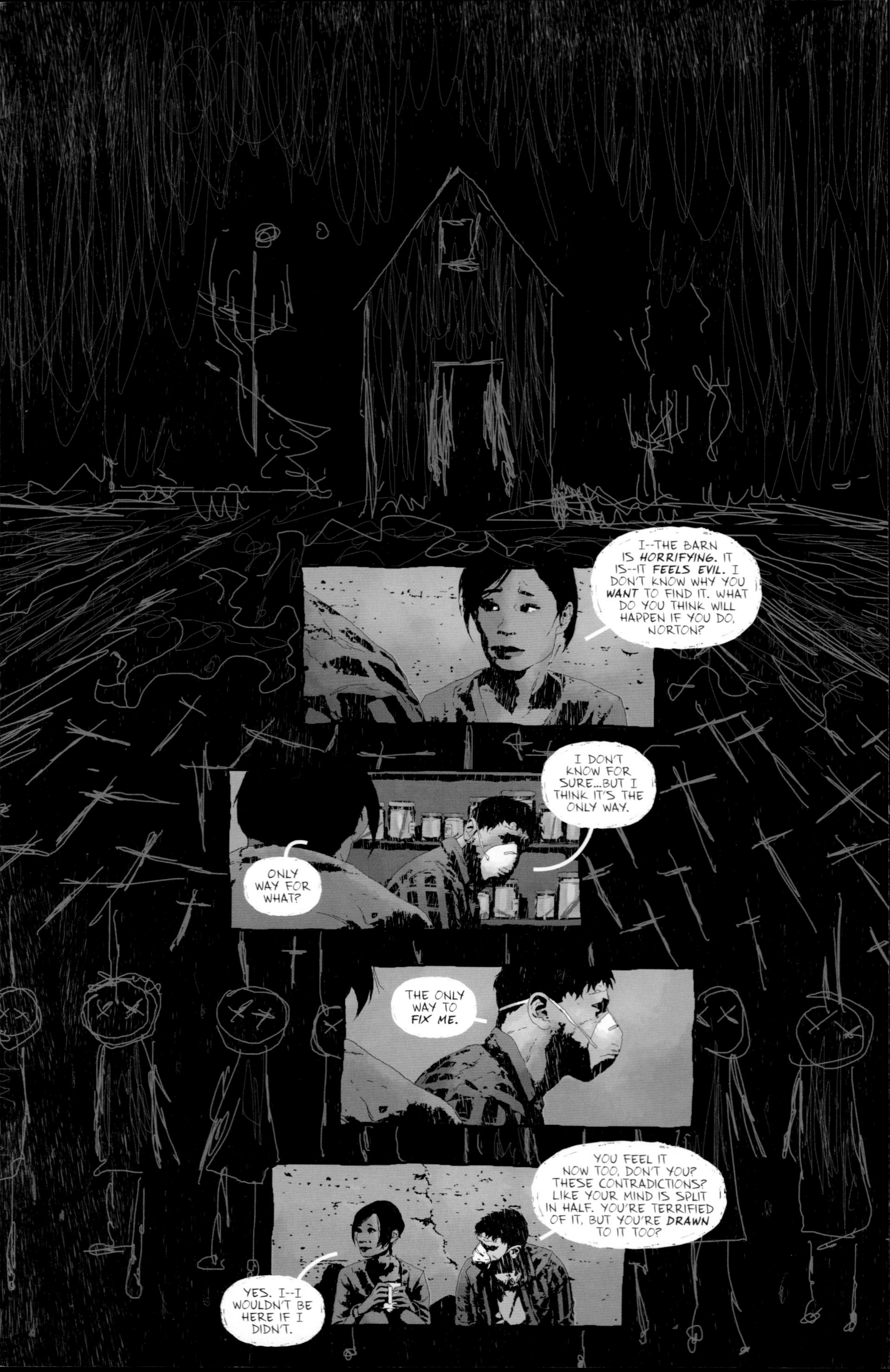

I--THE BARN IS HORRIFYING. IT IS--IT FEELS EVIL. I DON'T KNOW WHY YOU WANT TO FIND IT. WHAT DO YOU THINK WILL HAPPEN IF YOU DO, NORTON?
I DON'T KNOW FOR SURE...BUT I THINK IT'S THE ONLY WAY.
ONLY WAY FOR WHAT?
THE ONLY WAY TO FIX ME.
YOU FEEL IT NOW TOO, DON'T YOU? THESE CONTRADICTIONS? LIKE YOUR MIND IS SPLIT IN HALF. YOU'RE TERRIFIED OF IT, BUT YOU'RE DRAWN TO IT TOO?
YES. I--I WOULDN'T BE HERE IF I DIDN'T.

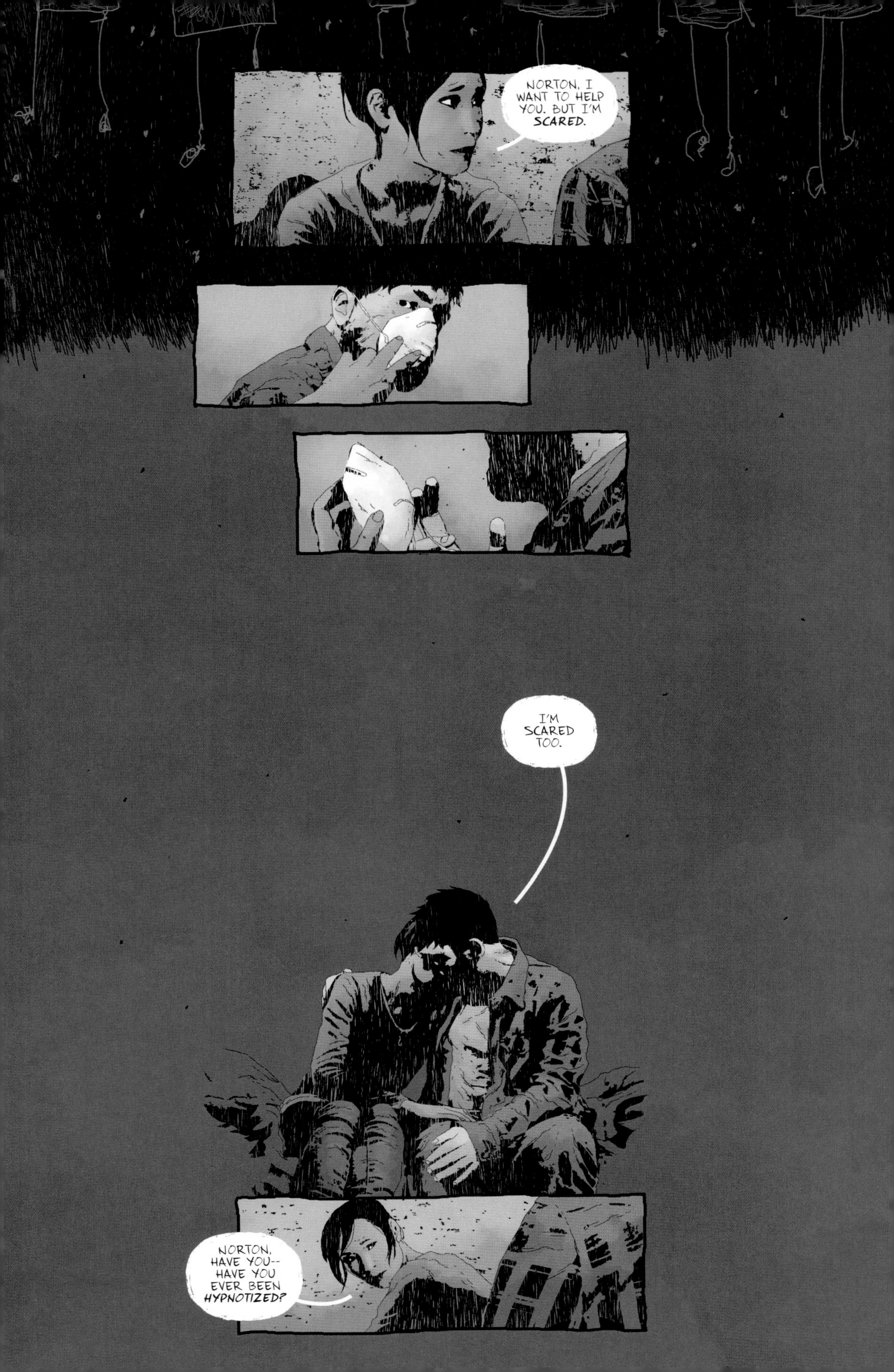
NORTON, I WANT TO HELP YOU. BUT I'M SCARED.
I'M SCARED TOO.
NORTON, HAVE YOU-- HAVE YOU EVER BEEN HYPNOTIZED?

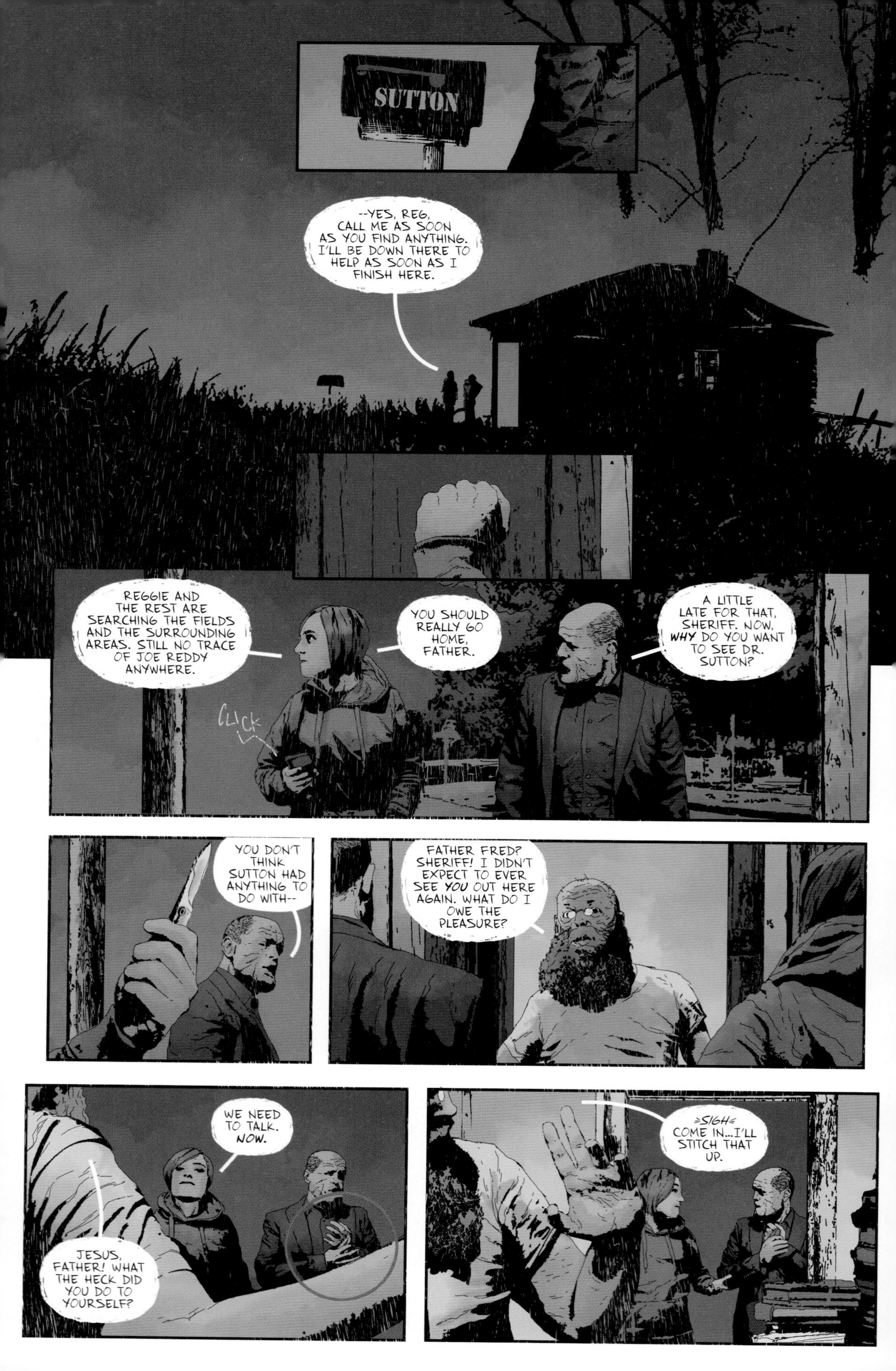
SUTTON
--YES, REG, CALL ME AS SOON AS YOU FIND ANYTHING. I'LL BE DOWN THERE TO HELP AS SOON AS I FINISH HERE.
REGGIE AND THE REST ARE SEARCHING THE FIELDS AND THE SURROUNDING AREAS. STILL NO TRACE OF JOE REDDY ANYWHERE.
YOU SHOULD REALLY GO HOME, FATHER.
A LITTLE LATE FOR THAT, SHERIFF. NOW, WHY DO YOU WANT TO SEE DR. SUTTON?
CLICK
YOU DON'T THINK SUTTON HAD ANYTHING TO DO WITH--
FATHER FRED? SHERIFF! I DIDN'T EXPECT TO EVER SEE YOU OUT HERE AGAIN. WHAT DO I OWE THE PLEASURE?
JESUS, FATHER! WHAT THE HECK DID YOU DO TO YOURSELF?
WE NEED TO TALK. NOW.
SIGH
COME IN...I'LL STITCH THAT UP.

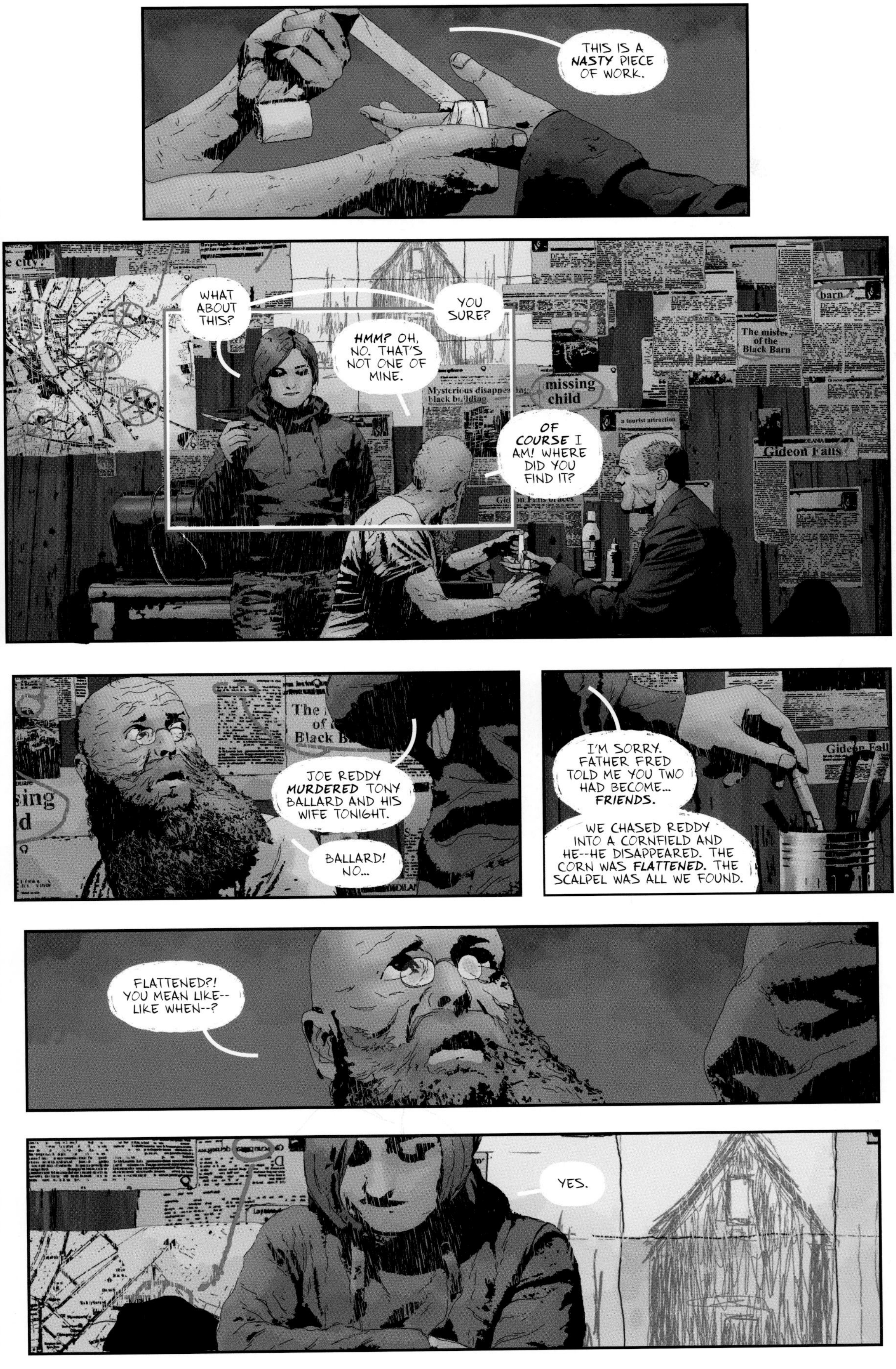
THIS IS A NASTY PIECE OF WORK.
WHAT ABOUT THIS?
YOU SURE?
HMM? OH, NO. THAT'S NOT ONE OF MINE.
OF COURSE I AM! WHERE DID YOU FIND IT?
JOE REDDY MURDERED TONY BALLARD AND HIS WIFE TONIGHT.
BALLARD! NO...
I'M SORRY. FATHER FRED TOLD ME YOU TWO HAD BECOME... FRIENDS.
WE CHASED REDDY INTO A CORNFIELD AND HE--HE DISAPPEARED. THE CORN WAS FLATTENED. THE SCALPEL WAS ALL WE FOUND.
FLATTENED?! YOU MEAN LIKE--LIKE WHEN--?
YES.

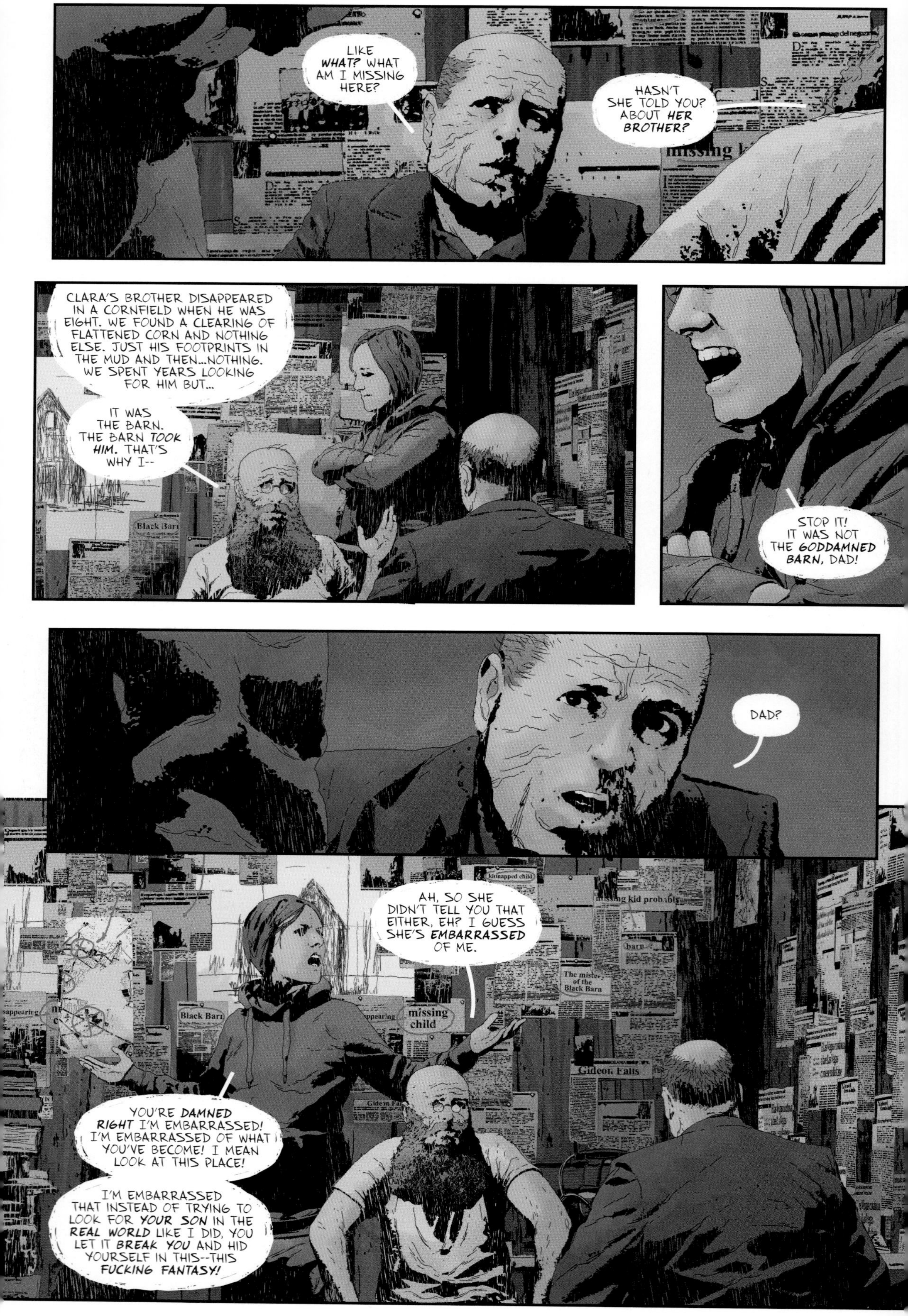
LIKE WHAT? WHAT AM I MISSING HERE?
HASN'T SHE TOLD YOU? ABOUT HER BROTHER?
CLARA'S BROTHER DISAPPEARED IN A CORNFIELD WHEN HE WAS EIGHT. WE FOUND A CLEARING OF FLATTENED CORN AND NOTHING ELSE. JUST HIS FOOTPRINTS IN THE MUD AND THEN...NOTHING. WE SPENT YEARS LOOKING FOR HIM BUT...
IT WAS THE BARN. THE BARN TOOK HIM. THAT'S WHY I--
STOP IT! IT WAS NOT THE GODDAMNED BARN, DAD!
DAD?
AH, SO SHE DIDN'T TELL YOU THAT EITHER, EH? I GUESS SHE'S EMBARRASSED OF ME.
YOU'RE DAMNED RIGHT I'M EMBARRASSED! I'M EMBARRASSED OF WHAT YOU'VE BECOME! I MEAN LOOK AT THIS PLACE!
I'M EMBARRASSED THAT INSTEAD OF TRYING TO LOOK FOR YOUR SON IN THE REAL WORLD LIKE I DID, YOU LET IT BREAK YOU AND HID YOURSELF IN THIS--THIS FUCKING FANTASY!

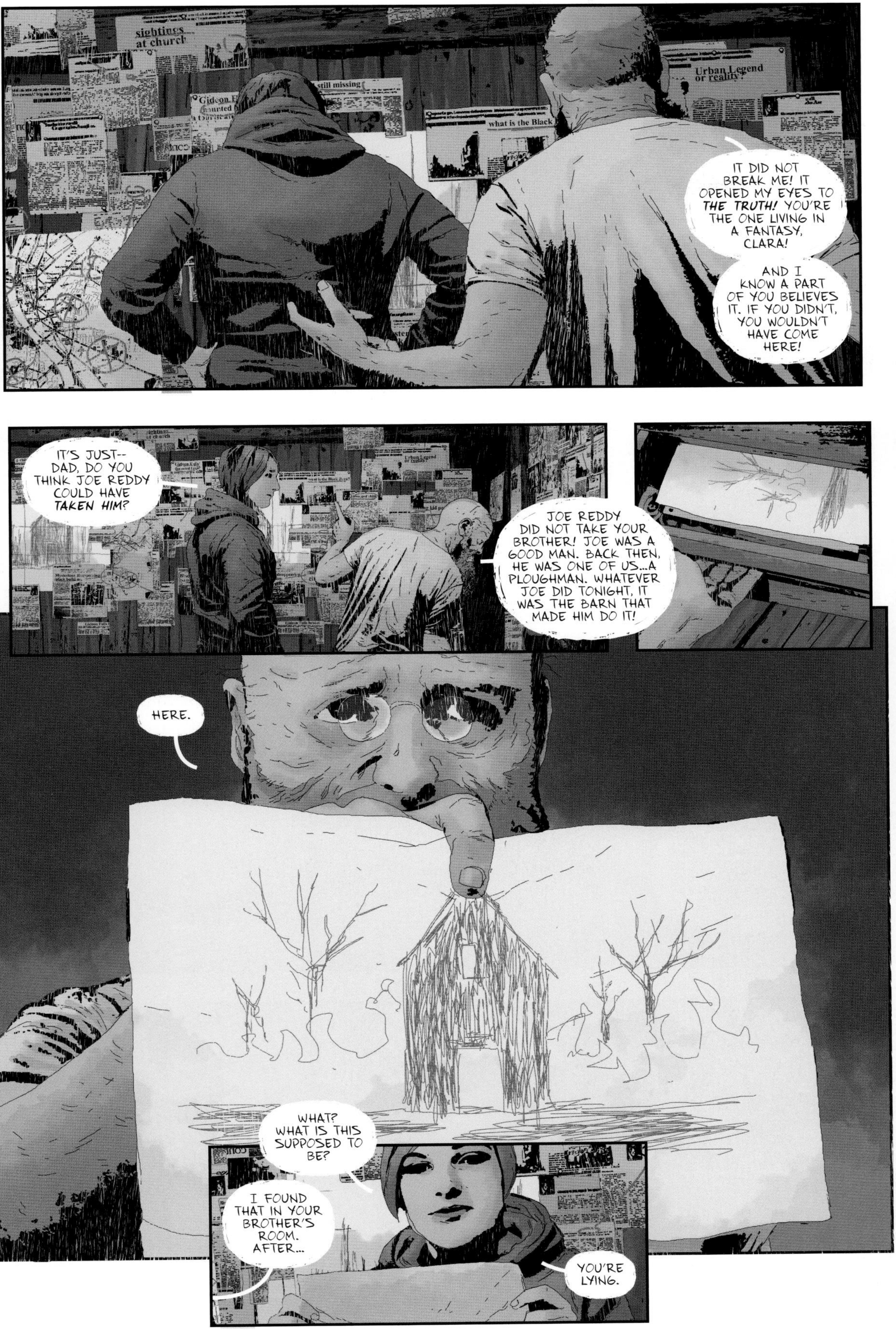
IT DID NOT BREAK ME! IT OPENED MY EYES TO THE TRUTH! YOU'RE THE ONE LIVING IN A FANTASY, CLARA!
AND I KNOW A PART OF YOU BELIEVES IT. IF YOU DIDN'T, YOU WOULDN'T HAVE COME HERE!
IT'S JUST-- DAD, DO YOU THINK JOE REDDY COULD HAVE TAKEN HIM?
JOE REDDY DID NOT TAKE YOUR BROTHER! JOE WAS A GOOD MAN. BACK THEN, HE WAS ONE OF US...A PLOUGHMAN. WHATEVER JOE DID TONIGHT, IT WAS THE BARN THAT MADE HIM DO IT!
HERE.
WHAT? WHAT IS THIS SUPPOSED TO BE?
I FOUND THAT IN YOUR BROTHER'S ROOM. AFTER...
YOU'RE LYING.

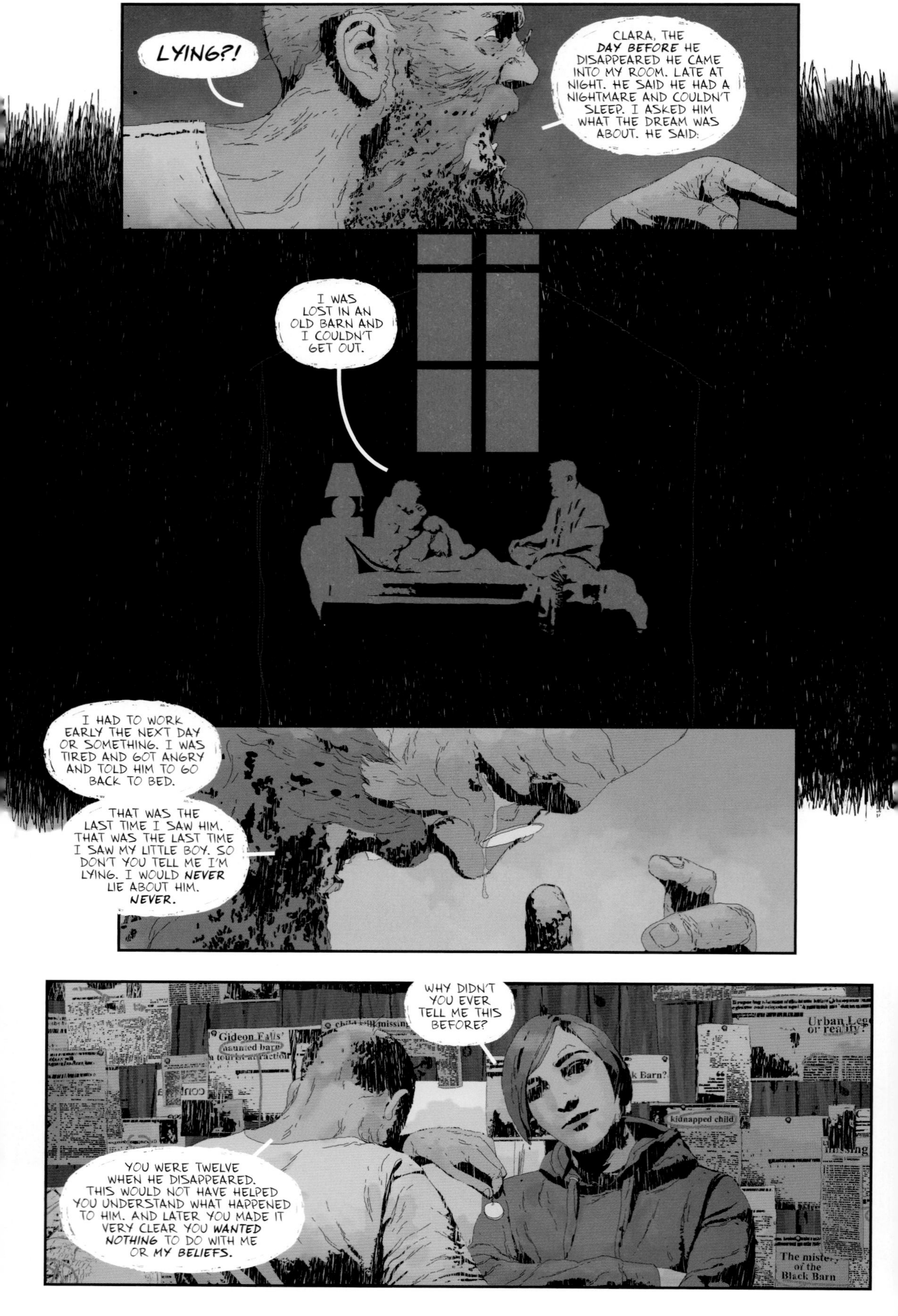
LYING?!
CLARA, THE DAY BEFORE HE DISAPPEARED HE CAME INTO MY ROOM. LATE AT NIGHT. HE SAID HE HAD A NIGHTMARE AND COULDN'T SLEEP. I ASKED HIM WHAT THE DREAM WAS ABOUT. HE SAID:
I WAS LOST IN AN OLD BARN AND I COULDN'T GET OUT.
I HAD TO WORK EARLY THE NEXT DAY OR SOMETHING. I WAS TIRED AND GOT ANGRY AND TOLD HIM TO GO BACK TO BED.
THAT WAS THE LAST TIME I SAW HIM. THAT WAS THE LAST TIME I SAW MY LITTLE BOY. SO DON'T YOU TELL ME I'M LYING. I WOULD NEVER LIE ABOUT HIM. NEVER.
WHY DIDN'T YOU EVER TELL ME THIS BEFORE?
YOU WERE TWELVE WHEN HE DISAPPEARED. THIS WOULD NOT HAVE HELPED YOU UNDERSTAND WHAT HAPPENED TO HIM. AND LATER YOU MADE IT VERY CLEAR YOU WANTED NOTHING TO DO WITH ME OR MY BELIEFS.
Gideon Falls'
haunted barn
a tourist attraction
kidnapped child
The mistery of the Black Barn

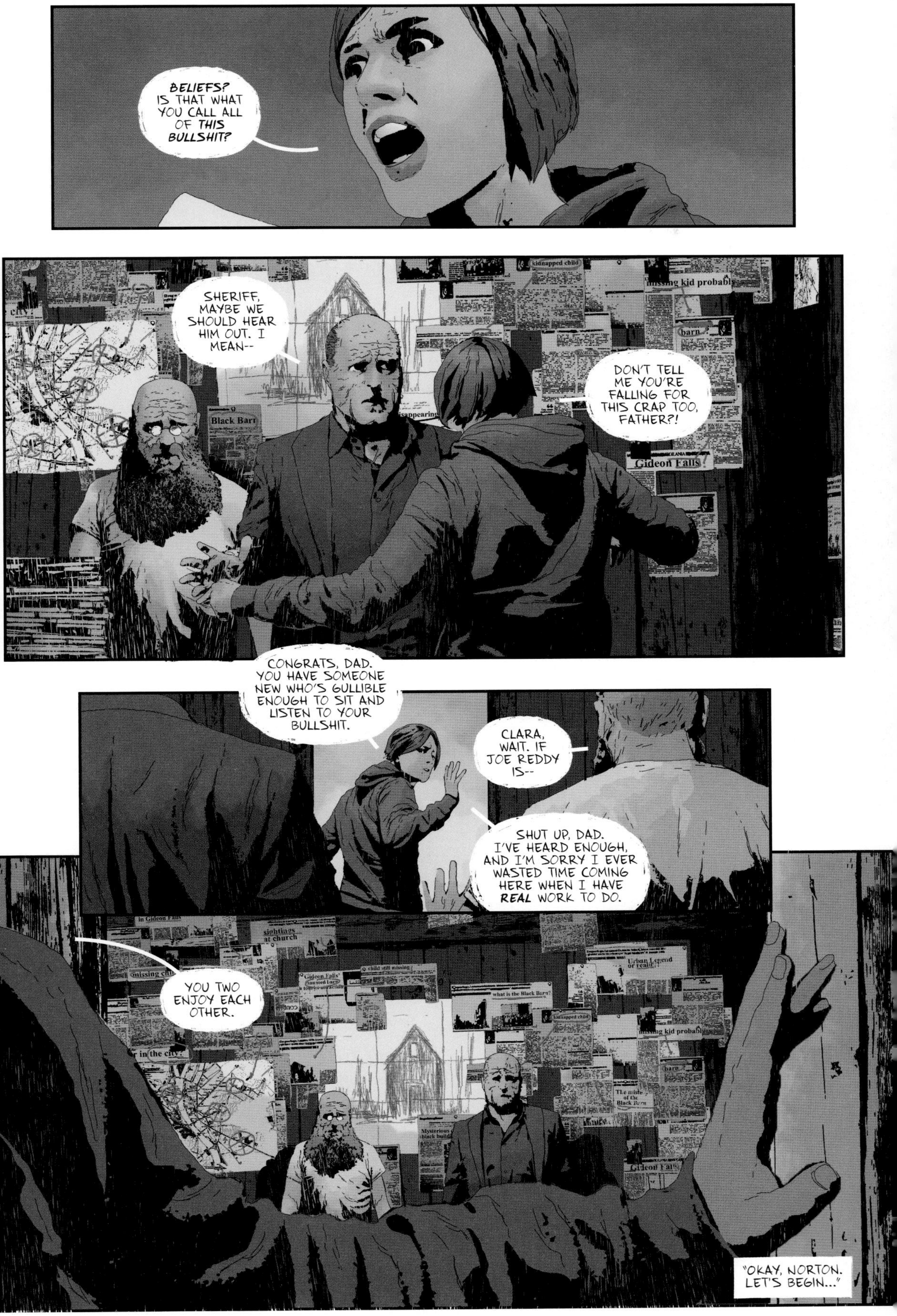
BELIEFS? IS THAT WHAT YOU CALL ALL OF THIS BULLSHIT?
SHERIFF, MAYBE WE SHOULD HEAR HIM OUT. I MEAN--
DON'T TELL ME YOU'RE FALLING FOR THIS CRAP TOO, FATHER?!
CONGRATS, DAD. YOU HAVE SOMEONE NEW WHO'S GULLIBLE ENOUGH TO SIT AND LISTEN TO YOUR BULLSHIT.
CLARA, WAIT. IF JOE REDDY IS--
SHUT UP, DAD. I'VE HEARD ENOUGH, AND I'M SORRY I EVER WASTED TIME COMING HERE WHEN I HAVE REAL WORK TO DO.
YOU TWO ENJOY EACH OTHER.
"OKAY, NORTON. LET'S BEGIN..."

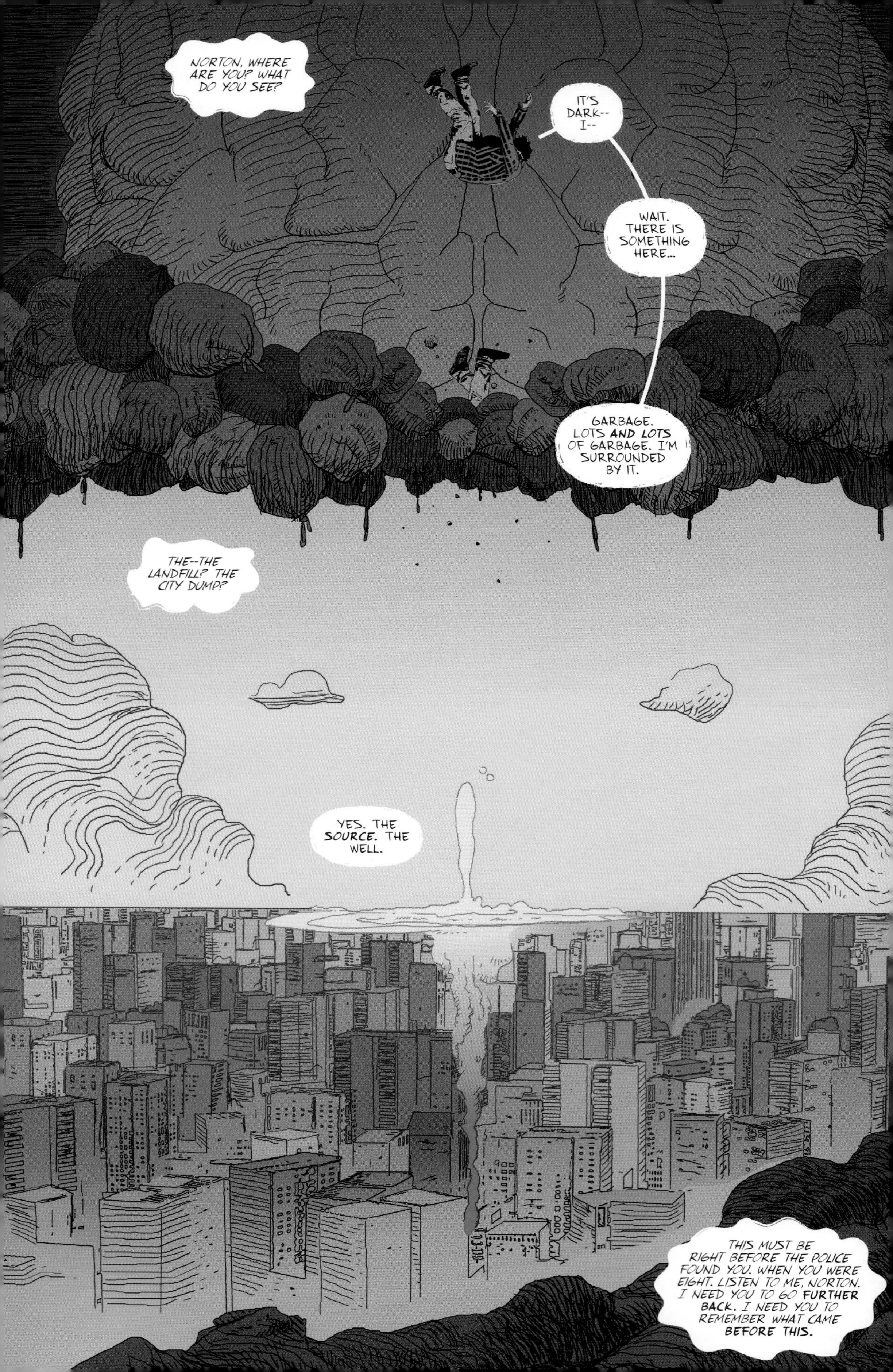

NORTON, WHERE ARE YOU? WHAT DO YOU SEE?
IT'S DARK-- I--
WAIT. THERE IS SOMETHING HERE...
GARBAGE. LOTS AND LOTS OF GARBAGE. I'M SURROUNDED BY IT.
THE--THE LANDFILL? THE CITY DUMP?
YES. THE SOURCE. THE WELL.
THIS MUST BE RIGHT BEFORE THE POLICE FOUND YOU. WHEN YOU WERE EIGHT. LISTEN TO ME, NORTON. I NEED YOU TO GO FURTHER BACK. I NEED YOU TO REMEMBER WHAT CAME BEFORE THIS.

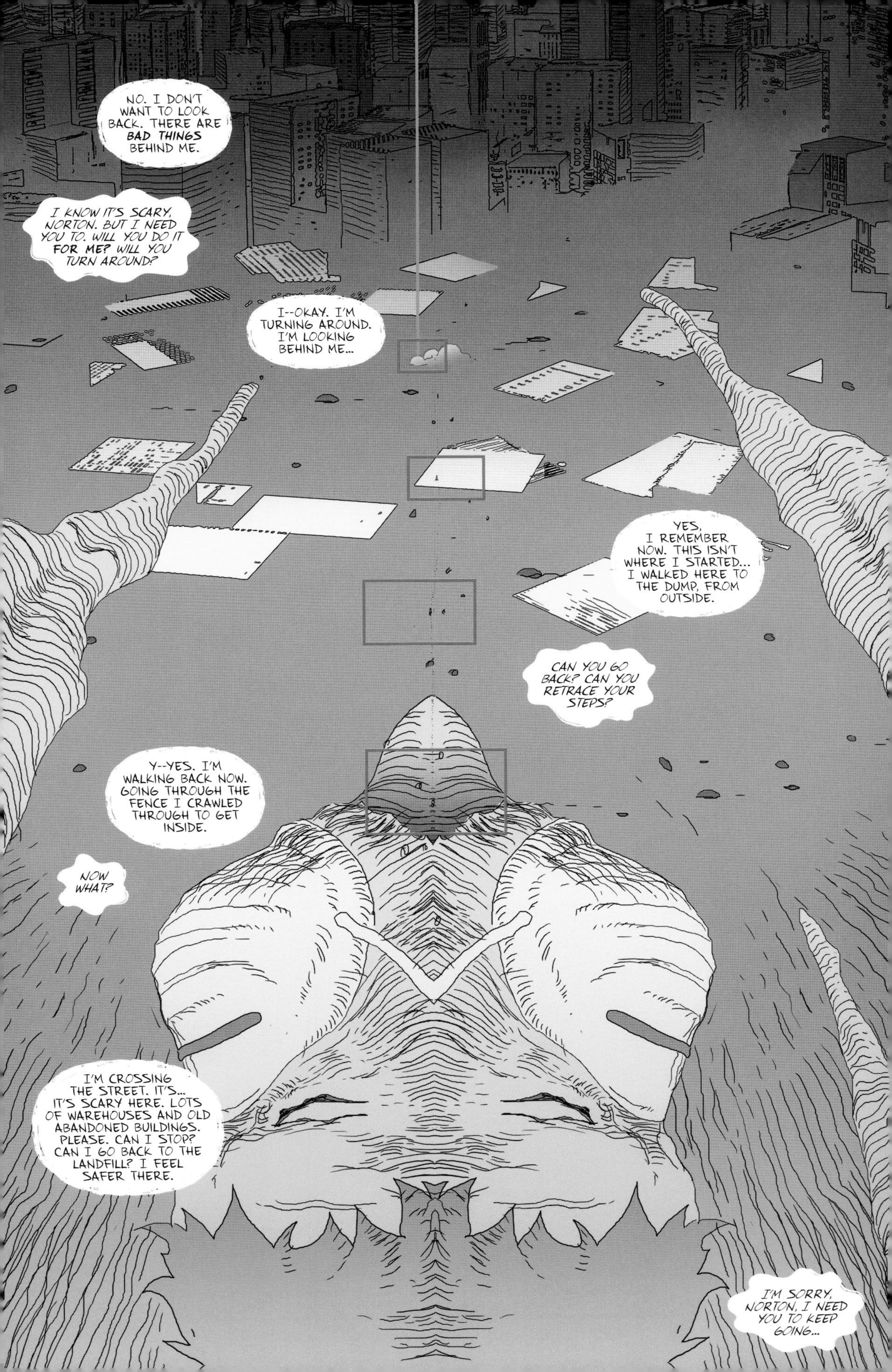
NO. I DON'T WANT TO LOOK BACK. THERE ARE **BAD THINGS** BEHIND ME.
I KNOW IT'S SCARY, NORTON. BUT I NEED YOU TO. WILL YOU DO IT **FOR ME?** WILL YOU TURN AROUND?
I--OKAY. I'M TURNING AROUND. I'M LOOKING BEHIND ME...
YES, I REMEMBER NOW. THIS ISN'T WHERE I STARTED... I WALKED HERE TO THE DUMP, FROM OUTSIDE.
CAN YOU GO BACK? CAN YOU RETRACE YOUR STEPS?
Y--YES. I'M WALKING BACK NOW. GOING THROUGH THE FENCE I CRAWLED THROUGH TO GET INSIDE.
NOW WHAT?
I'M CROSSING THE STREET. IT'S... IT'S SCARY HERE. LOTS OF WAREHOUSES AND OLD ABANDONED BUILDINGS. PLEASE. CAN I STOP? CAN I GO BACK TO THE LANDFILL? I FEEL SAFER THERE.
I'M SORRY, NORTON, I NEED YOU TO KEEP GOING...

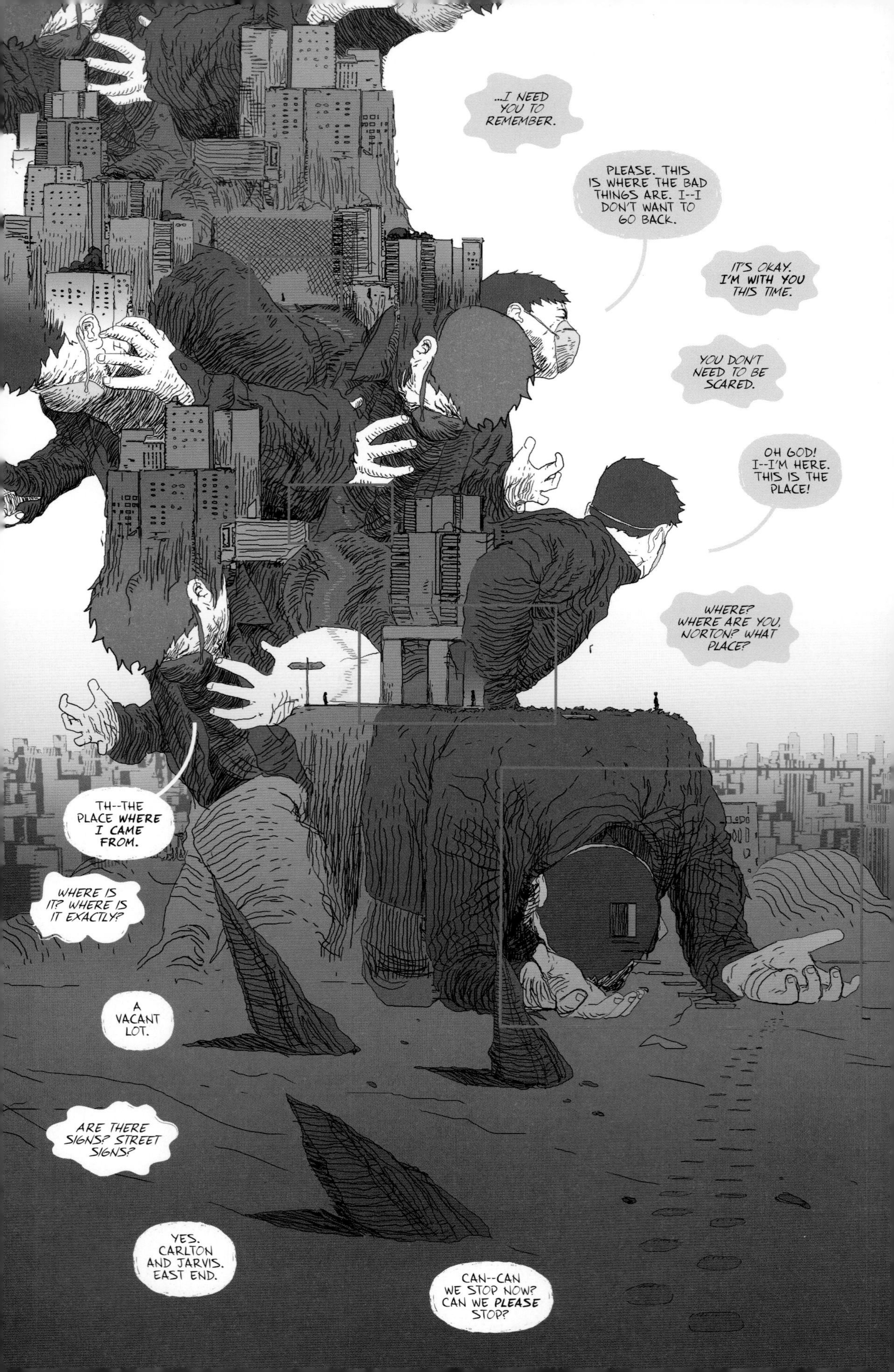
...I NEED YOU TO REMEMBER.
PLEASE. THIS IS WHERE THE BAD THINGS ARE. I--I DON'T WANT TO GO BACK.
IT'S OKAY. I'M WITH YOU THIS TIME.
YOU DON'T NEED TO BE SCARED.
OH GOD! I--I'M HERE. THIS IS THE PLACE!
WHERE? WHERE ARE YOU, NORTON? WHAT PLACE?
TH--THE PLACE WHERE I CAME FROM.
WHERE IS IT? WHERE IS IT EXACTLY?
A VACANT LOT.
ARE THERE SIGNS? STREET SIGNS?
YES. CARLTON AND JARVIS. EAST END.
CAN--CAN WE STOP NOW? CAN WE PLEASE STOP?

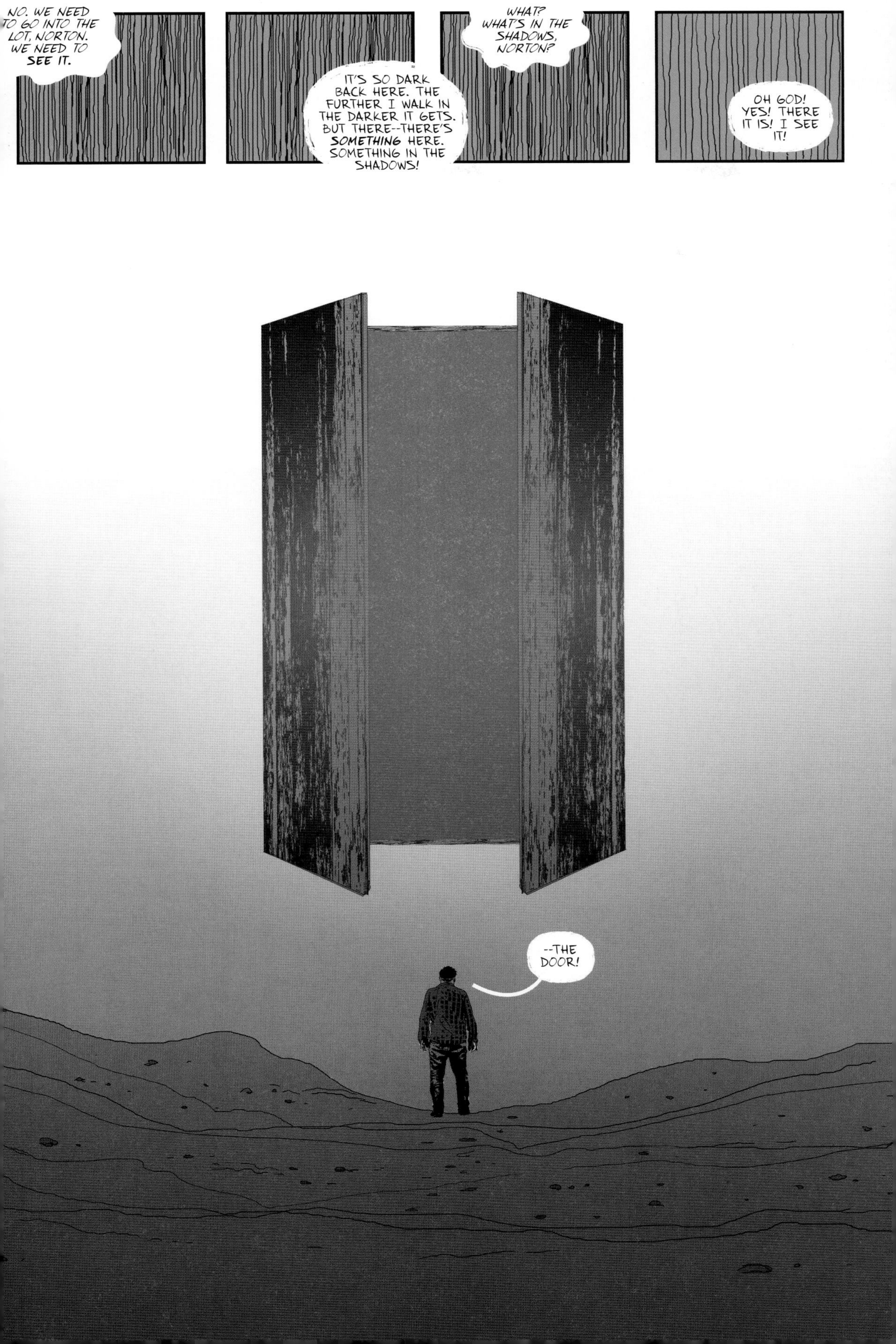
NO. WE NEED TO GO INTO THE LOT, NORTON. WE NEED TO SEE IT.
IT'S SO DARK BACK HERE. THE FURTHER I WALK IN THE DARKER IT GETS. BUT THERE--THERE'S SOMETHING HERE. SOMETHING IN THE SHADOWS!
WHAT? WHAT'S IN THE SHADOWS, NORTON?
OH GOD! YES! THERE IT IS! I SEE IT!
--THE DOOR!

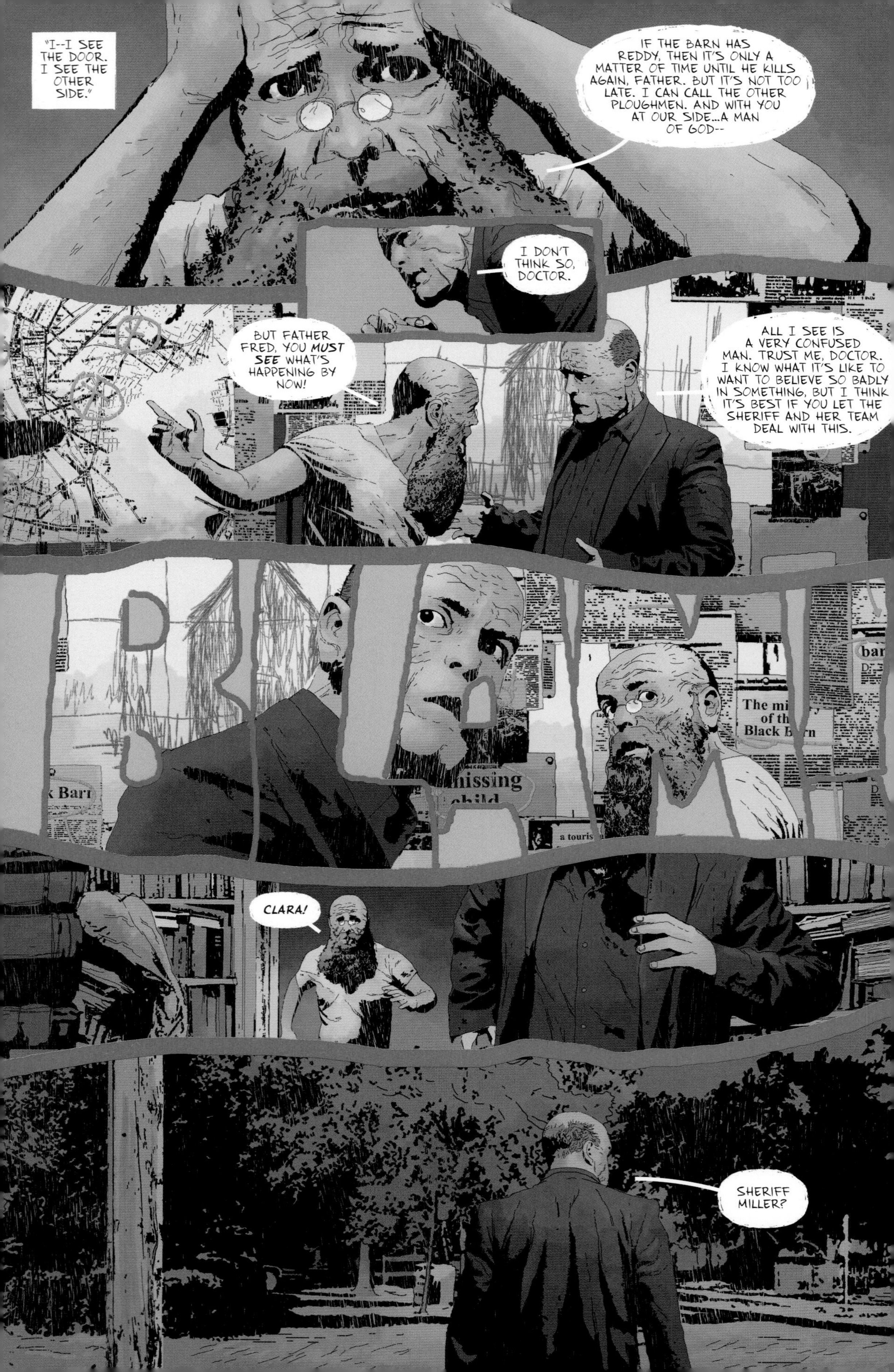
"I--I SEE THE DOOR. I SEE THE OTHER SIDE."
IF THE BARN HAS REDDY, THEN IT'S ONLY A MATTER OF TIME UNTIL HE KILLS AGAIN, FATHER. BUT IT'S NOT TOO LATE. I CAN CALL THE OTHER PLOUGHMEN. AND WITH YOU AT OUR SIDE...A MAN OF GOD--
I DON'T THINK SO, DOCTOR.
BUT FATHER FRED, YOU **MUST SEE** WHAT'S HAPPENING BY NOW!
ALL I SEE IS A VERY CONFUSED MAN. TRUST ME, DOCTOR. I KNOW WHAT IT'S LIKE TO WANT TO BELIEVE SO BADLY IN SOMETHING, BUT I THINK IT'S BEST IF YOU LET THE SHERIFF AND HER TEAM DEAL WITH THIS.
missing child
CLARA!
SHERIFF MILLER?

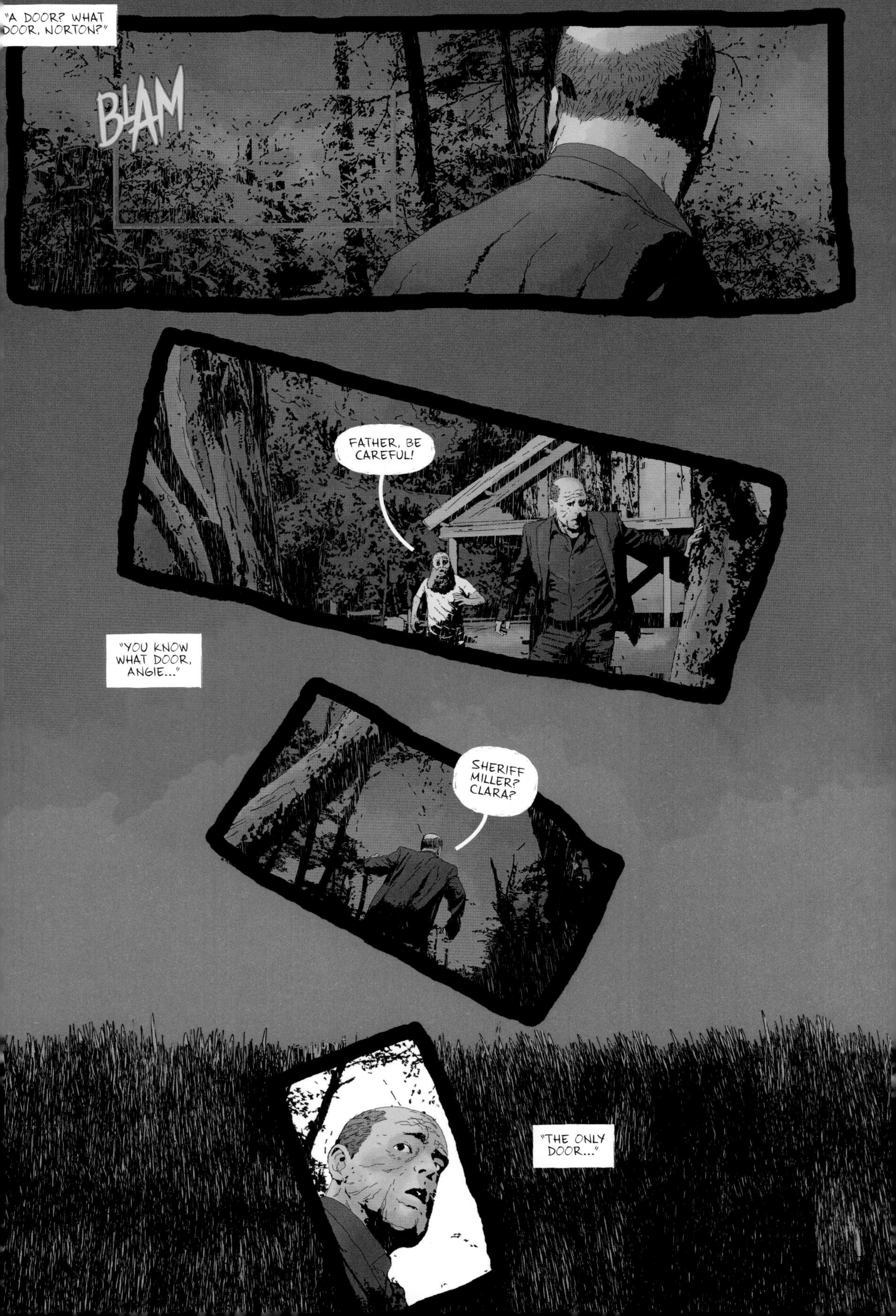
"A DOOR? WHAT DOOR, NORTON?"
BLAM
FATHER, BE CAREFUL!
"YOU KNOW WHAT DOOR, ANGIE..."
SHERIFF MILLER? CLARA?
"THE ONLY DOOR..."

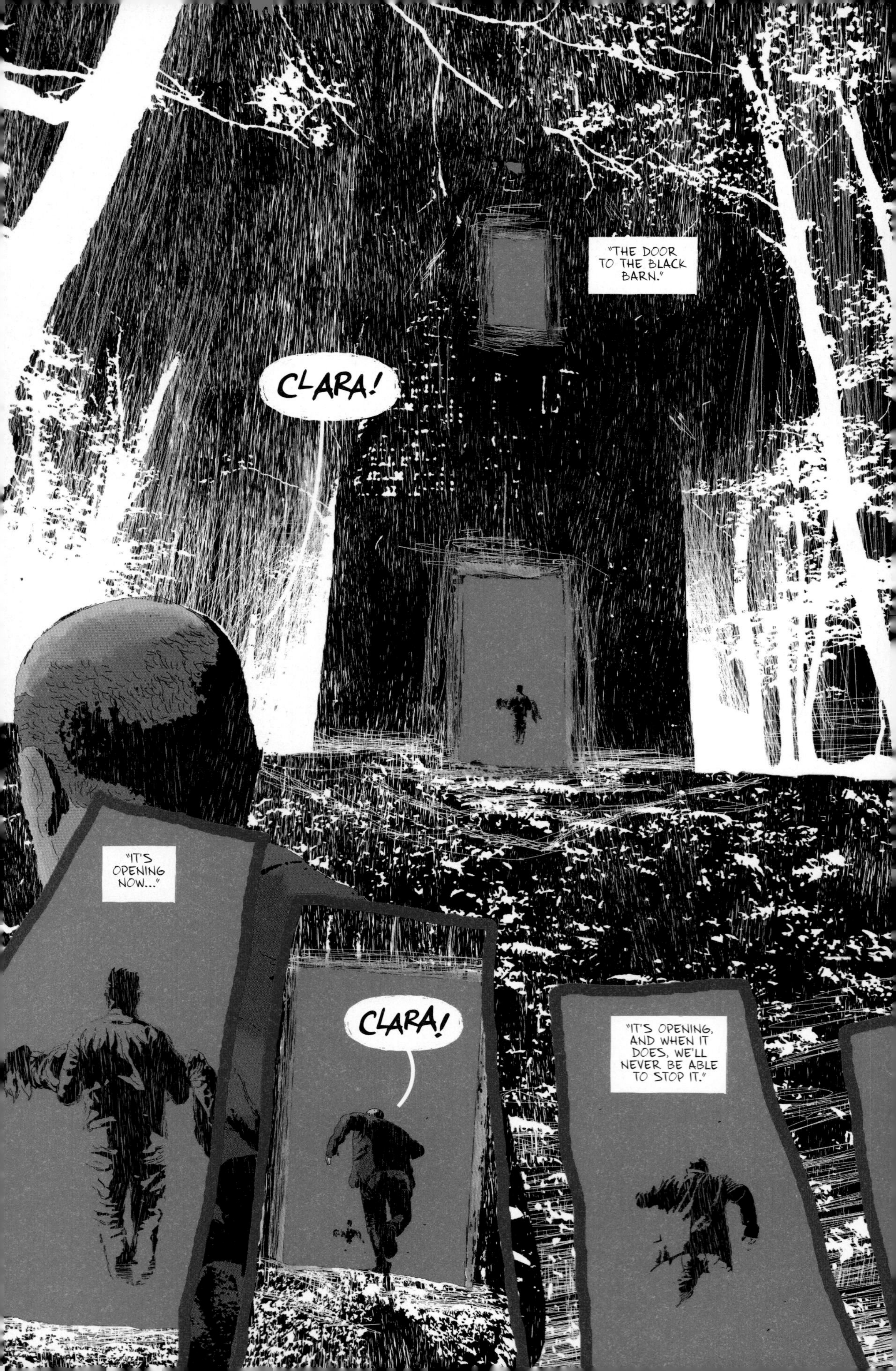
"THE DOOR TO THE BLACK BARN."
CLARA!
"IT'S OPENING NOW..."
CLARA!
"IT'S OPENING, AND WHEN IT DOES, WE'LL NEVER BE ABLE TO STOP IT."

GIDEON
FALLS

Six

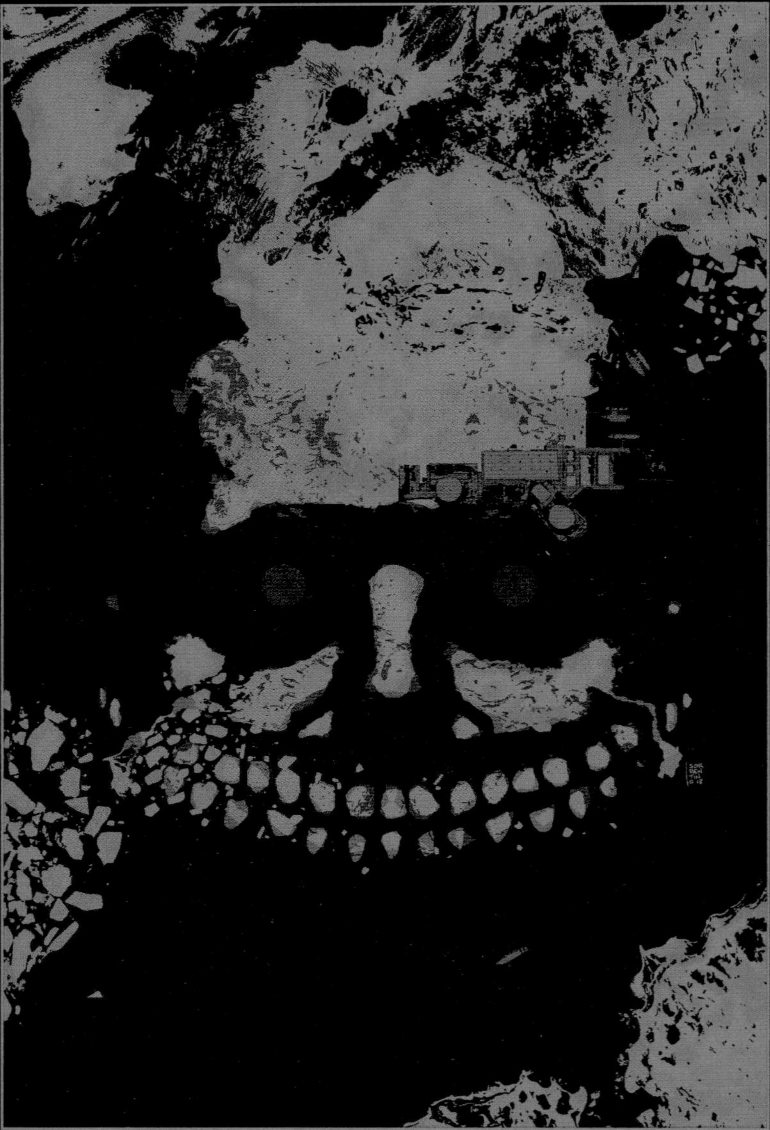

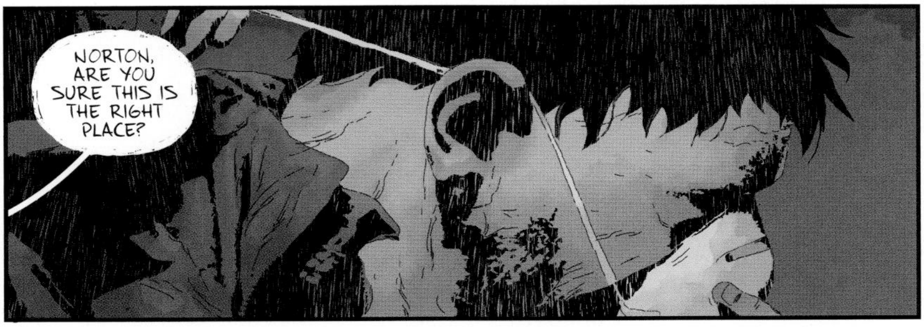
NORTON, ARE YOU SURE THIS IS THE RIGHT PLACE?

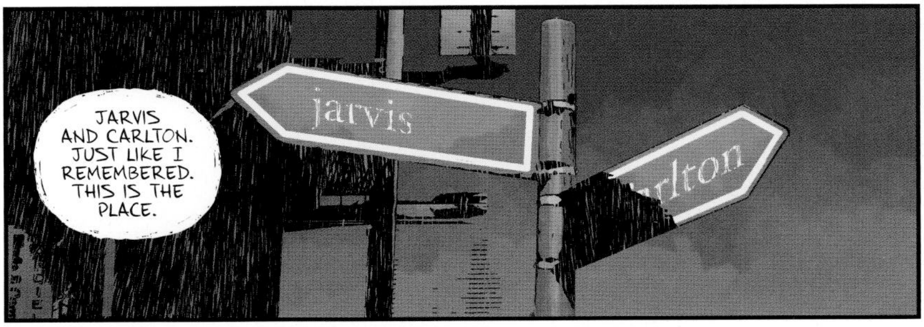
jarvis
JARVIS AND CARLTON. JUST LIKE I REMEMBERED. THIS IS THE PLACE.

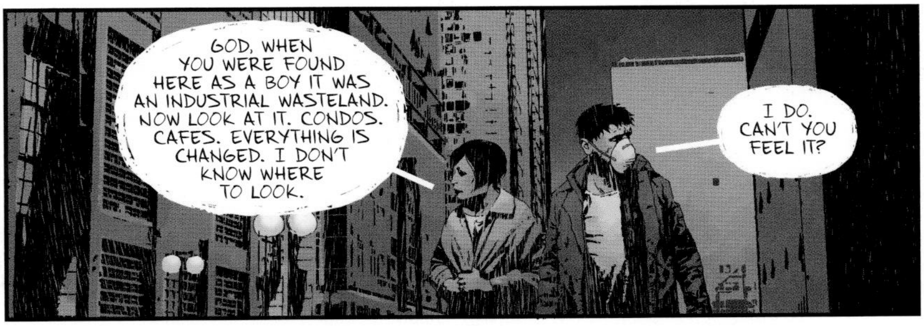
GOD, WHEN YOU WERE FOUND HERE AS A BOY IT WAS AN INDUSTRIAL WASTELAND. NOW LOOK AT IT. CONDOS. CAFES. EVERYTHING IS CHANGED. I DON'T KNOW WHERE TO LOOK.
I DO. CAN'T YOU FEEL IT?

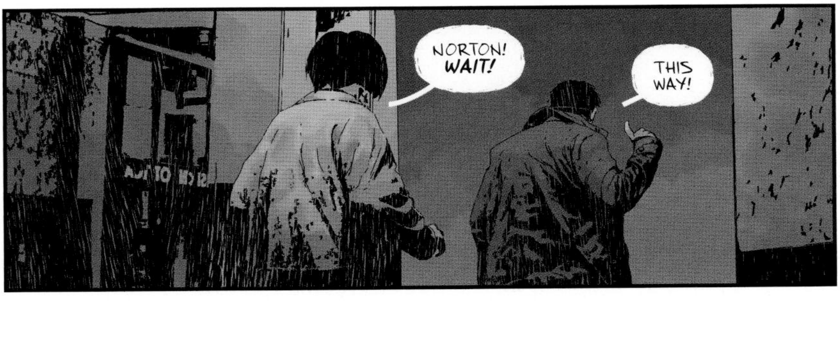
NORTON! **WAIT!**
THIS WAY!

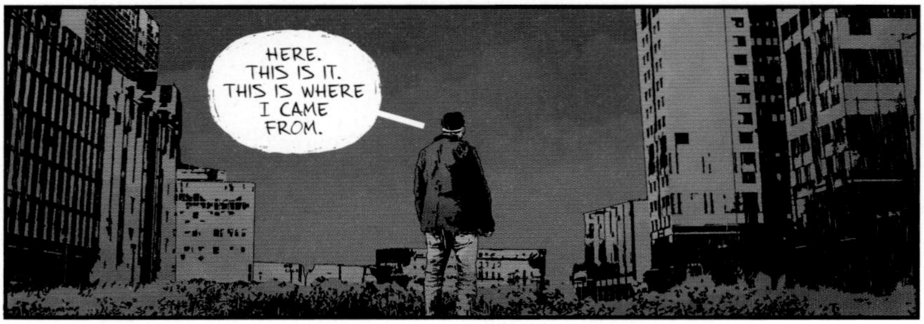
HERE. THIS IS IT. THIS IS WHERE I CAME FROM.

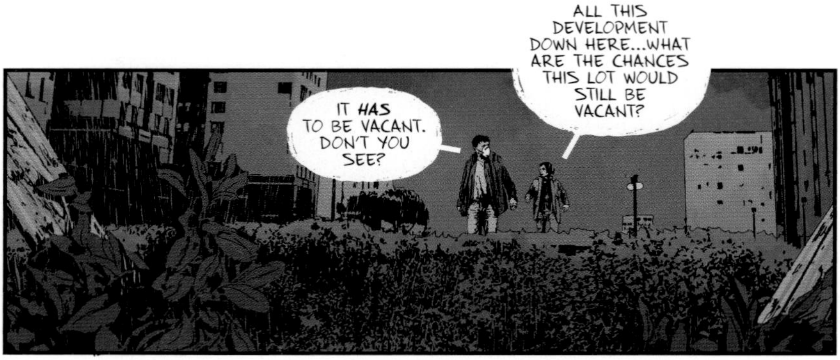
ALL THIS DEVELOPMENT DOWN HERE...WHAT ARE THE CHANCES THIS LOT WOULD STILL BE VACANT?
IT **HAS** TO BE VACANT. DON'T YOU SEE?

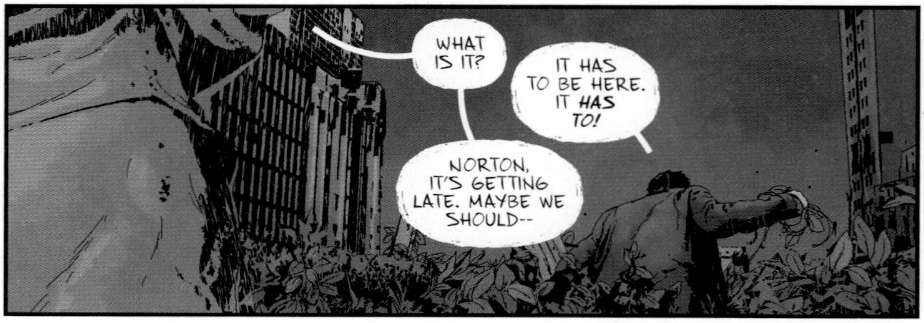
WHAT IS IT?
IT HAS TO BE HERE. IT **HAS TO!**
NORTON, IT'S GETTING LATE. MAYBE WE SHOULD--

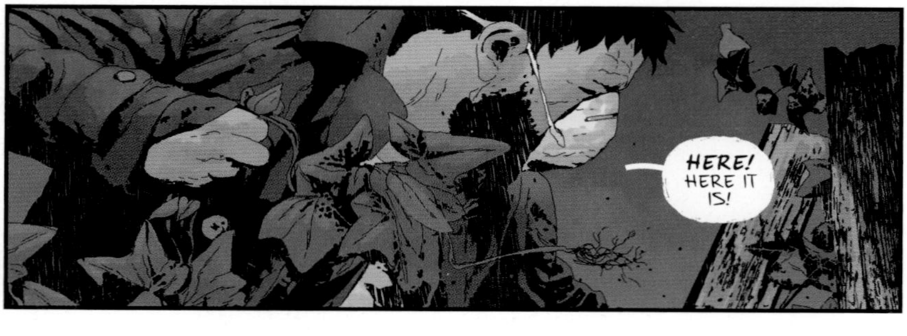
HERE! HERE IT IS!

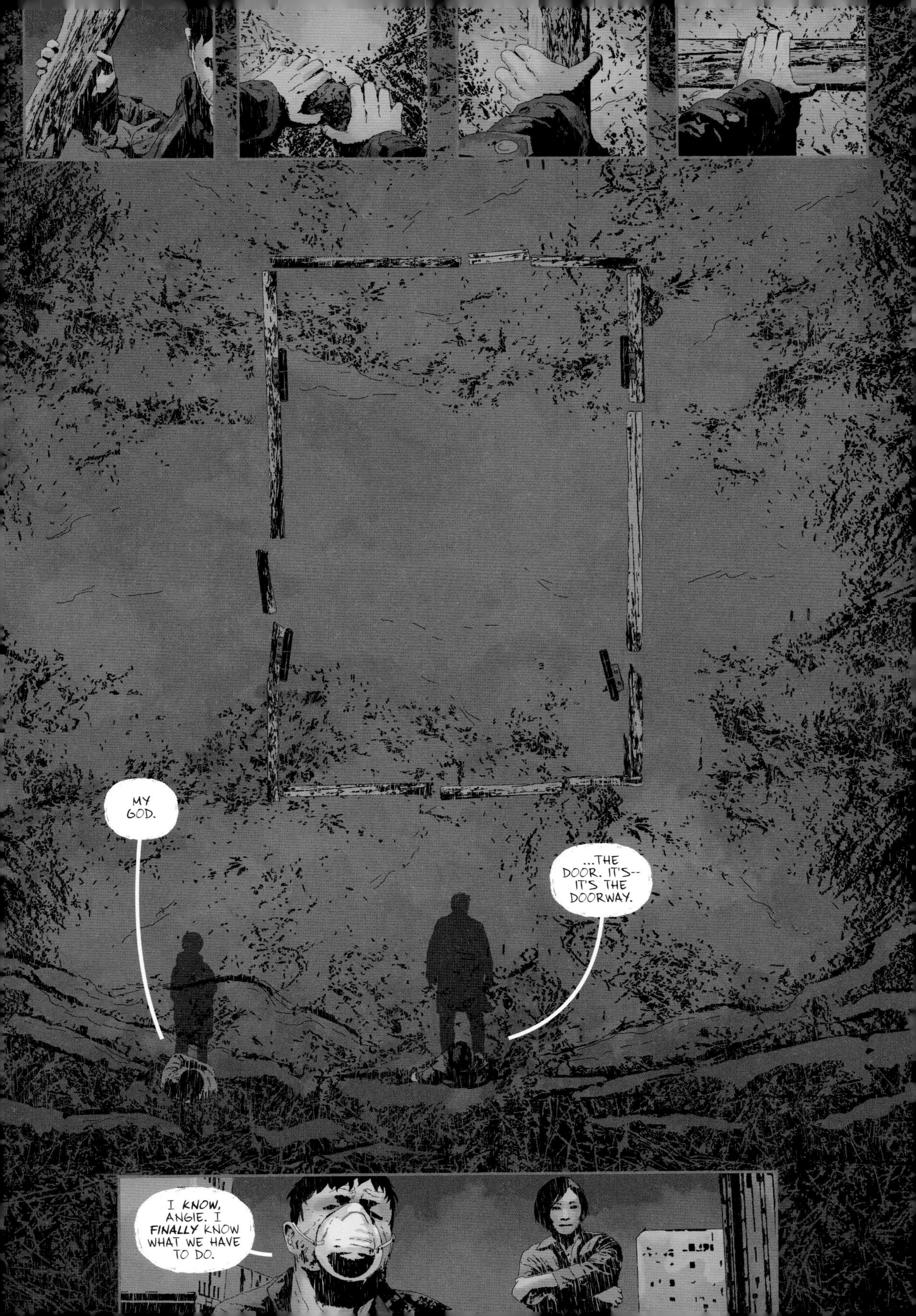
MY GOD.
...THE DOOR. IT'S-- IT'S THE DOORWAY.
I KNOW, ANGIE. I FINALLY KNOW WHAT WE HAVE TO DO.

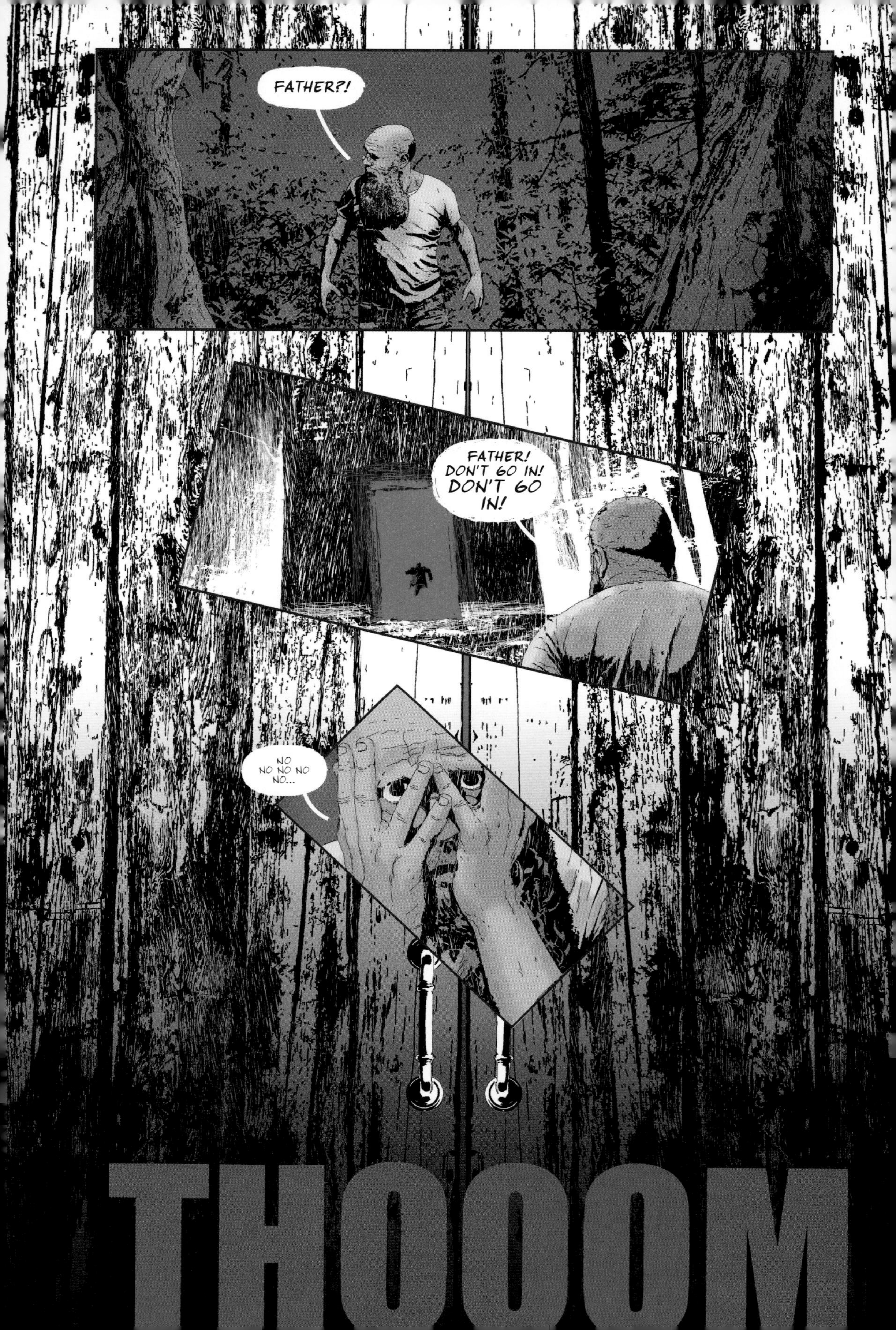
FATHER?!
FATHER! DON'T GO IN! DON'T GO IN!
NO NO NO NO NO...
THOOOM

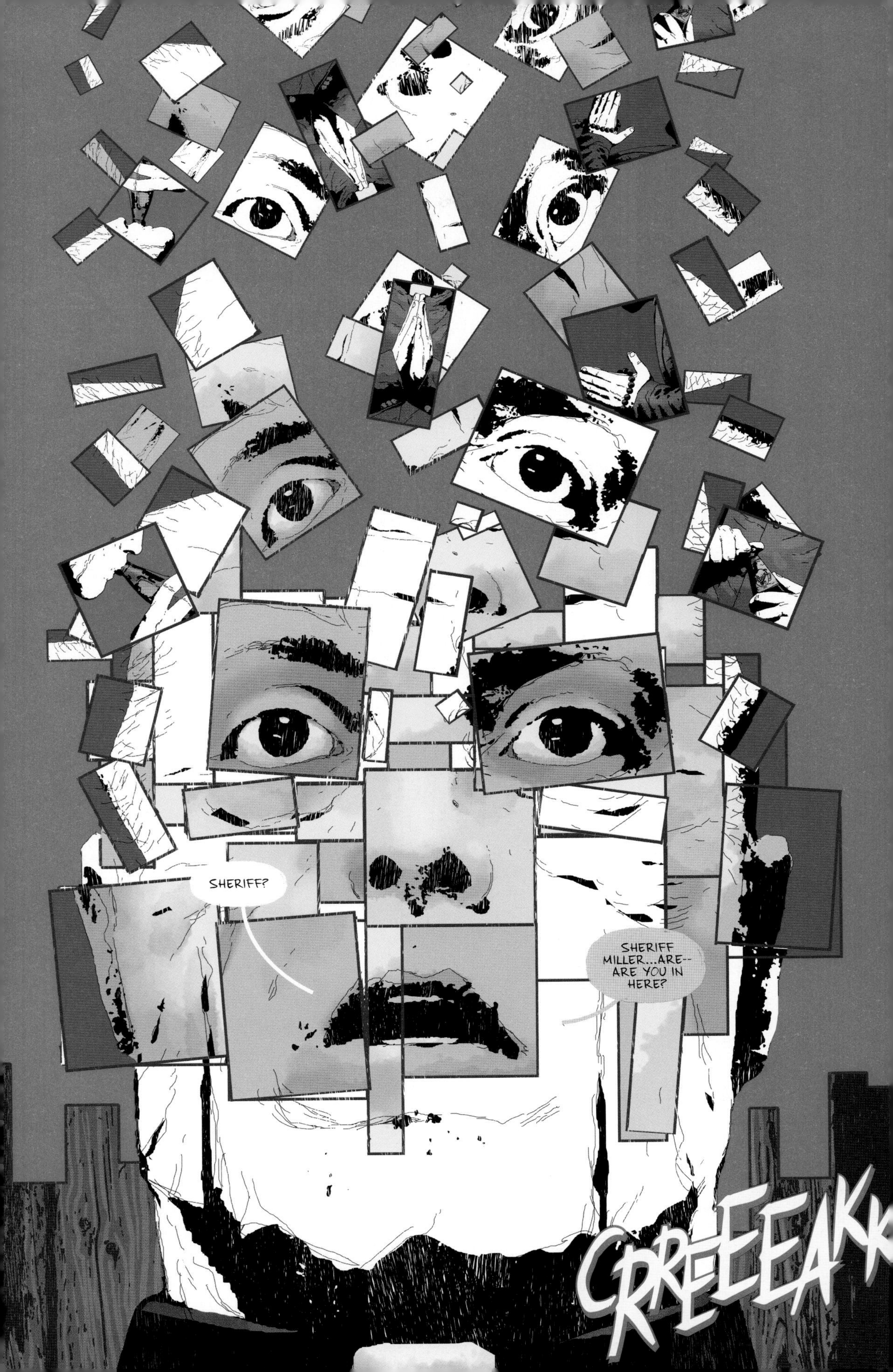
SHERIFF?
SHERIFF MILLER...ARE--ARE YOU IN HERE?
CREEEAKK

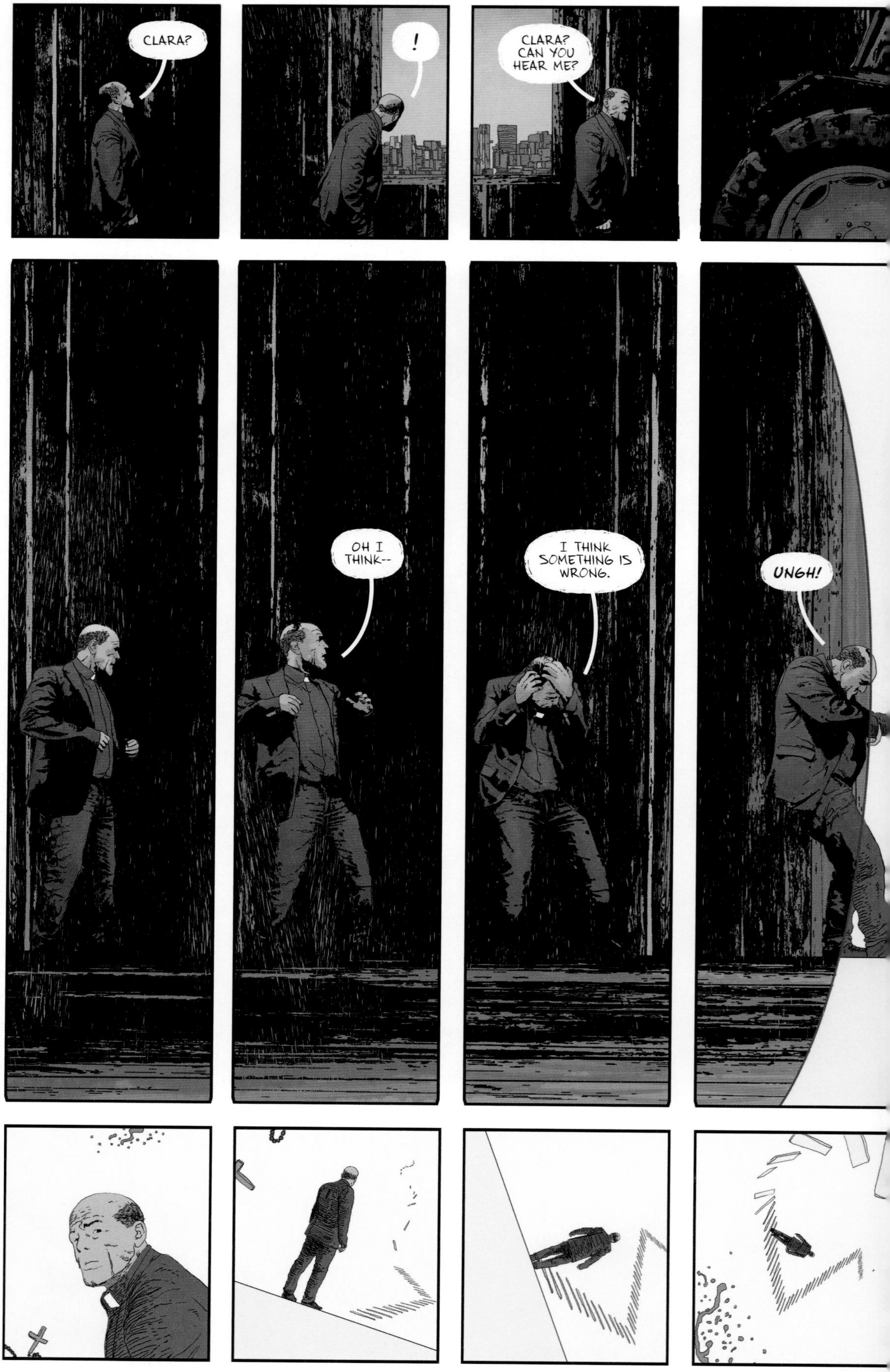

CLARA?
!
CLARA? CAN YOU HEAR ME?
OH I THINK--
I THINK SOMETHING IS WRONG.
UNGH!

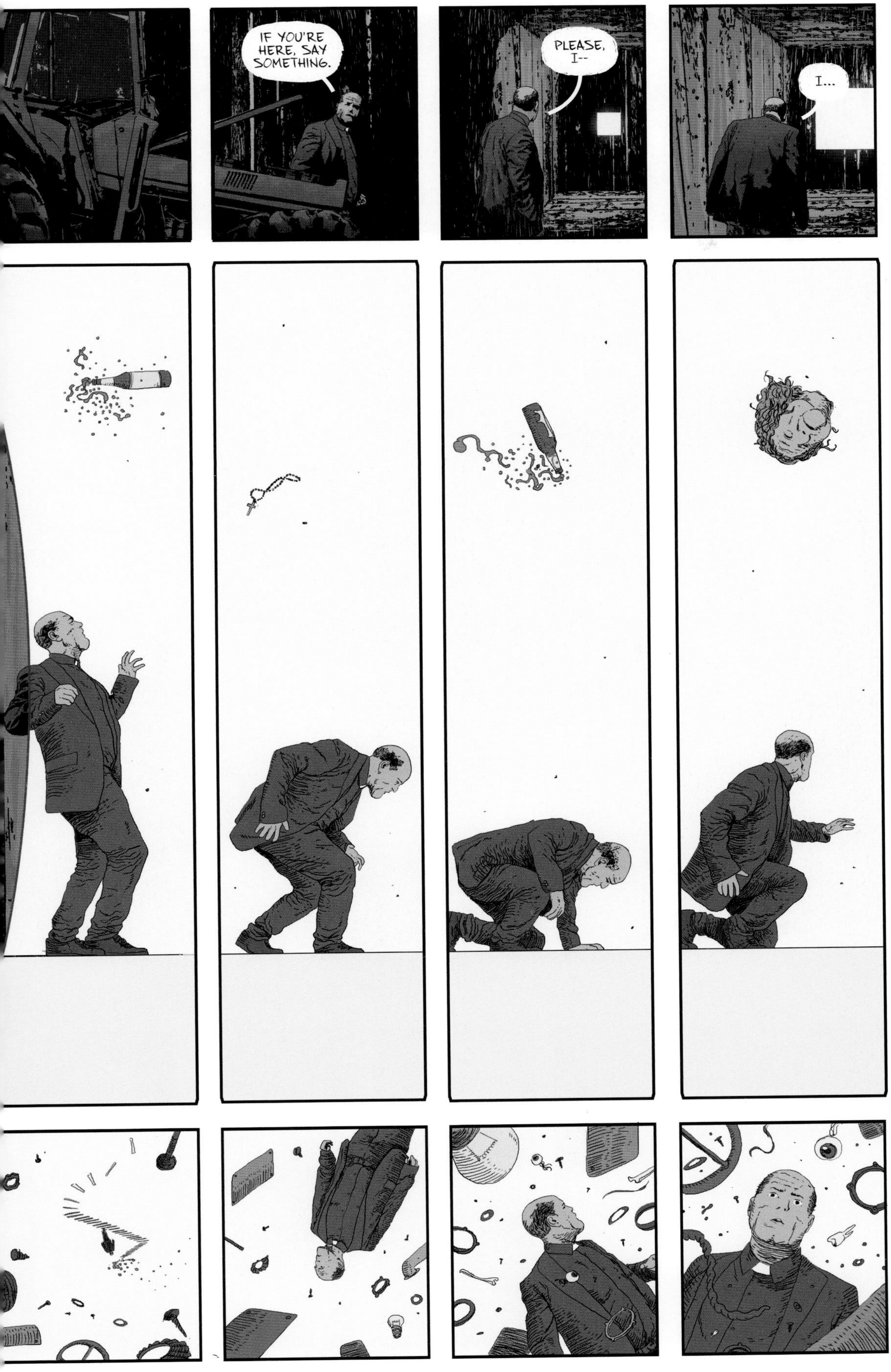
IF YOU'RE HERE, SAY SOMETHING.
PLEASE, I--
I...

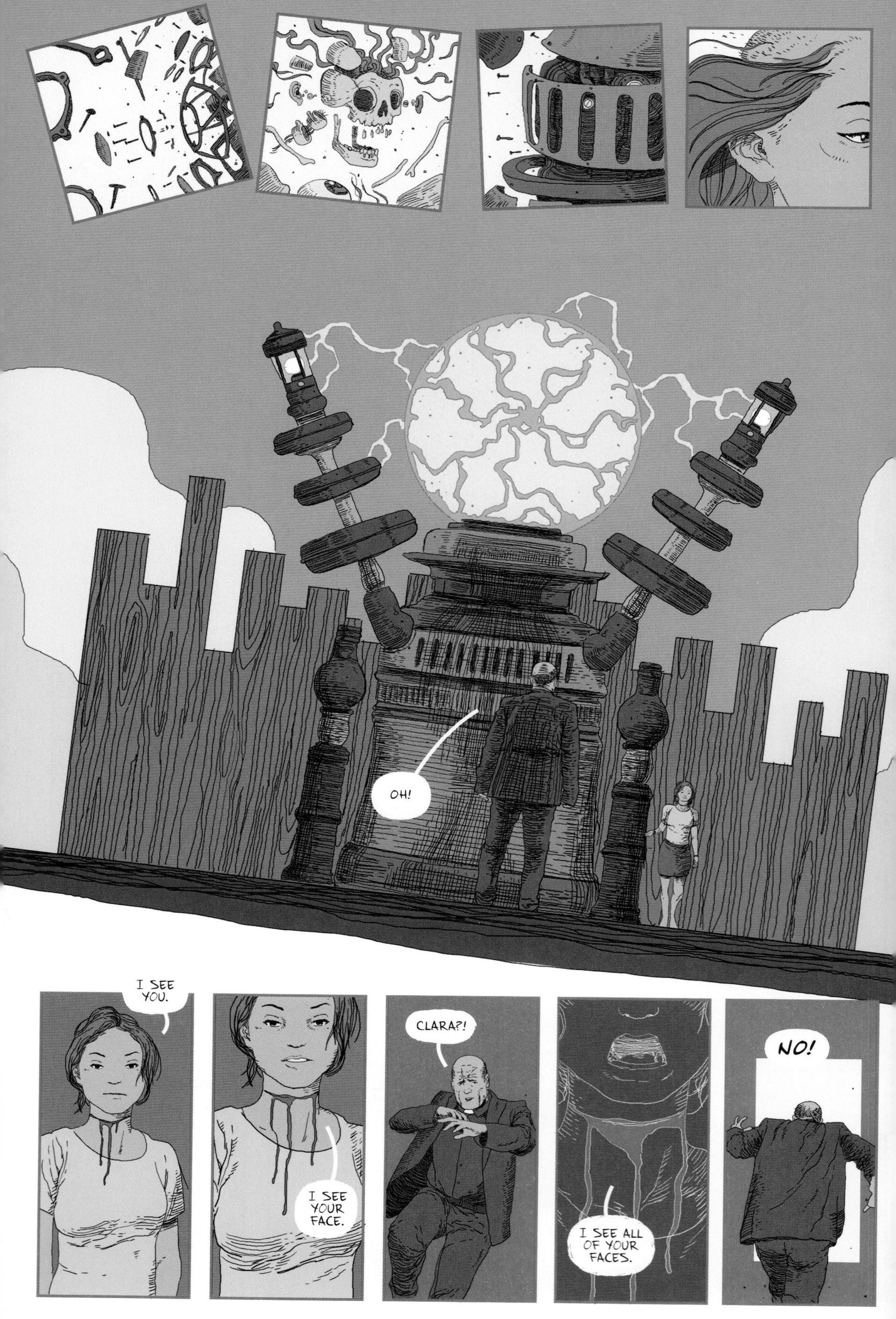
OH!
I SEE YOU.
I SEE YOUR FACE.
CLARA?!
I SEE ALL OF YOUR FACES.
NO!

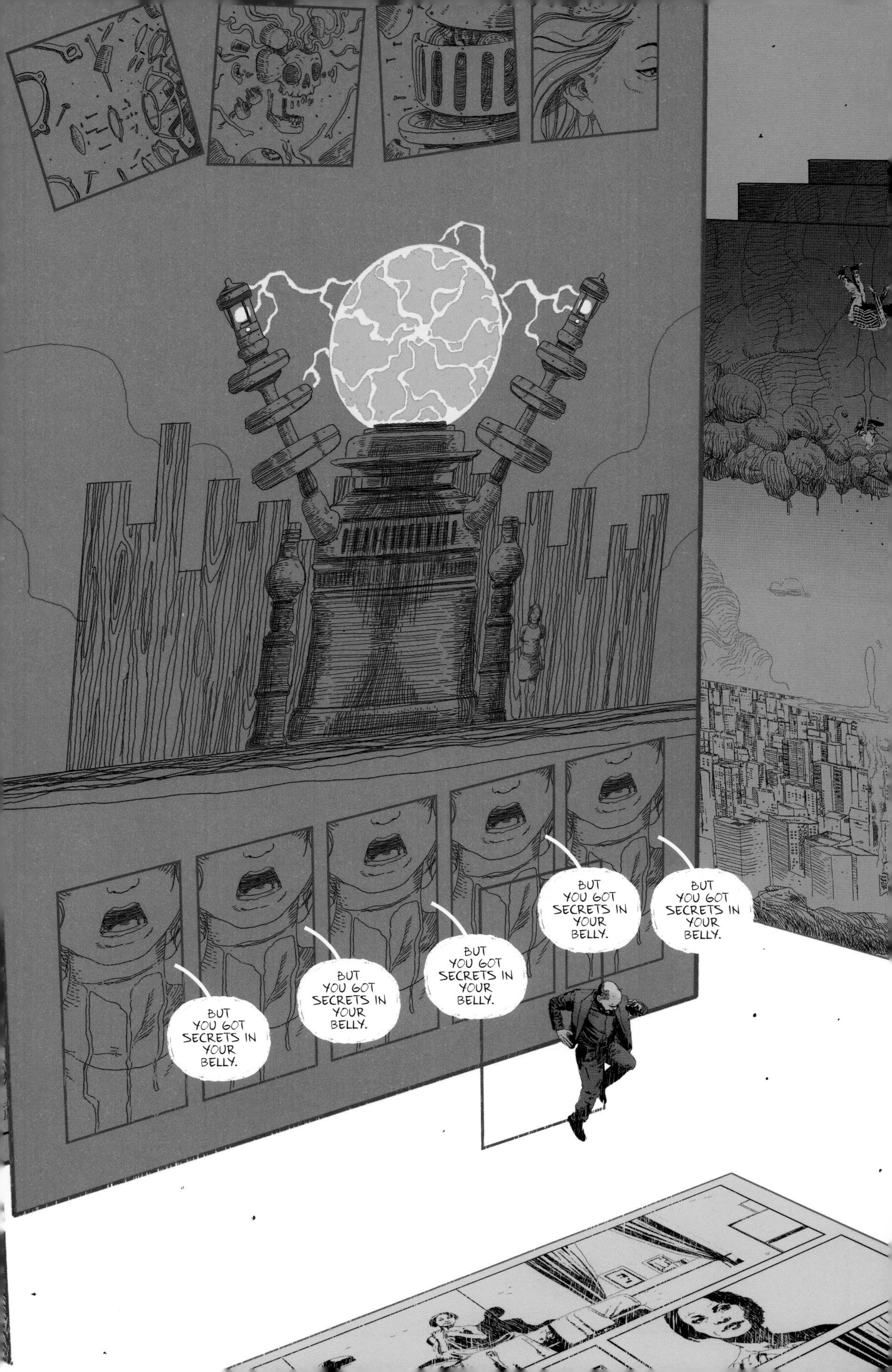
BUT YOU GOT SECRETS IN YOUR BELLY.
BUT YOU GOT SECRETS IN YOUR BELLY.
BUT YOU GOT SECRETS IN YOUR BELLY.
BUT YOU GOT SECRETS IN YOUR BELLY.
BUT YOU GOT SECRETS IN YOUR BELLY.

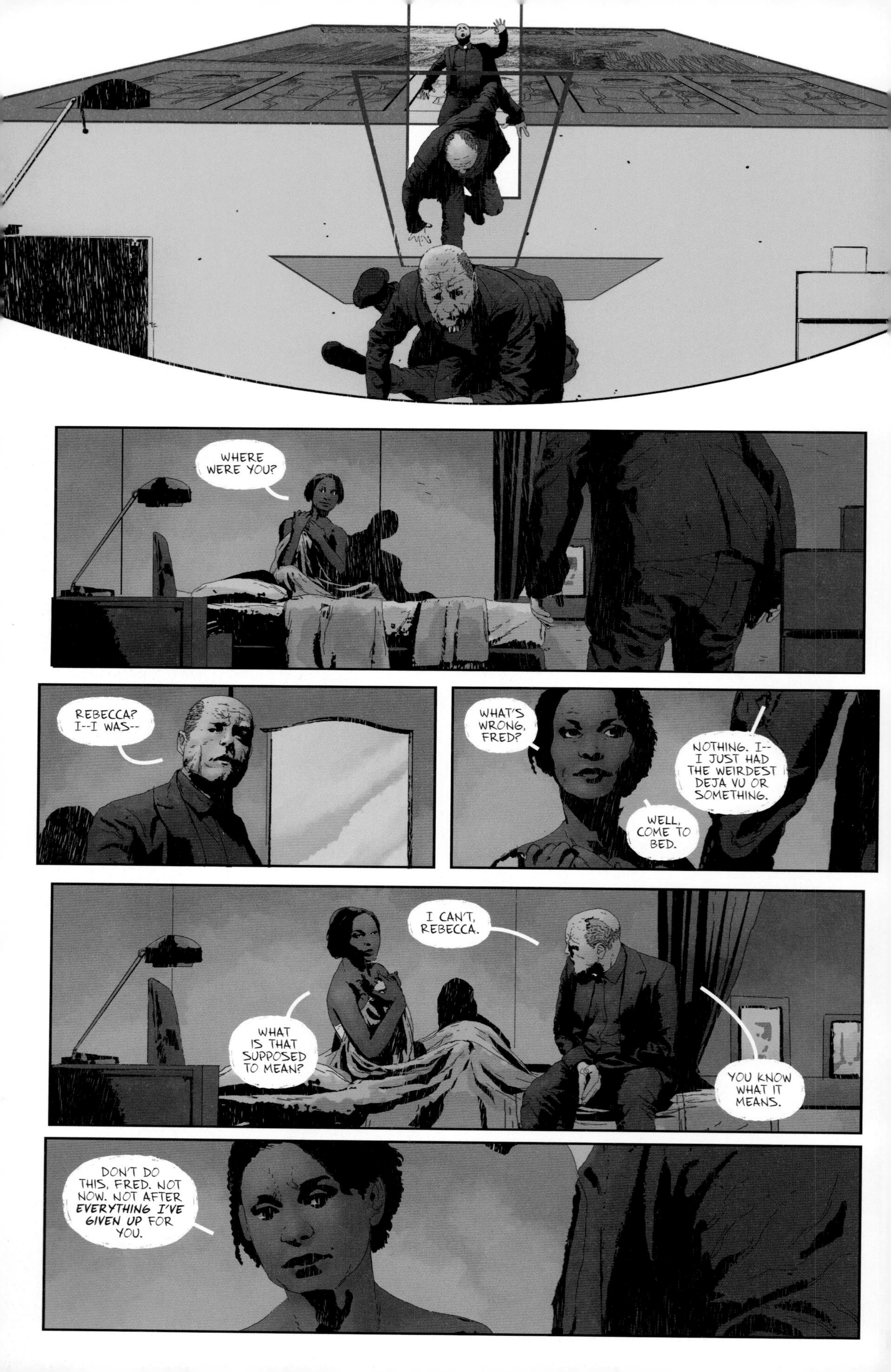
WHERE WERE YOU?
REBECCA? I--I WAS--
WHAT'S WRONG, FRED?
NOTHING. I-- I JUST HAD THE WEIRDEST DEJA VU OR SOMETHING.
WELL, COME TO BED.
I CAN'T, REBECCA.
WHAT IS THAT SUPPOSED TO MEAN?
YOU KNOW WHAT IT MEANS.
DON'T DO THIS, FRED. NOT NOW. NOT AFTER EVERYTHING I'VE GIVEN UP FOR YOU.

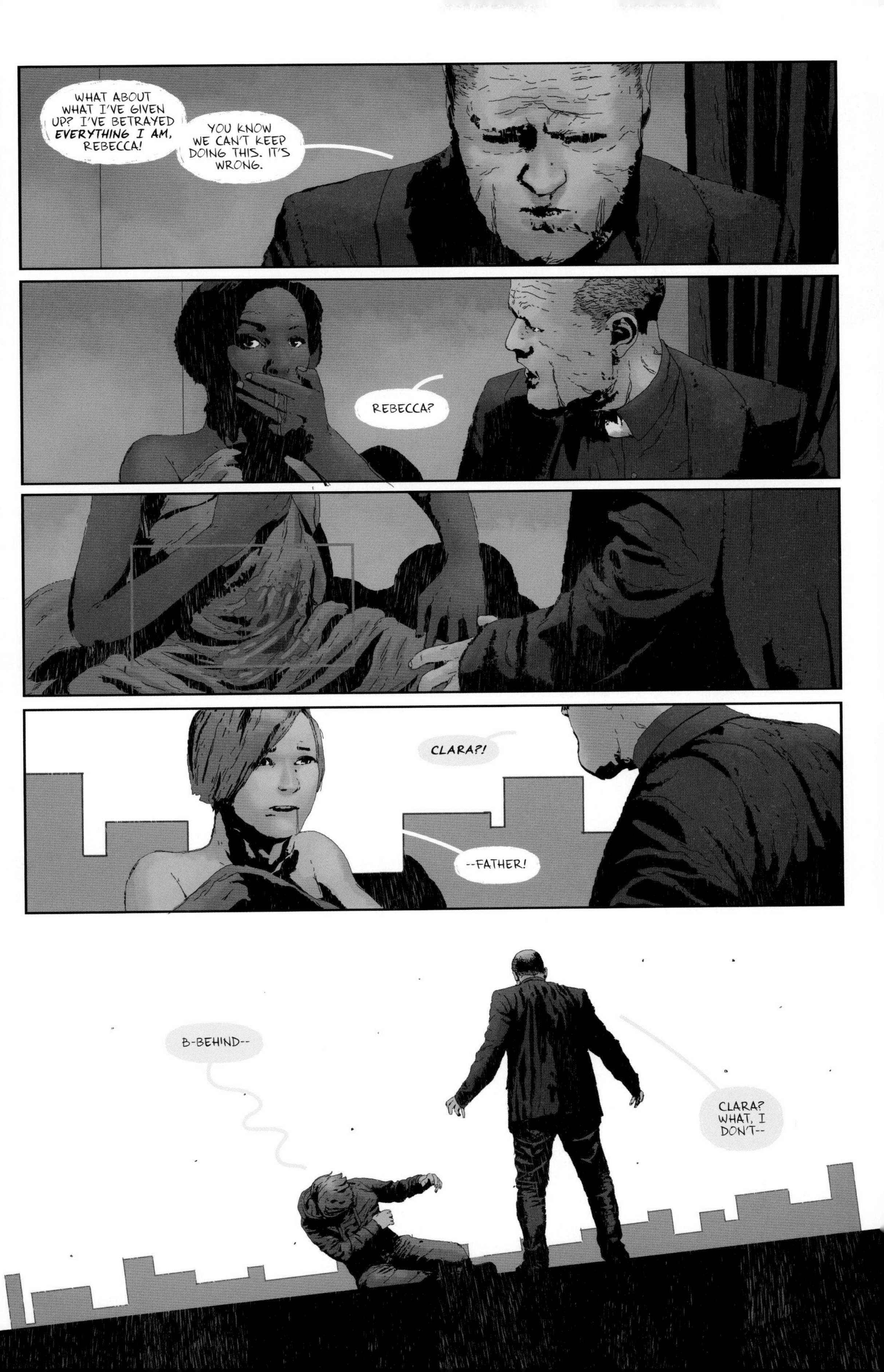
WHAT ABOUT WHAT I'VE GIVEN UP? I'VE BETRAYED EVERYTHING I AM, REBECCA!
YOU KNOW WE CAN'T KEEP DOING THIS. IT'S WRONG.
REBECCA?
CLARA?!
--FATHER!
B-BEHIND--
CLARA? WHAT, I DON'T--

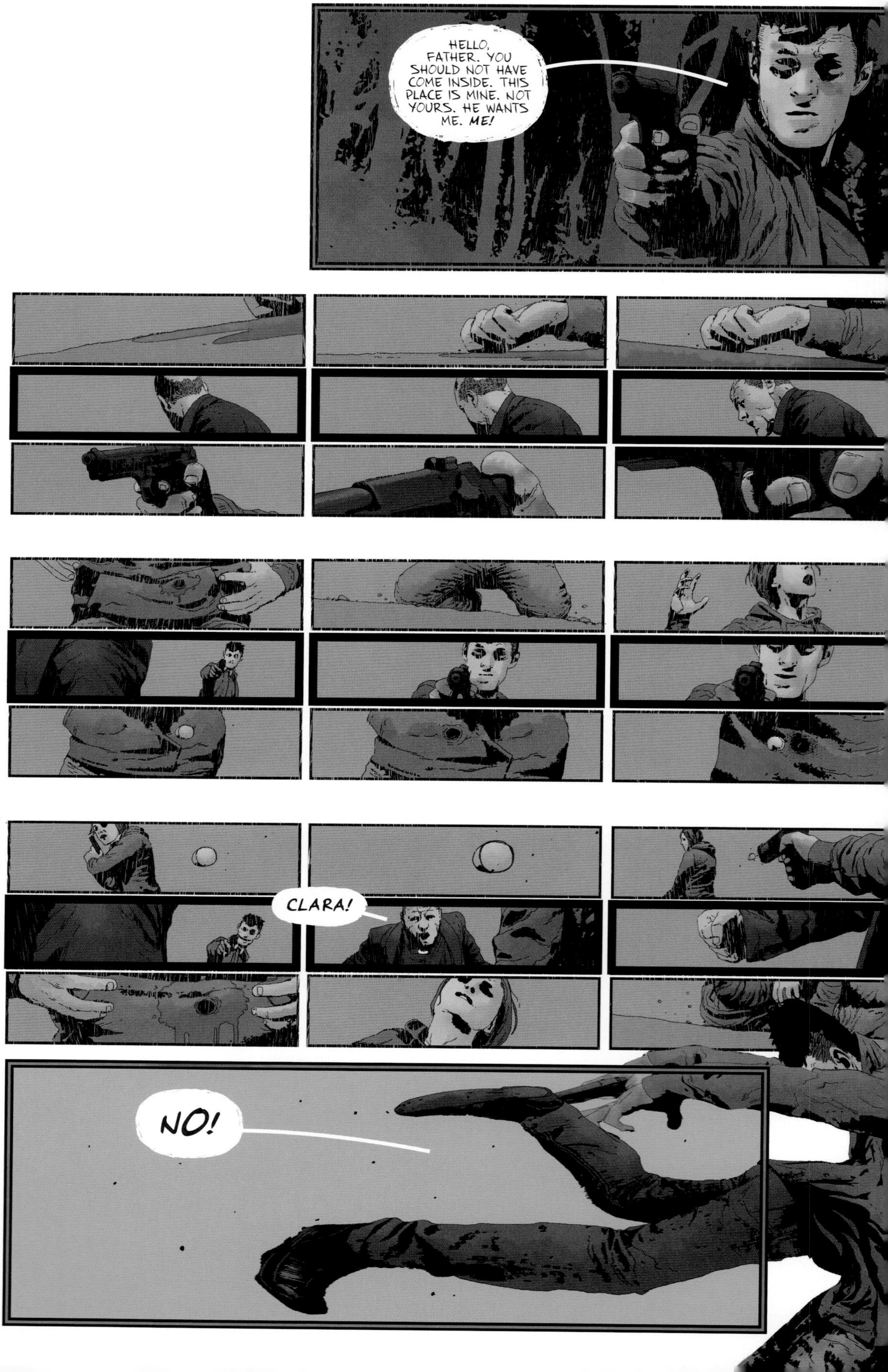
HELLO, FATHER. YOU SHOULD NOT HAVE COME INSIDE. THIS PLACE IS MINE. NOT YOURS. HE WANTS ME. ME!
CLARA!
NO!

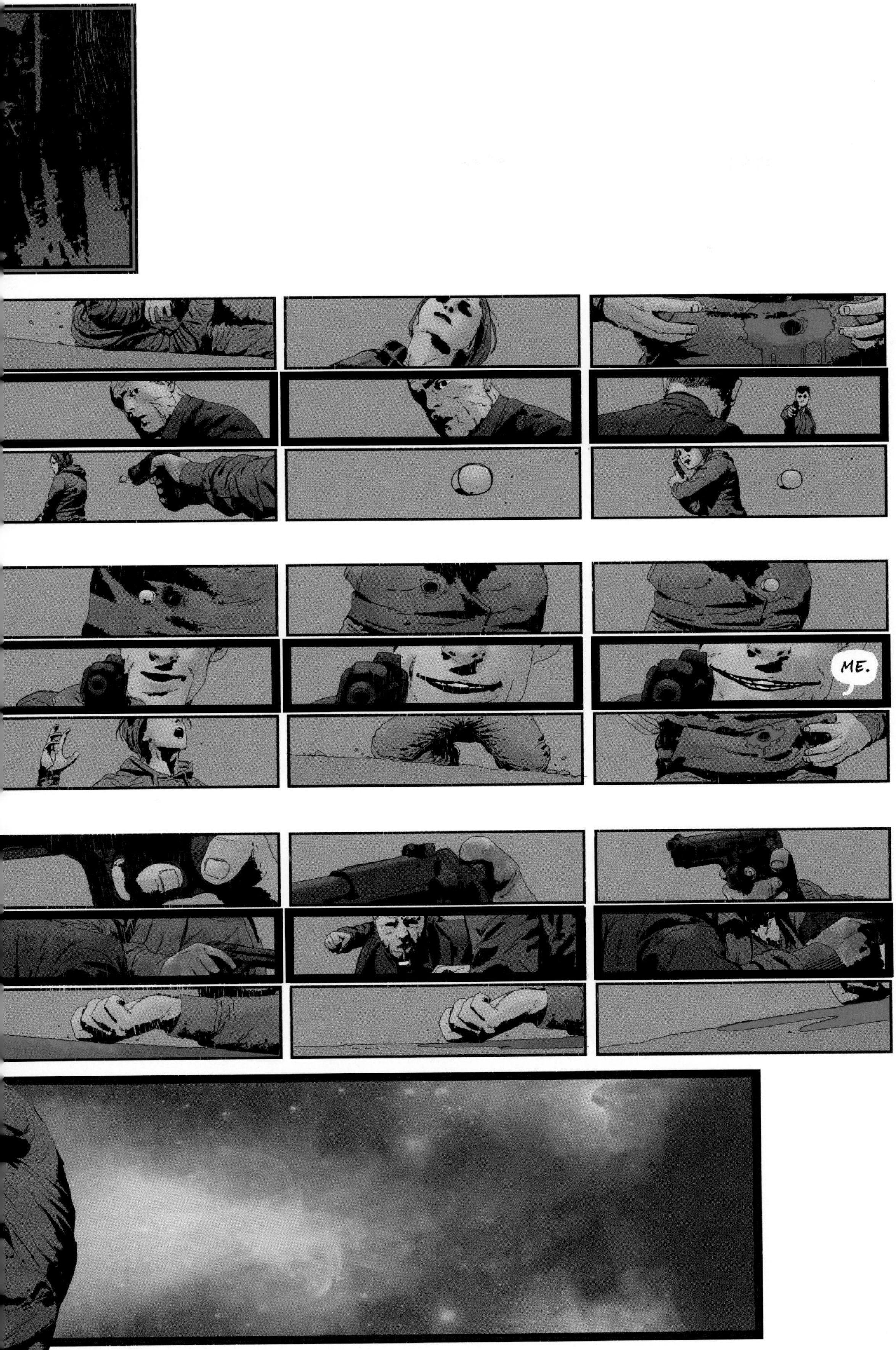
ME.

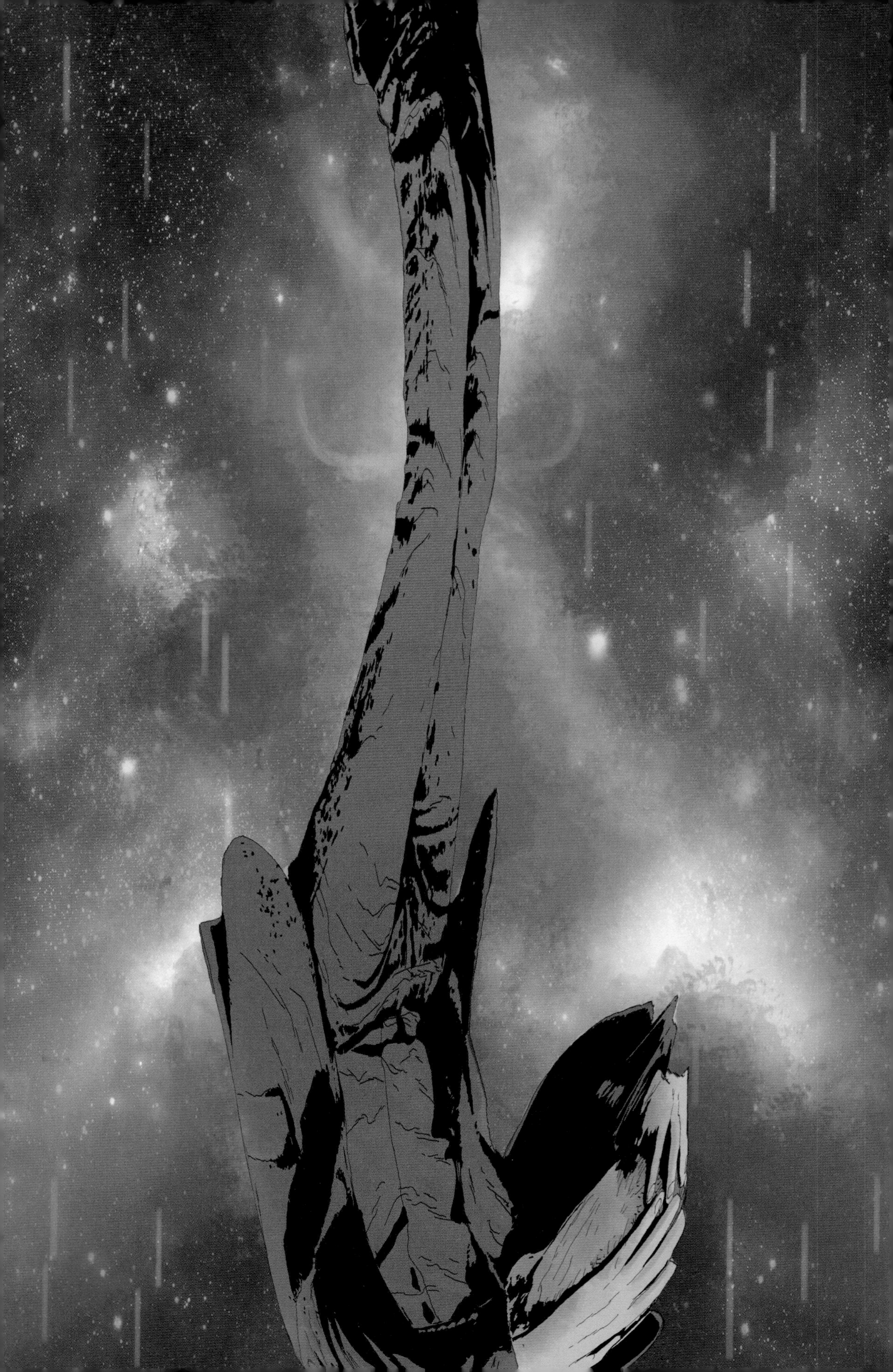

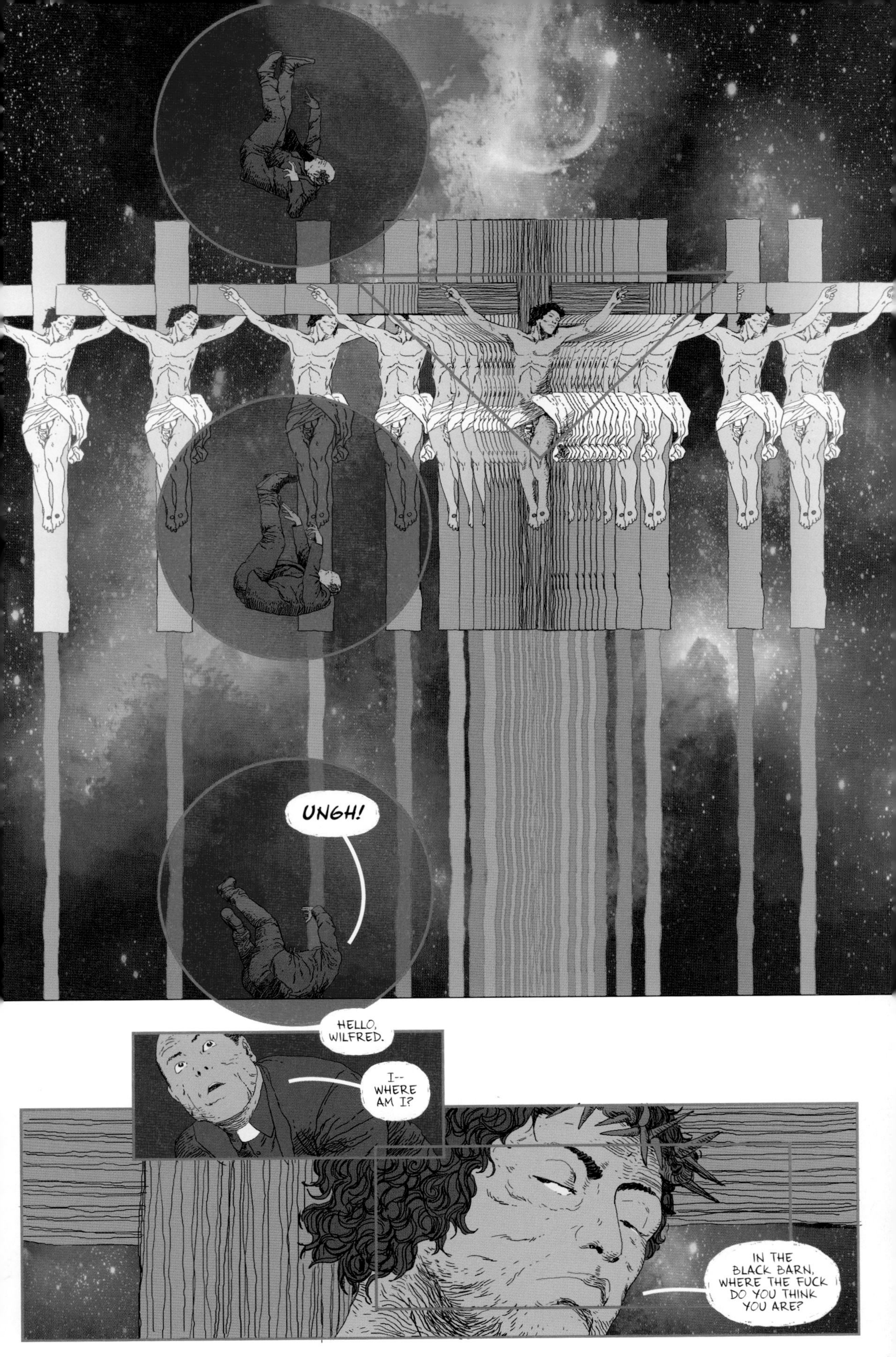
UNGH!
HELLO, WILFRED.
I-- WHERE AM I?
IN THE BLACK BARN, WHERE THE FUCK DO YOU THINK YOU ARE?

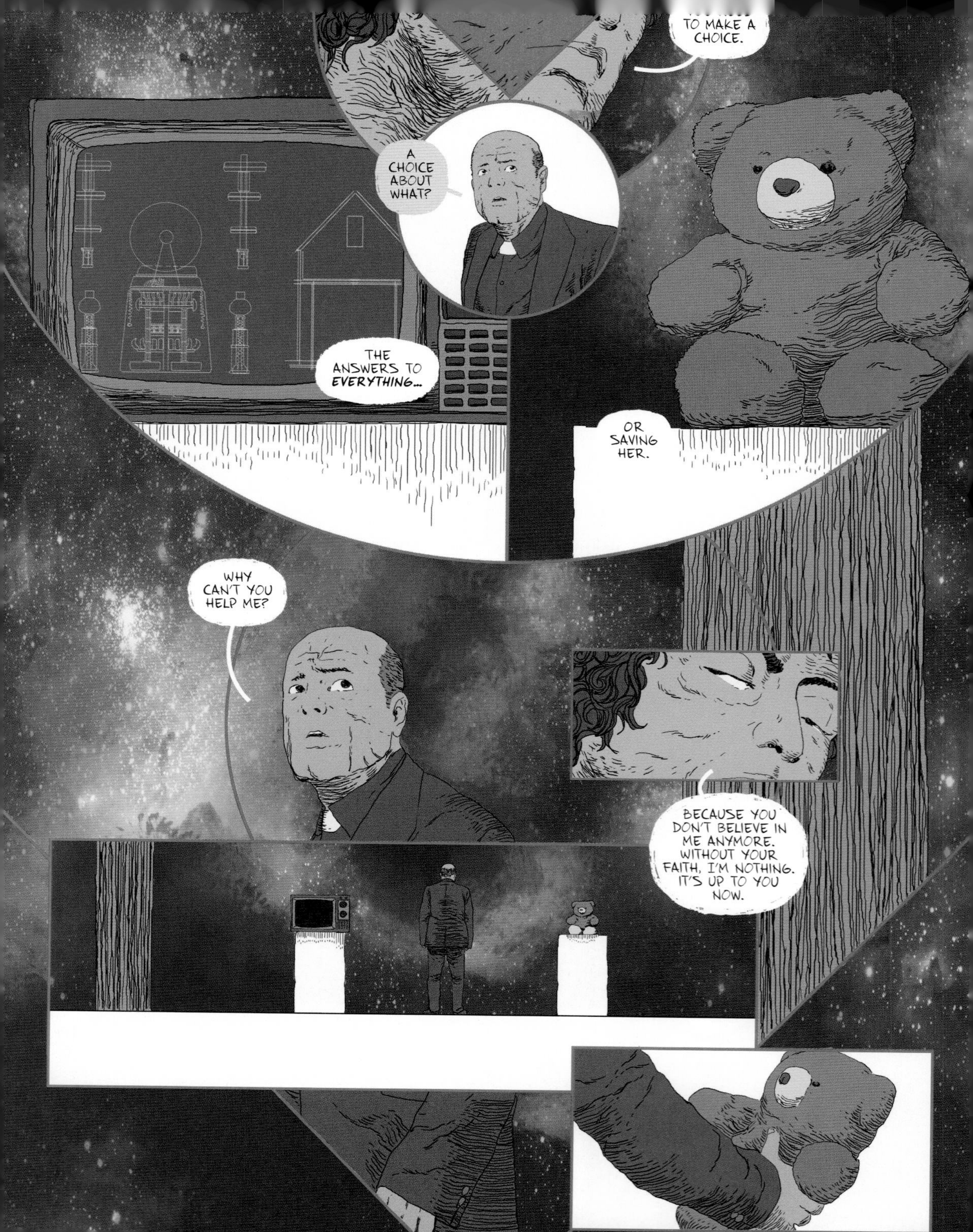
TO MAKE A CHOICE.
A CHOICE ABOUT WHAT?
THE ANSWERS TO *EVERYTHING*...
OR SAVING HER.
WHY CAN'T YOU HELP ME?
BECAUSE YOU DON'T BELIEVE IN ME ANYMORE. WITHOUT YOUR FAITH, I'M NOTHING. IT'S UP TO YOU NOW.

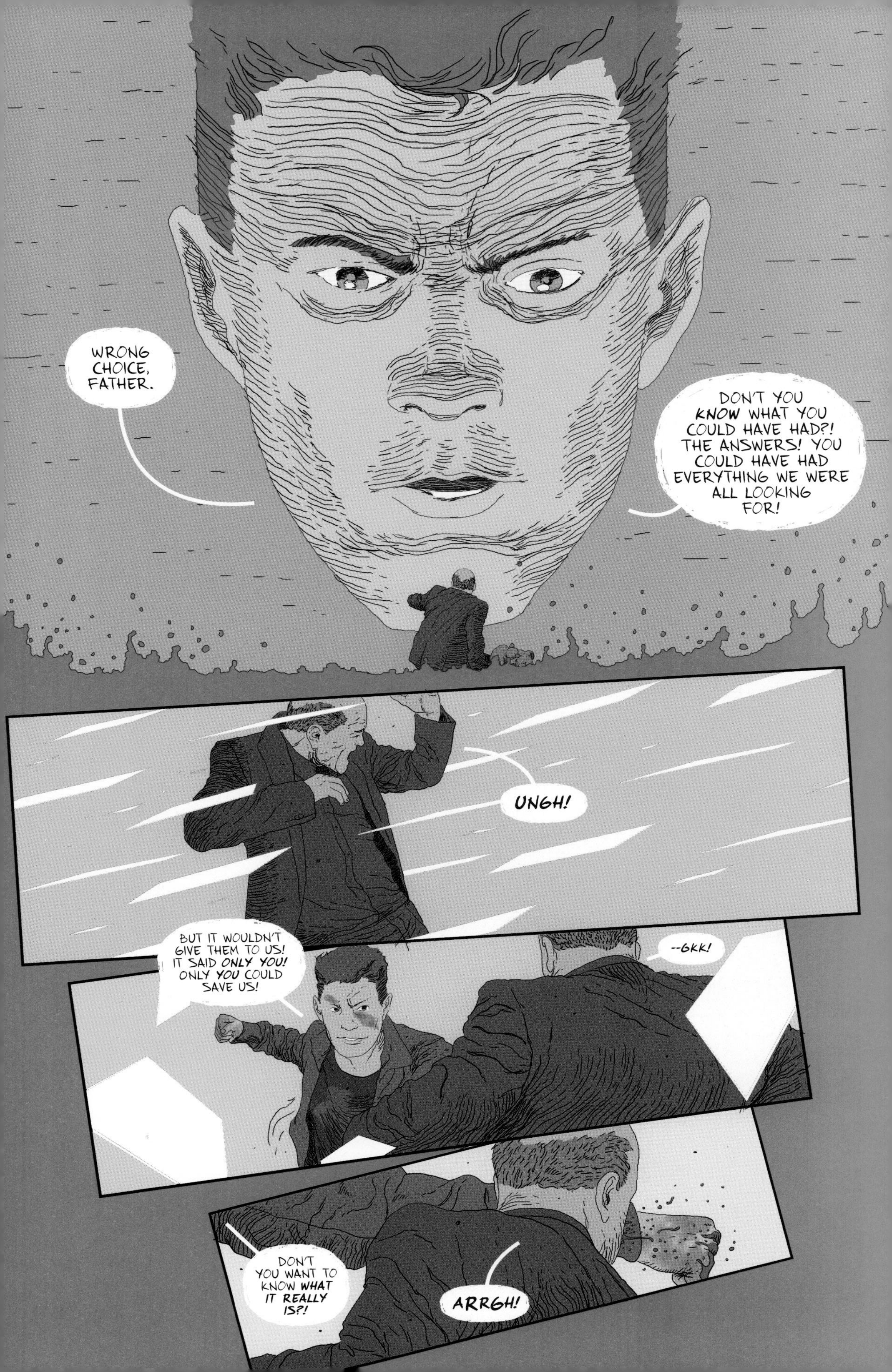
WRONG CHOICE, FATHER.
DON'T YOU KNOW WHAT YOU COULD HAVE HAD?! THE ANSWERS! YOU COULD HAVE HAD EVERYTHING WE WERE ALL LOOKING FOR!
UNGH!
BUT IT WOULDN'T GIVE THEM TO US! IT SAID ONLY YOU! ONLY YOU COULD SAVE US!
--GKK!
DON'T YOU WANT TO KNOW WHAT IT REALLY IS?!
ARRGH!

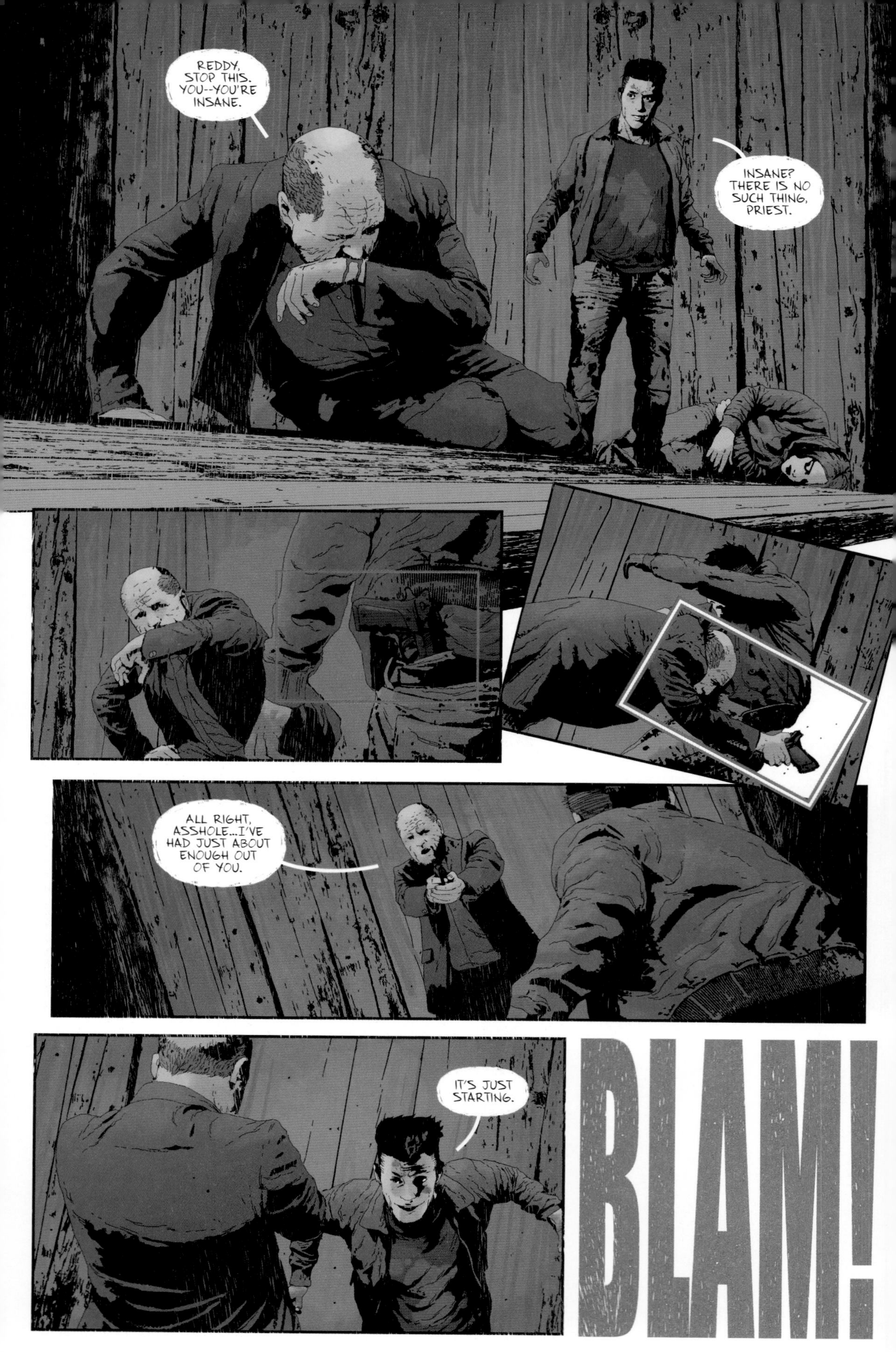
REDDY, STOP THIS. YOU--YOU'RE INSANE.
INSANE? THERE IS NO SUCH THING, PRIEST.
ALL RIGHT, ASSHOLE...I'VE HAD JUST ABOUT ENOUGH OUT OF YOU.
IT'S JUST STARTING.
BLAM!

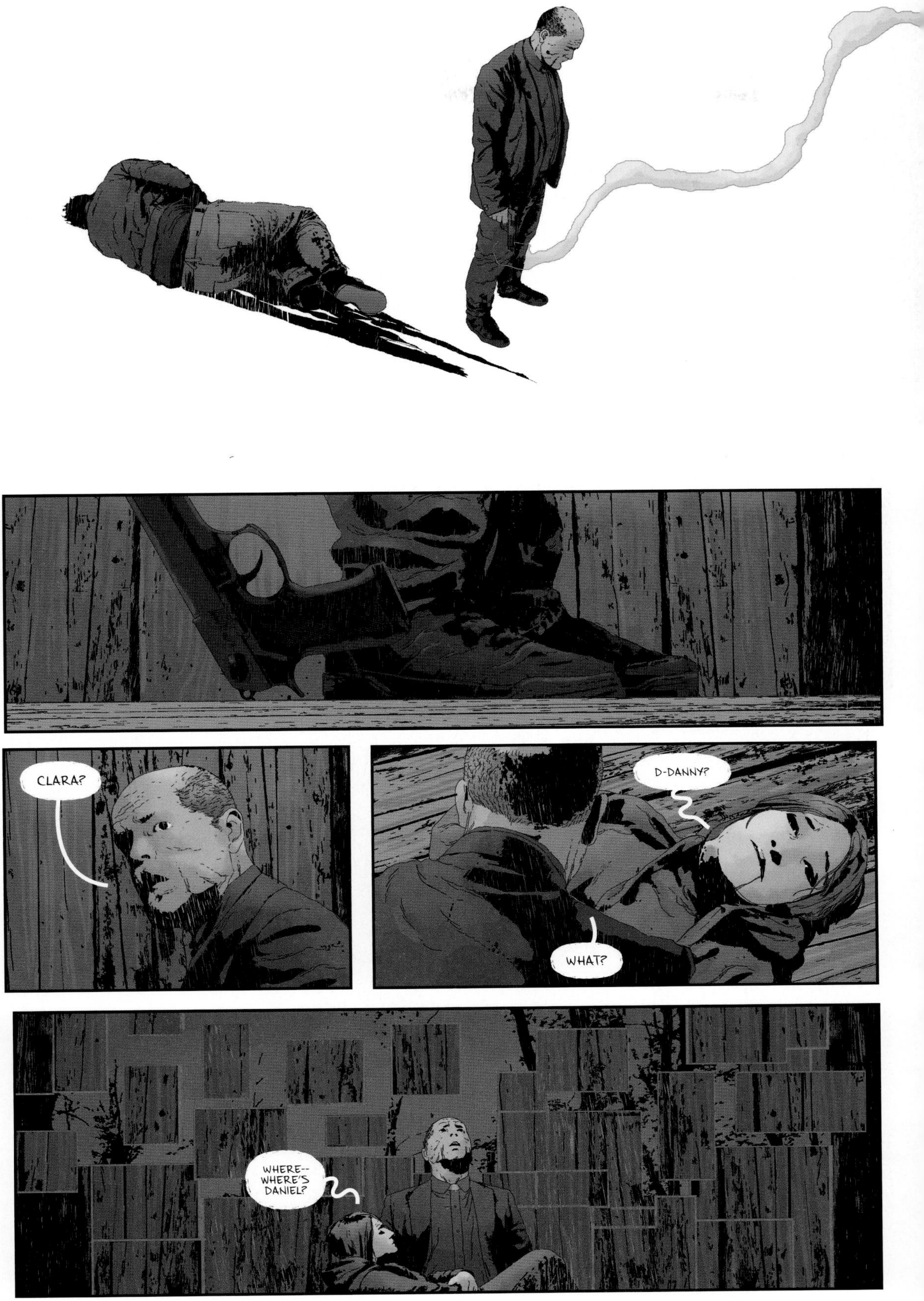
CLARA?
D-DANNY?
WHAT?
WHERE--
WHERE'S
DANIEL?

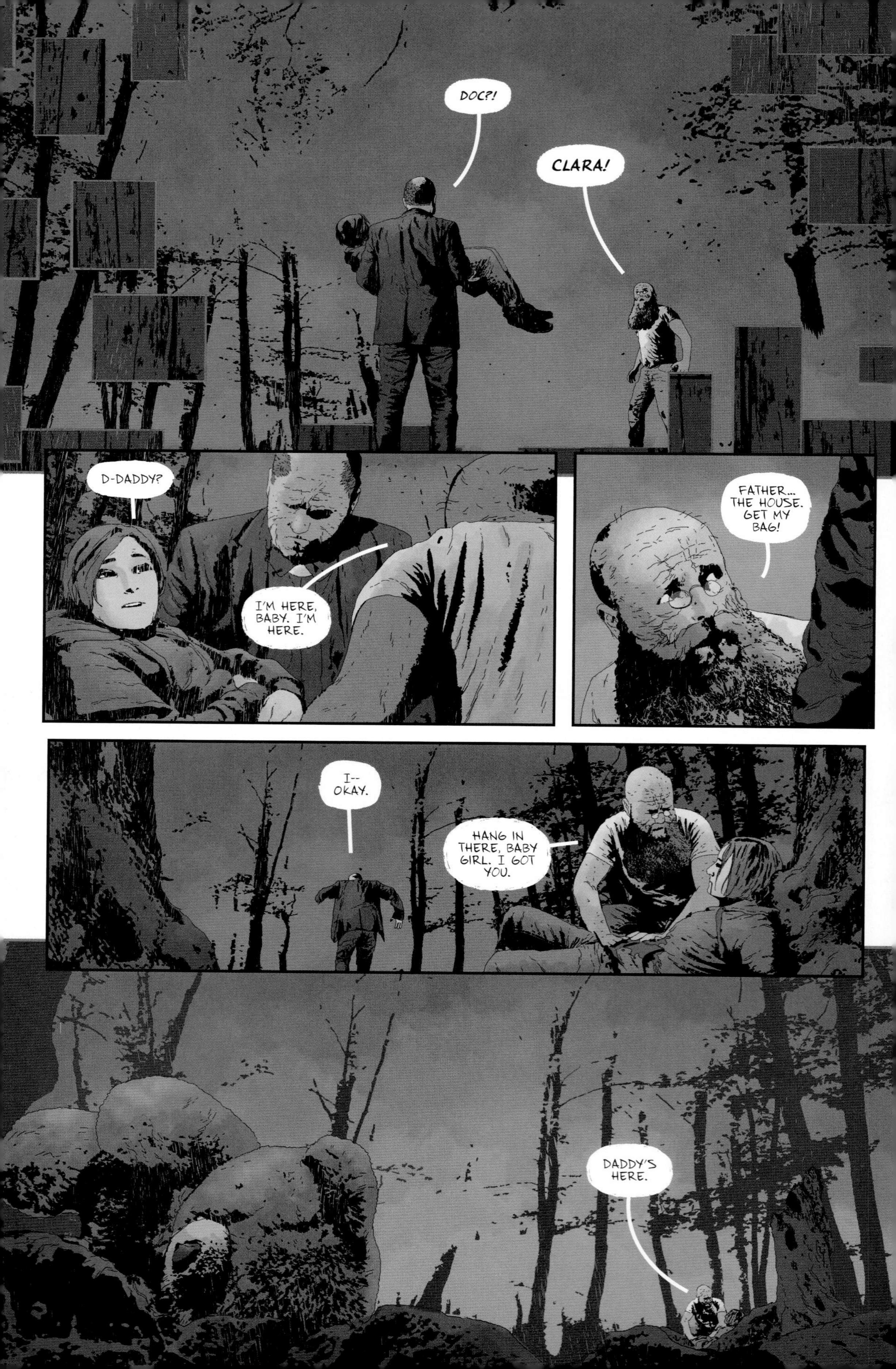
DOC?!
CLARA!
D-DADDY?
I'M HERE, BABY. I'M HERE.
FATHER... THE HOUSE. GET MY BAG!
I-- OKAY.
HANG IN THERE, BABY GIRL. I GOT YOU.
DADDY'S HERE.

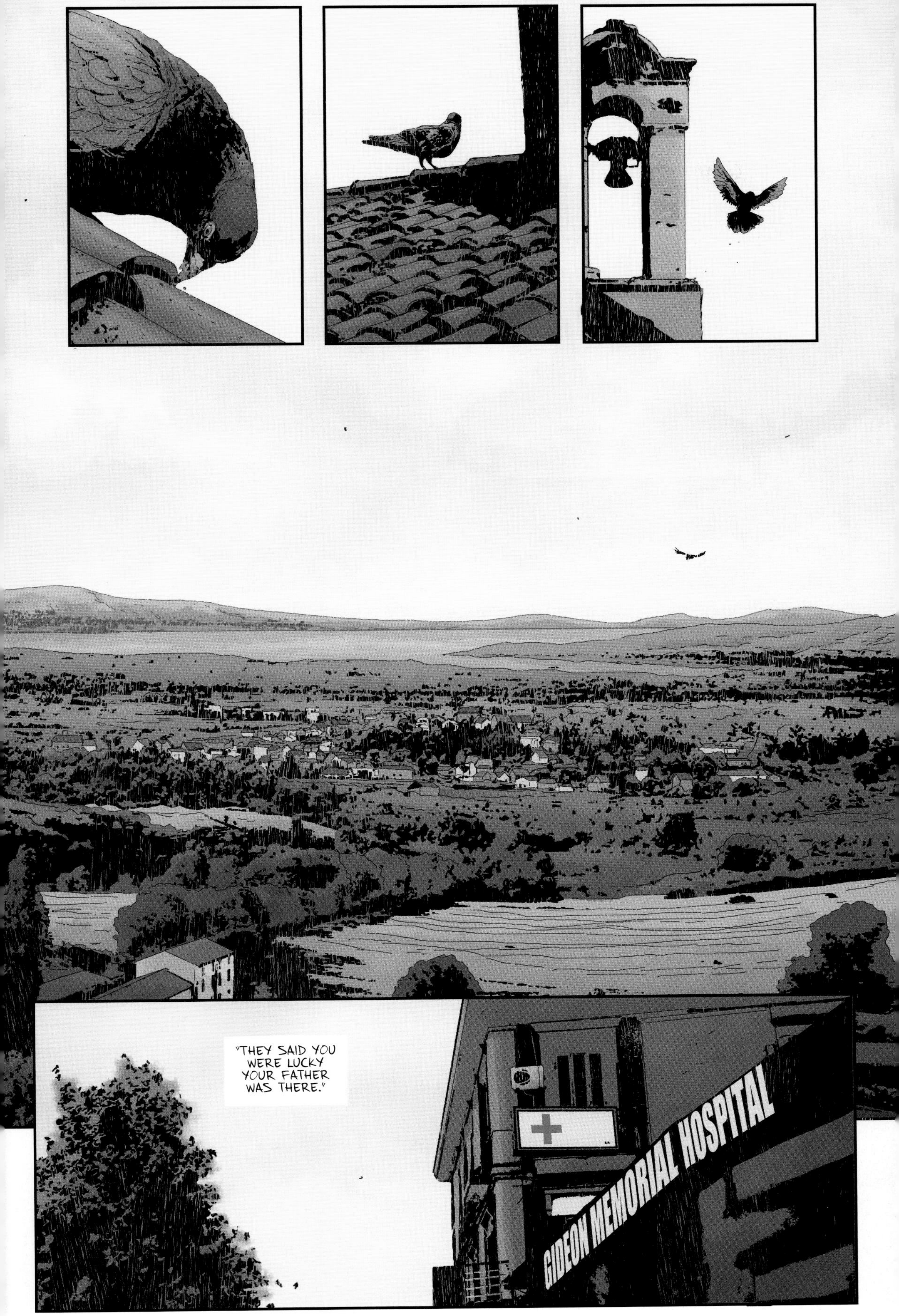
"THEY SAID YOU WERE LUCKY YOUR FATHER WAS THERE."
GIDEON MEMORIAL HOSPITAL

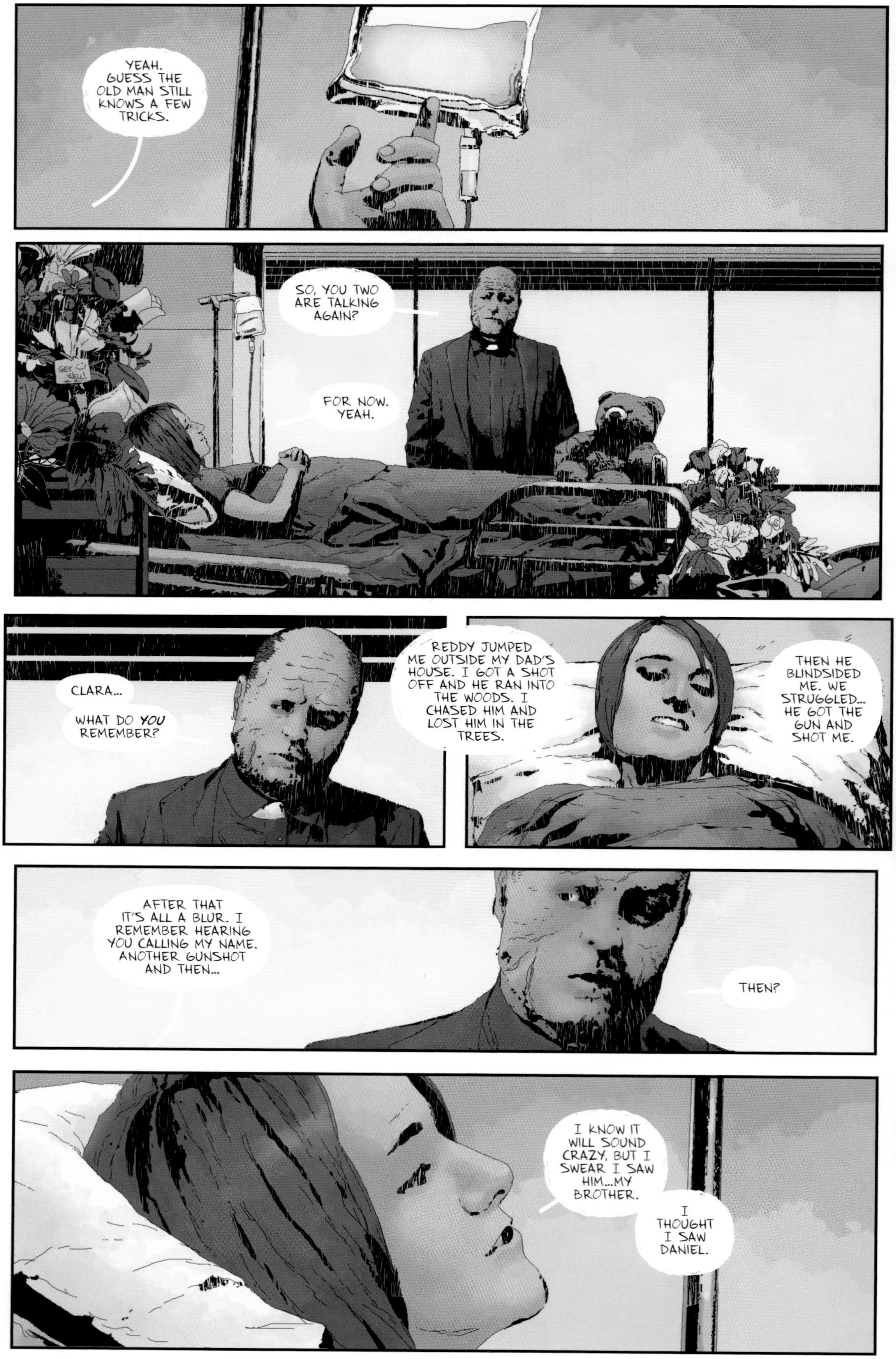
YEAH. GUESS THE OLD MAN STILL KNOWS A FEW TRICKS.
SO, YOU TWO ARE TALKING AGAIN?
FOR NOW. YEAH.
CLARA...
WHAT DO *YOU* REMEMBER?
REDDY JUMPED ME OUTSIDE MY DAD'S HOUSE. I GOT A SHOT OFF AND HE RAN INTO THE WOODS. I CHASED HIM AND LOST HIM IN THE TREES.
THEN HE BLINDSIDED ME. WE STRUGGLED... HE GOT THE GUN AND SHOT ME.
AFTER THAT IT'S ALL A BLUR. I REMEMBER HEARING YOU CALLING MY NAME. ANOTHER GUNSHOT AND THEN...
THEN?
I KNOW IT WILL SOUND CRAZY, BUT I SWEAR I SAW HIM...MY BROTHER.
I THOUGHT I SAW DANIEL.

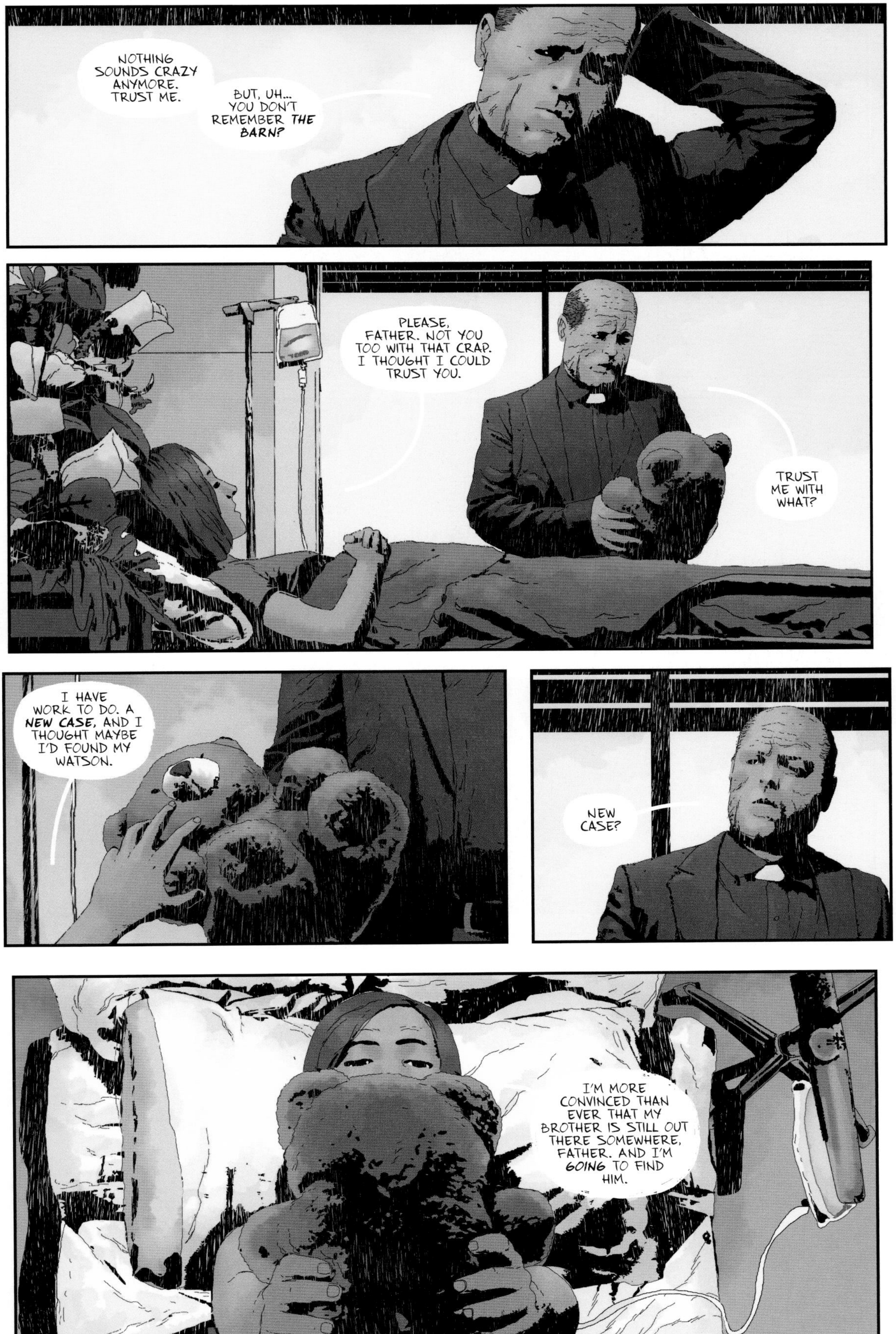
NOTHING SOUNDS CRAZY ANYMORE. TRUST ME.
BUT, UH... YOU DON'T REMEMBER THE BARN?
PLEASE, FATHER. NOT YOU TOO WITH THAT CRAP. I THOUGHT I COULD TRUST YOU.
TRUST ME WITH WHAT?
I HAVE WORK TO DO. A NEW CASE, AND I THOUGHT MAYBE I'D FOUND MY WATSON.
NEW CASE?
I'M MORE CONVINCED THAN EVER THAT MY BROTHER IS STILL OUT THERE SOMEWHERE, FATHER. AND I'M GOING TO FIND HIM.

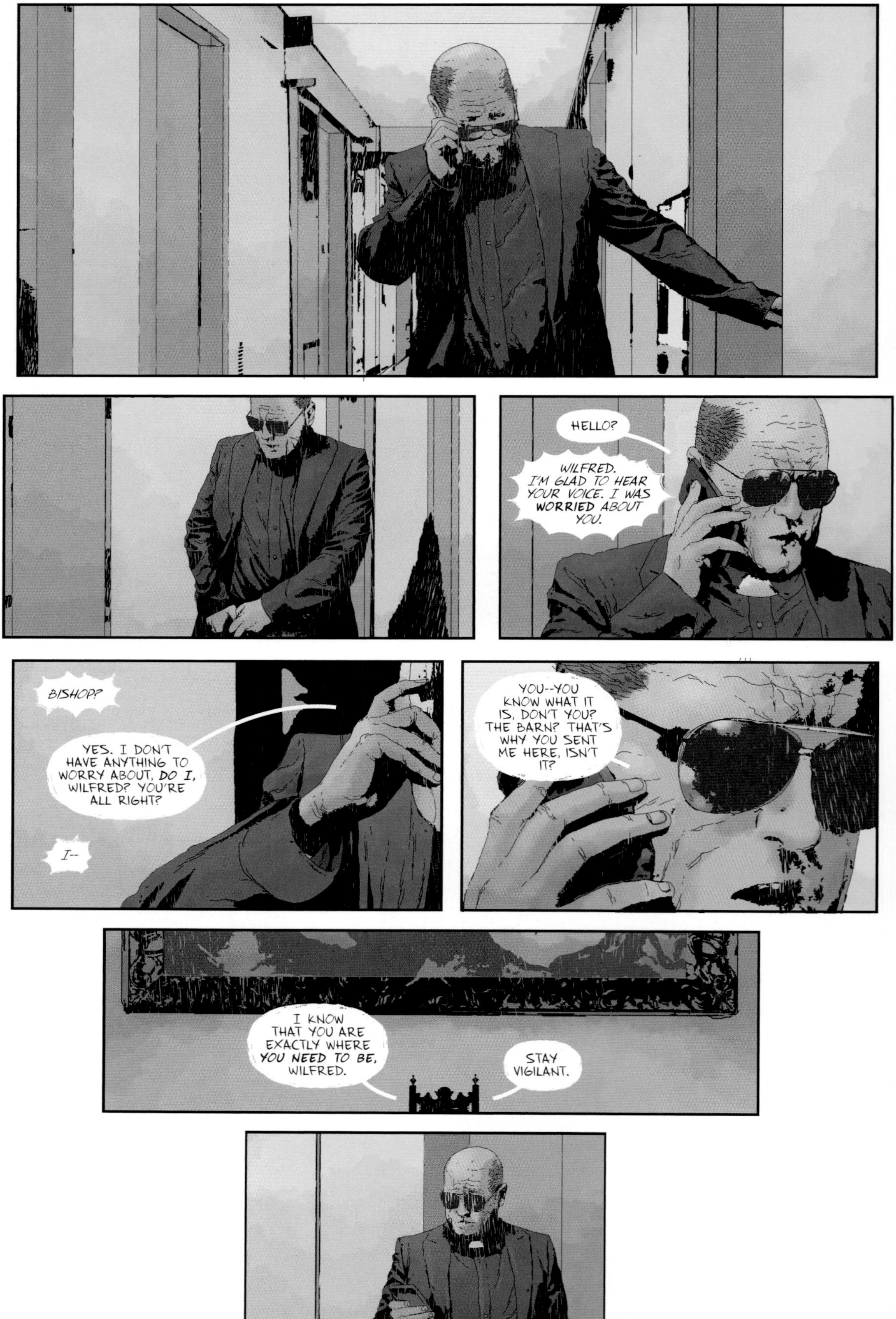
HELLO?
WILFRED. I'M GLAD TO HEAR YOUR VOICE. I WAS WORRIED ABOUT YOU.
BISHOP?
YES. I DON'T HAVE ANYTHING TO WORRY ABOUT, DO I, WILFRED? YOU'RE ALL RIGHT?
I--
YOU--YOU KNOW WHAT IT IS, DON'T YOU? THE BARN? THAT'S WHY YOU SENT ME HERE, ISN'T IT?
I KNOW THAT YOU ARE EXACTLY WHERE YOU NEED TO BE, WILFRED.
STAY VIGILANT.

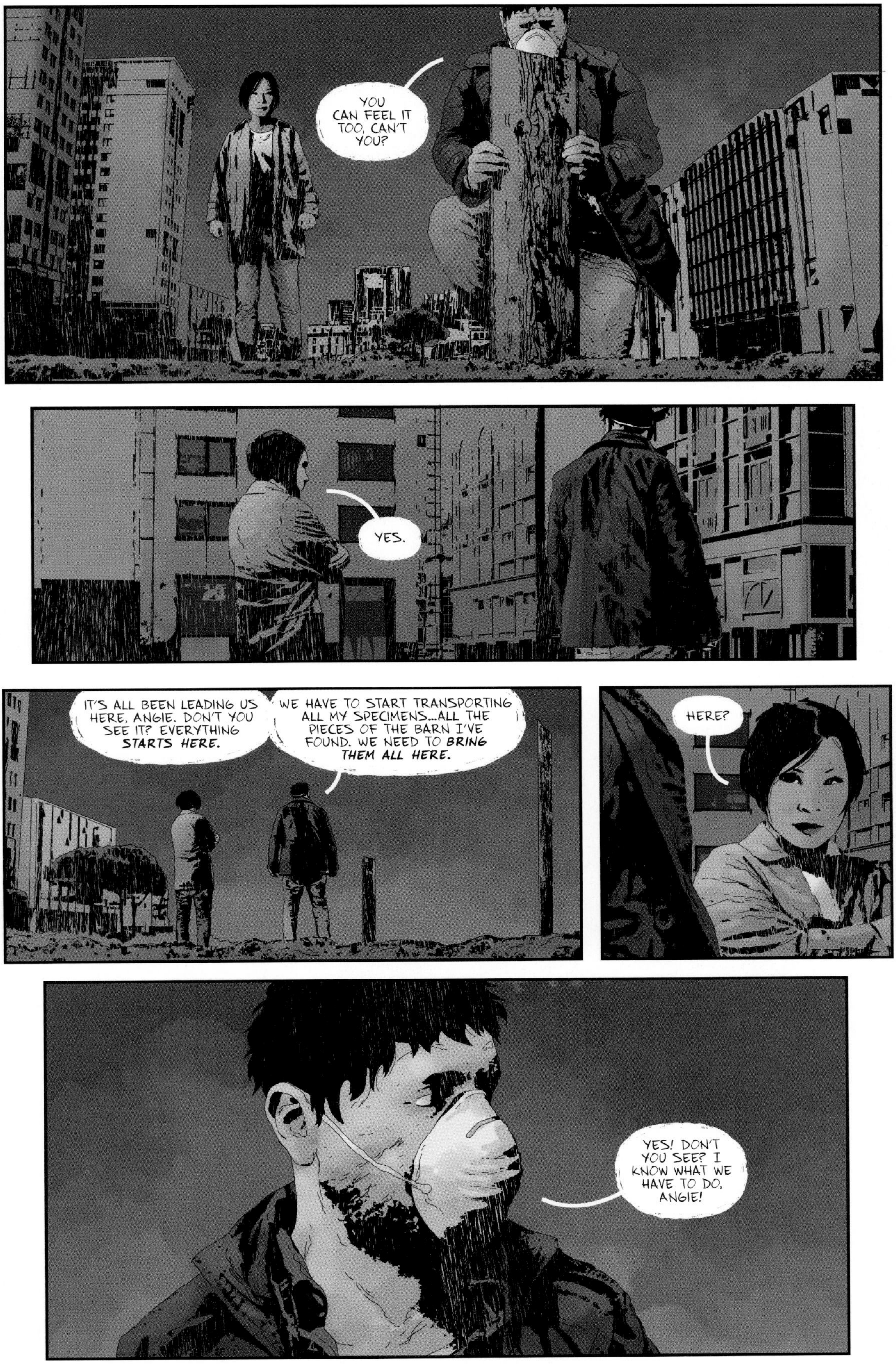
YOU CAN FEEL IT TOO, CAN'T YOU?
YES.
IT'S ALL BEEN LEADING US HERE, ANGIE. DON'T YOU SEE IT? EVERYTHING STARTS HERE.
WE HAVE TO START TRANSPORTING ALL MY SPECIMENS...ALL THE PIECES OF THE BARN I'VE FOUND. WE NEED TO BRING THEM ALL HERE.
HERE?
YES! DON'T YOU SEE? I KNOW WHAT WE HAVE TO DO, ANGIE!

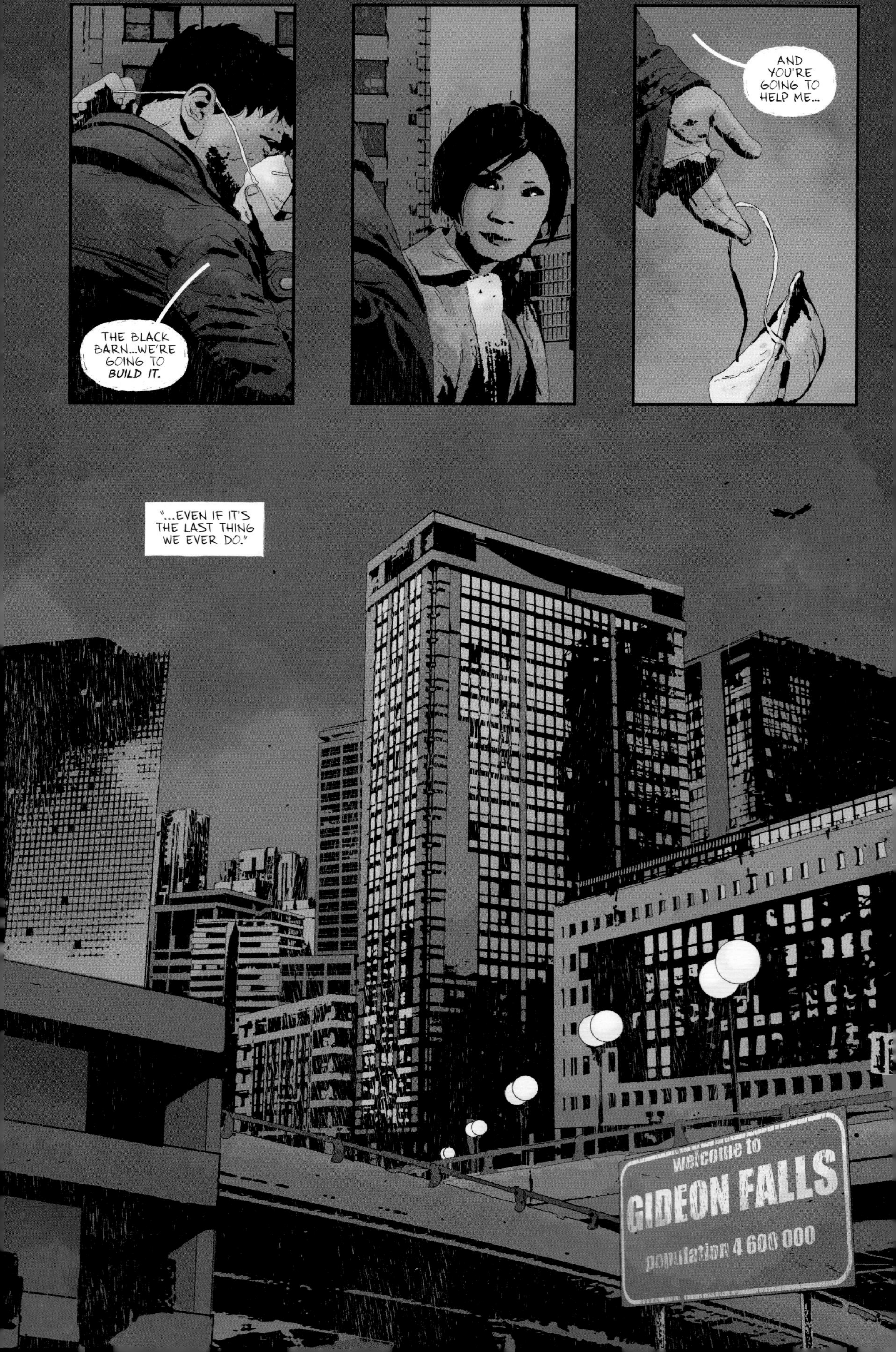
THE BLACK BARN...WE'RE GOING TO BUILD IT.
AND YOU'RE GOING TO HELP ME...
"...EVEN IF IT'S THE LAST THING WE EVER DO."
welcome to
GIDEON FALLS
population 4 600 000

COVER GALLERY

#1A - JEFF LEMIRE

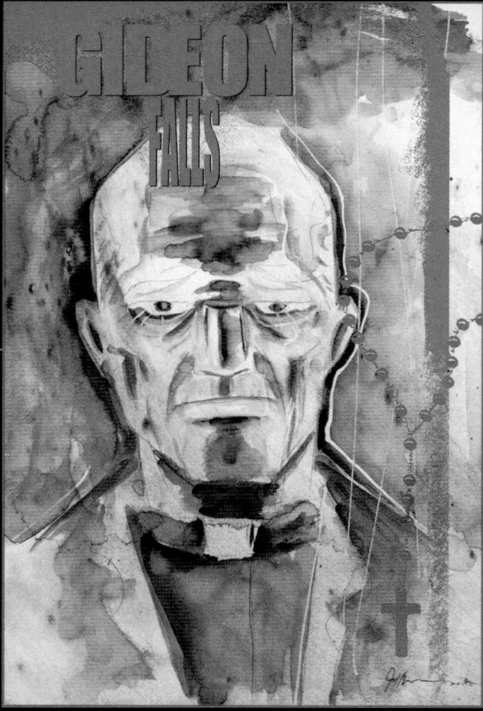
GIDEON
FALLS

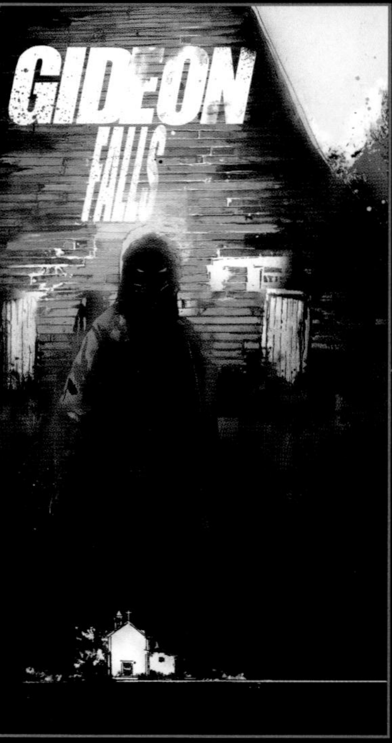
GIDEON
FALLS

#1B - JOCK

#1C - JEFF LEMIRE

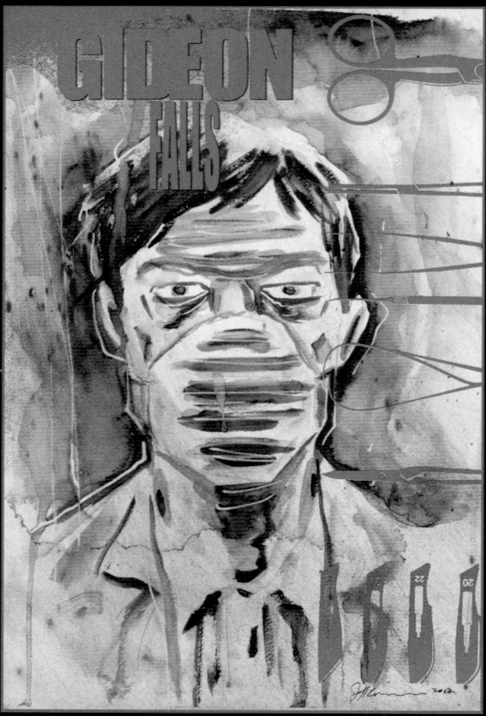
GIDEON
FALLS

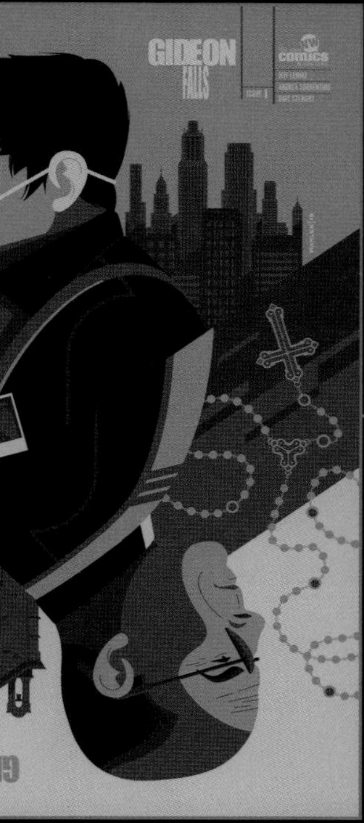
GIDEON
FALLS

#1D - TOM WHALEN

- CLIFF CHIANG

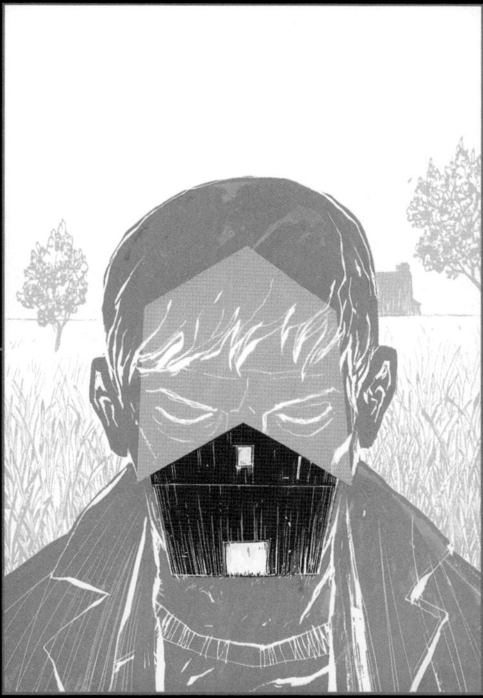

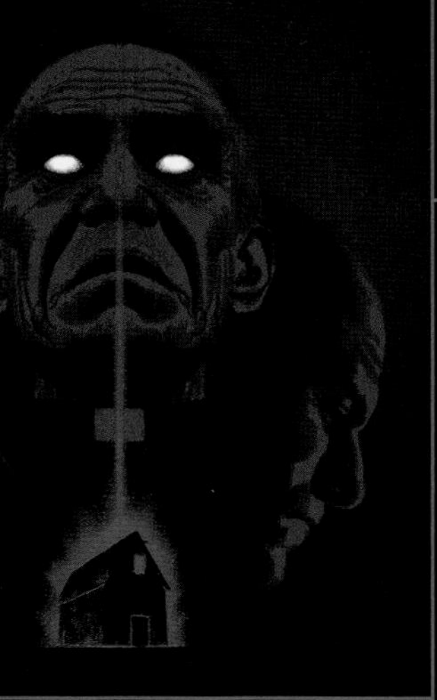

#3B - GREG SMALLWOOD

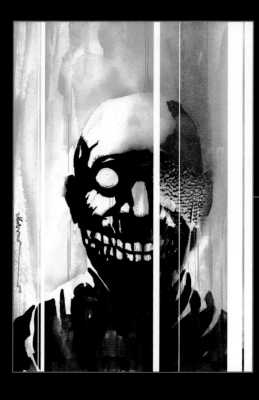

#4B - DUSTIN NGUYEN

ABSENCE OF LIGHT

#5B - SKOTTIE YOUNG

GIDEON
FALLS

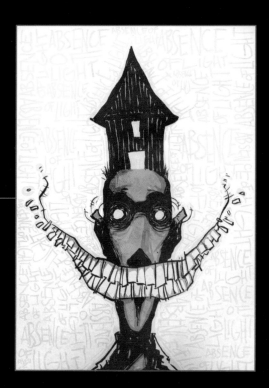

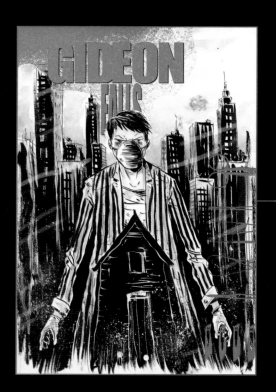

#6B - JEFF LEMIRE